THREE
SENTIMENTAL NOVELS

THREE
SENTIMENTAL NOVELS

LAURENCE STERNE
A Sentimental Journey
Through France and Italy

HENRY MACKENZIE
The Man of Feeling

THOMAS DAY
The History
of Sandford and Merton
(Abridged)

INTRODUCTION
Albert J. Kuhn
OHIO STATE UNIVERSITY

Holt, Rinehart and Winston, Inc.
NEW YORK · CHICAGO · SAN FRANCISCO · ATLANTA
DALLAS · MONTREAL · TORONTO · LONDON · SYDNEY

Introduction and Notes
Copyright © 1970 by Albert J. Kuhn
Library of Congress Catalog Card Number: 75–94349
SBN: 03-082758-2
Printed in the United States of America
1 2 3 4 5 6 7 8 9

Introduction

In 1782 the popular moral writer Miss Hannah More published a poem on "Sensibility." Her purpose was to define an ideal that had become an obsession of the times. What Reason had been to the Age of Pope and what Imagination was to become to the Age of Wordsworth Sensibility was to the last half of the eighteenth century. At the peak of its vogue from about 1770 to 1790, the term Sensibility included almost every noble human quality. He who possessed the trait was distinguished from the rest of mankind by being more finely sensitive to life, hence capable of greater pleasure (and pain) and, therefore, capable of greater virtue and happiness than others. Sensibility was an innate power of perception akin to but superior to genius or taste alone; it was the benevolent disposition to see good and beauty in the world and to make them prevail. Its origin and essence however were indefinable, according to Hannah More, who sought to display her own sensibility in the following apostrophes:

> Thy subtle essence still eludes the chains
> Of Definition, and defeats her pains.
> Sweet Sensibility! thou keen delight!
> Thou hasty moral! sudden sense of right!
> Thou untaught goodness! Virtue's precious seed!
> Thou sweet precursor of the gen'rous deed!
> Beauty's quick relish! Reason's radiant Morn,
> Which dawns soft light before Reflection's born.
> To those who know this not, no words can paint!
> And those who know thee, know all words are faint!

More soberly, John Donaldson, a minor artist and essayist, remarked in his *Harmony of Sensibility and Reason* (1780) that the union of these qualities of head and heart resulted not merely in the common virtues of love, pity, gratitude, and duty but also in "a certain elegance of soul, which renders kindness most kind, and pleasure most pleasing." True sensibility was genius and taste, the tenderness of friendship, and the exquisite endearments of love. Men's enjoyments and misfortunes, he went on to say, were "to be computed from their different degrees of feeling." Sensibility thus was the end and aim of life and he who acquired it was ennobled, and was ennobling in his society. The chief writers of the age, in Hannah More's judgment, who had depicted the ideals of sensibility were Samuel Richardson in his novels, Thomas Gray in his poetry, and Henry Mackenzie and Laurence Sterne in their works. Like her contemporaries generally, however, she had grave reservations about the indelicacies of Sterne's fiction. She included Dr. Johnson in her eulogy, but he, although he was her friend, would not have been complimented. He belonged to another generation in literary taste and had a different bias in his view of man and the world. The title of Donaldson's essay cited above indicates the effort to reconcile two contrary views and values of human nature. A few generalizations about these views may be helpful in appreciating aspects of the literature of the Age of Sensibility.

Broadly speaking, two views of human nature have dominated the history of moral theory. One holds that man is innately good, or at least not innately sinful, born by nature with an infinite capacity for attaining what is good, true, and beautiful. Human institutions of government, religion, manners, and society in general can corrupt and deflect him from his aim for virtue, but they cannot wholly destroy his natural tendency to noble thought and action. This view prizes the natural and spontaneous and rejects the artificial. It stresses man's capacity for feeling and imagination, his individuality, hence his alienation from society; and it looks to a hopeful future rather than to tradition and the past. The other view of human nature insists that the individual be subordinate to society and tradition, for it holds that man is by nature sinful and wayward and that human institutions, especially religion, redeem and civilize him. This view, therefore, stresses the values of reason and tradition in making man a social and moral creature, and it looks to the past to measure his progress. Its prophecies for the welfare of man are generally gloomy. Various labels, such as Optimism and Pessimism, Primitivism and Rationalism, or Romanticism and Classicism, among others, have been used to designate these views and values, but for purposes here it will be convenient to note aspects of these views for the followers of Thomas Hobbes, on the one hand, and the 3rd Earl of Shaftesbury, on the other.

For those in the early eighteenth century who believed in man's natural goodness and glorious prospects, the name of Hobbes was foremost in the list of philosophical villains. His *Leviathan* (1651) had spread the wicked doctrine that man was basically egoistic and that life in a state of nature was "nasty, brutish, and short." Hence, an authoritarian society was necessary for man's preservation. This belief omitted the agency of grace, of course, and Hobbes was charged with atheism. One of Hobbes' disciples, Bernard Mandeville, in a book published in 1714 on the origin and nature of virtue, showed with considerable wit and truth that man's selfish and aggressive character could be interpreted as a moral good because his getting and spending money for private vices led eventually to public wealth and prosperity, a benefit and a virtue. This egoistical utilitarianism had been Mandeville's answer to the theories of virtue proposed by Shaftesbury, who had written against Hobbes in 1711.

As a Platonist, Shaftesbury held that morality was not an expedient matter and certainly not motivated by selfish concerns. Virtue indeed, he thought, was its own reward. Man was born with an innate moral sense, an internal sense analogous to his five external ones. This internal sense directed man to virtuous goals; he was by nature altruistic, not egoistic, benevolent in his impulses, not selfish and vicious. The nature of this moral sense, with its derivatives "sentiment," "sympathy," and its most comprehensive label, "sensibility," was much elaborated during the eighteenth century, chiefly through the Scottish followers of Shaftesbury among whom the most influential was Francis Hutcheson. His *Enquiry into the Orig-*

inal of Our Ideas of Beauty and Virtue (1725) defended his master against Mandeville and, by extending the psychological and esthetical implications of the moral sense, led the way for the emphasis on sensibility above mere sense and on the man of feeling over the man of reason.

Shortly after Hutcheson's theory on virtue appeared, Swift's *Gulliver's Travels* was published, depicting a very different view of man's moral goodness. Throughout the four voyages indeed, Gulliver's education consisted mainly in his discovery of the cunning ways of man's sinfulness. Though reason was as self-evidently God's first law for man as motion was for the universe, in the end Gulliver found that human nature was more bestial than celestial. Man was less a rational animal than one merely capable of reason. This discovery brought Gulliver to a hatred of all mankind, including his own family, a misanthropy that, ironically, enabled Swift to show Gulliver's own unreasonableness. Pope, too, in his *Essay on Man* had preached the ideals of reason, order, and harmony implicit in the total order of nature, but we are apt to remember more vividly his satire on man's perversion of those ideals in *The Dunciad* and elsewhere. Dr. Johnson's *Rasselas* also explored the means and ends of human happiness. Rasselas had left the Happy Valley to discover what would fulfill man's yearning, but he found that neither reason nor imagination, riches nor retirement, love nor knowledge, nor a host of other things would suffice. What he discovered was the vanity of human wishes.

Where then was human happiness to be found? By 1755, when *Rasselas* was published, the faith in reason to minister to man's deepest needs was dead. In its place appeared a new idol, sensibility. Its chief characteristic had been described by Shaftesbury: the man of sensibility had an innate moral sense which motivated him to virtue, an end pleasing and rewarding in and for itself. Man's happiness consisted in being sympathetic and generous to others; it pleased his nature to be altruistic and benevolent. Since his pleasures were affective—literally, in contemporary usage, "sentimental" pleasures—it behooved man to develop, cultivate, and refine his sentimental nature. The emphasis at midcentury, in all endeavors of life, on "good nature," on gratitude, pity, love, and man's passions in general evidence this pursuit. Displays of feeling, especially tears, came to signify genuine sensibility, and sensibility employed in the right uses, it was believed, could reform the world. Sterne's rhapsody to it indicates its divine agency:

—Dear sensibility! source inexhausted of all that's precious in our joys, or costly in our sorrows! thou chainest thy martyr down upon his bed of straw—and 'tis thou who lifts him up to HEAVEN —eternal fountain of our feelings!—'tis here I trace thee—and this is thy divinity which stirs within me—not that, in some sad and sickening moments, *my soul shrinks back upon herself, and startles at destruction*—mere pomp of words!—but that I feel some generous joys and generous cares beyond myself—all comes from thee, great, great SENSORIUM of the world! which vibrates, if a hair of our heads but falls upon the ground, in the remotest desert of thy creation.

The religious address or prayer to sensibility is appropriate. By the middle of the eighteenth century the Evangelical movement, associated mainly with the Wesleys, had attracted multitudes of enthusiastical worshippers. For the Age of Pope and Swift, the term *enthusiast* meant a religious fanatic, a madman who assumed divine inspiration and grace to himself without the offices and tradition of the Established Church. The typical enthusiast of the times, however, was in fact a radical Protestant reacting against the rationalism and irrelevance of the orthodox faith. "We live," complained William Law, who was John Wesley's spiritual teacher, "in starving in the coldness and deadness of a formal, historical, hearsay religion." Salvation, he preached, was found not in learning nor intellectual subtlety but in the sensibility of man's own nature, in the inward experience of his need for redemption. Reason was powerless to redeem man; indeed it was the cause for man's first fall from God and remained the cause for his being divided within himself and from the Divine Being. A new sensibility of his spiritual plight was needed, an enthusiasm (meaning, in its root sense, *en theos:* in god) which kindled and inflamed in man a love of God. "This," Law declared, "is the enthusiasm in which every good Christian ought to endeavor to live and die." An enduring result of this new sensibility in religion of course was Methodism. Against this kind of enthusiasm, abuse and argument could not prevail, and in the last half of the century the religion of the heart was a matter for prayer and praise in the cathedrals as well as the chapels.

As Wesley and other preachers sought to revive the old or "primitive" Christianity, so the idea of a primitive, golden age of society in general appealed to the Age of Sensibility. The Rome that had been praised in the early part of the century as the height of polished civilization seemed to the succeeding generation to be the epitome of decadence and evil. The Goths, who had once been described as the ignorant barbarians who overran the Roman Empire, were now admired as noble savages. The legend of Odin, for example, which was attractive to the young Wordsworth, among others, as a theme for an epic poem, related how the brave Odin was persecuted by the Romans and driven far into the North, where he founded and ruled a noble race of liberty-loving people who, centuries later, avenged their leader by conquering the effeminate and luxury-loving Romans. This idealized or sentimental view of the past was expressed in many ways but especially by an interest in primitive man, like the American Indian, whose "savage grandeur" (in Thomas Day's phrase) was admired. In its application to educational theory, this ideal of the noble savage and "the return to nature" was largely the influence of Rousseau. His popular treatise *Émile* (1752) tried to show how a child's natural sensibilities could be developed so that he grew to a manhood of freedom and moral dignity. Rousseau argued that society frustrated and altered man's inclinations, but in a state of nature the virtues of duty, compassion, friendship, and the like, would develop ideally and practically.

In effect, then, sensibility was that natural yet exalted sense of feeling and being that, as its own reward, motivated man to moral action and esthetic experience. Inevitably, as with most obsessions, there was groundless optimism about the power of sensibility during the period. But the faith in it was not shallow or powerless, for the major characteristic of the Age of Sensibility was its humanitarianism. The sentiment Sterne expressed for a caged starling (or Burns for a field mouse) was the same kind of feeling that moved people to relieve the oppressed everywhere and to support the political revolutions in Europe and America. The sympathy for the Negro expressed by Day and others was very influential in the strong antislavery movement in England toward the end of the century. The rights of women were seriously advocated and heard, one indication of which was the number of female writers who were published and popular during the time. The education of children was a main concern, and Sunday schools date from this period, as do reform and philanthropic movements of many kinds. It was, in short, an effective age of protest and pity.

Sterne's *Sentimental Journey,* Mackenzie's *Man of Feeling,* and Day's *History of Sandford and Merton* are typical of the literature of sensibility. All three were widely read and admired and remained popular long after the vogue of sensibility had passed. In the decade immediately following their publication, for example, Sterne's novel went through five separate editions, in addition to collected editions of his works, Mackenzie's book had three separate editions, and Day's book, beside a number of abridged forms, had eight complete editions. For many decades Sandford and Merton were household words in England, and in America as well. All three works were much imitated (after his death Sterne's novel was even "continued") and translated well into the next century, when a reaction against sentimentality set in. Coleridge thought that Sterne's sentimentality had encouraged hypocrisy in English life, a view with which Thackeray agreed. Sterne's reputation, of course, has survived the Victorian Age, and his works are somewhat more justly appreciated in our time. But neither Mackenzie nor Day is much read today except by specialists of the period, and the reasons are apparent.

The literature of sensibility frequently exaggerated the power or manifestation of feeling, sentiment, sympathy, pity, in short, of sensibility, giving rise thereby to most of the negative connotations the term *sentimental* has for us today:

superficial, tearful, excessive, girlish emotion or behavior. From a modern point of view sentimental literature asks the reader to respond in excess of the justification, and at best may be described as ineffective and at worst dishonest. There are sentimental scenes in Day and Mackenzie that are ineffective— ironically, in view of their intent—because they are unnatural. No little boys are quite as bad or as good as Tommy Merton and Harry Sandford, even when we allow that Day was writing for children and purposely exaggerated his characters. Our credibility is strained when Tommy borrows a large sum of money to pay the debts of a poor farmer and his family who are about to be evicted, and says as he gives the farmer the money: "My good friend, you are very welcome to this; I freely give it to you, and I hope it will enable you to pay what you owe, and to preserve these poor little children." And when, in Mackenzie's novel, Harley and Miss Walton collapse in a heap of expired sensibility upon his declaration of his love for her, we are apt to be more amused than moved. So much weeping engages our pathological rather than esthetic interest. Even in Sterne, the master of "sentimental" writing, we are sometimes not sure whether the delicate irony or wry humor by which he offsets and counterbalances the sentiment of a scene is effectual. But the obvious excesses of sensibility in the individual novels are more than offset by their durable virtues.

As he was writing *A Sentimental Journey* in 1767, Sterne remarked to friends he was confident his book was an original one, "quite out of the beaten track," and that it would make them weep or he would give up "the business of sentimental writing." In his Journal in 1772, John Wesley exclaimed of the word *sentimental:* "What is that? It is not English; he might as well say *Continental*. It is not sense. It conveys no determinate idea; yet one fool makes many. And this nonsensical word (who would believe it?) is become a fashionable one." Wesley's outburst was prompted by the great popularity of the term since Sterne's novel had been published, and judging by that popularity the adjective *sentimental* was both English and made sense. Dr. Johnson did not include it in his *Dictionary* in 1755, but by then the term was fashionable if not clearly defined. For Sterne, *sentimental* was the expression for a moment or event experienced with a heightened or refined sensibility, an experience which could be moral or esthetic or both. His design in writing *A Sentimental Journey,* he told a friend, was "to teach us to love the world and our fellow creatures better than we do." Since the novel itself may not make that aim immediately obvious, it will be useful to discuss it briefly in the context of Sterne's literary career.

Like most talented but untitled men of his time, Sterne chose a career in the church, and his first ministerial duties were in a rural parish near the city of York, where his great grandfather had been an archbishop. That Sterne may not have been fitted temperamentally for this career is perhaps indicated by the story told of him that one Sunday, on the way to preach, his pointer dog sprang a covey of partridges, whereupon Sterne returned home to get his gun, leaving his congregation waiting for a sermon in vain. As an unknown country parson Sterne undertook to write a novel, "not to be fed but to be famous," he said of *The Life and Opinions of Tristram Shandy,* and famous he became, almost overnight. It was wagered in London that a letter addressed to "Tristram Shandy in Europe" would reach Sterne. The letter was delivered to him at his home in Yorkshire. In London and Paris he was the toast of the intellectual and social world, counting among his friends such people as David Garrick, William Pitt, Denis Diderot, and David Hume. But more flattering to him was his fame as the founder of an "ism," the philosophy of Shandyism.

The aim of literature in the eighteenth century was still the high moral one of instructing in a pleasing manner, and Sterne pleased and instructed by his wit and sentiment. Superficially, the wit of *Tristram Shandy* lies in the relation (and interrelation) of the family hobby-horses, of Walter's theory of names and noses that triumphs in logic but fails in life, of Uncle Toby's wordless world of fortifications and love, and of Tristram's dedication to putting into words the record of a life and opinions that outrun the speed of words to record them. Sentiment suffuses the book but is notorious in the Le Fever episode. A major characteristic of Sterne's genius, of course, is the delicate and inextricable tension or counterbalance of wit and sentiment in a sentence or a scene. Like the dynamic opposition of fancy and judgment in neoclassical poetics, from which a pleasing *concordia discors* results, the achievement of Sterne's style is, in general, of a witty intelligence saving sentiment from sentimentality and sentiment saving wit from triviality. *Tristram Shandy* is famous not because of plot (a modern critic has called it "the greatest shaggy-dog story in the language") nor because of wit, or sentiment, or style alone, but because of the memorable characters of Uncle Toby, Trim, Walter, and Tristram. The novelist of sensibility is concerned mainly with character, with looking inward and depicting what is typically yet uniquely human. In portraying the individuality of the Shandy household in their everyday, unheroic lives, Sterne created Shandyism, which, if not really a philosophy, is nevertheless a moral view of the world. Looking into this world, Sterne wrote a friend, would teach the reader "to laugh at its follies, to pity its errors, and despise its injustice."

Capitalizing on the popularity of *Tristram Shandy*, Sterne prepared for publication two volumes of his sermons, which appeared under the title of *The Sermons of Mr. Yorick*. The sermons were genuine and admirable as such, but in part their publication was a way of answering critics who cried out against what they believed was an unpriestlike fascination with sexuality in Tristram's life and opinions. The title for the sermons was also a good public relations device, keeping the image of Yorick-Sterne as a man of the cloth and "of infinite jest" before an eager audience. As volume by volume of Shandyism appeared during the next few years, Sterne's reputation grew ever greater, but his health, which had never been robust, suffered and he was forced to travel to the south of France in 1762 and again in 1765. These travels he turned to literary purpose in both his novels.

The modern age of tourism began in the eighteenth century when noblemen sent their sons on a grand tour of Europe as part of their education. As commerce and affluence made travel increasingly convenient, more and more travelers visited the fountains of Western culture and recorded their experiences. The novelist Tobias Smollett published a book about his travels through France and Italy in 1763. As Sterne characterizes him, Smollett was a supercilious, not a sentimental traveler because he was contemptuous of most things French and throughout his travels was obsessed by bad smells. Hence Sterne's reference to him as Smelfungus and his dismissing him in an indecent joke. By contrast, the sentimental traveler had set out, Yorick tells us, "upon a quiet journey of the heart in pursuit of NATURE, and those affections which arise out of her which make us love each other—and the world, better than we do." What we get is a most unusual travelogue indeed, for, instead of the wonders of Versailles or the like, it relates encounters with persons, often nameless, who move Yorick to acts of charity, or of chance meetings with women whose company he seeks to enjoy. It was his misfortune, Yorick had said, always to be falling in love, often against his will. The temptations of the heart are the main concern of his sentimental journey.

Sterne, his readers would have remembered from *Tristram Shandy,* was the master of *double-entendre,* in a single phrase or in a whole story, as that on noses. The account of the beautiful shopkeeper in Paris is Sterne's characteristic insinuation of a meaning beneath the surface level of his narrative. Yorick had set off to the opera and asked directions of the mistress of a shop. In looking into her eyes he forgets all but her charms, which he compliments so effectually that in a moment he is sitting by her side with his fingers on her pulse.

I had counted twenty pulsations, and was going on fast towards the fortieth, when her husband coming unexpected from a back parlour into the shop, put me a little out in my reckoning.—Twas nobody but her husband, she said—

The husband being a "nobody," and with encouragement from her, he tries on a pair of gloves, which under the circumstances are both gloves and not gloves. But, no: "It will not do, said I, shaking my head a little—No, said she, doing the same thing." Yorick's temptation has been conquered, at least temporarily. This air of eroticism pervading the novel is one of its most appealing textures, yet one of the most difficult to define. Sexuality in Sterne is neither sensual nor sentimental (in the modern sense of both words) but is a refined realism of both. It is the nature of the sentimental traveler to dwell upon the psychological rather than the physiological nature of love, which the reader can imagine for himself—as we are left to do at the end of the novel.

But, as in the scene above, the refined sentiments of the heart are made real by the sense of touch, and usually in a delightfully surprising or witty way. Early in the novel, Sterne alerts the reader in a metaphor of heart and hands (and italics) of the promise of Yorick's adventures: "What a large volume of adventures may be grasped within this little span of life by him who interests his heart in everything, and who having eyes to see, what time and chance are perpetually holding out to him as he journeyeth on his way, misses nothing he can *fairly* lay his hands on." This sentence epitomizes Yorick's sensual and sentimental adventures of love; and, in its pun on "grasped" and "fairly," and in the delay of its double meaning until the end, the sentence also epitomizes Sterne's style.

As these temptations of the heart fulfill Sterne's purpose of depicting our "gentler passions and affections," so the scenes that have to do mainly with charity, benevolence, and fellow-feeling fulfill his moral purpose of teaching us to "love the world more than we do." The episode of the caged starling is representative, and it illustrates, too, Sterne's structural skill in unifying the assorted travel experiences into an artistic whole. The unity of the novel lies not in the progression or events of the travels but in Yorick's experience of them. He had set out on his journey without a passport, and England being at war with France, he ran the risk of imprisonment as a spy. This possibility led him to reflect upon and to rationalize confinement in the Bastille as only a house "one couldn't get out of"—a chain of reasoning however that was interrupted by the plaintive cry of the caged bird, "I can't get out." This cry, mechanical as it was, made him reconsider the nature of liberty and to value it more truly than he had, which in turn sent him off to

Versailles in search of a passport. The journey there allows him to give the bird's history, and how upon his return to England he gave the starling to a lord, who sold it to a commoner. "But," as Yorick moralizes the result of the episode, "as all these wanted to *get in*—and my bird wanted to *get out*—he had almost as little store set by him in London as in Paris." Thus the fable ends in a satire on man's propensity to imprison himself. It also asserts the value of the feelings over the "conceits" of reason, and it gives us an affecting view of liberty, which man is always inclined to undervalue.

Sterne had already used the episode of Maria of Moulines in *Tristram Shandy,* but he came back to it again because it was the kind of sentimental writing for which he was admired. This scene in Sterne and the one like it in Mackenzie, of the forsaken and friendless maiden bereft of her senses because of her misfortunes in love, was to become a stock type in the literature of feeling. The tears Sterne sought to evoke in describing Maria's sorrow were the tears of moral sympathy, for to be moved as Yorick was moved was to portray both man's mortality and immortality. "I am positive I have a soul," Yorick asserts in regard to his sympathy for Maria, "nor can all the books with which materialists have pestered the world ever convince me to the contrary." Sterne's traveler is not jesting here. The materiality of the soul, hence its irrelevance, was the topic of notorious controversy during the age of scientific rationalism, but what writers could neither prove nor disprove by philosophical reasoning, Sterne felt he did prove in such adventures of his sentimental traveler. Following the Maria scene is Yorick's prayer to sensibility quoted above, in which this divine faculty is praised as relating us both to our fellow men and to God. Sensibility was the creative soul by which man refined his mortal being. It was at once the source, end, and test of man's moral and esthetic life.

Sterne's most successful rival in sentimental writing was Henry Mackenzie, a Scotsman, which is not surprising in view of the influential school of Scottish philosophers who wrote on the moral sense from Hutcheson on. Indeed, Sir Walter Scott thought that Mackenzie's fiction was better than Sterne's, but he may be forgiven his bias because Mackenzie was among the most eminent men of letters in Scotland during the last decades of the eighteenth century. Born in 1745 in Edinburgh in the year of the Jacobite Rebellion, he died in 1831 at the dawn of the Victorian era. The height of his literary fame spanned the period that has been called the Golden Age of Scotland—the age of Hume, Adam Smith, Burns, Scott, Blair, Robertson, among others—in which Mackenzie himself was hailed as "Ultimus Scotorum." His *Man of Feeling* was published in 1771 and was instantly successful. In the next few years he published two other novels, wrote several plays, and influential periodical essays, was an effective political journalist, and contributed in many ways to the cultural efflorescence of Scotland at this time. As a literary critic he was among the first to recognize Burns' genius, to help make German literature and the folk literature of Scotland better known, and to praise the merits of Alexander Pope when it was no longer fashionable to do so. For all the fame he received by being known as "the man of feeling," Mackenzie in person was described by one of his contemporaries as "a hard-headed, practical man, as full of practical wisdom as most of his fictitious characters are devoid of it, and this without impairing the affectionate softness of his heart. In person he was thin, shrivelled, and yellow, kiln dried with smoking, with something, when seen in profile, of the clever, wicked look of Voltaire."

It is likely that Mackenzie began his novel before Sterne's *Sentimental Journey* appeared in February, 1768, but it is evident that before *The Man of Feeling* was published in 1771, Sterne had influenced it directly or indirectly. Like Yorick, Harley is a sentimental traveler. The structure of the novel is Harley's adventures as he travels from his country home to London; the central interest in the story, as in Sterne's, is not a narrative of the events themselves but their effect upon the sensibility of the hero. Like Yorick, Harley sheds tears of moral elevation at doing acts of kindness and charity, but he is certainly no man of jest, and the love for a woman that animates and refines his sensibility in the end consumes him. Direct echoes of Sterne's influence can be detected probably in the style and substance of the opening chapter on travel (note, for example, Yorick's comparison of the English and French); and Harley's silent debate with his passions (p. 133) suggests that of Yorick's (p. 21). Also, Mackenzie imitates Sterne's manner of countering and releasing the emotional or sentimental intensity of a passage or scene by a witty antithesis. Other parallels of Harley's adventures, in Bedlam, with the misanthrope, and with the prostitute, can be found in the works of Fielding, Goldsmith, and Thomas Gray.

Still, Mackenzie's novel enjoyed its reputation largely for its originality, and this reputation was deserved. The novel, published anonymously, purports to be fragments of a history of Harley written by his friend—fragments because the curate who came by it (he preferred works of logic) used it for wadding for his gun. Therefore, the first person narrator serves Mackenzie both to tell Harley's story and to moralize about it. Mackenzie remarked that his purpose was to sketch "the life and sentiments of a man of more than usual sensibility," an undertaking he hoped was "uniformly subservient to the cause of virtue." Harley is a humanitarian and his experiences teach him how much in need the world is for common charity and kindness. He had gone to London with prospects for increasing his fortune, but he left the city a poorer and sadder man. For the man of feeling, in the literature of sensibility generally, London was the sink of iniquity, driving people to madness, misanthropy, and griefs of every sort. In meeting people bent upon or suffering from the city's vices, Harley grows more virtuous but less capable of living in the world. The central theme of *The Man of Feeling* is the contrast between the virtuous man of sensibility and the vicious worldliness of the great part of mankind. In the end Harley dies of the excess of feeling, but when directed to social ends that kind of sensibility, Mackenzie and the age believed, could redeem man's fallen nature.

What impressed Sir Walter Scott about Mackenzie's novel was "the tone of moral pathos" achieved and sustained in its representation of those "finer feelings to which ordinary hearts are callous. . . . In short, Mackenzie aimed at being the historian of feeling and has succeeded in the object of his ambition." With the added perspective of two hundred years of psychology, the modern reader will probably be less generous in his praise of *The Man of Feeling*. Scott's judgment remains valid, nevertheless. Despite the excessive tearfulness and misfortunes of the madwoman, or those of Old Edwards, there is in the portrayal of Harley's altruism and sensitivity a character that evokes our sense of moral pathos. Mackenzie intended an excess of feeling, what he called "a tincture of romantic enthusiasm," in his hero. "There are some feelings," Harley remarks in the end, "which perhaps are too tender to be suffered by the world. The world is in general selfish, interested, and unthinking, and throws the imputation of romance or melancholy on every temper more susceptible than its own." By depicting a man of fine yet morbid sensitivity who wishes to reform the world but cannot live in it, and who is consumed and dies by the passion that motivates him, Mackenzie foreshadows the romantic hero of the next generation.

By 1789, the year in which the last volume of Thomas Day's *History of Sandford and Merton* was published, the excesses of sensibility rather than its virtues were being stressed in literature. The following titles are indicative: *Excessive Sensibility* (1787); *Aurulia: The Victim of Sensibility* (1790); *Errors of Sensibility* (1793); and *Sense and Sensibility* (1811). The last, of course, was by Jane Austen and suggests both the counter and complementary nature of the two faculties. Thomas Day in his life and works sought to achieve the combined virtues of sense and sensibility. Born in London in 1748, educated at Oxford, Day early in life dedicated his considerable talents and fortune to the cause of human progress and freedom. His own chief virtue, according to a contemporary biographer, was that quality of sensibility or sympathetic imagination "which transposes into our own breasts the miseries or happiness of others, with the consequent desire to prevent the former and promote the latter." In the opinion of Richard Lovell Edgeworth, a lifelong friend, Thomas Day was "the most virtuous human being" he had ever known. Day's virtue showed itself mainly in acts of public utility and charity of many sorts. As a friend of John Wilkes and other critics of empire and political tyranny, he wrote pamphlets and poems in defense of individual liberty and of the American Revolution. He held very strong views against slavery, criticizing the colonists in that regard, and with his friend John Bicknell wrote a poem called "The Dying Negro," which received considerable attention. For a time he lived in Lichfield, and was intimate with a circle of celebrities that included Dr. Erasmus Darwin, famous then for his contributions to the arts and sciences but remembered now only as the grandfather of Charles Darwin. But Day disliked city life and settled on a country estate where he experimented with new agricultural methods and preached and practiced benevolence in his daily life.

One of Day's practical interests was education. Rousseau had impressed him deeply. In fact, so taken were Day and Edgeworth with the theory of education as detailed in *Émile* (they had also visited Rousseau), that they sought to teach his principles directly. Edgeworth describes his efforts thus: "I dressed my son without stockings, with his arms bare, and in a jacket and trousers such as are quite common at present, but which were at that time novel and extraordinary. I succeeded in making him fearless of danger, and, what is more difficult, capable of bearing privation of every sort. He had all the virtues of a child bred in the hut of a savage, and all the knowledge of things, which could well be acquired at an early age by a boy bred in civilized society." Not yet married, Day hoped to find a wife who would fulfill Rousseau's ideal of sense and sensibility, and to that end he adopted two girls aged eleven and twelve from an orphanage and set about bringing them up so that he might marry the most agreeable one. Some of the details of Day's experiment in their education—such as his unexpectedly firing off pistols close to their ears or suddenly dropping hot sealing wax on their bare arms in order to teach them to be fearless and hardy—were ridiculous, and luckily harmless. Because there are some traits of the human heart and mind that are not educable, neither of the girls turned out to be the ideal Day sought. The chief point of the experiment, however, was to develop the natural sensibilities and hence the natural virtues of children. Day believed with Rousseau that if children experienced the conditions supposed to be found in "the noble state of nature"—such as courage, compassion, endurance, fearlessness, spontaneity, and honesty—while at the same time they were protected from the vices of society, they would grow up into self-reliant and sensible human beings. The greatest threat to the civilized values of his time Day, and many others, saw as the "effeminacy" of manners and mind, brought about by wealth and pride of class, with the consequent chasm created between the rich and the poor. In this respect, as well as others, Day strikes a very modern note indeed. In countering these evils with a philosophy of nature and nobility, Day wrote his novel not only as "a work for the education of children" but for their elders as well.

Mr. Barlow, the teacher of Harry Sandford and Tommy Merton, is the spokesman for Day's ideas, declaring early in the story that he who undertakes the task of educating a child undertakes "the most important duty in society." The education of Tommy (for Harry has already been educated in the virtues of a state of nature) is primarily through imitation of Harry's deeds, and by means of the morals contained in the stories the children and Mr. Barlow read. As the spoiled rich boy, Tommy must unlearn his mistaken notions of what a "gentleman" is and must learn Harry's virtues as a poor but honest plowboy. These he learns after many misadventures and moral lessons. As published originally, the first volume (1783) ended with the tearful scene of Tommy's gift to the poor family who were about to be evicted. The second volume (1786) ended with the fight and separation of the two boys, and the third (1789) ended with their reconciliation and Tommy's having learned to practice that "greatness of character" that Mr. Barlow had stressed. Interspersed between these climactic episodes are moral tales and fables that Day either made up or adapted from various sources. Their purpose, in addition to their narrative interest, was to contrast virtue and vice, most typically, a noble life of endurance and courage contrasted with one of slothful and ignoble luxury. Therefore Day included many accounts of Laplanders, Scythians, Spartans, and the American Indian—the noble savage. He had, according to Edgeworth, "a deep-rooted prejudice in favor of savage life." But the savage life Day portrays emphasizes the virtues of sense and sensibility complementing each other in an ideal "manliness." For him, in short, education could bring out those virtues of sympathy that moved a Harley or Yorick to benevolence, and by adding to these the qualities of courage, duty, endurance, and the like, true greatness of character and a more virtuous civilization would result.

Day did not call his work a novel. Though it was not a "treatise on education" he said, he hoped no one who had not had experience in the education of children would belittle the book. Mackenzie had some doubts whether his novel was really a novel, and Sterne preferred to think of his work as original sentimental writing. No one probably will read any of the three novels for their plots. Commenting on the first popular sentimental novelist, Dr. Johnson declared: "Why, Sir, if you were to read Richardson for the story your impatience would be so much fretted that you would hang yourself."

Despite its lack of a "story," *A Sentimental Journey* deserves richly the status of a major classic that it currently has. Sterne succeeded, with inimitable wit and sentiment, in his purpose of describing those affections of the heart that make us love each other, and the world, better than we do. *The Man of Feeling* is a minor classic that deserves to be better known. Its tearfulness is too obvious, but the careful reader will note realities about the human condition, as Mackenzie saw it, that are deeper than tears. And, *The History of Sandford and Merton,* in part because of the reputation it once had, deserves not to be forgotten. The success it enjoyed, however, was not solely from its practical, pedagogical value. Day was a sharp observer of human affectation, especially in class and race prejudice, and characterized it frequently with effective irony. Like Sterne and Mackenzie, he exploited sentiment to create a moral view of the world.

A Note on the Texts

The text of *A Sentimental Journey* is based on the second edition published in 1768. *The Man of Feeling* is based on a new edition published in 1783, and *The History of Sandford and Merton,* which is here abridged, is taken from the third complete edition published in 1791. Spelling has been modernized in the novels, but the authors' punctuation, especially the dash, which is characteristic of the literature of sensibility, has been retained except in a few instances that might mislead the reader. Footnotes at the bottom of the text are the authors'; some notes on obscure words and references have been supplied at the end of the book.

Contents

LAURENCE STERNE

A Sentimental Journey Through France and Italy

—They order, said I, this matter better in France—

—You have been in France? said my gentleman, turning quick upon me with the most civil triumph in the world.— Strange! quoth I, debating the matter with myself, That one and twenty miles sailing, for 'tis absolutely no further from Dover to Calais, should give a man these rights—I'll look into them: so giving up the argument—I went straight to my lodgings, put up half a dozen shirts and a black pair of silk breeches—"the coat I have on, said I, looking at the sleeve, will do"—took a place in the Dover stage; and the packet sailing at nine the next morning—by three I had got sat down to my dinner upon a fricasee'd chicken, so incontestably in France, that had I died that night of an indigestion, the whole world could not have suspended the effects of the *Droits d'aubaine**—my shirts, and black pair of silk breeches—portmanteau and all must have gone to the king of France—even the little picture which I have so long worn, and so often have told thee, Eliza,[1] I would carry with me into my grave, would have been torn from my neck.—Ungenerous!—to seize upon the wreck of an unwary passenger, whom your subjects had beckoned to their coast—by heaven! SIRE, it is not well done;

* All the effects of strangers (Swiss and Scotch excepted) dying in France, are seized by virtue of this law, though the heir be upon the spot—the profit of these contingencies being farmed, there is no redress.

and much does it grieve me, 'tis the monarch of a people so civilized and courteous, and so renowned for sentiment and fine feelings, that I have to reason with——

But I have scarce set foot in your dominions—

CALAIS

When I had finished my dinner, and drank the king of France's health, to satisfy my mind that I bore him no spleen, but, on the contrary, high honour for the humanity of his temper —I rose up an inch taller for the accommodation.

—No—said I—the Bourbon is by no means a cruel race: they may be misled like other people; but there is a mildness in their blood. As I acknowledged this, I felt a suffusion of a finer kind upon my cheek—more warm and friendly to man, than what Burgundy (at least of two livres a bottle, which was such as I had been drinking) could have produced.

—Just God! said I, kicking my portmanteau aside, what is there in this world's goods which should sharpen our spirits, and make so many kind-hearted brethren of us, fall out so cruelly as we do by the way?

When man is at peace with man, how much lighter than a feather is the heaviest of metals in his hand! he pulls out his purse, and holding it airily and uncompressed, looks round him, as if he sought for an object to share it with.—In doing this, I felt every vessel in my frame dilate—the arteries beat all cheerily together, and every power which sustained life, performed it with so little friction, that 'twould have confounded the most *physical precieuse* in France: with all her materialism, she could scarce have called me a machine—

I'm confident, said I to myself, I should have overset her creed.

The accession of that idea, carried nature, at that time, as high as she could go—I was at peace with the world before, and this finished the treaty with myself—

—Now, was I a King of France, cried I—what a moment for an orphan to have begged his father's portmanteau of me!

THE MONK

Calais

I had scarce uttered the words, when a poor monk of the order of St. Francis came into the room to beg something for his convent. No man cares to have his virtues the sport of contingencies—or one man may be generous, as another man is puissant—*sed non, quo ad hanc*—or be it as it may—for there is no regular reasoning upon the ebbs and flows of our humours; they may depend upon the same causes, for aught I know, which influence the tides themselves—'twould oft be no discredit to us to suppose it was so: I'm sure at least for myself, that in many a case I should be more highly satisfied, to have it said by the world, "I had had an affair with the moon, in which there was neither sin nor shame," than have it pass altogether as my own act and deed, wherein there was so much of both.

—But be this as it may. The moment I cast my eyes upon him, I was predetermined not to give him a single sou; and accordingly I put my purse into my pocket—buttoned it up— set myself a little more upon my centre, and advanced up gravely to him: there was something, I fear, forbidding in my look: I have his figure this moment before my eyes, and think there was that in it which deserved better.

The monk, as I judged from the break in his tonsure, a few scattered white hairs upon his temples, being all that remained of it, might be about seventy—but from his eyes, and that sort of fire which was in them, which seemed more tempered by courtesy than years, could be no more than sixty— Truth might lie between—He was certainly sixty-five; and the general air of his countenance, notwithstanding something seemed to have been planting wrinkles in it before their time, agreed to the account.

It was one of those heads, which Guido[2] has often painted— mild, pale—penetrating, free from all commonplace ideas of

fat contented ignorance looking downwards upon the earth—
it looked forwards; but looked, as if it looked at something
beyond this world. How one of his order came by it, heaven
above, who let it fall upon a monk's shoulders, best knows:
but it would have suited a Bramin, and had I met it upon the
plains of Indostan, I had reverenced it.

The rest of his outline may be given in a few strokes; one
might put it into the hands of any one to design, for 'twas
neither elegant or otherwise, but as character and expression
made it so: it was a thin, spare form, something above the common size, if it lost not the distinction by a bend forwards in
the figure—but it was the attitude of Entreaty; and as it now
stands presented to my imagination, it gained more than it lost
by it.

When he had entered the room three paces, he stood still;
and laying his left hand upon his breast, (a slender white staff
with which he journeyed being in his right)—when I had got
close up to him, he introduced himself with the little story of
the wants of his convent, and the poverty of his order—and
did it with so simple a grace—and such an air of deprecation
was there in the whole cast of his look and figure—I was be-
witched not to have been struck with it—

—A better reason was, I had predetermined not to give
him a single sou.

THE MONK

Calais

—'Tis very true, said I, replying to a cast upwards with his
eyes, with which he had concluded his address—'tis very true
—and heaven be their resource who have no other but the
charity of the world, the stock of which, I fear, is no way
sufficient for the many *great claims* which are hourly made
upon it.

As I pronounced the words *great claims,* he gave a slight
glance with his eye downwards upon the sleeve of his tunic—

I felt the full force of the appeal—I acknowledge it, said I—a coarse habit, and that but once in three years, with meagre diet—are no great matters; and the true point of pity is, as they can be earned in the world with so little industry, that your order should wish to procure them by pressing upon a fund which is the property of the lame, the blind, the aged, and the infirm—the captive who lies down counting over and over again the days of his afflictions, languishes also for his share of it; and had you been of the *order of mercy,* instead of the order of St. Francis, poor as I am, continued I, pointing at my portmanteau, full cheerfully should it have been opened to you, for the ransom of the unfortunate—The monk made me a bow—but of all others, resumed I, the unfortunate of our own country, surely, have the first rights; and I have left thousands in distress upon our own shore—The monk gave a cordial wave with his head—as much as to say, No doubt there is misery enough in every corner of the world, as well as within our convent—But we distinguish, said I, laying my hand upon the sleeve of his tunic, in return for his appeal—we distinguish, my good father! betwixt those who wish only to eat the bread of their own labour—and those who eat the bread of other people's, and have no other plan in life, but to get through it in sloth and ignorance, *for the love of God.*

The poor Franciscan made no reply: a hectic of a moment passed across his cheek, but could not tarry—Nature seemed to have done with her resentments in him; he showed none—but letting his staff fall within his arm, he pressed both his hands with resignation upon his breast, and retired.

THE MONK

Calais

My heart smote me the moment he shut the door—Psha! said I with an air of carelessness, three several times—but it would not do: every ungracious syllable I had uttered, crowded back into my imagination: I reflected, I had no right over the poor Franciscan, but to deny him; and that the punishment of that was enough to the disappointed without the addition of unkind language—I considered his grey hairs—his courteous figure seemed to re-enter, and gently ask me what injury he had done me?—and why I could use him thus?—I would have given twenty livres for an advocate—I have behaved very ill, said I within myself; but I have only just set out upon my travels; and shall learn better manners as I get along.

THE DESOBLIGEANT

Calais

When a man is discontented with himself, it has one advantage however, that it puts him into an excellent frame of mind for making a bargain. Now there being no travelling through France and Italy without a chaise—and nature generally prompting us to the thing we are fittest for, I walked out into the coach-yard to buy or hire something of that kind to my purpose: an old Desobligeant* in the furthest corner of the court hit my fancy at first sight, so I instantly got into it, and finding it in tolerable harmony with my feelings, I ordered the waiter to call Monsieur Dessein the master of the hotel—but Monsieur Dessein being gone to vespers, and not caring to face the Franciscan, whom I saw on the opposite side of the court, in conference with a lady just arrived, at the inn—I drew the taffeta curtain betwixt us, and being determined to write my journey, I took out my pen and ink, and wrote the preface to it in the *Desobligeant*.

PREFACE

In the Desobligeant

It must have been observed by many a peripatetic philosopher, That nature has set up by her own unquestionable authority

---

* A chaise, so called in France, from its holding but one person.

certain boundaries and fences to circumscribe the discontent of man: she has effected her purpose in the quietest and easiest manner by laying him under almost insuperable obligations to work out his ease, and to sustain his sufferings at home. It is there only that she has provided him with the most suitable objects to partake of his happiness, and bear a part of that burden which, in all countries and ages, has ever been too heavy for one pair of shoulders. 'Tis true we are endued with an imperfect power of spreading our happiness sometimes beyond *her* limits, but 'tis so ordered, that, from the want of languages, connections, and dependencies, and from the difference in education, customs, and habits, we lie under so many impediments in communicating our sensations out of our own sphere, as often amount to a total impossibility.

It will always follow from hence, that the balance of sentimental commerce is always against the expatriated adventurer: he must buy what he has little occasion for at their own price—his conversation will seldom be taken in exchange for theirs without a large discount—and this, by the by, eternally driving him into the hands of more equitable brokers for such conversation as he can find, it requires no great spirit of divination to guess at his party—

This brings me to my point; and naturally leads me (if the see-saw of this *Desobligeant* will but let me get on) into the efficient as well as the final causes of travelling—

Your idle people that leave their native country and go abroad for some reason or reasons which may be derived from one of these general causes—

　　Infirmity of body,
　　Imbecility of mind, or
　　Inevitable necessity.

The first two include all those who travel by land or by water, labouring with pride, curiosity, vanity or spleen, subdivided and combined *in infinitum*.

The third class includes the whole army of peregrine martyrs; more especially those travellers who set out upon their travels with the benefit of the clergy, either as delinquents travelling under the direction of governors recommended by the magistrate—or young gentlemen transported by the cruelty of parents and guardians, and travelling under the direction of governors recommended by Oxford, Aberdeen and Glasgow.

There is a fourth class, but their number is so small that they would not deserve a distinction, was it not necessary in a work of this nature to observe the greatest precision and nicety, to avoid a confusion of character. And these men I speak of, are such as cross the seas, and sojourn in a land of strangers with a view of saving money for various reasons and upon various pretences: but as they might also save themselves and others a great deal of unnecessary trouble by saving their money at home—and as their reasons for travelling are the least complex of any other species of emigrants, I shall distinguish these gentlemen by the name of

Simple Travellers.

Thus the whole circle of travellers may be reduced to the following *Heads*.

Idle Travellers,
Inquisitive Travellers,
Lying Travellers,
   Proud Travellers,
   Vain Travellers,
   Splenetic Travellers.

Then follow the Travellers of Necessity.
The delinquent and felonious Traveller,
The unfortunate and innocent Traveller,
The simple Traveller,
And last of all (if you please) The

Sentimental Traveller (meaning thereby myself) who have travelled, and of which I am now sitting down to give an account—as much out of *Necessity,* and the *besoin de Voyager,* as any one in the class.

I am well aware, at the same time, as both my travels and

observations will be altogether of a different cast from any of my fore-runners; that I might have insisted upon a whole niche entirely to myself—but I should break in upon the confines of the *Vain* Traveller, in wishing to draw attention towards me, till I have some better grounds for it, than the mere *Novelty of my Vehicle*.

It is sufficient for my reader, if he has been a traveller himself, that with study and reflection hereupon he may be able to determine his own place and rank in the catalogue—it will be one step towards knowing himself; as it is great odds, but he retains some tincture and resemblance, of what he imbibed or carried out, to the present hour.

The man who first transplanted the grape of Burgundy to the Cape of Good Hope (observe he was a Dutchman) never dreamt of drinking the same wine at the Cape, that the same grape produced upon the French mountains—he was too phlegmatic for that—but undoubtedly he expected to drink some sort of vinous liquor; but whether good, bad, or indifferent—he knew enough of this world to know, that it did not depend upon his choice, but that which is generally called *chance* was to decide his success: however, he hoped for the best; and in these hopes, by an intemperate confidence in the fortitude of his head, and the depth of his discretion, Mynheer might possibly overset both in his new vineyard; and by discovering his nakedness, become a laughing-stock to his people.

Even so it fares with the poor Traveller, sailing and posting through the politer kingdoms of the globe in pursuit of knowledge and improvements.

Knowledge and improvements are to be got by sailing and posting for that purpose; but whether useful knowledge and real improvements, is all a lottery—and even where the adventurer is successful, the acquired stock must be used with caution and sobriety to turn to any profit—but as the chances run prodigiously the other way both as to the acquisition and application, I am of opinion, That a man would act as wisely, if he could prevail upon himself, to live contented without foreign knowledge or foreign improvements, especially if he lives in a country that has no absolute want of either—and indeed, much grief of heart has it oft and many a time cost me, when I have observed how many a foul step the inquisitive Traveller has measured to see sights and look into discoveries; all which, as Sancho Pança said to Don Quixote, they might have seen dry-shod at home. It is an age so full of light, that there is scarce a country or corner of Europe whose beams are not crossed and interchanged with others—knowledge in most of its branches, and in most affairs, is like music in an Italian street, whereof those may partake, who pay nothing—But there is no nation under heaven—and God is my record, (before whose tribunal I must one day come and give an account of this work)—that I do not speak it vauntingly—But there is no nation under heaven abounding with more variety of learning— where the sciences may be more fitly wooed, or more surely won than here—where art is encouraged, and will so soon rise high—where Nature (take her altogether) has so little to answer for—and, to close all, where there is more wit and variety of character to feed the mind with—Where then, my dear countrymen, are you going—

—We are only looking at this chaise, said they—Your most obedient servant, said I, skipping out of it, and pulling off my hat—We were wondering, said one of them, who, I found, was an *inquisitive traveller*—what could occasion its motion.—'Twas the agitation, said I coolly, of writing a preface —I never heard, said the other, who was a *simple traveller,* of a preface wrote in a *Desobligeant.*—It would have been better, said I, in a *Vis a Vis.*

—*As an Englishman does not travel to see Englishmen,* I retired to my room.

CALAIS

I perceived that something darkened the passage more than myself, as I stepped along it to my room; it was effectually Mons. Dessein, the master of the hotel, who had just returned

from vespers, and, with his hat under his arm, was most com-
plaisantly following me, to put me in mind of my wants. I had
wrote myself pretty well out of conceit with the *Desobligeant;*
and Mons. Dessein speaking of it, with a shrug, as if it would
no way suit me, it immediately struck my fancy that it belonged
to some *innocent traveller,* who, on his return home, had left
it to Mons. Dessein's honour to make the most of. Four months
had elapsed since it had finished its career of Europe in the
corner of Mons. Dessein's coach-yard; and having sallied out
from thence but a vampt-up business at the first, though it had
been twice taken to pieces on Mount Sennis, it had not profited
much by its adventures—but by none so little as the standing
so many months unpitied in the corner of Mons. Dessein's
coach-yard. Much indeed was not to be said for it—but
something might—and when a few words will rescue misery
out of her distress, I hate the man who can be a churl of them.

—Now was I the master of this hotel, said I, laying the
point of my fore-finger on Mons. Dessein's breast, I would
inevitably make a point of getting rid of this unfortunate
Desobligeant—it stands swinging reproaches at you every time
you pass by it——

Mon Dieu! said Mons. Dessein—I have no interest—Except the interest, said I, which men of a certain turn of mind
take, Mons. Dessein, in their own sensations—I'm persuaded,
to a man who feels for others as well as for himself, every
rainy night, disguise it as you will, must cast a damp upon
your spirits—You suffer, Mons. Dessein, as much as the
machine—

I have always observed when there is as much *sour* as
sweet in a compliment, that an Englishman is eternally at a
loss within himself, whether to take it, or let it alone: a Frenchman never is: Mons. Dessein made me a bow.

C'est bien vrai, said he—But in this case I should only exchange one disquietude for another, and with loss: figure to
yourself, my dear Sir, that in giving you a chaise which would
fall to pieces before you had got half way to Paris—figure to
yourself how much I should suffer, in giving an ill impression

of myself to a man of honour, and lying at the mercy, as I must do, *d'un homme d'esprit*.

The dose was made up exactly after my own prescription; so I could not help taking it—and returning Mons. Dessein his bow, without more casuistry we walked together towards his Remise, to take a view of his magazine of chaises.

IN THE STREET

Calais

It must needs be a hostile kind of a world, when the buyer (if it be but of a sorry post-chaise) cannot go forth with the seller thereof into the street to terminate the difference betwixt them, but he instantly falls into the same frame of mind and views his conventionist with the same sort of eye, as if he was going along with him to Hyde-park corner to fight a duel. For my own part, being but a poor sword's-man, and no way a match for Monsieur Dessein, I felt the rotation of all the movements within me, to which the situation is incident—I looked at Monsieur Dessein through and through—eyed him as he walked along in profile—then, *en face*—thought he looked like a Jew—then a Turk—disliked his wig—cursed him by my gods—wished him at the devil——

—And is all this to be lighted up in the heart for a beggarly account of three or four Louis d'ors, which is the most I can be over-reached in?—Base passion! said I, turning myself about, as a man naturally does upon a sudden reverse of sentiment—base, ungentle passion! thy hand is against every man, and every man's hand against thee—Heaven forbid! said she, raising her hand up to her forehead, for I had turned full in front upon the lady whom I had seen in conference with the monk—she had followed us unperceived—Heaven forbid indeed! said I, offering her my own—she had a black pair of silk gloves open only at the thumb and two fore-fingers, so accepted it without reserve—and I led her up to the door of the Remise.

Monsieur Dessein had *diabled* the key above fifty times before he found out he had come with a wrong one in his hand: we were as impatient as himself to have it opened; and so attentive to the obstacle, that I continued holding her hand almost without knowing it; so that Monsieur Dessein left us together with her hand in mine, and with our faces turned towards the door of the Remise, and said he would be back in five minutes.

Now a colloquy of five minutes, in such a situation, is worth one of as many ages, with your faces turned towards the street: in the latter case, 'tis drawn from the objects and occurrences without—when your eyes are fixed upon a dead blank— you draw purely from yourselves. A silence of a single moment upon Monsieur Dessein's leaving us, had been fatal to the situation—she had infallibly turned about—so I begun the conversation instantly.——

——But what were the temptations, (as I write not to apologize for the weaknesses of my heart in this tour,—but to give an account of them)—shall be described with the same simplicity, with which I felt them.

THE REMISE DOOR

Calais

When I told the reader that I did not care to get out of the *Desobligeant,* because I saw the monk in close conference with a lady just arrived at the inn—I told him the truth; but I did not tell him the whole truth; for I was full as much restrained by the appearance and figure of the lady he was talking to. Suspicion crossed my brain, and said, he was telling her what had passed: something jarred upon it within me—I wished him at his convent.

When the heart flies out before the understanding, it saves the judgment a world of pains—I was certain she was of a better order of beings—however, I thought no more of her, but went on and wrote my preface.

The impression returned, upon my encounter with her in

the street; a guarded frankness with which she gave me her hand, showed, I thought, her good education and her good sense; and as I led her on, I felt a pleasurable ductility about her, which spread a calmness over all my spirits——

——Good God! how a man might lead such a creature as this round the world with him!——

I had not yet seen her face—'twas not material; for the drawing was instantly set about, and long before we had got to the door of the Remise, *Fancy* had finished the whole head, and pleased herself as much with its fitting her goddess, as if she had dived into the TIBER for it——but thou art a seduced, and a seducing slut; and albeit thou cheatest us seven times a day with thy pictures and images, yet with so many charms dost thou do it, and thou deckest out thy pictures in the shapes of so many angels of light, 'tis a shame to break with thee.

When we had got to the door of the Remise, she withdrew her hand from across her forehead, and let me see the original —it was a face of about six and twenty—of a clear transparent brown, simply set off without rouge or powder—it was not critically handsome, but there was that in it, which in the frame of mind I was in, attached me much more to it—it was interesting; I fancied it wore the characters of a widowed look, and in that state of its declension, which had passed the two first paroxysms of sorrow, and was quietly beginning to reconcile itself to its loss—but a thousand other distresses might have traced the same lines; I wished to know what they had been—and was ready to enquire, (had the same *bon ton* of conversation permitted, as in the days of Esdras).—"*What aileth thee? and why art thou disquieted? and why is thy understanding troubled?*"—In a word, I felt benevolence for her; and resolved some way or other to throw in my mite of courtesy—if not of service.

Such were my temptations—and in this disposition to give way to them, was I left alone with the lady with her hand in mine, and with our faces both turned closer to the door of the Remise than what was absolutely necessary.

THE REMISE DOOR

Calais

This certainly, fair lady! said I, raising her hand up a little lightly as I begun, must be one of Fortune's whimsical doings: to take two utter strangers by their hands—of different sexes, and perhaps from different corners of the globe, and in one movement place them together in such a cordial situation, as Friendship herself could scarce have achieved for them, had she projected it for a month—

—And your reflection upon it, shows how much, Monsieur, she has embarrassed you by the adventure.—

When the situation is, what we would wish, nothing is so ill-timed as to hint at the circumstances which make it so: you thank Fortune, continued she—you had reason—the heart knew it, and was satisfied; and who but an English philosopher would have sent notices of it to the brain to reverse the judgment?

In saying this, she disengaged her hand with a look which I thought a sufficient commentary upon the text.

It is a miserable picture which I am going to give of the weakness of my heart, by owning, that it suffered a pain, which worthier occasions could not have inflicted.—I was mortified with the loss of her hand, and the manner in which I had lost it carried neither oil nor wine to the wound: I never felt the pain of a sheepish inferiority so miserably in my life.

The triumphs of a true feminine heart are short upon these discomfitures. In a very few seconds she laid her hand upon the cuff of my coat, in order to finish her reply; so some way or other, God knows how, I regained my situation.

——She had nothing to add.

I forthwith began to model a different conversation for the lady, thinking from the spirit as well as moral of this, that I had been mistaken in her character; but upon turning her

face towards me, the spirit which had animated the reply was
fled—the muscles relaxed, and I beheld the same unprotected
look of distress which first won me to her interest—melancholy!
to see such sprightliness the prey of sorrow.——I pitied her
from my soul: and though it may seem ridiculous enough to a
torpid heart,—I could have taken her into my arms, and
cherished her, though it was in the open street, without blushing.

The pulsations of the arteries along my fingers pressing
across hers, told her what was passing within me: she looked
down—a silence of some moments followed.

I fear, in this interval, I must have made some slight
efforts towards a closer compression of her hand, from a subtle
sensation I felt in the palm of my own—not as if she was going
to withdraw hers—but, as if she thought about it—and I had
infallibly lost it a second time, had not instinct more than
reason directed me to the last resource in these dangers—to
hold it loosely, and in a manner as if I was every moment
going to release it, of myself; so she let it continue, till Monsieur Dessein returned with the key; and in the mean time I set
myself to consider how I should undo the ill impressions which
the poor monk's story, in case he had told it her, must have
planted in her breast against me.

THE SNUFF-BOX

Calais

The good old monk was within six paces of us, as the idea of
him crossed my mind; and was advancing towards us a little
out of the line, as if uncertain whether he should break in
upon us or no.—He stopped, however, as soon as he came up
to us, with a word of frankness; and having a horn snuff-box in
his hand, he presented it open to me—You shall taste mine—
said I, pulling out my box (which was a small tortoise one)
and putting it into his hand—'Tis most excellent, said the monk;

Then do me the favour, I replied, to accept of the box and all, and when you take a pinch out of it, sometimes recollect it was the peace-offering of a man who once used you unkindly, but not from his heart.

The poor monk blushed as red as scarlet. *Mon Dieu!* said he, pressing his hands together—you never used me unkindly. —I should think, said the lady, he is not likely. I blushed in my turn; but from what movements, I leave to the few who feel to analyse—Excuse me, Madame, replied I—I treated him most unkindly; and from no provocations—'Tis impossible, said the lady.—My God! cried the monk, with a warmth of assevera-tion which seemed not to belong to him—the fault was in me, and in the indiscretion of my zeal—The lady opposed it, and I joined with her in maintaining it was impossible, that a spirit so regulated as his, could give offence to any.

I knew not that contention could be rendered so sweet and pleasurable a thing to the nerves as I then felt it.—We remained silent, without any sensation of that foolish pain which takes place, when in such a circle you look for ten minutes in one another's faces without saying a word. Whilst this lasted, the monk rubbed his horn-box upon the sleeve of his tunic; and as soon as it had acquired a little air of bright-ness by the friction—he made a low bow, and said, 'twas too late to say whether it was the weakness or goodness of our tempers which had involved us in this contest—but be it as it would—he begged we might exchange boxes.—In saying this, he presented his to me with one hand, as he took mine from me in the other; and having kissed it—with a stream of good nature in his eyes he put it into his bosom—and took his leave.

I guard this box, as I would the instrumental parts of my religion, to help my mind on to something better: in truth, I seldom go abroad without it; and oft and many a time have I called up by it the courteous spirit of its owner to regulate my own, in the justlings of the world; they had found full employment for his, as I learnt from his story, till about the forty-fifth year of his age, when upon some military services ill requited, and meeting at the same time with a disappointment in the tenderest of passions, he abandoned the sword and the sex together, and took sanctuary, not so much in his convent as in himself.

I feel a damp upon my spirits, as I am going to add, that in my last return through Calais, upon enquiring after Father Lorenzo, I heard he had been dead near three months, and was buried, not in his convent, but, according to his desire, in a little cemetery belonging to it, about two leagues off: I had a strong desire to see where they had laid him—when, upon pulling out his little horn-box, as I sat by his grave, and plucking up a nettle or two at the head of it, which had no business to grow there, they all struck together so forcibly upon my affections, that I burst into a flood of tears—but I am as weak as a woman; and I beg the world not to smile, but pity me.

THE REMISE DOOR

Calais

I had never quitted the lady's hand all this time; and had held it so long, that it would have been indecent to have let it go, without first pressing it to my lips: the blood and spirits, which had suffered a revulsion from her, crowded back to her, as I did it.

Now the two travellers who had spoke to me in the coach-yard, happening at that crisis to be passing by, and observing our communications, naturally took it into their heads that we must be *man and wife* at least; so stopping as soon as they came up to the door of the Remise, the one of them, who was the inquisitive traveller, asked us, if we set out for Paris the next morning?—I could only answer for myself, I said; and the lady added, she was for Amiens.—We dined there yesterday, said the simple traveller—You go directly through the town, added the other, in your road to Paris. I was going to return a thousand thanks for the intelligence, *that Amiens was in the road to Paris;* but, upon pulling out my poor monk's little horn-box to take a pinch of snuff—I made them a quiet bow, and wishing them a good passage to Dover—they left us alone—

—Now where would be the harm, said I to myself, if I was to beg of this distressed lady to accept of half of my chaise?—and what mighty mischief could ensue?

Every dirty passion, and bad propensity in my nature, took the alarm, as I stated the proposition—It will oblige you to have a third horse, said AVARICE, which will put twenty livres out of your pocket.——You know not who she is, said CAUTION—or what scrapes the affair may draw you into, whispered COWARDICE——

Depend upon it, Yorick! said DISCRETION, 'twill be said you went off with a mistress, and came by assignation to Calais for that purpose—

—You can never after, cried HYPOCRISY aloud, show your face in the world—or rise, quoth MEANNESS, in the church—or be anything in it, said PRIDE, but a lousy prebendary.

—But 'tis a civil thing, said I—and as I generally act from the first impulse, and therefore seldom listen to these cabals, which serve no purpose, that I know of, but to encompass the heart with adamant—I turned instantly about to the lady—

—But she had glided off unperceived, as the cause was pleading, and had made ten or a dozen paces down the street, by the time I had made the determination; so I set off after her with a long stride, to make her the proposal with the best address I was master of; but observing she walked with her cheek half resting upon the palm of her hand—with the slow, short-measured step of thoughtfulness, and with her eyes, as she went step by step, fixed upon the ground, it struck me, she was trying the same cause herself.—God help her! said I, she has some mother-in-law, or tartufish[3] aunt, or nonsensical old woman, to consult upon the occasion, as well as myself: so not caring to interrupt the process, and deeming it more gallant to take her at discretion than by surprise, I faced about, and took a short turn or two before the door of the Remise, whilst she walked musing on one side.

IN THE STREET

Calais

Having, on first sight of the lady, settled the affair in my fancy, "that she was of the better order of beings"—and then laid it down as a second axiom, as indisputable as the first, That she was a widow, and wore a character of distress—I went no further; I got ground enough for the situation which pleased me—and had she remained close beside my elbow till midnight, I should have held true to my system, and considered her only under that general idea.

She had scarce got twenty paces distant from me, ere something within me called out for a more particular enquiry—it brought on the idea of a further separation—I might possibly never see her more—the heart is for saving what it can; and I wanted the traces through which my wishes might find their way to her, in case I should never rejoin her myself: in a word, I wished to know her name—her family's—her condition; and as I knew the place to which she was going, I wanted to know from whence she came: but there was no coming at all this intelligence: a hundred little delicacies stood in the way. I formed a score of different plans—There was no such thing as a man's asking her directly—the thing was impossible.

A little French *debonaire* captain, who came dancing down the street, showed me, it was the easiest thing in the world; for popping in betwixt us, just as the lady was returning back to the door of the Remise, he introduced himself to my acquaintance, and before he had well got announced, begged I would do him the honour to present him to the lady—I had not been presented myself—so turning about to her, he did it just as well by asking her, if she had come from Paris?——No: she was going that route, she said.—*Vous n'etes pas de Londre?*——She was not, she replied.—Then Madame must have come through Flanders. *Apparemment vous etes Flammande?* said the French captain.—The lady answered she was.—

Peut-être, de Lisle? added he—She said, she was not of Lisle.
—Nor Arras?—nor Cambray?—nor Ghent?—nor Brussels?
She answered, she was of Brussels.

He had had the honour, he said, to be at the bombard-
ment of it last war—that it was finely situated, *pour cela*—
and full of noblesse when the Imperialists were driven out by
the French (the lady made a slight curtsy)—so giving her an
account of the affair, and of the share he had had in it—he
begged the honour to know her name—so made his bow.

——*Et Madame a son Mari?*—said he, looking back
when he had made two steps—and without staying for an
answer—danced down the street.

Had I served seven years apprenticeship to good breeding,
I could not have done as much.

THE REMISE

Calais

As the little French captain left us, Mons. Dessein came up
with the key of the Remise in his hand, and forthwith let us
into his magazine of chaises.

The first object which caught my eye, as Mons. Dessein
opened the door of the Remise, was another old tattered
Desobligeant: and notwithstanding it was the exact picture of
that which had hit my fancy so much in the coach-yard but an
hour before—the very sight of it stirred up a disagreeable
sensation within me now; and I thought 'twas a churlish beast
into whose heart the idea could first enter, to construct such
a machine; nor had I much more charity for the man who
could think of using it.

I observed the lady was as little taken with it as myself:
so Mons. Dessein led us on to a couple of chaises which stood
abreast, telling us, as he recommended them, that they had
been purchased by my Lord A. and B. to go the *grand tour,*
but had gone no further than Paris, so were in all respects as
good as new—They were too good—so I passed on to a third,

which stood behind, and forthwith began to chaffer for the price—But 'twill scarce hold two, said I, opening the door and getting in—Have the goodness, Madam, said Mons. Dessein, offering his arm, to step in—The lady hesitated half a second, and stepped in; and the waiter that moment beckoning to speak to Mons. Dessein, he shut the door of the chaise upon us, and left us.

THE REMISE

Calais

C'est bien comique, 'tis very droll, said the lady smiling, from the reflection that this was the second time we had been left together by a parcel of nonsensical contingencies—*c'est bien comique,* said she—

—There wants nothing, said I, to make it so, but the comic use which the gallantry of a Frenchman would put it to —to make love the first moment, and an offer of his person the second.

'Tis their *fort:* replied the lady.

It is supposed so at least—and how it has come to pass, continued I, I know not; but they have certainly got the credit of understanding more of love, and making it better than any other nation upon earth: but for my own part I think them errant bunglers, and in truth the worst set of marksmen that ever tried Cupid's patience.

—To think of making love by *sentiments!*

I should as soon think of making a genteel suit of clothes out of remnants:—and to do it—pop—at first sight by declaration—is submitting the offer and themselves with it, to be sifted, with all their *pours* and *contres,* by an unheated mind.

The lady attended as if she expected I should go on.

Consider then, Madam, continued I, laying my hand upon hers—

That grave people hate Love for the name's sake—
That selfish people hate it for their own—
Hypocrites for heaven's—
And that all of us, both old and young, being ten times
worse frightened than hurt by the very *report*—What a want
of knowledge in this branch of commerce a man betrays, whoever lets the word come out of his lips, till an hour or two at
least after the time, that his silence upon it becomes tormenting.
A course of small, quiet attentions, not so pointed as to alarm
—nor so vague as to be misunderstood,—with now and then
a look of kindness, and little or nothing said upon it—leaves
Nature for your mistress, and she fashions it to her mind.—

Then I solemnly declare, said the lady, blushing—you
have been making love to me all this while.

THE REMISE

Calais

Monsieur Dessein came back to let us out of the chaise, and
acquaint the lady, the Count de L— her brother was just
arrived at the hotel. Though I had infinite good will for the
lady, I cannot say, that I rejoiced in my heart at the event—
and could not help telling her so—for it is fatal to a proposal,
Madam, said I, that I was going to make to you—

—You need not tell me what the proposal was, said she,
laying her hand upon both mine, as she interrupted me.—
A man, my good Sir, has seldom an offer of kindness to make
to a woman, but she has a presentiment of it some moments
before—

Nature arms her with it, said I, for immediate preservation—But I think, said she, looking in my face, I had no evil
to apprehend—and to deal frankly with you, had determined
to accept it.—If I had—(she stopped a moment)—I believe
your good will would have drawn a story from me, which would
have made pity the only dangerous thing in the journey.

In saying this, she suffered me to kiss her hand twice, and with a look of sensibility mixed with a concern she got out of the chaise—and bid adieu.

IN THE STREET

Calais

I never finished a twelve-guinea bargain so expeditiously in my life: my time seemed heavy upon the loss of the lady, and knowing every moment of it would be as two, till I put myself into motion—I ordered post horses directly, and walked towards the hotel.

Lord! said I, hearing the town clock strike four, and recollecting that I had been little more than a single hour in Calais—

—What a large volume of adventures may be grasped within this little span of life by him who interests his heart in everything, and who having eyes to see, what time and chance are perpetually holding out to him as he journeyeth on his way, misses nothing he can *fairly* lay his hands on.—

—If this won't turn out something—another will—no matter—'tis an assay upon human nature—I get my labour for my pains—'tis enough—the pleasure of the experiment has kept my senses, and the best part of my blood awake, and laid the gross to sleep.

I pity the man who can travel from *Dan* to *Beersheba,* and cry, 'Tis all barren—And so it is; and so is all the world to him who will not cultivate the fruits it offers. I declare, said I, clapping my hands cheerily together, that was I in a desert, I would find out wherewith in it to call forth my affections—If I could not do better, I would fasten them upon some sweet myrtle, or seek some melancholy cypress to connect myself to —I would court their shade, and greet them kindly for their protection—I would cut my name upon them, and swear they were the loveliest trees throughout the desert: if their leaves withered, I would teach myself to mourn, and when they re-joiced, I would rejoice along with them.

The learned SMELFUNGUS[4] travelled from Boulogne to Paris—from Paris to Rome—and so on—but he set out with the spleen and jaundice, and every object he passed by was discoloured or distorted—He wrote an account of them, but 'twas nothing but the account of his miserable feelings.

I met Smelfungus in the grand portico of the Pantheon —he was just coming out of it—*'Tis nothing but a huge cock pit,** said he—I wish you had said nothing worse of the Venus of Medicis, replied I—for in passing through Florence, I had heard he had fallen foul upon the goddess, and used her worse than a common strumpet, without the least provocation in nature.

I popped upon Smelfungus again at Turin, in his return home; and a sad tale of sorrowful adventures had he to tell, "wherein he spoke of moving accidents by flood and field, and of the cannibals which each other eat: the Anthropophagi"— he had been flea'd alive, and bedeviled, and used worse than St. Bartholomew, at every stage he had come at—

—I'll tell it, cried Smelfungus, to the world. You had better tell it, said I, to your physician.

Mundungus, with an immense fortune, made the whole tour; going on from Rome to Naples—from Naples to Venice —from Venice to Vienna—to Dresden, to Berlin, without one generous connection or pleasurable anecdote to tell of; but he had travelled straight on looking neither to his right hand or his left, lest Love or Pity should seduce him out of his road.

Peace be to them! if it is to be found; but heaven itself, was it possible to get there with such tempers, would want objects to give it—every gentle spirit would come flying upon the wings of Love to hail their arrival—Nothing would the souls of Smelfungus and Mundungus hear of, but fresh anthems of joy, fresh raptures of love, and fresh congratulations of their common felicity—I heartily pity them: they have brought up no faculties for this work; and was the happiest mansion in

* *Vide* S—'s travels.

heaven to be allotted to Smelfungus and Mundungus, they would be so far from being happy, that the souls of Smelfungus and Mundungus would do penance there to all eternity.

MONTRIUL

I had once lost my portmanteau from behind my chaise, and twice got out in the rain, and one of the times up to the knees in dirt, to help the postillion to tie it on, without being able to find out what was wanting—Nor was it till I got to Montriul, upon the landlord's asking me if I wanted not a servant, that it occurred to me, that that was the very thing.

A servant! That I do most sadly, quoth I—Because, Monsieur, said the landlord, there is a clever young fellow, who would be very proud of the honour to serve an Englishman— But why an English one, more than any other?—They are so generous, said the landlord—I'll be shot if this is not a livre out of my pocket, quoth I to myself, this very night—But they have wherewithal to be so, Monsieur, added he—Set down one livre more for that, quoth I—It was but last night, said the landlord, *qu'un my Lord Anglois presentait un écu à la fille de chambre*—Tant pis, pour Madamoiselle Janatone, said I.

Now Janatone being the landlord's daughter, and the land-lord supposing I was young in French, took the liberty to inform me, I should not have said *tant pis*—but, *tant mieux*. *Tant mieux, toujours, Monsieur,* said he, when there is any thing to be got—*tant pis,* when there is nothing. It comes to the same thing, said I. *Pardonnez moi,* said the landlord.

I cannot take a fitter opportunity to observe once for all, that *tant pis* and *tant mieux* being two of the great hinges in French conversation, a stranger would do well to set himself right in the use of them, before he gets to Paris.

A prompt French Marquis at our ambassador's table de-manded of Mr H—, if he was H— the poet? No, said H— mildly—*Tant pis,* replied the Marquis.[5]

It is H— the historian, said another—*Tant mieux,* said

the Marquis. And Mr H——, who is a man of an excellent heart, returned thanks for both.

When the landlord had set me right in this matter, he called in La Fleur, which was the name of the young man he had spoke of——saying only first, That as for his talents, he would presume to say nothing——Monsieur was the best judge what would suit him; but for the fidelity of La Fleur, he would stand responsible in all he was worth.

The landlord delivered this in a manner which instantly set my mind to the business I was upon——and La Fleur, who stood waiting without, in that breathless expectation which every son of nature of us have felt in our turns, came in.

MONTRIUL

I am apt to be taken with all kinds of people at first sight; but never more so, than when a poor devil comes to offer his service to so poor a devil as myself; and as I know this weakness, I always suffer my judgment to draw back something on that very account——and this more or less, according to the mood I am in, and the case——and I may add the gender too, of the person I am to govern.

When La Fleur entered the room, after every discount I could make for my soul, the genuine look and air of the fellow determined the matter at once in his favour; so I hired him first——and then began to enquire what he could do: But I shall find out his talents, quoth I, as I want them——besides, a Frenchman can do everything.

Now poor La Fleur could do nothing in the world but beat a drum, and play a march or two upon the fife. I was determined to make his talents do; and can't say my weakness was ever so insulted by my wisdom, as in the attempt.

La Fleur had set out early in life, as gallantly as most Frenchmen do, with *serving* for a few years; at the end of which, having satisfied the sentiment, and found, moreover, that the honour of beating a drum was likely to be its own reward, as it opened no further track of glory to him——he

retired *à ses terres,* and lived *comme il plaisait à Dieu*—that
is to say, upon nothing.

—And so, quoth *Wisdome,* you have hired a drummer to
attend you in this tour of yours through France and Italy!
Psha! said I, and do not one half of our gentry go with a
humdrum *compagnon du voyage* the same round, and have the
piper and the devil and all to pay besides? When a man can
extricate himself with an *equivoque* in such an unequal match
—he is not ill off—But you can do something else, La Fleur?
said I—*O qu'oui!*—he could make spatterdashes,[6] and play
a little upon the fiddle—Bravo! said Wisdome—Why, I play a
bass myself, said I—we shall do very well. You can shave, and
dress a wig a little, La Fleur?—He had all the dispositions in
the world—It is enough for heaven! said I, interrupting him—
and ought to be enough for me—So supper coming in, and
having a frisky English spaniel on one side of my chair, and a
French valet, with as much hilarity in his countenance as ever
nature painted in one, on the other—I was satisfied to my
heart's content with my empire; and if monarchs knew what
they would be at, they might be as satisfied as I was.

MONTRIUL

As La Fleur went the whole tour of France and Italy with
me, and will be often upon the stage, I must interest the reader a
little further in his behalf, by saying, that I had never less
reason to repent of the impulses which generally do determine
me, than in regard to this fellow—he was a faithful, affectionate, simple soul as ever trudged after the heels of a philosopher; and notwithstanding his talents of drum-beating and
spatterdash-making, which, though very good in themselves,
happened to be of no great service to me, yet was I hourly
recompenced by the festivity of his temper—it supplied all
defects—I had a constant resource in his looks in all difficulties
and distresses of my own—I was going to have added, of his
too; but La Fleur was out of the reach of everything; for

whether 'twas hunger or thirst, or cold or nakedness, or watchings, or whatever stripes of ill luck La Fleur met with in our journeyings, there was no index in his physiognomy to point them out by—he was eternally the same; so that if I am a piece of a philosopher, which Satan now and then puts it into my head I am—it always mortifies the pride of the conceit, by reflecting how much I owe to the complexional philosophy of this poor fellow, for shaming me into one of a better kind. With all this, La Fleur had a small cast of the coxcomb—but he seemed at first sight to be more a coxcomb of nature than of art; and before I had been three days in Paris with him— he seemed to be no coxcomb at all.

MONTRIUL

The next morning La Fleur entering upon his employment, I delivered to him the key of my portmanteau with an inventory of my half a dozen shirts and silk pair of breeches; and bid him fasten all upon the chaise—get the horses put to—and desire the landlord to come in with his bill.

C'est un garçon de bonne fortune, said the landlord, pointing through the window to half a dozen wenches who had got round about La Fleur, and were most kindly taking their leave of him, as the postillion was leading out the horses. La Fleur kissed all their hands round and round again, and thrice he wiped his eyes, and thrice he promised he would bring them all pardons from Rome.

The young fellow, said the landlord, is beloved by all the town, and there is scarce a corner in Montriul where the want of him will not be felt: he has but one misfortune in the world, continued he, "He is always in love."—I am heartily glad of it, said I,—'twill save me the trouble every night of putting my breeches under my head. In saying this, I was making not so much La Fleur's eloge, as my own, having been in love with one princess or another almost all my life, and I hope I shall go on so, till I die, being firmly persuaded, that if ever I do a mean action, it must be in some interval betwixt one passion and another: whilst this interregnum lasts, I always perceive my heart locked up—I can scarce find in it, to give Misery a sixpence; and therefore I always get out of it as fast as I can, and the moment I am rekindled, I am all generosity and good will again; and would do anything in the world either for, or with anyone, if they will but satisfy me there is no sin in it.

—But in saying this—surely I am commending the passion—not myself.

A FRAGMENT

——The town of Abdera, notwithstanding Democritus lived there trying all the powers of irony and laughter to reclaim it, was the vilest and most profligate town in all Thrace. What for poisons, conspiracies, and assassinations—libels, pasquinades and tumults, there was no going there by day—'twas worse by night.

Now, when things were at the worst, it came to pass, that the *Andromeda* of Euripides being represented at Abdera, the whole orchestra was delighted with it: but of all the passages which delighted them, nothing operated more upon their imaginations, than the tender strokes of nature which the poet had wrought up in that pathetic speech of Perseus,

O Cupid! prince of God and men, &c.

Every man almost spoke pure iambics the next day and talked of nothing but Perseus his pathetic address—"O Cupid! prince of God and men"—in every street of Abdera, in every house— "O Cupid! Cupid!"—in every mouth, like the natural notes of some sweet melody which drops from it whether it will nor no —nothing but "Cupid! Cupid! prince of God and men"—The fire caught—and the whole city, like the heart of one man, opened itself to Love.

No pharmacopolist could sell one grain of hellebore— not a single armourer had a heart to forge one instrument of death—Friendship and Virtue met together, and kissed each other in the street—the golden age returned, and hung over the town of Abdera—every Abderite took his oaten pipe, and every Abderitish woman left her purple web, and chastely sat her down and listened to the song—

'Twas only in the power, says the Fragment, of the God whose empire extendeth from heaven to earth, and even to the depths of the sea, to have done this.

MONTRIUL

When all is ready, and every article is disputed and paid for in the inn, unless you are a little soured by the adventure, there is always a matter to compound at the door, before you can get into your chaise; and that is with the sons and daughters of poverty, who surround you. Let no man say, "let them go to the devil"—'tis a cruel journey to send a few miserables, and they have had sufferings enow without it: I always think it better to take a few sous out in my hand; and I would counsel every gentle traveller to do so likewise; he need not be so exact in setting down his motives for giving them—they will be registered elsewhere.

For my own part, there is no man gives so little as I do; for few that I know have so little to give: but as this was the first public act of my charity in France, I took the more notice of it.

A well-a-way! said I. I have but eight sous in the world, showing them in my hand, and there are eight poor men and eight poor women for 'em.

A poor tattered soul without a shirt on instantly withdrew his claim, by retiring two steps out of the circle, and making a disqualifying bow on his part. Had the whole parterre cried out, *Place aux dames,* with one voice, it would not have conveyed the sentiment of a deference for the sex with half the effect.

Just heaven! for what wise reasons hast thou ordered it,

that beggary and urbanity, which are at such variance in other countries, should find a way to be at unity in this?

—I insisted upon presenting him with a single sou, merely for his *politesse*.

A poor little dwarfish brisk fellow, who stood over-against me in the circle, putting something first under his arm, which had once been a hat, took his snuff-box out of his pocket, and generously offered a pinch on both sides of him: it was a gift of consequence, and modestly declined—The poor little fellow pressed it upon them with a nod of welcomeness—*Prenez en— prenez,* said he, looking another way; so they each took a pinch—Pity thy box should ever want one! said I to myself; so I put a couple of sous into it—taking a small pinch out of his box, to enhance their value, as I did it—He felt the weight of the second obligation more than that of the first—'twas doing him an honour—the other was only doing him a charity—and he made me a bow to the ground for it.

—Here! said I to an old soldier with one hand, who had been campaigned and worn out to death in the service—here's a couple of sous for thee. *Vive le Roi!* said the old soldier.

I had then but three sous left: so I gave one, simply *pour l'amour de Dieu,* which was the footing on which it was begged—The poor woman had a dislocated hip; so it could not be well, upon any other motive.

Mon cher et très charitable Monsieur—There's no opposing this, said I.

My Lord Anglois—the very sound was worth the money —so I gave *my last sou for it.* But in the eagerness of giving, I had overlooked a *pauvre honteux,* who had no one to ask a sou for him, and who, I believed, would have perished, ere he could have asked one for himself: he stood by the chaise a little without the circle, and wiped a tear from a face which I thought had seen better days—Good God! said I—and I have not one single sou left to give him—But you have a thousand! cried all the powers of nature, stirring within me—so I gave him—no matter what—I am ashamed to say *how much,* now —and was ashamed to think, how little, then: so if the reader can form any conjecture of my disposition, as these two fixed points are given him, he may judge within a livre or two what was the precise sum.

I could afford nothing for the rest, but, *Dieu vous benisse —Et le bon Dieu vous benisse encore*—said the old soldier, the dwarf, &c. The *pauvre honteux* could say nothing—he pulled out a little handkerchief, and wiped his face as he turned away—and I thought he thanked me more than them all.

THE BIDET

Having settled all these little matters, I got into my post-chaise with more ease than ever I got into a post-chaise in my life; and La Feur having got one large jack-boot on the far side of a little *bidet,** and another on this (for I count nothing of his legs)—he cantered away before me as happy and as perpendicular as a prince.—

—But what is happiness! what is grandeur in this painted scene of life! A dead ass, before we had got a league, put a sudden stop to La Fleur's career—his bidet would not pass by it—a contention arose betwixt them, and the poor fellow was kicked out of his jack-boots the very first kick.

La Fleur bore his fall like a French christian, saying neither more or less upon it, than, *Diable!* so presently got up and came to the charge again astride his bidet, beating him up to it as he would have beat his drum.

The bidet flew from one side of the road to the other, then back again—then this way—then that way, and in short every way but by the dead ass.—La Fleur insisted upon the thing—and the bidet threw him.

What's the matter, La Fleur, said I, with this bidet of thine?—*Monsieur,* said he, *c'est un cheval le plus opiniatré du monde*—Nay, if he is a conceited beast, he must go his own way, replied I—so La Fleur got off him, and giving him a good

*Post horse.

sound lash, the bidet took me at my word, and away he scampered back to Montriul.—*Peste!* said La Fleur.

It is not *mal à propos* to take notice here, that though La Fleur availed himself but of two different terms of exclamation in this encounter—namely, *Diable!* and *Peste!* that there are nevertheless three, in the French language; like the positive, comparative, and superlative, one or the other of which serve for every unexpected throw of the dice in life.

Le Diable! which is the first and positive degree, is generally used upon ordinary emotions of the mind, where small things only fall out contrary to your expectations—such as— the throwing once doublets[7]—La Fleur's being kicked off his horse, and so forth—cuckoldom, for the same reason, is always —*Le Diable!*

But in cases where the cast has something provoking in it, as in that of the bidet's running away after, and leaving La Fleur aground in jack-boots—'tis the second degree.

'Tis then *Peste!*

And for the third—

—But here my heart is wrung with pity and fellow-feeling, when I reflect what miseries must have been their lot, and how bitterly so refined a people must have smarted, to have forced them upon the use of it.——

Grant me, O ye powers which touch the tongue with eloquence in distress!—whatever is my *cast,* Grant me but decent words to exclaim in, and I will give my nature way.

—But as these were not to be had in France, I resolved to take every evil just as it befel me without any exclamation at all.

La Fleur, who had made no such covenant with himself, followed the bidet with his eyes till it was got out of sight— and then, you may imagine, if you please, with what word he closed the whole affair.

As there was no hunting down a frightened horse in jack-boots, there remained no alternative but taking La Fleur either behind the chaise, or into it.—

I preferred the latter, and in half an hour we got to the post-house at Nampont.

NAMPONT

The Dead Ass

—And this, said he, putting the remains of a crust into his wallet—and this, should have been thy portion, said he, hadst thou been alive to have shared it with me. I thought by the accent, it had been an apostrophe to his child; but 'twas to his ass, and to the very ass we had seen dead in the road, which had occasioned La Fleur's misadventure. The man seemed to lament it much; and it instantly brought into my mind Sancho's lamentation for his; but he did it with more true touches of nature.

The mourner was sitting upon a stone bench at the door, with the ass's pannel and its bridle on one side, which he took up from time to time—then laid them down—looked at them and shook his head. He then took his crust of bread out of his wallet again, as if to eat it; held it some time in his hand—then laid it upon the bit of his ass's bridle—looked wistfully at the little arrangement he had made—and then gave a sigh.

The simplicity of his grief drew numbers about him, and La Fleur amongst the rest, whilst the horses were getting ready; as I continued sitting in the post-chaise, I could see and hear over their heads.

—He said he had come last from Spain, where he had been from the furthest borders of Franconia; and had got so far on his return home, when his ass died. Every one seemed desirous to know what business could have taken so old and poor a man so far a journey from his own home.

It had pleased heaven, he said, to bless him with three sons, the finest lads in all Germany; but having in one week lost two of the eldest of them by the small-pox, and the youngest falling ill of the same distemper, he was afraid of being bereft of them all; and made a vow, if Heaven would not take him from him also, he would go in gratitude to St. Iago in Spain.

When the mourner got thus far on his story, he stopped to pay nature her tribute—and wept bitterly.

He said, Heaven had accepted the conditions, and that he had set out from his cottage with this poor creature, who had been a patient partner of his journey—that it had eat the same bread with him all the way, and was unto him as a friend.

Everybody who stood about, heard the poor fellow with concern—La Fleur offered him money.—The mourner said, he did not want it—it was not the value of the ass—but the loss of him.—The ass, he said, he was assured loved him—and upon this told them a long story of a mischance upon their passage over the Pyrenean mountains which had separated them from each other three days; during which time the ass had sought for him as much as he had sought the ass, and that they had neither scarce eat or drank till they met.

Thou hast one comfort, friend, said I, at least, in the loss of thy poor beast; I'm sure thou hast been a merciful master to him.—Alas! said the mourner, I thought so, when he was alive—but now that he is dead, I think otherwise.—I fear the weight of myself and my afflictions together have been too much for him—they have shortened the poor creature's days, and I fear I have them to answer for.—Shame on the world! said I to myself—Did we love each other, as this poor soul but loved his ass—'twould be something.—

NAMPONT

The Postillion

The concern which the poor fellow's story threw me into, required some attention: the postillion paid not the least to it, but set off upon the *pavé* in a full gallop.

The thirstiest soul in the most sandy desert of Arabia could not have wished more for a cup of cold water, than mine did for grave and quiet movements; and I should have had an high opinion of the postillion had he but stolen off with me in something like a pensive pace.—On the contrary, as the mourner finished his lamentation, the fellow gave an unfeeling lash to each of his beasts, and set off clattering like a thousand devils.

I called to him as loud as I could, for heaven's sake to go slower—and the louder I called, the more unmercifully he galloped.—The deuce take him and his galloping too—said I —he'll go on tearing my nerves to pieces till he has worked me into a foolish passion, and then he'll go slow, that I may enjoy the sweets of it.

The postillion managed the point to a miracle: by the time he had got to the foot of a steep hill about half a league from Nampont,—he had put me out of temper with him—and then with myself, for being so.

My case then required a different treatment; and a good rattling gallop would have been of real service to me.—

—Then, prithee get on—get on, my good lad, said I.

The postillion pointed to the hill—I then tried to return back to the story of the poor German and his ass—but I had broke the clue—and could no more get into it again, than the postillion could into a trot.—

—The deuce go, said I, with it all! Here am I sitting as candidly disposed to make the best of the worst, as ever wight was, and all runs counter.

There is one sweet lenitive at least for evils, which nature holds out to us; so I took it kindly at her hands, and fell asleep; and the first word which roused me was *Amiens*.

—Bless me! said I, rubbing my eyes—this is the very town where my poor lady is to come.

AMIENS

The words were scarce out of my mouth, when the Count de L***'s post-chaise, with his sister in it, drove hastily by: she had just time to make me a bow of recognition—and of that particular kind of it, which told me she had not yet done with me. She was as good as her look; for, before I had quite finished my supper, her brother's servant came into the room with a billet, in which she said she had taken the liberty to charge me with a letter, which I was to present myself to Madame R*** the first morning I had nothing to do at Paris. There was only added, she was sorry, but from what *penchant* she had not considered, that she had been prevented telling me her story—that she still owed it me; and if my route should ever lay through Brussels, and I had not by then forgot the name of Madame de L***—that Madame de L*** would be glad to discharge her obligation.

Then I will meet thee, said I, fair spirit! at Brussels—'tis only returning from Italy through Germany to Holland, by the route of Flanders, home—'twill scarce be ten posts out of my way; but were it ten thousand! with what a moral delight will it crown my journey, in sharing in the sickening incidents of a tale of misery told to me by such a sufferer? to see her weep! and though I cannot dry up the fountain of her tears, what an exquisite sensation is there still left, in wiping them away from off the cheeks of the first and fairest of women, as I'm sitting with my handkerchief in my hand in silence the whole night beside her.

There was nothing wrong in the sentiment; and yet I instantly reproached my heart with it in the bitterest and most reprobate of expressions.

It had ever, as I told the reader, been one of the singular blessings of my life, to be almost every hour of it miserably in love with some one; and my last flame happening to be blown out by a whiff of jealousy on the sudden turn of a corner, I had lighted it up afresh at the pure taper of Eliza but about three months before—swearing as I did it, that it should last me through the whole journey—Why should I dissemble the matter? I had sworn to her eternal fidelity—she had a right to my whole heart—to divide my affections was to lessen them —to expose them, was to risk them: where there is risk, there may be loss:—and what wilt thou have, Yorick! to answer to a heart so full of trust and confidence—so good, so gentle and unreproaching?

—I will not go to Brussels, replied I, interrupting myself—

but my imagination went on—I recalled her looks at that crisis of our separation when neither of us had power to say Adieu! I looked at the picture she had tied in a black ribband about my neck—and blushed as I looked at it—I would have given the world to have kissed it,—but was ashamed—And shall this tender flower, said I, pressing it between my hands—shall it be smitten to its very root—and smitten, Yorick! by thee, who hast promised to shelter it in thy breast?

Eternal fountain of happiness! said I, kneeling down upon the ground—be thou my witness—and every pure spirit which tastes it, be my witness also, That I would not travel to Brussels, unless Eliza went along with me, did the road lead me towards heaven.

In transports of this kind, the heart, in spite of the understanding, will always say too much.

THE LETTER

Amiens

Fortune had not smiled upon La Fleur; for he had been unsuccessful in his feats of chivalry—and not one thing had offered to signalize his zeal of my service from the time he had entered into it, which was almost four and twenty hours. The poor soul burned with impatience; and the Count de L***'s servant's coming with the letter, being the first practicable occasion which offered, La Fleur had laid hold of it; and in order to do honour to his master, had taken him into a back parlour in the Auberge, and treated him with a cup or two of the best wine in Picardy; and the Count de L***'s servant in return, and not to be behind hand in politeness with La Fleur, had taken him back with him to the Count's hotel. La Fleur's *prevenancy* (for there was a passport in his very looks) soon set every servant in the kitchen at ease with him; and as a Frenchman, whatever be his talents, has no sort of prudery in showing them, La Fleur, in less than five minutes, had pulled out his fife, and leading off the dance himself with the first note, set the *fille de chambre,* the *maitre d'hôtel,* the cook, the scullion, and all the household, dogs and cats, besides an old monkey, a dancing: I suppose there never was a merrier kitchen since the flood.

Madame de L***, in passing from her brother's apartments to her own, hearing so much jollity below stairs, rung up her *fille de chambre* to ask about it; and hearing it was the English gentleman's servant who had set the whole house merry with his pipe, she ordered him up.

As the poor fellow could not present himself empty, he had loadened himself in going upstairs with a thousand compliments to Madame de L***, on the part of his master—added a long apocrypha of enquiries about Madame de L***'s health—told her, that Monsieur his master was *au desespoire* for her re-establishment from the fatigues of her journey—and, to close all, that Monsieur had received the letter which Madame had done him the honour—And he has done me the honour, said Madame de L***, interrupting La Fleur, to send a billet in return.

Madame de L*** had said this with such a tone of reliance upon the fact, that La Fleur had not power to disappoint her expectations—he trembled for my honour—and possibly might not altogether be unconcerned for his own, as a man capable of being attached to a master who could be wanting *en égards vis-à-vis d'une femme;* so that when Madame de L*** asked La Fleur if he had brought a letter, *O qu'oui,* said La Fleur: so laying down his hat upon the ground, and taking hold of the flap of his right side pocket with his left hand, he began to search for the letter with his right—then contrary-wise—*Diable!*—then sought every pocket—pocket by pocket, round, not forgetting his fob—*Peste!*—then La Fleur emptied them upon the floor—pulled out a dirty cravat—a handkerchief—a comb—a whip-lash—a night-cap—then gave a peep into his hat—*Quelle étourderie!* He had left the letter upon the table in the Auberge—he would run for it, and be back with it in three minutes.

I had just finished my supper when La Fleur came in to

give me an account of his adventure: he told the whole story simply as it was; and only added, that if Monsieur had forgot (*par hazard*) to answer Madame's letter, the arrangement gave him an opportunity to recover the *faux pas*—and if not, that things were only as they were.

Now I was not altogether sure of my *etiquette,* whether I ought to have wrote or no; but if I had—a devil himself could not have been angry: 'twas but the officious zeal of a well-meaning creature for my honour; and however he might have mistook the road—or embarrassed me in so doing—his heart was in no fault—I was under no necessity to write—and what weighed more than all—he did not look as if he had done amiss.

—'Tis all very well, La Fleur, said I—'Twas sufficient. La Fleur flew out of the room like lightning, and returned with pen, ink, and paper, in his hand; and coming up to the table, laid them close before me, with such a delight in his countenance, that I could not help taking up the pen.

I begun and begun again; and though I had nothing to say, and that nothing might have been expressed in half a dozen lines, I made half a dozen different beginnings, and could no way please myself.

In short, I was in no mood to write.

La Fleur stepped out and brought a little water in a glass to dilute my ink—then fetched sand and seal-wax—It was all one: I wrote, and blotted, and tore off, and burnt, and wrote again—*Le Diable l'emporte!* said I half to myself—I cannot write this self-same letter; throwing the pen down despairingly as I said it.

As soon as I had cast down the pen, La Fleur advanced with the most respectful carriage up to the table, and making a thousand apologies for the liberty he was going to take, told me he had a letter in his pocket wrote by a drummer in his regiment to a corporal's wife, which, he durst say, would suit the occasion.

I had a mind to let the poor fellow have his humour—Then prithee, said I, let me see it.

La Fleur instantly pulled out a little dirty pocket-book

crammed full of small letters and billet-doux in a sad condition, and laying it upon the table, and then untying the string which held them all together, run them over one by one, till he came to the letter in question—*La voilà!* said he, clapping his hands: so unfolding it first, he laid it before me, and retired three steps from the table whilst I read it.

THE LETTER

Madame,

Je suis penetré de la douleur la plus vive, et reduit en même temps au desespoir ce retour imprevû du Corporal qui rend notre entrevue de ce soir la chose du monde la plus impossible.

Mais vive la joie! et toute la mienne sera de penser à vous.

L'amour n'est *rien* sans sentiment.

Et le sentiment est encore *moins* sans amour.

On dit qu'on ne doit jamais se desesperer.

On dit aussi que Monsieur le Corporal monte la garde Mercredi: alors ce sera mon tour.

Chacun a son tour.

En attendant—Vive l'amour! et vive la bagatelle!

Je suis, Madame,

Avec toutes les sentiments les plus respecteux et les plus tendres tout à vous,

Jacques Roque

It was but changing the Corporal into the Count—and saying nothing about mounting guard on Wednesday—and the letter was neither right or wrong—so to gratify the poor fellow, who stood trembling for my honour, his own, and the honour of his letter,—I took the cream gently off it, and whipping it up in my own way—I sealed it up and sent him with it to Madame de L***—and the next morning we pursued our journey to Paris.

PARIS

When a man can contest the point by dint of equipage, and carry on all floundering before him with half a dozen lackies and a couple of cooks—'tis very well in such a place as Paris—he may drive in at which end of a street he will.

A poor prince who is weak in cavalry, and whose whole infantry does not exceed a single man, had best quit the field; and signalize himself in the cabinet, if he can get up into it—I say *up into it*—for there is no descending perpendicular amongst 'em with a "*Me voici! mes enfants*"—here I am—whatever many may think.

I own my first sensations, as soon as I was left solitary and alone in my own chamber in the hotel, were far from being so flattering as I had préfigured them. I walked up gravely to the window in my dusty black coat, and looking through the glass saw all the world in yellow, blue, and green, running at the ring of pleasure.—The old with broken lances, and in helmets which had lost their vizards—the young in armour bright which shone like gold, beplumed with each gay feather of the east—all—all tilting at it like fascinated knights in tournaments of yore for fame and love.—

Alas, poor Yorick! cried I, what art thou doing here? On the very first onset of all this glittering clatter, thou art reduced to an atom—seek—seek some winding alley, with a tourniquet at the end of it, where chariot never rolled or flambeau shot its rays—there thou mayest solace thy soul in converse sweet with some kind *grisset*[8] of a barber's wife, and get into such coteries!—

—May I perish! if I do, said I, pulling out the letter which I had to present to Madame de R***.—I'll wait upon this lady, the very first thing I do. So I called La Fleur to go seek me a barber directly—and come back and brush my coat.

THE WIG

Paris

When the barber came, he absolutely refused to have anything to do with my wig: 'twas either above or below his art: I had nothing to do, but to take one ready made of his own recommendation.

——But I fear, friend! said I, this buckle won't stand.—You may immerge it, replied he, into the ocean, and it will stand—

What a great scale is everything upon in this city! thought I—The utmost stretch of an English periwig-maker's ideas could have gone no further than to have "dipped it into a pail of water"—What difference! 'tis like time to eternity.

I confess I do hate all cold conceptions, as I do the puny ideas which engender them; and am generally so struck with the great works of nature, that for my own part, if I could help it, I never would make a comparison less than a mountain at least. All that can be said against the French sublime in this instance of it, is this—that the grandeur is *more* in the *word;* and *less* in the *thing.* No doubt the ocean fills the mind with vast ideas; but Paris being so far inland, it was not likely I should run post a hundred miles out of it, to try the experiment —the Parisian barber meant nothing.—

The pail of water standing besides the great deep, makes certainly but a sorry figure in speech—but 'twill be said—it has one advantage—'tis in the next room, and the truth of the buckle may be tried in it without more ado, in a single moment.

In honest truth, and upon a more candid revision of the matter, *The French expression professes more than it performs.*

I think I can see the precise and distinguishing marks of national characters more in these nonsensical *minutiæ,* than in the most important matters of state; where great men of all nations talk and stalk so much alike, that I would not give ninepence to choose amongst them.

I was so long in getting from under my barber's hands, that it was too late of thinking of going with my letter to Madame R*** that night: but when a man is once dressed at all points for going out, his reflections turn to little account; so taking down the name of the Hotel de Modene where I lodged, I walked forth without any determination where to go—I shall consider of that, said I, as I walk along.

THE PULSE

Paris

Hail ye small sweet courtesies of life, for smooth do ye make the road of it! like grace and beauty which beget inclinations to love at first sight; 'tis ye who open this door and let the stranger in.

—Pray, Madame, said I, have the goodness to tell me which way I must turn to go to the Opera comique:—Most willingly, Monsieur, said she, laying aside her work—

I had given a cast with my eye into half a dozen shops as I came along in search of a face not likely to be disordered by such an interruption; till at last, this hitting my fancy, I had walked in.

She was working a pair of ruffles as she sat in a low chair on the far side of the shop facing the door—

——*Très volontiers;* most willingly, said she, laying her work down upon a chair next her, and rising up from the low chair she was sitting in, with so cheerful a movement and so cheerful a look, that had I been laying out fifty Louis d'ors with her, I should have said—"This woman is grateful."

You must turn, Monsieur, said she, going with me to the door of the shop, and pointing the way down the street I was to take—you must turn first to your left hand—*mais prenez garde*—there are two turns; and be so good as to take the second—then go down a little way and you'll see a church, and when you are past it, give yourself the trouble to turn directly to the right, and that will lead you to the foot of the *Pont Neuf,* which you must cross—and there, anyone will do himself the pleasure to show you—

She repeated her instructions three times over to me with the same good natured patience the third time as the first;—and if *tones and manners* have a meaning, which certainly they have, unless to hearts which shut them out—she seemed really interested, that I should not lose myself.

I will not suppose it was the woman's beauty, notwithstanding she was the handsomest Grisset, I think, I ever saw, which had much to do with the sense I had of her courtesy; only I remember, when I told her how much I was obliged to her, that I looked very full in her eyes,—and that I repeated my thanks as often as she had done her instructions.

I had not got ten paces from the door, before I found I had forgot every tittle of what she had said—so looking back, and seeing her still standing in the door of the shop as if to look whether I went right or not—I returned back, to ask her whether the first turn was to my right or left—for that I had absolutely forgot.—Is it possible! said she, half laughing.— 'Tis very possible, replied I, when a man is thinking more of a woman, than of her good advice.

As this was the real truth—she took it, as every woman takes a matter of right, with a slight curtsy.

—*Attendez!* said she, laying her hand upon my arm to detain me, whilst she called a lad out of the back-shop, to get ready a parcel of gloves. I am just going to send him, she said, with a packet into that quarter, and if you will have the complaisance to step in, it will be ready in a moment, and he shall attend you to the place.—So I walked in with her to the far side of the shop, and taking up the ruffle in my hand which she laid upon the chair, as if I had a mind to sit, she sat down herself in her low chair, and I instantly sat myself down besides her.

—He will be ready, Monsieur, said she, in a moment— And in that moment, replied I, most willingly would I say something very civil to you for all these courtesies. Any one may do a casual act of good nature, but a continuation of them shows it is a part of the temperature; and certainly, added I, if it is the same blood which comes from the heart, which descends to the extremes (touching her wrist) I am sure you must have one of the best pulses of any woman in the world— Feel it, said she, holding out her arm. So laying down my hat, I took of her fingers in one hand, and applied the two fore-fingers of my other to the artery.—

—Would to heaven! my dear Eugenius,[9] thou hadst passed by, and beheld me sitting in my black coat, and in my lack-a-day-sical manner, counting the throbs of it, one by one, with as much true devotion as if I had been watching the critical ebb or flow of her fever—How wouldst thou have laughed and moralized upon my new profession?—and thou shouldst have laughed and moralized on—Trust me, my dear Eugenius, I should have said, "there are worse occupations in this world *than feeling a woman's pulse*."—But a Grisset's! thou wouldst have said—and in an open shop! Yorick—

—So much the better: for when my views are direct, Eugenius, I care not if all the world saw me feel it.

THE HUSBAND

Paris

I had counted twenty pulsations, and was going on fast towards the fortieth, when her husband coming unexpected from a back parlour into the shop, put me a little out in my reckoning.—'Twas nobody but her husband, she said—so I began a fresh score—Monsieur is so good, quoth she, as he passed us by, as to give himself the trouble of feeling my pulse—The husband took off his hat, and making me a bow, said, I did him too much honour—and having said that, he put on his hat and walked out.

Good God! said I to myself, as he went out—and can this man be the husband of this woman?

Let it not torment the few who know what must have been the grounds of this exclamation, if I explain it to those who do not.

In London a shopkeeper and a shopkeeper's wife seem

to be one bone and one flesh: in the several endowments of mind and body, sometimes the one, sometimes the other has it, so as in general to be upon a par, and to tally with each other as nearly as man and wife need to do.

In Paris, there are scarce two orders of beings more different: for the legislative and executive powers of the shop not resting in the husband, he seldom comes there—in some dark and dismal room behind, he sits commerceless in his thrum night-cap, the same rough son of Nature that Nature left him.

The genius of a people where nothing but the monarchy is *salique,* having ceded this department, with sundry others, totally to the women—by a continual higgling with customers of all ranks and sizes from morning to night, like so many rough pebbles shook long together in a bag, by amicable collisions, they have worn down their asperities and sharp angles, and not only become round and smooth, but will receive, some of them, a polish like a brilliant—Monsieur *le Mari* is little better than the stone under your feet—

—Surely—surely man! it is not good for thee to sit alone—thou wast made for social intercourse and gentle greetings, and this improvement of our natures from it, I appeal to, as my evidence.

——And how does it beat, Monsieur? said she.—With all the benignity, said I, looking quietly in her eyes, that I expected——She was going to say something civil in return—but the lad came into the shop with the gloves—*A propos,* said I; I want a couple of pair myself.

THE GLOVES

Paris

The beautiful Grisset rose up when I said this, and going behind the counter, reached down a parcel and untied it: I advanced to the side over-against her: they were all too large. The beautiful Grisset measured them one by one across my hand—It would not alter the dimensions—She begged I would try a single pair, which seemed to be the least—she held it open—my hand slipped into it at once—It will not do, said I, shaking my head a little—No, said she, doing the same thing.

There are certain combined looks of simple subtlety—where whim, and sense, and seriousness, and nonsense, are so blended, that all the languages of Babel set loose together could not express them—they are communicated and caught so instantaneously, that you can scarce say which party is the infecter. I leave it to your men of words to swell pages about it—it is enough in the present to say again, the gloves would not do; so folding our hands within our arms, we both lolled upon the counter—it was narrow, and there was just room for the parcel to lay between us.

The beautiful Grisset looked sometimes at the gloves, then side-ways to the window, then at the gloves—and then at me. I was not disposed to break silence—I followed her example: so I looked at the gloves, then to the window, then at the gloves, and then at her—and so on alternately.

I found I lost considerably in every attack—she had a quick black eye, and shot through two such long and silken eyelashes with such penetration, that she looked into my very heart and reins—It may seem strange, but I could actually feel she did—

—It is no matter, said I, taking up a couple of the pairs next to me, and putting them into my pocket.

I was sensible the beautiful Grisset had not asked above a single livre above the price—I wished she had asked a livre more, and was puzzling my brains how to bring the matter about—Do you think, my dear Sir, said she, mistaking my embarrassment, that I could ask a *sou* too much of a stranger—and of a stranger whose politeness, more than his want of gloves, has done me the honour to lay himself at my mercy?—*M'en croyez capable?*—Faith! not I, said I; and if you were, you are welcome—So counting the money into her hand, and with a lower bow than one generally makes to a shopkeeper's wife, I went out, and her lad with his parcel followed me.

THE TRANSLATION

Paris

There was nobody in the box I was let into but a kindly old French officer. I love the character, not only because I honour the man whose manners are softened by a profession which makes bad men worse; but that I once knew one—for he is no more—and why should I not rescue one page from violation by writing his name in it, and telling the world it was Captain Tobias Shandy,[10] the dearest of my flock and friends, whose philanthropy I never think of at this long distance from his death—but my eyes gush out with tears. For his sake, I have a predilection for the whole corps of veterans; and so I strode over the two back rows of benches, and placed myself beside him.

The old officer was reading attentively a small pamphlet, it might be the book of the opera, with a large pair of spectacles. As soon as I sat down, he took his spectacles off, and putting them into a shagreen case, returned them and the book into his pocket together. I half rose up, and made him a bow.

Translate this into any civilized language in the world—the sense is this:

"Here's a poor stranger come into the box—he seems as if he knew nobody; and is never likely, was he to be seven years in Paris, if every man he comes near keeps his spectacles on his nose—'tis shutting the door of conversation absolutely in his face—and using him worse than a German."

The French officer might as well have said it all aloud; and if he had, I should in course have put the bow I made him into French too, and told him, "I was sensible of his attention, and returned him a thousand thanks for it."

There is not a secret so aiding to the progress of sociality, as to get master of this *short hand,* and be quick in rendering the several turns of looks and limbs, with all their inflections and delineations, into plain words. For my own part, by long habitude, I do it so mechanically, that when I walk the streets of London, I go translating all the way; and have more than once stood behind in the circle, where not three words have been said, and have brought off twenty different dialogues with me, which I could have fairly wrote down and sworn to.

I was going one evening to Martini's concert at Milan, and was just entering the door of the hall, when the Marquesina di F was coming out in a sort of a hurry—she was almost upon me before I saw her; so I gave a spring to one side to let her pass—She had done the same, and on the same side too; so we ran our heads together: she instantly got to the other side to get out: I was just as unfortunate as she had been; for I had sprung to that side, and opposed her passage again— We both flew together to the other side, and then back—and so on—it was ridiculous; we both blushed intolerably; so I did at last the thing I should have done at first—I stood stock still, and the Marquesina had no more difficulty. I had no power to go into the room, till I had made her so much reparation as to wait and follow her with my eye to the end of the passage—She looked back twice, and walked along it rather side-ways, as if she would make room for anyone coming up-stairs to pass her—No, said I—that's a vile translation: the Marquesina has a right to the best apology I can make her; and that opening is left for me to do it in—so I ran and begged pardon for the embarrassment I had given her, saying it was my intention to have made her way. She answered, she was guided by the same intention towards me—so we reciprocally thanked each other. She was at the top of the stairs; and seeing no *chichesbee*[11] near her, I begged to hand her to her coach— so we went down the stairs, stopping at every third step to talk of the concert and the adventure—Upon my word, Madame, said I, when I had handed her in, I made six different efforts to let you go out—And I made six efforts, replied she, to let you enter—I wish to heaven you would make a seventh, said I— With all my heart, said she, making room—Life is too short to be long about the forms of it—so I instantly stepped in, and she carried me home with her—And what became of the concert, St. Cecilia, who, I suppose, was at it, knows more than I.

I will only add, that the connection which arose out of that translation, gave me more pleasure than any one I had the honour to make in Italy.

THE DWARF

Paris

I had never heard the remark made by anyone in my life, except by one; and who that was, will probably come out in this chapter; so that being pretty much unprepossessed, there must have been grounds for what struck me the moment I cast my eyes over the *parterre*—and that was, the unaccountable sport of nature in forming such numbers of dwarfs—No doubt, she sports at certain times in almost every corner of the world; but in Paris, there is no end to her amusements—The goddess seems almost as merry as she is wise.

As I carried my idea out of the *opera comique* with me, I measured everybody I saw walking in the streets by it— Melancholy application! especially where the size was extremely little—the face extremely dark—the eyes quick—the nose long—the teeth white—the jaw prominent—to see so many miserables, by force of accidents driven out of their own proper class into the very verge of another, which it gives me pain to write down—every third man a pigmy!—some by ricketty heads and hump backs—others by bandy legs—a third set arrested by the hand of Nature in the sixth and seventh years of their growth—a fourth, in their perfect and natural state, like dwarf apple-trees; from the first rudiments and stamina of their existence, never meant to grow higher.

A medical traveller might say, 'tis owing to undue bandages—a splenetic one, to want of air—and an inquisitive traveller, to fortify the system, may measure the height of their houses—the narrowness of their streets, and in how few feet square in the sixth and seventh stories such numbers of the *Bourgoisie* eat and sleep together; but I remember, Mr. Shandy the elder, who accounted for nothing like anybody else, in speaking one evening of these matters, averred, that children, like other animals, might be increased almost to any size, provided they came right into the world; but the misery was, the citizens of Paris were so cooped up, that they had not actually room enough to get them—I do not call it getting anything, said he—'tis getting nothing—Nay, continued he, rising in his argument, 'tis getting worse than nothing, when all you have got, after twenty or five and twenty years of the tenderest care and most nutritious aliment bestowed upon it, shall not at last be as high as my leg. Now, Mr. Shandy being very short, there could be nothing more said upon it.

As this is not a work of reasoning, I leave the solution as I found it, and content myself with the truth only of the remark, which is verified in every lane and by-lane of Paris. I was walking down that which leads from the Carousal to the Palais Royal, and observing a little boy in some distress at the side of the gutter, which ran down the middle of it, I took hold of his hand, and helped him over. Upon turning up his face to look at him after, I perceived he was about forty— Never mind, said I; some good body will do as much for me when I am ninety.

I feel some little principles within me, which incline me to be merciful towards this poor blighted part of my species, who have neither size or strength to get on in the world—I cannot bear to see one of them trod upon; and had scarce got seated beside my old French officer, ere the disgust was exercised, by seeing the very thing happen under the box we sat in.

At the end of the orchestra, and betwixt that and the first side-box, there is a small esplanade left, where, when the house is full, numbers of all ranks take sanctuary. Though you stand, as in the parterre, you pay the same price as in the orchestra. A poor defenceless being of this order had got thrust somehow or other into this luckless place—the night was hot, and he was surrounded by beings two feet and a half higher than himself. The dwarf suffered inexpressibly on all sides; but the thing which incommoded him most, was a tall corpulent German, near seven feet high, who stood directly betwixt him and all possibility of his seeing either the stage or the actors. The poor dwarf did all he could to get a peep at what was going forwards, by seeking for some little opening betwixt the German's arm and his body, trying first one side, then the other; but the German stood square in the most unaccommodating posture that can be imagined—the dwarf might well have been placed at the bottom of the deepest draw-well in Paris; so he civilly reached up his hand to the German's sleeve, and told him his distress—The German turned his head back, looked down upon him as Goliath did upon David—and unfeelingly resumed his posture.

I was just then taking a pinch of snuff out of my monk's little horn-box—And how would thy meek and courteous spirit, my dear monk! so tempered to *bear and forbear!*—how sweetly would it have lent an ear to this poor soul's complaint!

The old French officer, seeing me lift up my eyes with an emotion, as I made the apostrophe, took the liberty to ask me what was the matter—I told him the story in three words; and added, how inhuman it was.

By this time the dwarf was driven to extremes, and in his first transports, which are generally unreasonable, had told the German he would cut off his long queue with his knife—The German looked back coolly, and told him he was welcome if he could reach it.

An injury sharpened by insult, be it to who it will, makes every man of sentiment a party: I could have leaped out of the box to have redressed it.—The old French officer did it with much less confusion; for leaning a little over, and nodding to a sentinel, and pointing at the same time with his finger at the distress—the sentinel made his way to it.—There was no occasion to tell the grievance—the thing told itself; so thrusting back the German instantly with his musket—he took the poor dwarf by the hand, and placed him before him.—This is noble! said I, clapping my hands together—And yet you would not permit this, said the old officer, in England.

—In England, dear Sir, said I, *we sit all at our ease.*[12]

The old French officer would have set me at unity with myself, in case I had been at variance,—by saying it was a *bon mot*—and as a *bon mot* is always worth something at Paris, he offered me a pinch of snuff.

THE ROSE

Paris

It was now my turn to ask the old French officer "What was the matter?" for a cry of *"Haussez les mains, Monsieur l'Abbé,"* re-echoed from a dozen different parts of the parterre, was as unintelligible to me, as my apostrophe to the monk had been to him.

He told me, it was some poor Abbé in one of the upper loges, who he supposed had got planted perdu behind a couple of grissets in order to see the opera, and that the parterre espying him, were insisting upon his holding up both his hands during the representation.—And can it be supposed, said I, that an ecclesiastic would pick the grissets' pockets? The old French officer smiled, and whispering in my ear, opened a door of knowledge which I had no idea of——

Good God! said I, turning pale with astonishment—is it possible, that a people so smit with sentiments should at the same time be so unclean, and so unlike themselves—*Quelle grossièreté!* added I.

The French officer told me, it was an illiberal sarcasm at the church, which had begun in the theatre about the time the *Tartuffe* was given in it, by Moliere—but, like other remains of Gothic manners, was declining—Every nation, continued he, have their refinements and *grossièretés,* in which they take the lead, and lose it of one another by turns—that he had been in most countries, but never in one where he found not some delicacies, which others seemed to want. *Le* POUR *et le* CONTRE *se trouvent en chaque nation;* there is a balance, said he, of good and bad everywhere; and nothing but the knowing it is so can emancipate one half of the world from the prepossessions which it holds against the other—that the advantage of travel, as it regarded the *sçavoir vivre,* was by seeing a great deal both of men and manners; it taught us mutual toleration; and mutual toleration, concluded he, making me a bow, taught us mutual love.

The old French officer delivered this with an air of such candour and good sense, as coincided with my first favourable impressions of his character—I thought I loved the man; but I fear I mistook the object—'twas my own way of thinking—the difference was, I could not have expressed it half so well.

It is alike troublesome to both the rider and his beast— if the latter goes pricking up his ears and starting all the way at every object which he never saw before—I have as little torment of this kind as any creature alive; and yet I honestly confess, that many a thing gave me pain, and that I blushed at many a word the first month—which I found inconsequent and perfectly innocent the second.

Madame de Rambouliet, after an acquaintance of about six weeks with her, had done me the honour to take me in her coach about two leagues out of town—Of all women, Madame de Rambouliet is the most correct; and I never wish to see one of more virtues and purity of heart—In our return back, Madame de Rambouliet desired me to pull the cord—I asked her, if she wanted anything—*Rien que pisser,* said Madame de Rambouliet——

Grieve not, gentle traveller, to let Madame de Rambouliet p—ss on—And ye fair mystic nymphs! go each one *pluck your rose,*[13] and scatter them in your path—for Madame de Rambouliet did no more—I handed Madame de Rambouliet out of the coach; and had I been the priest of the chaste CASTALIA, I could not have served at her fountain with a more respectful decorum.

THE FILLE DE CHAMBRE

Paris

What the old French officer had delivered upon travelling, bringing Polonius's advice to his son upon the same subject into my head—and that bringing in *Hamlet;* and *Hamlet*, the rest of Shakespear's works, I stopped at the Quai de Conti, in my return home, to purchase the whole set.

The bookseller said he had not a set in the world— *Comment!* said I; taking one up out of a set which lay upon the counter betwixt us.—He said, they were sent him only to be got bound, and were to be sent back to Versailles in the morning to the Count de B****

—And does the Count de B****, said I, read Shakespear? *C'est un Esprit fort,* replied the bookseller.—He loves English books; and what is more to his honour, Monsieur, he loves the English too. You speak this so civilly, said I, that 'tis enough to oblige an Englishman to lay out a Louis d'or or two at your shop—the bookseller made a bow, and was going to say something, when a young decent girl of about twenty, who by her air and dress seemed to be *fille de chambre* to some devout woman of fashion, came into the shop and asked for *Les Egarements du Cœur & de l'Esprit:* the bookseller gave her the book directly; she pulled out a little green satin purse run round with a ribband of the same colour, and putting her finger and thumb into it, she took out the money, and paid for it. As I had nothing more to stay me in the shop, we both walked out at the door together.

—And what have you to do, my dear, said I, with *The Wanderings of the Heart,* who scarce know yet you have one? nor till love has first told you it, or some faithless shepherd has made it ache, can'st thou ever be sure it is so.—*Le Dieu m'en guard!* said the girl.—With reason, said I; for if it is a good one, 'tis pity it should be stolen; 'tis a little treasure to thee, and gives a better air to your face, than if it was dressed out with pearls.

The young girl listened with a submissive attention, holding her satin purse by its ribband in her hand all the time— 'Tis a very small one, said I, taking hold of the bottom of it— she held it towards me—and there is very little in it, my dear, said I; but be but as good as thou art handsome, and heaven will fill it. I had a parcel of crowns in my hand to pay for

Shakespear; and as she had let go the purse entirely, I put a single one in; and tying up the ribband in a bow-knot, returned it to her.

The young girl made me more a humble curtsy than a low one—'twas one of those quiet, thankful sinkings where the spirit bows itself down—the body does no more than tell it. I never gave a girl a crown in my life which gave me half the pleasure.

My advice, my dear, would not have been worth a pin to you, said I, if I had not given this along with it: but now, when you see the crown, you'll remember it—so don't, my dear, lay it out in ribbands.

Upon my word, Sir, said the girl, earnestly, I am incapable —in saying which, as is usual in little bargains of honour, she gave me her hand—*En verité, Monsieur, je mettrai cet argent apart,* said she.

When a virtuous convention is made betwixt man and woman, it sanctifies their most private walks: so notwithstanding it was dusky, yet as both our roads lay the same way, we made no scruple of walking along the Quai de Conti together.

She made me a second curtsy in setting off, and before we got twenty yards from the door, as if she had not done enough before, she made a sort of little stop to tell me again— she thanked me.

It was a small tribute, I told her, which I could not avoid paying to virtue, and would not be mistaken in the person I had been rendering it to for the world—but I see innocence, my dear, in your face—and foul befal the man who ever lays a snare in its way!

The girl seemed affected some way or other with what I said—she gave a low sigh—I found I was not impowered to enquire at all after it—so said nothing till I got to the corner of the Rue de Nevers, where we were to part.

—But is this the way, my dear, said I, to the hotel de Modene? she told me it was—or, that I might go by the Rue de Guineygaude, which was the next turn.—Then I'll go, my dear, by the Rue de Guineygaude, said I, for two reasons; first,

I shall please myself, and next, I shall give you the protection of my company as far on your way as I can. The girl was sensible I was civil—and said, she wished the hotel de Modene was in the Rue de St. Pierre—You live there? said I.—She told me she was *fille de chambre* to Madame R****—Good God! said I, 'tis the very lady for whom I have brought a letter from Amiens—The girl told me that Madame R****, she believed, expected a stranger with a letter, and was impatient to see him—so I desired the girl to present my compliments to Madame R****, and say I would certainly wait upon her in the morning.

We stood still at the corner of the Rue de Nevers whilst this passed—We then stopped a moment whilst she disposed of her *Egarements de Cœur, &c.* more commodiously than carrying them in her hand—they were two volumes; so I held the second for her whilst she put the first into her pocket; and then she held her pocket, and I put in the other after it.

'Tis sweet to feel by what fine-spun threads our affections are drawn together.

We set off afresh, and as she took her third step, the girl put her hand within my arm—I was just bidding her—but she did it of herself with that undeliberating simplicity, which showed it was out of her head that she had never seen me before. For my own part, I felt the conviction of consanguinity so strongly, that I could not help turning half round to look in her face, and see if I could trace out anything in it of a family likeness—Tut! said I, are we not all relations?

When we arrived at the turning up of the Rue de Guineygaude, I stopped to bid her adieu for good and all: the girl would thank me again for my company and kindness—She bid me adieu twice—I repeated it as often; and so cordial was the parting between us, that had it happened anywhere else, I'm not sure but I should have signed it with a kiss of charity, as warm and holy as an apostle.

But in Paris, as none kiss each other but the men—I did what amounted to the same thing—

—I bid God bless her.

THE PASSPORT

Paris

When I got home to my hotel, La Fleur told me I had been enquired after by the Lieutenant de Police—The deuce take it! said I—I know the reason. It is time the reader should know it, for in the order of things in which it happened, it was omitted; not that it was out of my head; but that, had I told it then, it might have been forgot now—and now is the time I want it.

I had left London with so much precipitation, that it never entered my mind that we were at war with France; and had reached Dover, and looked through my glass at the hills beyond Boulogne, before the idea presented itself; and with this in its train, that there was no getting there without a passport. Go but to the end of a street, I have a mortal aversion for returning back no wiser than I set out; and as this was one of the greatest efforts I had ever made for knowledge, I could less bear the thoughts of it: so hearing the Count de **** had hired the packet, I begged he would take me in his *suite*. The Count had some little knowledge of me, so made little or no difficulty—only said, his inclination to serve me could reach no further than Calais, as he was to return by way of Brussels to Paris: however, when I had once passed there, I might get to Paris without interruption; but that in Paris I must make friends and shift for myself.—Let me get to Paris, Monsieur le Count, said I—and I shall do very well. So I embarked, and never thought more of the matter.

When La Fleur told me the Lieutenant de Police had been enquiring after me—the thing instantly recurred—and by the time La Fleur had well told me, the master of the hotel came into my room to tell me the same thing, with this addition to it, that my passport had been particularly asked after: the master of the hotel concluded with saying, He hoped I had one.— Not I, faith! said I.

The master of the hotel retired three steps from me, as from an infected person, as I declared this—and poor La

Fleur advanced three steps towards me, and with that sort of movement which a good soul makes to succour a distressed one—the fellow won my heart by it; and from that single *trait,* I knew his character as perfectly, and could rely upon it as firmly, as if he had served me with fidelity for seven years.

Mon seigneur! cried the master of the hotel—but recollecting himself as he made the exclamation, he instantly changed the tone of it—If Monsieur, said he, has not a passport (*apparemment*) in all likelihood he has friends in Paris who can procure him one.—Not that I know of, quoth I, with an air of indifference.—Then *certes,* replied he, you'll be sent to the Bastile or the Chatelet, *au moins.*—Poo! said I, the king of France is a good-natured soul—he'll hurt nobody.—*Cela n'empeche pas,* said he—you will certainly be sent to the Bastile to-morrow morning.—But I've taken your lodgings for a month, answered I, and I'll not quit them a day before the time for all the kings of France in the world. La Fleur whispered in my ear, That nobody could oppose the king of France.

Pardi! said my host, *ces Messieurs Anglois sont des gens très extraordinaires*—and having both said and sworn it—he went out.

THE PASSPORT

The Hotel at Paris

I could not find in my heart to torture La Fleur's with a serious look upon the subject of my embarrassment, which was the reason I had treated it so cavalierly: and to show him how light it lay upon my mind, I dropt the subject entirely; and whilst he waited upon me at supper, talked to him with more than usual gaiety about Paris, and of the opera comique.— La Fleur had been there himself, and had followed me through the streets as far as the bookseller's shop; but seeing me come out with the young *fille de chambre,* and that we walked down the Quai de Conti together, La Fleur deemed it unnecessary to follow me a step further—so making his own reflections upon it, he took a shorter cut—and got to the hotel in time to be informed of the affair of the Police against my arrival.

As soon as the honest creature had taken away, and gone down to sup himself, I then began to think a little seriously about my situation.——

—And here, I know, Eugenius, thou wilt smile at the remembrance of a short dialogue which passed betwixt us the moment I was going to set out—I must tell it here.

Eugenius, knowing that I was as little subject to be over-burthened with money as thought, had drawn me aside to interrogate me how much I had taken care for; upon telling him the exact sum, Eugenius shook his head, and said it would not do; so pulled out his purse in order to empty it into mine.—I've enough in conscience, Eugenius, said I.—Indeed, Yorick, you have not, replied Eugenius—I know France and Italy better than you.—But you don't consider, Eugenius, said I, refusing his offer, that before I have been three days in Paris, I shall take care to say or do something or other for which I shall get clapped up into the Bastile, and that I shall live there a couple of months entirely at the king of France's expence.—I beg pardon, said Eugenius, drily: really I had forgot that resource.

Now the event I treated gaily came seriously to my door.

Is it folly, or nonchalance, or philosophy, or pertinacity—or what is it in me, that, after all, when La Fleur had gone downstairs, and I was quite alone, that I could not bring down my mind to think of it otherwise than I had then spoken of it to Eugenius?

—And as for the Bastile! the terror is in the word—Make the most of it you can, said I to myself, the Bastile is but another word for a tower—and a tower is but another word for a house you can't get out of—Mercy on the gouty! for they are in it twice a year—but with nine livres a day, and pen and ink and paper, and patience, albeit a man can't get out, he may do very well within—at least for a month or six weeks; at the end of which, if he is a harmless fellow, his innocence appears, and he comes out a better and wiser man than he went in.

I had some occasion (I forget what) to step into the court-yard, as I settled this account; and remember I walked downstairs in no small triumph with the conceit of my reasoning—Beshrew the *sombre* pencil! said I, vauntingly—for I envy not its powers, which paints the evils of life with so hard and deadly a colouring. The mind sits terrified at the objects she has magnified herself, and blackened; reduce them to their proper size and hue, she overlooks them—'Tis true, said I, correcting the proposition—the Bastile is not an evil to be despised—but strip it of its towers—fill up the fossé—unbarricade the doors—call it simply a confinement, and suppose 'tis some tyrant of a distemper—and not of a man which holds you in it—the evil vanishes, and you bear the other half without complaint.

I was interrupted in the hey-day of this soliloquy, with a voice which I took to be of a child, which complained "it could not get out."—I looked up and down the passage, and seeing neither man, woman, or child, I went out without further attention.

In my return back through the passage, I heard the same words repeated twice over; and looking up, I saw it was a starling hung in a little cage.—"I can't get out—I can't get out," said the starling.

I stood looking at the bird: and to every person who came through the passage it ran fluttering to the side towards which they approached it, with the same lamentation of its captivity—"I can't get out," said the starling——God help thee! said I, but I'll let thee out, cost what it will; so I turned about the cage to get to the door; it was twisted and double twisted so fast with wire, there was no getting it open without pulling the cage to pieces—I took both hands to it.

The bird flew to the place where I was attempting his deliverance, and thrusting his head through the trellis, pressed his breast against it, as if impatient——I fear, poor creature! said I, I cannot set thee at liberty—"No," said the starling—"I can't get out—I can't get out," said the starling.

I vow, I never had my affections more tenderly awakened; or do I remember an incident in my life, where the dissipated spirits, to which my reason had been a bubble, were so suddenly called home. Mechanical as the notes were, yet so true in tune to nature were they chanted, that in one moment they overthrew all my systematic reasonings upon the Bastile; and I heavily walked upstairs, unsaying every word I had said in going down them.

Disguise thyself as thou wilt, still slavery! said I—still thou art a bitter draught; and though thousands in all ages have been made to drink of thee, thou art no less bitter on that account.—'Tis thou, thrice sweet and gracious goddess, addressing myself to LIBERTY, whom all in public or in private worship, whose taste is grateful, and ever wilt be so, till NATURE herself shall change—no *tint* of words can spot thy snowy mantle, or chymic power turn thy sceptre into iron—with thee to smile upon him as he eats his crust, the swain is happier than his monarch, from whose court thou art exiled—Gracious heaven! cried I, kneeling down upon the last step but one in my ascent—grant me but health, thou great Bestower of it, and give me but this fair goddess as my companion—and shower down thy mitres, if it seems good unto thy divine providence, upon those heads which are aching for them.

THE CAPTIVE

Paris

The bird in his cage pursued me into my room; I sat down close to my table, and leaning my head upon my hand, I began to figure to myself the miseries of confinement. I was in a right frame for it, and so I gave full scope to my imagination.

I was going to begin with the millions of my fellow-creatures born to no inheritance but slavery; but finding, however affecting the picture was, that I could not bring it near me, and that the multitude of sad groups in it did but distract me——

—I took a single captive, and having first shut him up in his dungeon, I then looked through the twilight of his grated door to take his picture.

I beheld his body half wasted away with long expectation and confinement, and felt what kind of sickness of the heart it was which arises from hope deferred. Upon looking nearer I saw him pale and feverish: in thirty years the western breeze had not once fanned his blood—he had seen no sun, no moon in all that time—nor had the voice of friend or kinsman breathed through his lattice—his children—

—But here my heart began to bleed—and I was forced to go on with another part of the portrait.

He was sitting upon the ground upon a little straw, in the furthest corner of his dungeon, which was alternately his chair and bed: a little calendar of small sticks were laid at the head notched all over with the dismal days and nights he had passed there—he had one of these little sticks in his hand, and with a rusty nail he was etching another day of misery to add to the heap. As I darkened the little light he had, he lifted up a hopeless eye towards the door, then cast it down, shook his head, and went on with his work of affliction. I heard his chains upon his legs, as he turned his body to lay his little stick upon the bundle—He gave a deep sigh—I saw the iron enter into his soul—I burst into tears—I could not sustain the picture of confinement which my fancy had drawn—I started up from my chair, and calling La Fleur, I bid him bespeak me a *remise,* and have it ready at the door of the hotel by nine in the morning.

I'll go directly, said I, myself to Monsieur Le Duc de Choiseul.

La Fleur would have put me to bed; but not willing he should see any thing upon my cheek which would cost the honest fellow a heartache—I told him I would go to bed myself—and bid him go do the same.

THE STARLING

Road to Versailles

I got into my *remise* the hour I proposed: La Fleur got up behind, and I bid the coachman make the best of his way to Versailles.

As there was nothing in this road, or rather nothing which I look for in travelling, I cannot fill up the blank better than with a short history of this self-same bird, which became the subject of the last chapter.

Whilst the honourable Mr **** was waiting for a wind at Dover it had been caught upon the cliffs, before it could well fly, by an English lad who was his groom; who not caring to destroy it, had taken it in his breast into the packet—and by course of feeding it, and taking it once under his protection, in a day or two grew fond of it, and got it safe along with him to Paris.

At Paris the lad had laid out a livre in a little cage for the starling, and as he had little to do better the five months his master stayed there, he taught it in his mother's tongue the four simple words—(and no more)—to which I owned myself so much its debtor.

Upon his master's going on for Italy, the lad had given it to the master of the hotel—But his little song for liberty, being in an *unknown* language at Paris, the bird had little or no store set by him—so La Fleur bought both him and his cage for me for a bottle of Burgundy.

In my return from Italy I brought him with me to the country in whose language he had learned his notes—and telling the story of him to Lord A—Lord A begged the bird of me—in a week Lord A gave him to Lord B—Lord B made a present of him to Lord C—and Lord C's gentleman sold him to Lord D's for a shilling—Lord D gave him to Lord E— and so on—half round the alphabet—From that rank he passed into the lower house, and passed the hands of as many commoners—But as all these wanted to *get in*—and my bird wanted to *get out*—he had almost as little store set by him in London as in Paris.

It is impossible but many of my readers must have heard of him; and if any by mere chance have ever seen him—I beg leave to inform them, that that bird was my bird—or some vile copy set up to represent him.

I have nothing further to add upon him, but that from that time to this, I have borne this poor starling as the crest to my arms.—Thus:

—And let the herald's officers twist his neck about if they dare.

THE ADDRESS

Versailles

I should not like to have my enemy take a view of my mind, when I am going to ask protection of any man; for which reason I generally endeavour to protect myself: but this going

to Monsieur Le Duc de C**** was an act of compulsion—
had it been an act of choice, I should have done it, I suppose,
like other people.

How many mean plans of dirty address, as I went along,
did my servile heart form! I deserved the Bastile for every one
of them.

Then nothing would serve me, when I got within sight
of Versailles, but putting words and sentences together, and
conceiving attitudes and tones to wreath myself into Monsieur
Le Duc de C****'s good graces—This will do, said I—Just
as well, retorted I again, as a coat carried up to him by an
adventurous tailor, without taking his measure—Fool! continued I—see Monsieur Le Duc's face first—observe what
character is written in it—take notice in what posture he stands
to hear you—mark the turns and expressions of his body and
limbs—And for the tone—the first sound which comes from his
lips will give it you—and from all these together you'll compound an address at once upon the spot, which cannot disgust
the Duke—the ingredients are his own, and most likely to go
down.

Well! said I, I wish it well over—Coward again! as if
man to man was not equal throughout the whole surface of
the globe: and if in the field—why not face to face in the
cabinet too? And trust me, Yorick, whenever it is not so man
is false to himself, and betrays his own succours ten times
where nature does it once. Go to the Duc de C**** with the
Bastile in thy looks—My life for it, thou wilt be sent to Paris
in about half an hour, with an escort.

I believe so, said I—Then I'll go to the Duke, by heaven!
with all the gaiety and debonairness in the world.——

——And there you are wrong again, replied I—A heart at
ease, Yorick, flies into no extremes—'tis ever on its center.——
Well! Well! cried I, as the coachman turned in at the gates, I
find I shall do very well: and by the time he had wheeled
round the court, and brought me up to the door, I found myself
so much the better for my own lecture, that I neither ascended
the steps like a victim to justice, who was to part with life upon

the topmost—nor did I mount them with a skip and a couple of strides, as I do when I fly up, Eliza! to thee, to meet it.

As I entered the door of the saloon, I was met by a person who possibly might be the maitre d'hotel, but had more the air of one of the under secretaries, who told me the Duc de C**** was busy—I am utterly ignorant, said I, of the forms of obtaining an audience, being an absolute stranger, and what is worse in the present conjuncture of affairs, being an Englishman too.—He replied, that did not increase the difficulty.—I made him a slight bow, and told him, I had something of importance to say to Monsieur le Duc. The secretary looked towards the stairs, as if he was about to leave me to carry up this account to someone—But I must not mislead you, said I; for what I have to say is of no manner of importance to Monsieur le Duc de C****,—but of great importance to myself. —*C'est une autre affaire,* replied he—Not at all, said I, to a man of gallantry.—But pray, good Sir, continued I, when can a stranger hope to have *accesse?*—In not less than two hours, said he, looking at his watch. The number of equipages in the court-yard seemed to justify the calculation, that I could have no nearer a prospect—and as walking backwards and forwards in the saloon, without a soul to commune with, was for the time as bad as being in the Bastile itself, I instantly went back to my *remise,* and bid the coachman drive me to the Cordon Bleu, which was the nearest hotel.

I think there is a fatality in it—I seldom go to the place I set out for.

LE PATISSER

Versailles

Before I had got half-way down the street, I changed my mind: as I am at Versailles, thought I, I might as well take a view of the town; so I pulled the cord, and ordered the coachman to drive round some of the principal streets—I suppose the town is not very large, said I.—The coachman begged pardon for setting me right, and told me it was very superb, and that numbers of the first dukes and marquises and counts had hotels—The Count de B**** of whom the bookseller at the Quai de Conti had spoke so handsomely the night before, came instantly into my mind.—And why should I not go, thought I, to the Count de B****, who has so high an idea of English books, and Englishmen, and tell him my story? so I changed my mind a second time—In truth it was the third; for I had intended that day for Madame de R**** in the Rue St. Pierre, and had devoutly sent her word by her *fille de chambre* that I would assuredly wait upon her—but I am governed by circumstances—I cannot govern them: so seeing a man standing with a basket on the other side of the street, as if he had something to sell, I bid La Fleur go up to him and enquire for the Count's hotel.

La Fleur returned a little pale; and told me it was a Chevalier de St Louis selling *pâtés*—It is impossible, La Fleur! said I.—La Fleur could no more account for the phenomenon than myself; but persisted in his story: he had seen the croix set in gold, with its red ribband, he said, tied to his button-hole—and had looked into the basket, and seen the *pâtés* which the Chevalier was selling; so could not be mistaken in that.

Such a reverse in man's life awakens a better principle than curiosity: I could not help looking for some time at him, as I sat in the *remise*—the more I looked at him, his croix, and his basket, the stronger they wove themselves into my brain—I got out of the *remise* and went towards him.

He was begirt with a clean linen apron which fell below his knees, and with a sort of a bib that went half-way up his breast; upon the top of this, but a little below the hem, hung his croix. His basket of little *pâtés* was covered over with a white damask napkin; another of the same kind was spread at the bottom; and there was a look of *propreté* and neatness throughout, that one might have bought his *pâtés* of him, as much from appetite as sentiment.

He made an offer of them to neither; but stood still with them at the corner of a hotel, for those to buy who chose it without solicitation.

He was about forty-eight—of a sedate look, something approaching to gravity. I did not wonder.—I went up rather to the basket than him, and having lifted up the napkin, and taken one of his *pâtés* into my hand—I begged he would explain the appearance which affected me.

He told me in a few words, that the best part of his life had passed in the service, in which, after spending a small patrimony, he had obtained a company and the croix with it; but that at the conclusion of the last peace, his regiment being reformed, and the whole corps, with those of some other regiments, left without any provision, he found himself in a wide world without friends, without a livre—and indeed, said he, without any thing but this—(pointing, as he said it, to his croix)—The poor Chevalier won my pity, and he finished the scene with winning my esteem too.

The king, he said, was the most generous of princes, but his generosity could neither relieve or reward every one, and it was only his misfortune to be amongst the number. He had a little wife, he said, whom he loved, who did the *patisserie;* and added, he felt no dishonour in defending her and himself from want in this way—unless Providence had offered him a better.

It would be wicked to withhold a pleasure from the good, in passing over what happened to this poor Chevalier of St Louis about nine months after.

It seems he usually took his stand near the iron gates which lead up to the palace, and as his croix had caught the eye of numbers, numbers had made the same enquiry which I had done—He had told them the same story, and always with so much modesty and good sense, that it had reached at last the king's ears—who hearing the Chevalier had been a gallant officer, and respected by the whole regiment as a man of honour and integrity—he broke up his little trade by a pension of fifteen hundred livres a year.

As I have told this to please the reader, I beg he will

allow me to relate another out of its order, to please myself—the two stories reflect light upon each other—and 'tis a pity they should be parted.

THE SWORD

Rennes

When states and empires have their periods of declension, and feel in their turns what distress and poverty is—I stop not to tell the causes which gradually brought the house of d'E**** in Britany into decay. The Marquis d'E**** had fought up against his condition with great firmness; wishing to preserve, and still show to the world, some little fragments of what his ancestors had been—their indiscretions had put it out of his power. There was enough left for the little exigencies of *obscurity*—But he had two boys who looked up to him for *light*—he thought they deserved it.—He had tried his sword—it could not open the way—the *mounting*[14] was too expensive —and simple œconomy was not a match for it—there was no resource but commerce.

In any other province in France, save Britany, this was smiting the root for ever of the little tree his pride and affection wished to see re-blossom—But in Britany, there being a provision for this, he availed himself of it; and taking an occasion when the states were assembled at Rennes, the Marquis, attended with his two boys, entered the court; and having pleaded the right of an ancient law of the duchy, which, though seldom claimed, he said, was no less in force; he took his sword from his side—Here, said he, take it; and be trusty guardians of it, till better times put me in condition to reclaim it.

The president accepted the Marquis's sword—he stayed a few minutes to see it deposited in the archives of his house, and departed.

The Marquis and his whole family embarked the next day for Martinico, and in about nineteen or twenty years of successful application to business, with some unlooked-for bequests from distant branches of his house, returned home to re-claim his nobility and to support it.

It was an incident of good fortune which will never happen to any traveller but a sentimental one, that I should be at Rennes at the very time of this solemn requisition: I call it solemn—it was so to me.

The Marquis entered the court with his whole family: he supported his lady—his eldest son supported his sister, and his youngest was at the other extreme of the line next his mother —he put his handkerchief to his face twice—

—There was a dead silence. When the Marquis had ap-proached within six paces of the tribunal, he gave the Mar-chioness to his youngest son, and advancing three steps before his family—he reclaimed his sword. His sword was given him, and the moment he got it into his hand he drew it almost out of the scabbard—'twas the shining face of a friend he had once given up—he looked attentively along it, beginning at the hilt, as if to see whether it was the same—when observing a little rust which it had contracted near the point, he brought it near his eye, and bending his head down over it, I think I saw a tear fall upon the place: I could not be deceived by what followed.

"I shall find," said he, "some *other way* to get it off."

When the Marquis had said this, he returned his sword into its scabbard, made a bow to the guardians of it—and, with his wife and daughter and his two sons following him, walked out.

O how I envied him his feelings!

THE PASSPORT

Versailles

I found no difficulty in getting admittance to Monsieur le Count de B****. The set of Shakespears was laid upon the table, and he was tumbling them over. I walked up close to the table, and giving first such a look at the books as to make him conceive I knew what they were—I told him I had come without anyone to present me, knowing I should meet with a friend in his apartment who, I trusted, would do it for me—It is my countryman the great Shakespear, said I, pointing to his works—*et ayez la bonté, mon cher ami,* apostrophizing his spirit, added I, *de me faire cet honneur là.*—

The Count smiled at the singularity of the introduction; and seeing I looked a little pale and sickly, insisted upon my taking an arm-chair: so I sat down; and to save him conjectures upon a visit so out of all rule, I told him simply of the incident in the bookseller's shop, and how that had impelled me rather to go to him with the story of a little embarrassment I was under, than to any other man in France—And what is your embarrassment? Let me hear it, said the Count. So I told him the story just as I have told it the reader—

—And the master of my hotel, said I, as I concluded it, will needs have it, Monsieur le Count, that I shall be sent to the Bastile—but I have no apprehensions, continued I—for in falling into the hands of the most polished people in the world, and being conscious I was a true man, and not come to spy the nakedness of the land, I scarce thought I laid at their mercy.—It does not suit the gallantry of the French, Monsieur le Count, said I, to show it against invalids.

An animated blush came into the Count de B****'s cheeks, as I spoke this—*Ne craignez rien*—Don't fear, said he—Indeed I don't, replied I again—Besides, continued I, a little sportingly, I have come laughing all the way from London to Paris, and I do not think Monsieur le Duc de Choiseul is such an enemy to mirth, as to send me back crying for my pains.

—My application to you, Monsieur le Count de B**** (making him a low bow) is to desire he will not.

The Count heard me with great good-nature, or I had not said half as much—and once or twice said—*C'est bien dit.* So I rested my cause there—and determined to say no more about it.

The Count led the discourse: we talked of indifferent

things—of books and politics, and men—and then of women—
God bless them all! said I, after much discourse about them—
there is not a man upon earth who loves them so much as I do:
after all the foibles I have seen, and all the satires I have read
against them, still I love them; being firmly persuaded that a
man who has not a sort of an affection for the whole sex, is
incapable of ever loving a single one as he ought.

Heh bien! Monsieur l'Anglois, said the Count, gaily—
You are not come to spy the nakedness of the land—I believe
you—*ni encore,* I dare say, *that* of our women—But permit
me to conjecture—if, *par hazard,* they fell into your way, that
the prospect would not affect you.

I have something within me which cannot bear the shock
of the least indecent insinuation: in the sportability of chit-chat
I have often endeavoured to conquer it, and with infinite pain
have hazarded a thousand things to a dozen of the sex together
—the least of which I could not venture to a single one, to
gain heaven.

Excuse me, Monsieur le Count, said I—as for the nakedness of your land, if I saw it, I should cast my eyes over it with
tears in them—and for that of your women (blushing at the
idea he had excited in me) I am so evangelical in this, and
have such a fellow feeling for whatever is *weak* about them,
that I would cover it with a garment, if I knew how to throw it
on—But I could wish, continued I, to spy the *nakedness* of
their hearts, and through the different disguises of customs,
climates, and religion, find out what is good in them to fashion
my own by—and therefore am I come.

It is for this reason, Monsieur le Count, continued I, that
I have not seen the Palais Royal—nor the Luxembourg—nor
the Façade of the Louvre—nor have attempted to swell the
catalogues we have of pictures, statues, and churches—I conceive every fair being as a temple, and would rather enter in,
and see the original drawings and loose sketches hung up in
it, than the transfiguration of Raphael itself.

The thirst of this, continued I, as impatient as that which
inflames the breast of the connoisseur, has led me from my

own home into France—and from France will lead me through Italy—'tis a quiet journey of the heart in pursuit of NATURE, and those affections which arise out of her, which make us love each other—and the world, better than we do.

The Count said a great many civil things to me upon the occasion; and added very politely how much he stood obliged to Shakespear for making me known to him—But, *à-propos,* said he—Shakespear is full of great things—he forgot a small punctilio of announcing your name—it puts you under a necessity of doing it yourself.

THE PASSPORT

Versailles

There is not a more perplexing affair in life to me, than to set about telling anyone who I am—for there is scarce anybody I cannot give a better account of than of myself; and I have often wished I could do it in a single word—and have an end of it. It was the only time and occasion in my life, I could accomplish this to any purpose—for Shakespear lying upon the table, and recollecting I was in his books, I took up *Hamlet,* and turning immediately to the grave-diggers scene in the fifth act, I laid my finger upon YORICK, and advancing the book to the Count, with my finger all the way over the name— Me, *Voici!* said I.

Now whether the idea of poor Yorick's skull was put out of the Count's mind by the reality of my own, or by what magic he could drop a period of seven or eight hundred years, makes nothing in this account—'tis certain the French conceive better than they combine—I wonder at nothing in this world, and the less at this; inasmuch as one of the first of our own church, for whose candour and paternal sentiments I have the highest veneration, fell into the same mistake in the very same case.— "He could not bear," he said, "to look into sermons wrote by the king of Denmark's jester."—Good, my lord! said I—but there are two Yoricks. The Yorick your lordship thinks of has been dead and buried eight hundred years ago; he flourished in Horwendillus's court—the other Yorick is myself, who have flourished, my lord, in no court—He shook his head—Good God! said I, you might as well confound Alexander the Great, with Alexander the Coppersmith, my lord—'Twas all one, he replied—

—If Alexander king of Macedon could have translated your lordship, said I, I'm sure your lordship would not have said so.

The poor Count de B**** fell but into the same *error*—
—*Et, Monsieur, est-il Yorick?* cried the Count.—*Je le suis,* said I.—*Vous?—Moi—moi qui ai l'honneur de vous parler, Monsieur le Compte—Mon Dieu!* said he, embracing me—*Vous êtes Yorick.*

The Count instantly put the Shakespear into his pocket, and left me alone in his room.

THE PASSPORT

Versailles

I could not conceive why the Count de B**** had gone so abruptly out of the room, any more than I could conceive why he had put the Shakespear into his pocket—*Mysteries which must explain themselves are not worth the loss of time which a conjecture about them takes up:* 'twas better to read Shakespear; so taking up *Much Ado about Nothing,* I transported myself instantly from the chair I sat in to Messina in Sicily, and got so busy with Don Pedro and Benedick and Beatrice, that I thought not of Versailles, the Count, or the Passport.

Sweet pliability of man's spirit, that can at once surrender itself to illusions, which cheat expectation and sorrow of their weary moments!——Long—long since had ye numbered out my days, had I not trod so great a part of them upon this enchanted ground: when my way is too rough for my feet, or too steep for my strength, I get off it, to some smooth velvet path which fancy has scattered over with rose-buds of delights; and having taken a few turns in it, come back strengthened and refreshed—When evils press sore upon me, and there is no retreat from them in this world, then I take a new course— I leave it—and as I have a clearer idea of the Elysian fields than I have of heaven, I force myself, like Æneas, into them —I see him meet the pensive shade of his forsaken Dido— and wish to recognize it—I see the injured spirit wave her head, and turn off silent from the author of her miseries and dis-honours—I lose the feelings for myself in hers, and in those affections which were wont to make me mourn for her when I was at school.

Surely this is not walking in a vain shadow—nor does man disquiet himself in vain *by it*—he oftener does so in trusting the issue of his commotions to reason only.—I can safely say for myself, I was never able to conquer any one single bad sensation in my heart so decisively, as by beating up as fast as I could for some kindly and gentle sensation, to fight it upon its own ground.

When I had got to the end of the third act, the Count de B**** entered with my passport in his hand. Mons. Le Duc de C****, said the Count, is as good a prophet, I dare say, as he is a statesman—*Un homme qui rit,* said the Duke, *ne sera jamais dangereux.*—Had it been for anyone but the king's jester, added the Count, I could not have got it these two hours.——*Pardonnez moi, Monsieur le Compte,* said I—I am not the king's jester.—But you are Yorick?—Yes.—*Et vous plaisantez?*——I answered, Indeed I did jest—but was not paid for it—'twas entirely at my own expence.

We have no jester at court, Mons. le Count, said I; the last we had was in the licentious reign of Charles II—since which time our manners have been so gradually refining, that our court at present is so full of patriots, who wish for *nothing* but the honours and wealth of their country—and our ladies are all so chaste, so spotless, so good, so devout—there is nothing for a jester to make a jest of—

Voilà un persiflage! cried the Count.

THE PASSPORT

Versailles

As the passport was directed to all lieutenant-governors, governors, and commandants of cities, generals of armies, justiciaries, and all officers of justice, to let Mr. Yorick, the king's jester, and his baggage, travel quietly along—I own the triumph of obtaining the passport was not a little tarnished by the figure I cut in it—But there is nothing unmixed in this world; and some of the gravest of our divines have carried it so far as to affirm that enjoyment itself was attended even with a sigh—and that the greatest *they knew of* terminated *in a general way,* in little better than a convulsion.

I remember the grave and learned Bevoriskius, in his commentary upon the generations from Adam, very naturally breaks off in the middle of a note to give an account to the world of a couple of sparrows upon the out-edge of his window, which had incommoded him all the time he wrote, and at last had entirely taken him off from his genealogy.

—'Tis strange! writes Bevoriskius; but the facts are certain, for I have had the curiosity to mark them down one by one with my pen—but the cock-sparrow during the little time that I could have finished the other half this note, has actually interrupted me with the reiteration of his caresses three and twenty times and a half.

How merciful, adds Bevoriskus, is heaven to his creatures!

Ill fated Yorick! that the gravest of thy brethren should be able to write that to the world, which stains thy face with crimson, to copy in even thy study.

But this is nothing to my travels—So I twice—twice beg pardon for it.

CHARACTER

Versailles

And how do you find the French? said the Count de B****, after he had given me the passport.

The reader may suppose, that after so obliging a proof of courtesy, I could not be at a loss to say something handsome to the enquiry.

—*Mais passe, pour cela*—Speak frankly, said he; do you find all the urbanity in the French which the world give us the honour of?—I had found everything, I said, which confirmed it—*Vraiment,* said the Count.—*Les Français sont polis.*—To an excess, replied I.

The Count took notice of the word *excesse;* and would have it I meant more than I said. I defended myself a long time as well as I could against it—he insisted I had a reserve, and that I would speak my opinion frankly.

I believe, Mons. le Count, said I, that man has a certain compass, as well as an instrument; and that the social and other calls have occasion by turns for every key in him; so that if you begin a note too high or too low, there must be a want either in the upper or under part, to fill up the system of harmony.—The Count de B**** did not understand music, so desired me to explain it some other way. A polished nation, my dear Count, said I, makes every one its debtor; and besides, urbanity itself, like the fair sex, has so many charms, it goes against the heart to say it can do ill; and yet, I believe, there is but a certain line of perfection that man, take him altogether, is impowered to arrive at—if he gets beyond, he rather exchanges qualities than gets them. I must not presume to say, how far this has affected the French in the subject we are speaking of—but should it ever be the case of the English, in the progress of their refinements, to arrive at the same polish which distinguishes the French, if we did not lose the *politesse de cœur,* which inclines men more to humane actions than courteous ones—we should at least lose that distinct variety and originality of character, which distinguishes them, not only from each other, but from all the world besides.

I had a few king William's shillings as smooth as glass in my pocket; and forseeing they would be of use in the illustration of my hypothesis, I had got them into my hand, when I had proceeded so far—

See, Monsieur le Count, said I, rising up, and laying them before him upon the table—by jingling and rubbing one against another for seventy years together in one body's pocket or another's, they are become so much alike you can scarce distinguish one shilling from another.

The English, like ancient medals, kept more apart, and passing but few people's hands, preserve the first sharpnesses which the fine hand of nature has given them—they are not so pleasant to feel—but in return, the legend is so visible, that at the first look you see whose image and superscription they bear.—But the French, Mons. le Count, added I, wishing to soften what I had said, have so many excellencies, they can the better spare this—they are a loyal, a gallant, a generous, an ingenious, and good tempered people as is under heaven—if they have a fault—they are too *serious*.

Mon Dieu! cried the Count, rising out of his chair.

Mais vous plaisantez, said he, correcting his exclamation. —I laid my hand upon my breast, and with earnest gravity assured him it was my most settled opinion.

The Count said he was mortified, he could not stay to hear my reasons, being engaged to go that moment to dine with the Duc de C*****.

But if it is not too far to come to Versailles to eat your soup with me, I beg, before you leave France, I may have the pleasure of knowing you retract your opinion—or, in what manner you support it.—But if you do support it, Mons. Anglois, said he, you must do it with all your powers, because you have the whole world against you.—I promised the Count I would do myself the honour of dining with him before I set out for Italy—so took my leave.

THE TEMPTATION

Paris

When I alighted at the hotel, the porter told me a young woman with a band-box had been that moment enquiring for me.—I do not know, said the porter, whether she is gone or no. I took the key of my chamber of him, and went upstairs; and when I had got within ten steps of the top of the landing before my door, I met her coming easily down.

It was the fair *fille de chambre* I had walked along the Quai de Conti with: Madame de R**** had sent her upon some commissions to a *merchande de modes* within a step or two of the hotel de Modene; and as I had failed in waiting upon her, had bid her enquire if I had left Paris; and if so, whether I had not left a letter addressed to her.

As the fair *fille de chambre* was so near my door she turned back, and went into the room with me for a moment or two whilst I wrote a card.

It was a fine still evening, in the latter end of the month of May—the crimson window-curtains (which were of the same colour of those of the bed) were drawn close—the sun was setting, and reflected through them so warm a tint into the fair *fille de chambre's* face—I thought she blushed—the idea of it made me blush myself—we were quite alone; and that super-induced a second blush before the first could get off.

There is a sort of a pleasing half-guilty blush, where the blood is more in fault than the man—'tis sent impetuous from the heart, and virtue flies after it—not to call it back, but to make the sensation of it more delicious to the nerves—'tis associated.—

But I'll not describe it.—I felt something at first within me which was not in strict unison with the lesson of virtue I had given her the night before—I sought five minutes for a card—I knew I had not one.——I took up a pen—I laid it down again—my hand trembled—the devil was in me.

I know as well as anyone, he is an adversary, whom if we resist he will fly from us—but I seldom resist him at all; from a terror, that though I may conquer, I may still get a hurt in the combat—*so* I give up the triumph for security; and instead of thinking to make him fly, I generally fly myself.

The fair *fille de chambre* came close up to the bureau where I was looking for a card—took up first the pen I cast down, then offered to hold me the ink: she offered it so sweetly, I was going to accept it—but I durst not—I have nothing, my dear, said I, to write upon.—Write it, said she, simply, upon any thing.—

I was just going to cry out, Then I will write it, fair girl! upon thy lips.—

—If I do, said I, I shall perish—so I took her by the hand, and led her to the door, and begged she would not forget the lesson I had given her—She said, indeed she would not—and as she uttered it with some earnestness, she turned about, and gave me both her hands, closed together, into mine—it was impossible not to compress them in that situation—I wished to let them go; and all the time I held them, I kept arguing within myself against it—and still I held them on.—In two minutes I found I had all the battle to fight over again—and I felt my legs and every limb about me tremble at the idea.

The foot of the bed was within a yard and a half of the place where we were standing—I had still hold of her hands—and how it happened I can give no account, but I neither asked her—nor drew her—nor did I think of the bed—but so it did happen, we both sat down.

I'll just show you, said the fair *fille de chambre,* the little purse I have been making today to hold your crown. So she put her hand into her right pocket, which was next me, and felt for it for some time—then into the left—"She had lost it."— I never bore expectation more quietly—it was in her right pocket at last—she pulled it out; it was of green taffeta, lined with a little bit of white quilted satin, and just big enough to hold the crown—she put it into my hand—it was pretty; and I held it ten minutes with the back of my hand resting upon her lap looking sometimes at the purse, sometimes on one side of it.

A stitch or two had broke out in the gathers of my stock[15] —the fair *fille de chambre,* without saying a word, took out her little hussive, threaded a small needle, and sewed it up— I foresaw it would hazard the glory of the day; and as she passed her hand in silence across and across my neck in the manœuvre, I felt the laurels shake which fancy had wreathed about my head.

A strap had given way in her walk, and the buckle of her shoe was just falling off—See, said the *fille de chambre,* holding up her foot—I could not for my soul but fasten the buckle in return, and putting in the strap—and lifting up the other foot with it, when I had done, to see both were right—in doing it too suddenly—it unavoidably threw the fair *fille de chambre* off her center—and then——

THE CONQUEST

Yes—and then—Ye whose clay-cold heads and lukewarm hearts can argue down or mask your passions, tell me, what trespass is it that man should have them? or how his spirit stands answerable to the Father of spirits, but for his conduct under them?

If nature has so wove her web of kindness, that some threads of love and desire are entangled with the piece, must the whole web be rent in drawing them out?—Whip me such stoics, great Governor of nature! said I to myself—Wherever thy Providence shall place me for the trials of my virtue— whatever is my danger—whatever is my situation—let me feel the movements which rise out of it, and which belong to me as a man, and if I govern them as a good one, I will trust the issues to thy justice; for, thou hast made us, and not we ourselves.

As I finished my address, I raised the fair *fille de chambre* up by the hand, and led her out of the room—she stood by me till I locked the door and put the key in my pocket—*and then*

—the victory being quite decisive—and not till then, I pressed my lips to her cheek, and, taking her by the hand again, led her safe to the gate of the hotel.

THE MYSTERY

Paris

If a man knows the heart, he will know it was impossible to go back instantly to my chamber—it was touching a cold key with a flat third to it, upon the close of a piece of music, which had called forth my affections—therefore, when I let go the hand of the *fille de chambre,* I remained at the gate of the hotel for some time, looking at everyone who passed by, and forming conjectures upon them, till my attention got fixed upon a single object which confounded all kind of reasoning upon him.

It was a tall figure, of a philosophic, serious, adust look, which passed and repassed sedately along the street, making a turn of about sixty paces on each side of the gate of the hotel —the man was about fifty-two—had a small cane under his arm—was dressed in a dark drab-coloured coat, waistcoat and breeches, which seemed to have seen some years service—they were still clean, and there was a little air of frugal *propreté* throughout him. By his pulling off his hat, and his attitude of accosting a good many in his way, I saw he was asking charity; so I got a sou or two out of my pocket ready to give him, as he took me in his turn—he passed by me without asking any-thing—and yet did not go five steps further before he asked charity of a little woman—I was much more likely to have given of the two.—He had scarce done with the woman, when he pulled off his hat to another who was coming the same way. —An ancient gentleman came slowly—and, after him, a young smart one—He let them both pass, and asked nothing: I stood observing him half an hour, in which time he had made a dozen turns backwards and forwards, and found that he invariably pursued the same plan.

There were two things very singular in this, which set my brain to work, and to no purpose—the first was, why the man should *only* tell his story to the sex—and secondly—what kind of story it was, and what species of eloquence it could be, which softened the hearts of the women, which he knew 'twas to no purpose to practise upon the men.

There were two other circumstances which entangled this mystery—the one was, he told every woman what he had to say in her ear, and in a way which had much more the air of a secret than a petition—the other was, it was always successful—he never stopped a woman, but she pulled out her purse, and immediately gave him something.

I could form no system to explain the phenomenon.

I had got a riddle to amuse me for the rest of the evening, so I walked upstairs to my chamber.

THE CASE OF CONSCIENCE

Paris

I was immediately followed up by the master of the hotel, who came into my room to tell me I must provide lodgings elsewhere.—How so, friend? said I.—He answered, I had had a young woman locked up with me two hours that evening in my bed-chamber, and 'twas against the rules of his house.— Very well, said I, we'll all part friends then—for the girl is no worse—and I am no worse—and you will be just as I found you.—It was enough, he said, to overthrow the credit of his hotel—*Voyez vous, Monsieur,* said he, pointing to the foot of the bed we had been sitting upon.—I own it had something of the appearance of an evidence; but my pride not suffering me to enter into any detail of the case, I exhorted him to let his soul sleep in peace, as I resolved to let mine do that night, and that I would discharge what I owed him at breakfast.

I should not have minded, *Monsieur,* said he, if you had had twenty girls—'Tis a score more, replied I, interrupting him, than I ever reckoned upon—Provided, added he, it had been but in a morning—And does the difference of the time of the day at Paris make a difference in the sin?—It made a difference, he said, in the scandal.—I like a good distinction in my heart, and cannot say I was intolerably out of temper with the man.— I own it is necessary, re-assumed the master of the hotel, that a stranger at Paris should have the opportunities presented to him of buying lace and silk stockings and ruffles, *et tout cela*— and 'tis nothing if a woman comes with a band-box.—O' my conscience, said I, she had one; but I never looked into it.—— Then, *Monsieur,* said he, has bought nothing.——Not one earthly thing, replied I.—Because, said he, I could recommend one to you who would use you *en conscience*.—But I must see her this night, said I.—He made me a low bow and walked down.

Now shall I triumph over this *Maitre d'hotel,* cried I— and what then?—Then I shall let him see I know he is a dirty fellow.—And what then?—What then!—I was too near myself to say it was for the sake of others.—I had no good answer left—there was more of spleen than principle in my project, and I was sick of it before the execution.

In a few minutes the Grisset came in with her box of lace—I'll buy nothing however, said I, within myself.

The Grisset would show me everything—I was hard to please: she would not seem to see it; she opened her little magazine, laid all her laces one after another before me— unfolded and folded them up again one by one with the most patient sweetness—I might buy—or not—she would let me have everything at my own price—the poor creature seemed anxious to get a penny; and laid herself out to win me, and not so much in a manner which seemed artful, as in one I felt simple and caressing.

If there is not a fund of honest cullibility in man, so much the worse—my heart relented, and I gave up my second resolution as quietly as the first—Why should I chastise one for the trespass of another?—If thou art tributary to this tyrant of an host, thought I, looking up in her face, so much harder is thy bread.

If I had not had more than four Louis d'ors in my purse,

there was no such thing as rising up and showing her the door, till I had first laid three of them out in a pair of ruffles.

—The master of the hotel will share the profit with her— no matter—then I have only paid as many a poor soul has *paid* before me for an act he *could* not do, or think of.

THE RIDDLE

Paris

When La Fleur came up to wait upon me at supper, he told me how sorry the master of the hotel was for his affront to me in bidding me change my lodgings.

A man who values a good night's rest will not lie down with enmity in his heart if he can help it—So I bid La Fleur tell the master of the hotel, that I was sorry on my side for the occasion I had given him—and you may tell him, if you will, La Fleur, added I, that if the young woman should call again, I shall not see her.

This was a sacrifice not to him, but myself, having re- solved, after so narrow an escape, to run no more risks, but to leave Paris, if it was possible, with all the virtue I entered in.

C'est deroger à noblesse, Monsieur, said La Fleur, making me a bow down to the ground as he said it—*Et encore Mon- sieur,* said he, may change his sentiments—and if (*par hazard*) he should like to amuse himself—I find no amusement in it, said I, interrupting him—

Mon Dieu! said La Fleur—and took away.

In an hour's time he came to put me to bed, and was more than commonly officious—something hung upon his lips to say to me, or ask me, which he could not get off: I could not con- ceive what it was; and indeed gave myself little trouble to find it out, as I had another riddle so much more interesting upon my mind, which was that of the man's asking charity before the door of the hotel—I would have given anything to have got to the bottom of it; and that, not out of curiosity—'tis so low a principle of enquiry, in general, I would not purchase the gratification of it with a two-sous piece—but a secret, I thought, which so soon and so certainly softened the heart of every woman you came near, was a secret at least equal to the philosopher's stone:[16] had I had both the Indies, I would have given up one to have been master of it.

I tossed and turned it almost all night long in my brains to no manner of purpose; and when I awoke in the morning, I found my spirit as much troubled with my *dreams,* as ever the king of Babylon had been with his; and I will not hesitate to affirm, it would have puzzled all the wise men of Paris, as much as those of Chaldea, to have given its interpretation.

LE DIMANCHE

Paris

It was Sunday; and when La Fleur came in, in the morning, with my coffee and roll and butter, he had got himself so gallantly arrayed, I scarce knew him.

I had covenanted at Montriul to give him a new hat with a silver button and loop, and four Louis d'ors *pour s'adoniser,* when we got to Paris; and the poor fellow, to do him justice, had done wonders with it.

He had bought a bright, clean, good scarlet coat, and a pair of breeches of the same—They were not a crown worse, he said, for the wearing—I wished him hanged for telling me— They looked so fresh, that though I knew the thing could not be done, yet I would rather have imposed upon my fancy with thinking I had bought them new for the fellow, than that they had come out of the Rue de Friperie.

This is a nicety which makes not the heart sore at Paris.

He had purchased moreover a handsome blue satin waistcoat, fancifully enough embroidered—this was indeed something the worse for the service it had done, but 'twas clean scoured—the gold had been touched up, and upon the whole was rather showy than otherwise—and as the blue was not violent, it suited with the coat and breeches very well: he had squeezed out of the money, moreover, a new bag and a solitaire;[17] and had insisted with the *fripier* upon a gold pair of garters to his breeches knees—He had purchased muslin ruffles, *bien brodées,* with four livres of his own money—and a pair of white silk stockings for five more—and, to top all, nature had given him a handsome figure, without costing him a sou.

He entered the room thus set off, with his hair dressed in the first style, and with a handsome *bouquet* in his breast—in a word, there was that look of festivity in everything about him, which at once put me in mind it was Sunday—and by combining both together, it instantly struck me, that the favour he wished to ask of me the night before, was to spend the day as everybody in Paris spent it besides. I had scarce made the conjecture, when La Fleur, with infinite humility, but with a look of trust, as if I should not refuse him, begged I would grant him the day, *pour faire le galant vis-à-vis de sa maîtresse.*

Now it was the very thing I intended to do myself *vis-à-vis* Madame de R****—I had retained the *remise* on purpose for it, and it would not have mortified my vanity to have had a servant so well dressed as La Fleur was to have got up behind it: I never could have worse spared him.

But we must *feel,* not argue in these embarrassments— the sons and daughters of service part with Liberty, but not with Nature, in their contacts; they are flesh and blood, and have their little vanities and wishes in the midst of the house of bondage, as well as their task-masters—no doubt they have set their self-denials at a price—and their expectations are so unreasonable, that I would often disappoint them, but that their condition puts it so much in my power to do it.

Behold—Behold, I am thy servant—disarms me at once of the powers of a master—

—Thou shalt go, La Fleur! said I.—

—And what mistress, La Fleur, said I, canst thou have picked up in so little a time at Paris? La Fleur laid his hand upon his breast, and said 'twas a *petite demoiselle* at Monsieur le Count de B****'s.—La Fleur had a heart made for society; and, to speak the truth of him, let as few occasions slip him as his master—so that somehow or other; but how—

heaven knows—he had connected himself with the *demoiselle* upon the landing of the stair-case, during the time I was taken up with my passport; and as there was time enough for me to win the Count to my interest, La Fleur had contrived to make it do to win the maid to his—The family, it seems, was to be at Paris that day, and he had made a party with her, and two or three more of the Count's household, upon the *boulevards*.

Happy people! that once a week at least are sure to lay down all your cares together; and dance and sing, and sport away the weights of grievance, which bow down the spirit of other nations to the earth.

THE FRAGMENT

Paris

La Fleur had left me something to amuse myself with for the day more than I had bargained for, or could have entered either into his head or mine.

He had brought the little print of butter upon a currant leaf; and as the morning was warm, and he had a good step to bring it, he had begged a sheet of waste paper to put betwixt the currant leaf and his hand—As that was plate sufficient, I bade him lay it upon the table as it was, and as I resolved to stay within all day, I ordered him to call upon the *traiteur* to bespeak my dinner, and leave me to breakfast by myself.

When I had finished the butter, I threw the current leaf out of the window, and was going to do the same by the waste paper—but stopping to read a line first, and that drawing me on to a second and third—I thought it better worth; so I shut the window, and drawing a chair up to it, I sat down to read it.

It was the old French of Rabelais's time, and for aught I knew might have been wrote by him—it was moreover in a Gothic letter, and that so faded and gone off by damps and length of time, it cost me infinite trouble to make anything of it—I threw it down; and then wrote a letter to Eugenius— then I took it up again, and embroiled my patience with it afresh—and then to cure that, I wrote a letter to Eliza.—Still it kept hold of me; and the difficulty of understanding it increased but the desire.

I got my dinner; and after I had enlightened my mind with a bottle of Burgundy, I at it again—and after two or three hours poring upon it, with almost as deep attention as ever Gruter or Jacob Spon[18] did upon a nonsensical inscription, I thought I made sense of it; but to make sure of it, the best way, I imagined, was to turn it into English, and see how it would look then—so I went on leisurely, as a trifling man does, sometimes writing a sentence—then taking a turn or two— and then looking how the world went, out of the window; so that it was nine o'clock at night before I had done it—I then began to read it as follows.

THE FRAGMENT

Paris

——Now as the notary's wife disputed the point with the notary with too much heat—I wish, said the notary, throwing down the parchment, that there was another notary here only to set down and attest all this—

—And what would you do then, Monsieur? said she, rising hastily up—the notary's wife was a little fume of a woman, and the notary thought it well to avoid a hurricane by a mild reply—I would go, answered he, to bed.—You may go to the devil, answered the notary's wife.

Now there happening to be but one bed in the house, the other two rooms being unfurnished, as is the custom at Paris, and the notary not caring to lie in the same bed with a woman who had but that moment sent him pell-mell to the devil, went forth with his hat and cane and short cloak, the night being very windy, and walked out ill at ease towards the *Pont Neuf*.

Of all the bridges which ever were built, the whole world who have passed over the *Pont Neuf* must own, that it is the noblest—the finest—the grandest—the lightest—the longest—

the broadest that ever conjoined land and land together upon
the face of the terraqueous globe——

*By this, it seems, as if the author of the fragment had not
been a Frenchman.*

The worst fault which divines and the doctors of the
Sorbonne can allege against it, is, that if there is but a cap-full
of wind in or about Paris, 'tis more blasphemously *sacre Dieu*'d
there than in any other aperture of the whole city—and with
reason, good and cogent Messieurs; for it comes against you
without crying *garde d'eau,* and with such unpremeditable puffs,
that of the few who cross it with their hats on, not one in
fifty but hazards two livres and a half, which is its full worth.

The poor notary, just as he was passing by the sentry,
instinctively clapped his cane to the side of it, but in raising it
up, the point of his cane catching hold of the loop of the
sentinel's hat, hoisted it over the spikes of the balustrade clear
into the Seine——

—'Tis an ill wind, said a boatsman, who catched it, *which
blows nobody any good*.

The sentry, being a Gascon, incontinently twirled up his
whiskers, and levelled his harquebuss.

Harquebusses in those days went off with matches; and
an old woman's paper lanthorn at the end of the bridge happened to be blown out, she had borrowed the sentry's match
to light it—it gave a moment's time for the Gascon's blood to
run cool, and turn the accident better to his advantage—*'Tis
an ill wind,* said he, catching off the notary's castor,[19] and
legitimating the capture with the boatman's adage.

The poor notary crossed the bridge, and passing along
the Rue de Dauphine into the fauxbourgs of St. Germain,
lamented himself as he walked along in this manner:

Luckless man that I am! said the notary, to be the sport
of hurricanes all my days—to be born to have the storm of
ill language levelled against me and my profession wherever I
go—to be forced into marriage by the thunder of the church
to a tempest of a woman—to be driven forth out of my house
by domestic winds, and despoiled of my castor by pontific ones

—to be here, bare-headed, in a windy night, at the mercy of the ebbs and flows of accidents—where am I to lay my head?—miserable man! what wind in the two-and-thirty points of the whole compass can blow unto, thee, as it does to the rest of thy fellow-creatures, good!

As the notary was passing on by a dark passage, complaining in this sort, a voice called out to a girl, to bid her run for the next notary—now the notary being the next, and availing himself of his situation, walked up the passage to the door, and passing through an old sort of a saloon, was ushered into a large chamber dismantled of everything but a long military pike—a breast-plate—a rusty old sword, and bandoleer, hung up equidistant in four different places against the wall.

An old personage, who had heretofore been a gentleman, and unless decay of fortune taints the blood along with it was a gentleman at that time, lay supporting his head upon his hand in his bed; a little table with a taper burning was set close beside it, and close by the table was placed a chair—the notary sat him down in it; and pulling out his ink-horn and a sheet or two of paper which he had in his pocket, he placed them before him, and dipping his pen in his ink, and leaning his breast over the table, he disposed everything to make the gentleman's last will and testament.

Alas! Monsieur le Notaire, said the gentleman, raising himself up a little, I have nothing to bequeath which will pay the expence of bequeathing, except the history of myself, which I could not die in peace unless I left it as a legacy to the world; the profits arising out of it, I bequeath to you for the pains of taking it from me—it is a story so uncommon, it must be read by all mankind—it will make the fortunes of your house—the notary dipped his pen into his ink-horn—Almighty director of every event in my life! said the old gentleman, looking up earnestly and raising his hands toward heaven—thou whose hand has led me on through such a labyrinth of strange passages down into this scene of desolation, assist the decaying memory of an old, infirm, and broken-hearted man, direct my tongue, by the spirit of thy eternal truth, that this stranger may set down naught but what is written in that BOOK, from whose records, said he, clasping his hands together, I am to be condemned or acquitted!—the notary held up the point of his pen betwixt the taper and his eye——

—It is a story, Monsieur le Notaire, said the gentleman, which will rouse up every affection in nature—it will kill the humane, and touch the heart of cruelty herself with pity——

—The notary was inflamed with a desire to begin, and put his pen a third time into his ink-horn—and the old gentleman turning a little more towards the notary, began to dictate his story in these words——

—And where is the rest of it, La Fleur? said I, as he just then entered the room.

THE FRAGMENT
AND THE BOUQUET*

Paris

When La Fleur came up close to the table, and was made to comprehend what I wanted, he told me there were only two other sheets of it which he had wrapt round the stalks of a *bouquet* to keep it together, which he had presented to the *demoiselle* upon the *boulevards*—Then, prithee, La Fleur, said I, step back to her to the Count de B****'s hotel and *see if you canst get it*—There is no doubt of it, said La Fleur—and away he flew.

In a very little time the poor fellow came back quite out of breath, with deeper marks of disappointment in his looks than could arise from the simple irreparability of the fragment —*Juste ciel!* in less than two minutes that the poor fellow had taken his last tender farewell of her—his faithless mistress had given his *gage d'amour* to one of the Count's footmen—the footman to a young sempstress—and the sempstress to a fiddler, with my fragment at the end of it—Our misfortunes were involved together—I gave a sigh—and La Fleur echoed it back again to my ear—

* Nosegay.

—How perfidious! cried La Fleur—How unlucky! said I.—

—I should not have been mortified, Monsieur, quoth La Fleur, if she had lost it—Nor I, La Fleur, said I, had I found it. Whether I did or no, will be seen hereafter.

THE ACT OF CHARITY

Paris

The man who either disdains or fears to walk up a dark entry may be an excellent good man, and fit for a hundred things; but he will not do to make a good sentimental traveller. I count little of the many things I see pass at broad noon-day in large and open streets.—Nature is shy, and hates to act before spectators; but in such an unobserved corner, you sometimes see a single short scene of hers worth all the sentiments of a dozen French plays compounded together—and yet they are *absolutely* fine;—and whenever I have a more brilliant affair upon my hands than common, as they suit a preacher just as well as a hero, I generally make my sermon out of 'em—and for the text—"Capadosia, Pontus and Asia, Phrygia and Pamphilia"—is as good as any one in the Bible.

There is a long dark passage issuing out from the opera comique into a narrow street; 'tis trod by a few who humbly wait for a *fiacre*,* or wish to get off quietly o'foot when the opera is done. At the end of it, towards the theatre, 'tis lighted by a small candle, the light of which is almost lost before you get half-way down, but near the door—'tis more for ornament than use: you see it as a fixed star of the least magnitude; it burns—but does little good to the world, that we know of.

In returning along this passage, I discerned, as I approached within five or six paces of the door, two ladies standing arm in arm, with their backs against the wall, waiting, as I imagined, for a *fiacre*—as they were next the door, I thought they had a prior right; so edged myself up within a yard or

* Hackney-coach.

little more of them, and quietly took my stand—I was in black, and scarce seen.

The lady next me was a tall lean figure of a woman of about thirty-six; the other of the same size and make, of about forty; there was no mark of wife or widow in any one part of either of them—they seemed to be two upright vestal sisters, unsapped by caresses, unbroke in upon by tender salutations: I could have wished to have made them happy—their happiness was destined, that night, to come from another quarter.

A low voice, with a good turn of expression, and sweet cadence at the end of it, begged for a twelve-sous piece betwixt them, for the love of heaven. I thought it singular, that a beggar should fix the quota of an alms—and that the sum should be twelve times as much as what is usually given in the dark. They both seemed astonished at it as much as myself.—Twelve sous! said one—A twelve-sous piece! said the other—and made no reply.

The poor man said, He knew not how to ask less of ladies of their rank, and bowed down his head to the ground.

Poo! said they—we have no money.

The beggar remained silent for a moment or two, and renewed his supplication.

Do not, my fair young ladies, said he, stop your good ears against me—Upon my word, honest man! said the younger, we have no change——Then God bless you, said the poor man, and multiply those joys which you can give to others without change!——I observed the elder sister put her hand into her pocket—I'll see, said she, if I have a sou.—A sou! give twelve, said the supplicant; Nature has been bountiful to you, be bountiful to a poor man.

I would, friend, with all my heart, said the younger, if I had it.

My fair charitable! said he, addressing himself to the elder—What is it but your goodness and humanity which makes your bright eyes so sweet, that they outshine the morning even in this dark passage? and what was it which made the Marquis de Santerre and his brother say so much of you both as they just passed by?

The two ladies seemed much affected; and impulsively at the same time they both put their hands into their pocket, and each took out a twelve-sous piece.

The contest betwixt them and the poor supplicant was no more—it was continued betwixt themselves, which of the two should give the twelve-sous piece in charity—and to end the dispute, they both gave it together, and the man went away.

THE RIDDLE EXPLAINED

Paris

I stepped hastily after him: it was the very man whose success in asking charity of the women before the door of the hotel had so puzzled me—and I found at once his secret, or at least the basis of it—'twas flattery.

Delicious essence! how refreshing art thou to nature! how strongly are all its powers and all its weaknesses on thy side! how sweetly dost thou mix with the blood, and help it through the most difficult and tortuous passages to the heart!

The poor man, as he was not straitened for time, had given it here in a larger dose: 'tis certain he had a way of bringing it into less form, for the many sudden cases he had to do with in the streets; but how he contrived to correct, sweeten, concentrate, and quality it—I vex not my spirit with the enquiry—it is enough, the beggar gained two twelve-sous pieces—and they can best tell the rest, who have gained much greater matters by it.

PARIS

We get forwards in the world not so much by doing services, as receiving them: you take a withering twig, and put it in the ground; and then you water it, because you have planted it.

Mons. le Count de B****, merely because he had done

me one kindness in the affair of my passport, would go on and do me another, the few days he was at Paris, in making me known to a few people of rank; and they were to present me to others, and so on.

I had got master of my *secret* just in time to turn these honours to some little account; otherwise, as is commonly the case, I should have dined or supped a single time or two round, and then by *translating* French looks and attitudes into plain English, I should presently have seen, that I had got hold of the *couvert** of some more entertaining guest; and in course, should have resigned all my places one after another, merely upon the principle that I could not keep them.—As it was, things did not go much amiss.

I had the honour of being introduced to the old Marquis de B****: in days of yore he had signalized himself by some small feats of chivalry in the *Cour d'amour,* and had dressed himself out to the idea of tilts and tournaments ever since—the Marquis de B**** wished to have it thought the affair was somewhere else than in his brain. "He could like to take a trip to England," and asked much of the English ladies. Stay where you are, I beseech you, Mons. le Marquis, said I— Les Messrs. Anglois can scarce get a kind look from them as it is.—The Marquis invited me to supper.

Mons. P**** the farmer-general, was just as inquisitive about our taxes.—They were very considerable, he heard—If we knew but how to collect them, said I, making him a low bow.

I could never have been invited to Mons. P****'s concerts upon any other terms.

I had been misrepresented to Madame de Q**** as an *esprit*—Madame de Q**** was an *esprit* herself; she burnt with impatience to see me, and hear me talk. I had not taken my seat, before I saw she did not care a sou whether I had any wit or no—I was let in, to be convinced she had.—I call heaven to witness I never once opened the door of my lips.

Madame de Q**** vowed to every creature she met, "She

* Plate, napkin, knife, fork, and spoon.

had never had a more improving conversation with a man in her life."

There are three epochas in the empire of a French woman —She is coquette—then deist—then *devôte:* the empire during these is never lost—she only changes her subjects: when thirty-five years and more have unpeopled her dominions of the slaves of love, she re-peoples it with slaves of infidelity—and then with the slaves of the Church.

Madame de V*** was vibrating betwixt the first of these epochas: the colour of the rose was shading fast away—she ought to have been a deist five years before the time I had the honour to pay my first visit.

She placed me upon the same sofa with her, for the sake of disputing the point of religion more closely—In short, Madame de V*** told me she believed nothing.

I told Madame de V*** it might be her principle; but I was sure it could not be her interest to level the outworks, without which I could not conceive how such a citadel as hers could be defended—that there was not a more dangerous thing in the world, than for a beauty to be a deist—that it was a debt I owed my creed, not to conceal it from her—that I had not been five minutes sat upon the sofa beside her, but I had begun to form designs—and what is it, but the sentiments of religion, and the persuasion they had existed in her breast, which could have checked them as they rose up?

We are not adamant, said I, taking hold of her hand—and there is need of all restraints, till age in her own time steals in and lays them on us—but, my dear lady, said I, kissing her hand—'tis too—too soon—

I declare I had the credit all over Paris of unperverting Madame de V***.—She affirmed to Mons. D*** and the Abbé M***, that in one half hour I had said more for revealed religion, than all their Encyclopedia had said against it—I was listed directly into Madame de V***'s *Coterie*—and she put off the epocha of deism for two years.

I remember it was in this *Coterie,* in the middle of a discourse, in which I was showing the necessity of a *first cause,* that the young Count de Faineant took me by the hand to the furthest corner of the room, to tell me my *solitaire* was pinned too strait about my neck—It should be *plus badinant,* said the Count, looking down upon his own—but a word, Mons. Yorick, *to the wise—*

—And from the wise, Mons. le Count, replied I, making him a bow—*is enough.*

The Count de Faineant embraced me with more ardour than ever I was embraced by mortal man.

For three weeks together, I was of every man's opinion I met.—*Pardi! ce Mons. Yorick a autant d'esprit que nous autres.* —*Il raisonne bien,* said another.——*C'est un bon enfant,* said a third.—And at this price I could have eaten and drank and been merry all the days of my life at Paris; but 'twas a dishonest *reckoning*—I grew ashamed of it—it was the gain of a slave—every sentiment of honour revolted against it—the higher I got, the more I was forced upon my *beggarly system*— the better the *Coterie*—the more children of Art—I languished for those of Nature: and one night after a most vile prostitution of myself to half a dozen different people, I grew sick—went to bed—ordered La Fleur to get me horses in the morning to set out for Italy.

MARIA

Moulines

I never felt what the distress of plenty was in any one shape till now—to travel it through the Bourbonnois, the sweetest part of France—in the hey-day of the vintage, when Nature is pouring her abundance into everyone's lap, and every eye is lifted up—a journey through each step of which music beats time to *Labour,* and all her children are rejoicing as they carry in their clusters—to pass through this with my affections flying out, and kindling at every group before me— and every one of 'em was pregnant with adventures.

Just heaven!—it would fill up twenty volumes—and alas! I have but a few small pages left of this to crowd it into—and half of these must be taken up with the poor Maria my friend, Mr. Shandy[20] met with near Moulines.

The story he had told of that disordered maid affected me not a little in the reading; but when I got within the neighbourhood where she lived, it returned so strong into my mind, that I could not resist an impulse which prompted me to go half a league out of the road to the village where her parents dwelt to enquire after her.

'Tis going, I own, like the Knight of the Woeful Countenance,[21] in quest of melancholy adventures—but I know not how it is, but I am never so perfectly conscious of the existence of a soul within me, as when I am entangled in them.

The old mother came to the door, her looks told me the story before she opened her mouth—She had lost her husband; he had died, she said, of anguish, for the loss of Maria's senses about a month before.—She had feared at first, she added, that it would have plundered her poor girl of what little understanding was left—but, on the contrary, it had brought her more to herself—still she could not rest—her poor daughter, she said, crying, was wandering somewhere about the road—

—Why does my pulse beat languid as I write this? and what made La Fleur, whose heart seemed only to be tuned to joy, to pass the back of his hand twice across his eyes, as the woman stood and told it? I beckoned to the postillion to turn back into the road.

When we had got within half a league of Moulines, at a little opening in the road leading to a thicket, I discovered poor Maria sitting under a poplar—she was sitting with her elbow in her lap, and her head leaning on one side within her hand—a small brook ran at the foot of the tree.

I bid the postillion go on with the chaise to Moulines—and La Fleur to bespeak my supper—and that I would walk after him.

She was dressed in white, and much as my friend described her, except that her hair hung loose, which before was twisted within a silk net.—She had, superadded likewise to her jacket, a pale green ribband which fell across her shoulder to the waist; at the end of which hung her pipe.—Her goat had been as faithless as her lover; and she had got a little dog in lieu of him, which she had kept tied by a string to her girdle; as I looked at her dog, she drew him towards her with the string.—"Thou shalt not leave me, Sylvio," said she. I looked in Maria's eyes, and saw she was thinking more of her father than of her lover or her little goat; for as she uttered them the tears trickled down her cheeks.

I sat down close by her; and Maria let me wipe them away as they fell with my handkerchief—I then steeped it in my own—and then in hers—and then in mine—and then I wiped hers again—and as I did it, I felt such undescribable emotions within me, as I am sure could not be accounted for from any combinations of matter and motion.

I am positive I have a soul; nor can all the books with which materialists have pestered the world ever convince me of the contrary.

MARIA

When Maria had come a little to herself, I asked her if she remembered a pale thin person of a man who had sat down betwixt her and her goat about two years before? She said, she was unsettled much at that time, but remembered it upon two accounts—that ill as she was she saw the person pitied her; and next, that her goat had stolen his handkerchief, and she had beat him for the theft—she had washed it, she said, in the brook, and kept it ever since in her pocket to restore it to him in case she should ever see him again, which, she added, he had half promised her. As she told me this she took the handkerchief out of her pocket to let me see it; she had folded it up neatly in a couple of vine leaves, tied round with a tendril—on opening it, I saw an S marked in one of the corners.

She had since that, she told me, strayed as far as Rome, and walked round St. Peter's once—and returned back—that she found her way alone across the Apennines—had travelled over all Lombardy without money—and through the flinty roads of Savoy without shoes—how she had borne it, and how she had got supported, she could not tell—but *God tempers the wind,* said Maria, to the shorn lamb.

Shorn indeed! and to the quick, said I; and wast thou in my own land, where I have a cottage, I would take thee to it and shelter thee: thou shouldst eat of my own bread, and drink of my own cup—I would be kind to thy Sylvio—in all thy weaknesses and wanderings I would seek after thee and bring thee back—when the sun went down I would say my prayers, and when I had done thou shouldst play thy evening song upon thy pipe; nor would the incense of my sacrifice be worse accepted for entering heaven along with that of a broken heart.

Nature melted within me, as I uttered this; and Maria observing, as I took out my handkerchief, that it was steeped too much already to be of use, would needs go wash it in the stream.—And where will you dry it, Maria? said I—I'll dry it in my bosom, said she—'twill do me good.

And is your heart still so warm, Maria? said I.

I touched upon the string on which hung all her sorrows —she looked with wistful disorder for some time in my face; and then, without saying anything, took her pipe, and played her service to the Virgin—The string I had touched ceased to vibrate—in a moment or two Maria returned to herself—let her pipe fall—and rose up.

And where you are going, Maria? said I.—She said to Moulines.—Let us go, said I, together.—Maria put her arm within mine, and lengthening the string, to let the dog follow— in that order we entered Moulines.

MARIA

Moulines

Though I hate salutations and greetings in the market-place, yet when we got into the middle of this, I stopped to take my last look and last farewell of Maria.

Maria, though not tall, was nevertheless of the first order

of fine forms—affliction had touch'd her looks with something that was scarce earthly—still she was feminine—and so much was there about her of all that the heart wishes, or the eye looks for in woman, that could the traces be ever worn out of her brain, and those of Eliza's out of mine, she should *not only eat of my bread and drink of my own cup,* but Maria should lay in my bosom, and be unto me as a daughter.

Adieu, poor luckless maiden!—imbibe the oil and wine which the compassion of a stranger, as he journeyeth on his way, now pours into thy wounds—the Being who has twice bruised thee can only bind them up for ever.

THE BOURBONNOIS

There was nothing from which I had painted out for myself so joyous a riot of the affections, as in this journey in the vintage, through this part of France; but pressing through this gate of sorrow to it, my sufferings had totally unfitted me: in every scene of festivity I saw Maria in the background of the piece, sitting pensive under her poplar; and I had got almost to Lyons before I was able to cast a shade across her—

—Dear sensibility! source inexhausted of all that's precious in our joys, or costly in our sorrows! thou chainest thy martyr down upon his bed of straw—and 'tis thou who lifts him up to HEAVEN—eternal fountain of our feelings!—'tis here I trace thee—and this is thy divinity which stirs within me— not that, in some sad and sickening moments, *my soul shrinks back upon herself, and startles at destruction*—mere pomp of words!—but that I feel some generous joys and generous cares beyond myself—all comes from thee, great, great SENSORIUM of the world! which vibrates, if a hair of our heads but falls upon the ground, in the remotest desert of thy creation.— Touched with thee, Eugenius draws my curtain when I languish —hears my tale of symptoms, and blames the weather for the disorder of his nerves. Thou givest a portion of it sometimes to the roughest peasant who traverses the bleakest mountains— he finds the lacerated lamb of another's flock—This moment I behold him leaning with his head against his crook, with piteous inclination looking down upon it!—Oh! had I come one moment sooner!—it bleeds to death—his gentle heart bleeds with it——

Peace to thee, generous swain!—I see thou walkest off with anguish—but thy joys shall balance it—for happy is thy cottage —and happy is the sharer of it—and happy are the lambs which sport about you.

THE SUPPER

A shoe coming loose from the fore-foot of the thill-horse, at the beginning of the ascent of mount Taurira, the postillion dismounted, twisted the shoe off, and put it in his pocket; as the ascent was of five or six miles, and that horse our main dependence, I made a point of having the shoe fastened on again, as well as we could; but the postillion had thrown away the nails, and the hammer in the chaise-box being of no great use without them, I submitted to go on.

He had not mounted half a mile higher, when coming to a flinty piece of road, the poor devil lost a second shoe, and from off his other fore-foot; I then got out of the chaise in good earnest; and seeing a house about a quarter of a mile to the left-hand, with a great deal to do I prevailed upon the postillion to turn up to it. The look of the house, and of everything about it, as we drew nearer, soon reconciled me to the disaster.—It was a little farmhouse surrounded with about twenty acres of vineyard, about as much corn—and close to the house, on one side, was a *potagerie* of an acre and a half, full of everything which could make plenty in a French peasant's house—and on the other side was a little wood which furnished wherewithal to dress it. It was about eight in the evening when I got to the house—so I left the postillion to manage his point as he could—and for mine, I walked directly into the house.

The family consisted of an old grey-headed man and his wife, with five or six sons and sons-in-law, and their several wives, and a joyous genealogy out of 'em.

They were all sitting down together to their lentil-soup; a large wheaten loaf was in the middle of the table; and a flaggon of wine at each end of it promised joy through the stages of the repast—'twas a feast of love.

The old man rose up to meet me, and with a respectful cordiality would have me sit down at the table; my heart was sat down the moment I entered the room; so I sat down at once like a son of the family; and to invest myself in the character as speedily as I could, I instantly borrowed the old man's knife, and taking up the loaf, cut myself a hearty luncheon; and as I did it, I saw a testimony in every eye, not only of an honest welcome, but of a welcome mixed with thanks that I had not seemed to doubt it.

Was it this; or tell me, Nature, what else it was which made this morsel so sweet—and to what magic I owe it, that the draught I took of their flaggon was so delicious with it, that they remain upon my palate to this hour?

If the supper was to my taste—the grace that followed it was much more so.

THE GRACE

When supper was over, the old man gave a knock upon the table with the haft of his knife, to bid them prepare, for the dance: the moment the signal was given, the women and girls ran all together into a back apartment to tie up their hair— and the young men to the door to wash their faces, and change their sabots;[22] and in three minutes every soul was ready upon a little esplanade before the house to begin—The old man and his wife came out last, and, placing me betwixt them, sat down upon a sofa of turf by the door.

The old man had some fifty years ago been no mean performer upon the vielle—and, at the age he was then of, touched it well enough for the purpose. His wife sung now and then a little to the tune—then intermitted—and joined her old man again as their children and grandchildren danced before them.

It was not till the middle of the second dance, when, from some pauses in the movement wherein they all seemed to look up, I fancied I could distinguish an elevation of spirit different from that which is the cause or the effect of simple jollity—In a word, I thought I beheld *Religion* mixing in the dance—but as I had never seen her so engaged, I should have looked upon it now, as one of the illusions of an imagination which is eternally misleading me, had not the old man, as soon as the dance ended, said, that this was their constant way; and that all his life long he had made it a rule, after supper was over, to call out his family to dance and rejoice; believing, he said, that a cheerful and contented mind was the best sort of thanks to heaven that an illiterate peasant could pay—

—Or a learned prelate either, said I.

THE CASE OF DELICACY

When you have gained the top of mount Taurira, you run presently down to Lyons—adieu then to all rapid movements! 'Tis a journey of caution; and it fares better with sentiments, not to be in a hurry with them; so I contracted with a voiturin[23] to take his time with a couple of mules, and convey me in my own chaise safe to Turin through Savoy.

Poor, patient, quiet, honest people! fear not; your poverty, the treasury of your simple virtues, will not be envied you by the world, nor will your valleys be invaded by it.—Nature! in the midst of thy disorders, thou art still friendly to the scantiness thou hast created—with all thy great works about thee, little hast thou left to give, either to the scythe or to the sickle —but to that little thou grantest safety and protection; and sweet are the dwellings which stand so sheltered.

Let the way-worn traveller vent his complaints upon the sudden turns and dangers of your roads—your rocks—your precipices—the difficulties of getting up—the horrors of getting down—mountains impracticable—and cataracts, which roll down great stones from their summits, and block up his road. —The peasants had been all day at work in removing a fragment of this kind between St. Michael and Madane; and by the time my voiturin got to the place, it wanted full two hours of completing before a passage could any how be gained: there was nothing but to wait with patience—'twas a wet and tempestuous night; so that by the delay, and that together, the voiturin found himself obliged to take up five miles short of his stage at a little decent kind of an inn by the road side.

I forthwith took possession of my bed-chamber—got a good fire—ordered supper; and was thanking heaven it was no worse—when a voiture arrived with a lady in it and her servant-maid.

As there was no other bed-chamber in the house, the hostess, without much nicety, led them into mine, telling them as she ushered them in, that there was nobody in it but an English gentleman—that there were two good beds in it, and a closet within the room which held another—the accent in which she spoke of this third bed did not say much for it—however, she said, there were three beds, and but three people—and she durst say, the gentleman would do anything to accommodate matters.—I left not the lady a moment to make a conjecture about it—so instantly made a declaration I would do anything in my power.

As this did not amount to an absolute surrender of my bed-chamber, I still felt myself so much the proprietor, as to have a right to do the honours of it—so I desired the lady to sit down—pressed her into the warmest seat—called for more wood—desired the hostess to enlarge the plan of the supper, and to favour us with the very best wine.

The lady had scarce warmed herself five minutes at the fire, before she began to turn her head back, and give a look at the beds; and the oftener she cast her eyes that way, the more they returned perplexed—I felt for her—and for myself; for in a few minutes, what by her looks, and the case itself, I found myself as much embarrassed as it was possible the lady could be herself.

That the beds we were to lay in were in one and the same room, was enough simply by itself to have excited all this—but the position of them, for they stood parallel, and so very close to each other as only to allow space for a small wicker chair betwixt them, rendered the affair still more oppressive to us— they were fixed up moreover near the fire, and the projection of the chimney on one side, and a large beam which crossed the room on the other, formed a kind of recess for them that was no way favourable to the nicety of our sensations—if anything could have added to it, it was, that the two beds were both of 'em so very small, as to cut us off from every idea of the lady and the maid lying together; which in either of them, could it have been feasible, my lying beside them, though a thing not to be wished, yet there was nothing in it so terrible which the imagination might not have passed over them without torment.

As for the little room within, it offered little or no consolation to us; 'twas a damp cold closet, with a half-dismantled window-shutter, and with a window which had neither glass or oil-paper in it to keep out the tempest of the night. I did not endeavour to stifle my cough when the lady gave a peep into it; so it reduced the case in course to this alternative—that the lady should sacrifice her health to her feelings, and take up with the closet herself, and abandon the bed next to mine to her maid—or that the girl should take the closet, &c. &c.

The lady was a Piedmontese of about thirty, with a glow of health in her cheeks: the maid was a Lyonoise of twenty, and as brisk and lively a French girl as ever moved.—There were difficulties every way—and the obstacle of the stone in the road which brought us into the distress, great as it appeared whilst the peasants were removing it, was but a pebble to what lay in our ways now—I have only to add, that it did not lessen the weight which hung upon our spirits, that we were both too delicate to communicate what we felt to each other upon the occasion.

We sat down to supper; and had we not had more generous wine to it than a little inn in Savoy could have furnished, our tongues had been tied up, till necessity herself had set them at liberty—but the lady having a few bottles of Burgundy in her voiture sent down her fille de chambre for a couple of them; so that by the time supper was over, and we were left alone, we felt ourselves inspired with a strength of mind sufficient to talk, at least, without reserve upon our situation. We turned it every way, and debated and considered it in all kind of lights in the course of a two hours negotiation; at the end of which the articles were settled finally betwixt us, and stipulated for in form and manner of a treaty of peace—and I believe with as much religion and good faith on both sides, as in any treaty which as yet had the honour of being handed down to posterity.

They were as follows:

First. As the right of the bed-chamber is in Monsieur—and he thinking the bed next to the fire to be the warmest, he insists upon the concession on the lady's side of taking up with it.

Granted, on the part of Madame; with a proviso, That as the curtains of that bed are of a flimsy transparent cotton, and appear likewise too scanty to draw close, that the fille de chambre shall fasten up the opening, either by corking pins, or needle and thread, in such manner as shall be deemed a sufficient barrier on the side of Monsieur.

2dly. It is required on the part of Madame, that Monsieur shall lay the whole night through in his robe de chambre.

Rejected: inasmuch as Monsieur is not worth a robe de chambre; he having nothing in his portmanteau but six shirts and a black silk pair of breeches.

The mentioning the silk pair of breeches made an entire change of the article—for the breeches were accepted as an equivalent for the robe de chambre; and so it was stipulated and agreed upon that I should lie in my black silk breeches all night.

3dly. It was insisted upon, and stipulated for by the lady, that after Monsieur was got to bed, and the candle and fire extinguished, that Monsieur should not speak one single word the whole night.

Granted; provided Monsieur's saying his prayers might not be deemed an infraction of the treaty.

There was but one point forgot in this treaty, and that was the manner in which the lady and myself should be obliged to undress and get to bed—there was but one way of doing it, and that I leave to the reader to devise; protesting as I do it, that if it is not the most delicate in nature, 'tis the fault of his own imagination—against which this is not my first complaint.

Now when we were got to bed, whether it was the novelty of the situation, or what it was, I know not, but so it was, I could not shut my eyes; I tried this side and that, and turned and turned again, till a full hour after midnight, when nature and patience both wearing out—O my God! said I—

—You have broke the treaty, Monsieur, said the lady, who had no more slept than myself.—I begged a thousand pardons—but insisted it was no more than an ejaculation—she maintained 'twas an entire infraction of the treaty—I maintained it was provided for in the clause of the third article.

The lady would by no means give up her point, though she weakened her barrier by it; for in the warmth of the dispute, I could hear two or three corking pins fall out of the curtain to the ground.

Upon my word and honour, Madame, said I—stretching my arm out of bed by way of asseveration—

—(I was going to have added, that I would not have trespassed against the remotest idea of decorum for the world)—

—But the fille de chambre hearing there were words between us, and fearing that hostilities would ensue in course, had crept silently out of her closet, and it being totally dark, had stolen so close to our beds, that she had got herself into the narrow passage which separated them, and had advanced so far up as to be in a line betwixt her mistress and me—

So that when I stretched out my hand, I caught hold of the fille de chambre's—

HENRY MACKENZIE

The Man of Feeling

INTRODUCTION

My dog had made a point on a piece of fallow-ground, and led the curate and me two or three hundred yards over that and some stubble adjoining, in a breathless state of expectation, on a burning first of September.

It was a false point, and our labour was vain: yet, to do Rover justice (for he's an excellent dog, though I have lost his pedigree), the fault was none of his, the birds were gone: the curate showed me the spot where they had lain basking, at the root of an old hedge.

I stopped and cried Hem! The curate is fatter than I; he wiped the sweat from his brow.

There is no state where one is apter to pause and look round one, than after such a disappointment. It is even so in life. When we have been hurrying on, impelled by some warm wish or other, looking neither to the right hand nor to the left— we find of a sudden that all our gay hopes are flown; and the only slender consolation that some friend can give us, is to point where they were once to be found. And lo! if we are not of that combustible race, who will rather beat their heads in spite, than wipe their brows with the curate, we look round and say, with the nauseated listlessness of the king of Israel, "All is vanity and vexation of spirit."

I looked round with some such grave apophthegm in my mind when I discovered, for the first time, a venerable pile, to which the enclosure belonged. An air of melancholy hung about it. There was a languid stillness in the day, and a single crow, that perched on an old tree by the side of the gate, seemed to delight in the echo of its own croaking.

I leaned on my gun and looked; but I had not breath

enough to ask the curate a question. I observed carving on the
bark of some of the trees: 'twas indeed the only mark of human
art about the place, except that some branches appeared to
have been lopped, to give a view of the cascade, which was
formed by a little rill at some distance.

Just at that instant I saw pass between the trees, a young
lady with a book in her hand. I stood upon a stone to observe
her; but the curate sat him down on the grass, and leaning his
back where I stood, told me, "That was the daughter of a
neighbouring gentleman of the name of WALTON, whom he had
seen walking there more than once.

"Some time ago," he said, "one HARLEY lived there, a
whimsical sort of a man I am told, but I was not then in the
cure; though, if I had a turn for such things, I might know a
good deal of his history, for the greatest part of it is still in my
possession."

"His history!" said I. "Nay, you may call it what you
please," said the curate; "for indeed it is no more a history than
it is a sermon. The way I came by it was this: some time ago, a
grave, oddish kind of a man boarded at a farmer's in this
parish: the country people called him The Ghost; and he was
known by the slouch in his gait, and the length of his stride. I
was but little acquainted with him, for he never frequented any
of the clubs hereabouts. Yet for all he used to walk a-nights,
he was as gentle as a lamb at times; for I have seen him playing at teetotum[1] with the children, on the great stone at the
door of our churchyard.

"Soon after I was made curate, he left the parish, and
went nobody knows whither; and in his room was found a
bundle of papers, which was brought to me by his landlord. I
began to read them, but I soon grew weary of the task; for,
besides that the hand is intolerably bad, I could never find the
author in one strain for two chapters together; and I don't believe there's a single syllogism from beginning to end."

"I should be glad to see this medley," said I. "You shall
see it now," answered the curate, "for I always take it along
with me a-shooting." "How came it so torn?" " 'Tis excellent
wadding," said the curate.—This was a plea of expediency I

was not in a condition to answer; for I had actually in my pocket great part of an edition of one of the German Illustris- simi, for the very same purpose. We exchanged books; and by that means (for the curate was a strenuous logician) we prob- ably saved both.

When I returned to town, I had leisure to peruse the ac- quisition I had made: I found it a bundle of little episodes, put together without art, and of no importance on the whole, with something of nature, and little else in them. I was a good deal affected with some very trifling passages in it; and had the name of a Marmontel, or a Richardson, been on the title-page— 'tis odds that I should have wept: But

One is ashamed to be pleased with the works of one knows not whom.

CHAPTER XI*

*Of Bashfulness—A Character—His Opinion
on that Subject*

There is some rust about every man at the beginning;
though in some nations (among the French, for instance) the
ideas of the inhabitants, from climate, or what other cause you
will, are so vivacious, so eternally on the wing, that they must,
even in small societies, have a frequent collision; the rust therefore will wear off sooner: but in Britain, it often goes with a
man to his grave; nay, he dares not even pen a *hic jacet* to
speak out for him after his death.

"Let them rub it off by travel," said the baronet's brother,
who was a striking instance of excellent metal, shamefully
rusted. I had drawn my chair near his. Let me paint the honest
old man: 'tis but one passing sentence to preserve his image
in my mind.

He sat in his usual attitude, with his elbow rested on his
knee, and his fingers pressed to his cheek. His face was shaded
by his hand; yet it was a face that might once have been well
accounted handsome; its features were manly and striking, and
a certain dignity resided on his eye-brows, which were the
largest I remember to have seen. His person was tall and well-
made; but the indolence of his nature had now inclined it to
corpulency.

His remarks were few, and made only to his familiar
friends; but they were such as the world might have heard with

* The reader will remember that the Editor is accountable only
for scattered chapters and fragments of chapters; the curate must
answer for the rest. The number at the top, when the chapter was
entire, he has given as it originally stood, with the title which its author
had affixed to it.

veneration: and his heart, uncorrupted by its ways, was ever warm in the cause of virtue and his friends.

He is now forgotten and gone! The last time I was at Silton Hall, I saw his chair stand in its corner by the fire-side; there was an additional cushion on it, and it was occupied by my young lady's favourite lap-dog. I drew near unperceived, and pinched its ears in the bitterness of my soul; the creature howled, and ran to its mistress. She did not suspect the author of its misfortune, but she bewailed it in the most pathetic terms; and kissing its lips, laid it gently on her lap, and covered it with a cambric handkerchief. I sat in my old friend's seat; I heard the roar of mirth and gaiety around me: poor Ben Silton! I gave thee a tear then: accept of one cordial drop that falls to thy memory now.

"They should wear it off by travel."—Why, it is true, said I, that will go far; but then it will often happen, that in the velocity of a modern tour, and amidst the materials through which it is commonly made, the friction is so violent, that not only the rust, but the metal too, will be lost in the progress.

"Give me leave to correct the expression of your metaphor," said Mr. Silton: "that is not always rust which is produced by the inactivity of the body on which it preys; such, perhaps, is the case with me, though indeed I was never cleared from my youth; but (taking it in its first stage) it is rather an encrustation, which nature has given for purposes of the greatest wisdom."

"You are right," I returned; "and sometimes, like certain precious fossils, there may be hid under it gems of the purest brilliancy."

"Nay, farther," continued Mr. Silton, "there are two distinct sorts of what we call bashfulness; this, the awkwardness of a booby, which a few steps into the world will convert into the pertness of a coxcomb; that, a consciousness, which the most delicate feelings produce, and the most extensive knowledge cannot always remove."

From the incidents I have already related, I imagine it will be concluded that Harley was of the latter species of bashful animals; at least, if Mr. Silton's principle is just, it may be argued on this side: for the gradation of the first mentioned sort, it is certain, he never attained. Some part of his external appearance was modelled from the company of those gentlemen, whom the antiquity of a family, now possessed of bare £250 a year, entitled its representative to approach: these indeed were not many; great part of the property in his neighbourhood being in the hands of merchants, who had got rich by their lawful calling abroad, and the sons of stewards, who had got rich by their lawful calling at home: persons so perfectly versed in the ceremonial of thousands, tens of thousands, and hundreds of thousands (whose degrees of precedency are plainly demonstrable from the first page of the Complete Accomptant, or Young Man's Best Pocket Companion) that a bow at church from them to such a man as Harley—would have made the parson look back into his sermon for some precept of Christian humility.

CHAPTER XII

Of Worldly Interests

There are certain interests which the world supposes every man to have, and which therefore are properly enough termed worldly; but the world is apt to make an erroneous estimate: ignorant of the dispositions which constitute our happiness or misery, it brings to an undistinguished scale the means of the one, as connected with power, wealth, or grandeur, and of the other with their contraries. Philosophers and poets have often protested against this decision; but their arguments have been despised as declamatory, or ridiculed as romantic.

There are never wanting to a young man some grave and prudent friends to set him right in this particular, if he need it; to watch his ideas as they arise, and point them to those objects which a wise man should never forget.

Harley did not want for some monitors of this sort. He was frequently told of men whose fortunes enabled them to command all the luxuries of life, whose fortunes were of their own acquirement: his envy was excited by a description of their happiness, and his emulation by a recital of the means which had procured it.

Harley was apt to hear those lectures with indifference; nay, sometimes they got the better of his temper; and as the instances were not always amiable, provoked, on his part, some reflections, which I am persuaded his good-nature would else have avoided.

Indeed, I have observed one ingredient, somewhat necessary in a man's composition towards happiness, which people of feeling would do well to acquire; a certain respect for the follies of mankind: for there are so many fools whom the opinion of the world entitles to regard, whom accident has placed in heights of which they are unworthy, that he who cannot restrain his contempt, or indignation at the sight, will be too often quarrelling with the disposal of things, to relish that share which is allotted to himself. I do not mean, however, to insinuate this to have been the case with Harley; on the contrary, if we might rely on his own testimony, the conceptions he had of pomp and grandeur served to endear the state which Providence had assigned him.

He lost his father, the last surviving of his parents, as I have already related, when he was a boy. The good man, from a fear of offending, as well as from a regard to his son, had named him a variety of guardians; one consequence of which was, that they seldom met at all to consider the affairs of their ward; and when they did meet, their opinions were so opposite, that the only possible method of conciliation, was the mediatory power of a dinner and a bottle, which commonly interrupted, not ended, the dispute; and after that interruption ceased, left the consulting parties in a condition not very proper for adjusting it. His education therefore had been but indifferently attended to; and after being taken from a country school, at which he had been boarded, the young gentleman was suffered to be his own master in the subsequent branches of literature, with some assistance from the parson of the parish in languages and philosophy, and from the exciseman in arithmetic and bookkeeping. One of his guardians, indeed, who, in his youth, had been an inhabitant of the Temple, set him to read Coke upon Lyttelton; a book which is very properly put into the hands of beginners in that science, as its simplicity is accommodated to their understandings, and its size to their inclination. He profited but little by the perusal; but it was not without its use in the family: for his maiden aunt applied it commonly to the laudable purpose of pressing her rebellious linens to the folds she had allotted them.

There were particularly two ways of increasing his fortune, which might have occurred to people of less foresight than the counsellors we have mentioned. One of these was, the prospect of his succeeding to an old lady, a distant relation, who was known to be possessed of a very large sum in the stocks: but in this their hopes were disappointed; for the young man was so untoward in his disposition, that, notwithstanding the instructions he daily received, his visits rather tended to alienate than gain the good-will of his kinswoman. He sometimes looked grave when the old lady told the jokes of her youth; he often refused to eat when she pressed him, and was seldom or never provided with sugar-candy or liquorice when she was seized with a fit of coughing: nay, he had once the rudeness to fall asleep while she was describing the composition and virtues of her favourite cholic-water. In short, he accommodated himself so ill to her humour, that she died, and did not leave him a farthing.

The other method pointed out to him, was an endeavour to get a lease of some crown-lands, which lay contiguous to his little paternal estate. This, it was imagined, might be easily procured, as the crown did not draw so much rent as Harley could afford to give, with very considerable profit to himself; and the then lessee had rendered himself so obnoxious to the ministry, by the disposal of his vote at an election, that he could not expect a renewal. This, however, needed some interest with the great, which Harley or his father never possessed.

His neighbour, Mr. Walton, having heard of this affair, generously offered his assistance to accomplish it. He told him, that though he had long been a stranger to courtiers, yet he believed there were some of them who might pay regard to his recommendation; and that, if he thought it worth the while to take a London journey upon the business, he would furnish him with a letter of introduction to a baronet of his acquaintance, who had a great deal to say with the first lord of the treasury.

When his friends heard of this offer, they pressed him with the utmost earnestness to accept of it. They did not fail to enumerate the many advantages which a certain degree of spirit and assurance gives a man who would make a figure in the world: they repeated their instances of good fortune in others, ascribed them all to a happy forwardness of disposition; and made so copious a recital of the disadvantages which attend the opposite weakness, that a stranger, who had heard them, would have been led to imagine, that in the British code there was some disqualifying statute against any citizen who should be convicted of—modesty.

Harley, though he had no great relish for the attempt, yet could not resist the torrent of motives that assaulted him; and as he needed but little preparation for his journey, a day, not very distant, was fixed for his departure.

CHAPTER XIII

The Man of Feeling in Love

The day before that on which he set out, he went to take leave of Mr. Walton.—We would conceal nothing;—there was another person of the family to whom also the visit was intended, on whose account, perhaps, there were some tenderer feelings in the bosom of Harley, than his gratitude for the friendly notice of that gentleman (though he was seldom deficient in that virtue) could inspire. Mr. Walton had a daughter; and such a daughter! we will attempt some description of her by and by.

Harley's notions of the καλον, or beautiful, were not always to be defined, nor indeed such as the world would always assent to, though we could define them. A blush, a phrase of affability to an inferior, a tear at a moving tale, were to him, like the Cestus of Cytherea, unequalled in conferring beauty. For all these Miss Walton was remarkable; but as these, like the above-mentioned Cestus, are perhaps still more powerful when the wearer is possessed of some degree of beauty, commonly so called, it happened, that, from this cause, they had more than usual power in the person of that young lady.

She was now arrived at that period of life which takes, or is supposed to take, from the flippancy of girlhood those sprightlinesses with which some good-natured old maids oblige the world at three-score. She had been ushered into life (as that word is used in the dialect of St. James's) at seventeen, her father being then in parliament, and living in London: at seventeen, therefore, she had been a universal toast; her health, now she was four-and-twenty, was only drank by those who knew her face at least. Her complexion was mellowed into a paleness,

127

which certainly took from her beauty; but agreed, at least Harley used to say so, with the pensive softness of her mind. Her eyes were of that gentle hazel colour which is rather mild than piercing; and, except when they were lighted up by good-humour, which was frequently the case, were supposed by the fine gentlemen to want fire. Her air and manner were elegant in the highest degree, and were as sure of commanding respect as their mistress was far from demanding it. Her voice was inexpressibly soft; it was, according to that incomparable simile of Otway's,

>   "like the shepherd's pipe upon the mountains,
> When all his little flock's at feed before him."

The effect it had upon Harley, he himself used to paint ridiculously enough; and ascribed it to powers, which few believed, and nobody cared for.

Her conversation was always cheerful, but rarely witty; and without the smallest affectation of learning, had as much sentiment in it as would have puzzled a Turk, upon his principles of female materialism, to account for. Her beneficence was unbounded; indeed the natural tenderness of her heart might have been argued, by the frigidity of a casuist, as detracting from her virtue in this respect, for her humanity was a feeling, not a principle: but minds like Harley's are not very apt to make this distinction, and generally give our virtue credit for all that benevolence which is instinctive in our nature.

As her father had for some years retired to the country, Harley had frequent opportunities of seeing her. He looked on her for some time merely with that respect and admiration which her appearance seemed to demand, and the opinion of others conferred upon her: from this cause, perhaps, and from that extreme sensibility of which we have taken frequent notice, Harley was remarkably silent in her presence. He heard her sentiments with peculiar attention, sometimes with looks very expressive of approbation; but seldom declared his opinion on the subject, much less made compliments to the lady on the justness of her remarks.

From this very reason it was, that Miss Walton frequently

took more particular notice of him than of other visitors, who, by the laws of precedency, were better entitled to it: it was a mode of politeness she had peculiarly studied, to bring to the line of that equality, which is ever necessary for the ease of our guests, those whose sensibility had placed them below it.

Harley saw this; for though he was a child in the drama of the world, yet was it not altogether owing to a want of knowledge of his part; on the contrary, the most delicate consciousness of propriety often kindled that blush which marred the performance of it: this raised his esteem something above what the most sanguine descriptions of her goodness had been able to do; for certain it is, that notwithstanding the laboured definitions which very wise men have given us of the inherent beauty of virtue, we are always inclined to think her handsomest when she condescends to smile upon ourselves.

It would be trite to observe the easy gradation from esteem to love: in the bosom of Harley there scarce needed a transition; for there were certain seasons when his ideas were flushed to a degree much above their common complexion. In times not credulous of inspiration, we should account for this from some natural cause; but we do not mean to account for it at all; it were sufficient to describe its effects; but they were sometimes so ludicrous, as might derogate from the dignity of the sensations which produced them to describe. They were treated indeed as such by most of Harley's sober friends, who often laughed very heartily at the awkward blunders of the real Harley, when the different faculties, which should have prevented them, were entirely occupied by the ideal. In some of these paroxysms of fancy, Miss Walton did not fail to be introduced; and the picture which had been drawn amidst the surrounding objects of unnoticed levity was now singled out to be viewed through the medium of romantic imagination: it was improved of course, and esteem was a word inexpressive of the feelings which it excited.

CHAPTER XIV

He Sets Out on His Journey—The Beggar and His Dog

He had taken leave of his aunt on the eve of his intended departure; but the good lady's affection for her nephew interrupted her sleep, and early as it was next morning when Harley came downstairs to set out, he found her in the parlour with a tear on her cheek, and her caudle-cup in her hand. She knew enough of physic to prescribe against going abroad of a morning with an empty stomach. She gave her blessing with the draught; her instructions she had delivered the night before. They consisted mostly of negatives; for London, in her idea, was so replete with temptations that it needed the whole armour of her friendly cautions to repel their attacks.

Peter stood at the door. We have mentioned this faithful fellow formerly: Harley's father had taken him up an orphan, and saved him from being cast on the parish; and he had ever since remained in the service of him and of his son. Harley shook him by the hand as he passed, smiling, as if he had said, "I will not weep." He sprung hastily into the chaise that waited for him: Peter folded up the step. "My dear master," said he, shaking the solitary lock that hung on either side of his head, "I have been told as how London is a sad place." He was choked with the thought, and his benediction could not be heard:—but it shall be heard, honest Peter! where these tears will add to its energy.

In a few hours Harley reached the inn where he proposed breakfasting, but the fulness of his heart would not suffer him to eat a morsel. He walked out on the road, and gaining a little height, stood gazing on the quarter he had left. He looked for his wonted prospect, his fields, his woods, and his hills: they were lost in the distant clouds! He pencilled them on the clouds, and bade them farewell with a sigh!

He sat down on a large stone to take out a little pebble from his shoe, when he saw, at some distance, a beggar approaching him. He had on a loose sort of coat, mended with different-coloured rags, amongst which the blue and the russet were the predominant. He had a short knotty stick in his hand, and on the top of it was stuck a ram's horn; his knees (though he was no pilgrim) had worn the stuff of his breeches; he wore no shoes, and his stockings had entirely lost that part of them which should have covered his feet and ankles; in his face, however, was the plump appearance of good humour; he walked a good round pace, and a crook-legged dog trotted at his heels.

"Our delicacies," said Harley to himself, "are fantastic; they are not in nature! that beggar walks over the sharpest of these stones barefooted, whilst I have lost the most delightful dream in the world, from the smallest of them happening to get into my shoes."—The beggar had by this time come up, and, pulling off a piece of hat, asked charity of Harley; the dog began to beg too:—it was impossible to resist both; and, in truth, the want of shoes and stockings had made both unnecessary, for Harley had destined sixpence for him before. The beggar, on receiving it, poured forth blessings without number; and, with a sort of smile on his countenance, said to Harley, "that if he wanted to have his fortune told"—Harley turned his eye briskly on the beggar: it was an unpromising look for the subject of a prediction, and silenced the prophet immediately. "I would much rather learn," said Harley, "what it is in your power to tell me: your trade must be an entertaining one; sit down on this stone, and let me know something of your profession; I have often thought of turning fortune-teller for a week or two myself."

"Master," replied the beggar, "I like your frankness much; God knows I had the humour of plain-dealing in me from a child, but there is no doing with it in this world; we must live as we can, and lying is, as you call it, my profession, but I was in some sort forced to the trade, for I dealt once in telling truth.

"I was a labourer, sir, and gained as much as to make me live: I never laid by indeed: for I was reckoned a piece of a wag, and your wags, I take it, are seldom rich, Mr. Harley."

"So," said Harley, "you seem to know me."

"Ay, there are few folks in the country that I don't know something of: how should I tell fortunes else?"

"True; but to go on with your story: you were a labourer, you say, and a wag; your industry, I suppose, you left with your old trade, but your humour you preserve to be of use to you in your new."

"What signifies sadness, sir? a man grows lean on't: but I was brought to my idleness by degrees; first I could not work, and it went against my stomach to work ever after. I was seized with a jail fever at the time of the assizes being in the county where I lived; for I was always curious to get acquainted with the felons, because they are commonly fellows of much mirth and little thought, qualities I had ever an esteem for. In the height of this fever, Mr. Harley, the house where I lay took fire, and burnt to the ground; I was carried out in that condition, and lay all the rest of my illness in a barn. I got the better of my disease, however, but I was so weak that I spit blood whenever I attempted to work. I had no relation living that I knew of, and I never kept a friend above a week, when I was able to joke; I seldom remained above six months in a parish, so that I might have died before I had found a settlement in any: thus I was forced to beg my bread, and a sorry trade I found it, Mr. Harley. I told all my misfortunes truly, but they were seldom believed; and the few who gave me a halfpenny as they passed, did it with a shake of the head, and an injunction not to trouble them with a long story. In short, I found that people don't care to give alms without some security for their money; a wooden leg or a withered arm is a sort of draught upon heaven for those who choose to have their money placed to account there; so I changed my plan, and, instead of telling my own misfortunes, began to prophesy happiness to others. This I found by much the better way: folks will always listen when the tale is their own; and of many who say they do not believe in fortune-telling, I have known few on whom it had not a very sensible effect. I pick up the names of their acquaintance; amours and little squabbles are easily gleaned among servants and neighbours; and indeed people themselves are the best intelligencers in the world for our purpose: they dare not puzzle us for their own sakes, for everyone is anxious to hear what they wish to believe, and they who repeat it, to laugh at it when they have done, are generally more serious than their hearers are apt to imagine. With a tolerable good memory, and some share of cunning, with the help of walking a-nights over heaths and church-yards, with this, and showing the tricks of that there dog, whom I stole from the serjeant of a marching regiment (and by the way, he can steal too upon occasion), I make shift to pick up a livelihood. My trade, indeed, is none of the honestest; yet people are not much cheated neither who give a few halfpence for a prospect of happiness, which I have heard some persons say is all a man can arrive at in this world.——But I must bid you good day, sir, for I have three miles to walk before noon, to inform some boarding-school young ladies whether their husbands are to be peers of the realm, or captains in the army: a question which I promised to answer them by that time."

Harley had drawn a shilling from his pocket; but Virtue bade him consider on whom he was going to bestow it.——Virtue held back his arm:——but a milder form, a younger sister of Virtue's, not so severe as Virtue, nor so serious as Pity, smiled upon him; his fingers lost their compression;——nor did Virtue offer to catch the money as it fell. It had no sooner reached the ground than the watchful cur (a trick he had been taught) snapped it up; and, contrary to the most approved method of stewardship, delivered it immediately into the hands of his master.

•   •   •   •   •   •

CHAPTER XIX

*He Makes a Second Expedition to the Baronet's—The
Laudable Ambition of a Young Man to be Thought
Something by the World*

We have related, in a former chapter, the little success of
his first visit to the great man, for whom he had the introductory
letter from Mr. Walton. To people of equal sensibility, the influence of those trifles we mentioned on his deportment will
not appear surprising; but to his friends in the country they
could not be stated, nor would they have allowed them any
place in the account. In some of their letters, therefore, which
he received soon after, they expressed their surprise at his not
having been more urgent in his application, and again recommended the blushless assiduity of successful merit.

He resolved to make another attempt at the baronet's; fortified with higher notions of his own dignity, and with less apprehension of repulse. In his way to Grosvenor Square he began to
ruminate on the folly of mankind, who affixed those ideas of
superiority to riches, which reduced the minds of men, by
nature equal with the more fortunate, to that sort of servility
which he felt in his own. By the time he had reached the Square,
and was walking along the pavement which led to the baronet's,
he had brought his reasoning on the subject to such a point, that
the conclusion, by every rule of logic, should have led him to a
thorough indifference in his approaches to a fellow-mortal,
whether that fellow-mortal was possessed of six or six thousand
pounds a year. It is probable, however, that the premises had
been improperly formed: for it is certain, that when he ap-

proached the great man's door he felt his heart agitated by an unusual pulsation.

He had almost reached it, when he observed a young gentleman coming out, dressed in a white frock and a red laced waistcoat, with a small switch in his hand, which he seemed to manage with a particular good grace. As he passed him on the steps, the stranger very politely made him a bow, which Harley returned, though he could not remember ever having seen him before. He asked Harley, in the same civil manner, if he was going to wait on his friend the baronet. "For I was just calling," said he, "and am sorry to find that he is gone for some days into the country."

Harley thanked him for his information, and was turning from the door, when the other observed that it would be proper to leave his name, and very obligingly knocked for that purpose.

"Here is a gentleman, Tom, who meant to have waited on your master."

"Your name, if you please, sir?"

"Harley."

"You'll remember, Tom, Harley."

The door was shut.—"Since we are here," said he, "we shall not lose our walk if we add a little to it by a turn or two in Hyde Park." He accompanied this proposal with a second bow, and Harley accepted of it by another in return.

The conversation, as they walked, was brilliant on the side of his companion. The playhouse, the opera, with every occurrence in high life, he seemed perfectly master of; and talked of some reigning beauties of quality in a manner the most feeling in the world. Harley admired the happiness of his vivacity; and, opposite as it was to the reserve of his own nature, began to be much pleased with its effects.

Though I am not of opinion with some wise men, that the existence of objects depends on idea, yet I am convinced that their appearance is not a little influenced by it. The optics of some minds are so unhappily constructed as to throw a certain shade on every picture that is presented to them, while those of others (of which number was Harley), like the mirrors of the ladies, have a wonderful effect in bettering their complexions. Through such a medium perhaps he was looking on his present companion.

When they had finished their walk, and were returning by the corner of the Park, they observed a board hung out of a window signifying, "An excellent ORDINARY on Saturdays and Sundays." It happened to be Saturday, and the table was covered.

"What if we should go in and dine here, if you happen not to be engaged, sir?" said the young gentleman. "It is not impossible but we shall meet with some original or other; it is a sort of humour I like hugely." Harley made no objection, and the stranger showed him the way into the parlour.

He was placed, by the courtesy of his introductor, in an arm-chair that stood at one side of the fire. Over against him was seated a man of a grave considering aspect, with that look of sober prudence which indicates what is commonly called a warm man. He wore a pretty large wig, which had once been white, but was now of a brownish yellow; his coat was one of those modest-coloured drabs which mock the injuries of dust and dirt; two jack-boots concealed, in part, the well-mended knees of an old pair of buckskin breeches; while the spotted handkerchief round his neck preserved at once its owner from catching cold, and his neckcloth from being dirtied. Next him sat another man, with a tankard in his hand and a quid of tobacco in his cheek, whose eye was rather more vivacious, and whose dress was something smarter.

The first-mentioned gentleman took notice that the room had been so lately washed, as not to have had time to dry; and remarked that wet lodging was unwholesome for man or beast. He looked round at the same time for a poker to stir the fire with, which, he at last observed to the company, the people of the house had removed, in order to save their coals. This difficulty, however, he overcame by the help of Harley's stick, saying, "that as they should, no doubt, pay for their fire in some shape or other, he saw no reason why they should not have the use of it while they sat."

The door was now opened for the admission of dinner. "I don't know how it is with you, gentlemen," said Harley's new acquaintance, "but I am afraid I shall not be able to get down a morsel at this horrid mechanical hour of dining." He sat down, however, and did not show any want of appetite by his eating. He took upon him the carving of the meat, and criticised on the goodness of the pudding.

When the table-cloth was removed, he proposed calling for some punch, which was readily agreed to; he seemed at first inclined to make it himself, but afterwards changed his mind, and left that province to the waiter, telling him to have it pure West Indian, or he could not taste a drop of it.

When the punch was brought he undertook to fill the glasses and call the toasts.—"The king."—The toast naturally produced politics. It is the privilege of Englishmen to drink the king's health, and to talk of his conduct. The man who sat opposite to Harley (and who by this time, partly from himself, and partly from his acquaintance on his left hand, was discovered to be a grazier) observed, "That it was a shame for so many pensioners to be allowed to take the bread out of the mouth of the poor."

"Ay, and provisions," said his friend, "were never so dear in the memory of man; I wish the king and his counsellors would look to that."

"As for the matter of provisions, neighbour Wrightson," he replied, "I am sure the prices of cattle——"

A dispute would have probably ensued, but it was prevented by the spruce toastmaster, who gave a sentiment, and turning to the two politicians, "Pray, gentlemen," said he, "let us have done with these musty politics: I would always leave them to the beer-suckers in Butcher Row.[2] Come, let us have something of the fine arts. That was a damn'd hard match between the Nailor and Tim Bucket. The knowing ones were cursedly taken in there! I lost a cool hundred myself, faith."

At mention of the cool hundred, the grazier threw his eyes

aslant, with a mingled look of doubt and surprise; while the man at his elbow looked arch, and gave a short emphatical sort of cough.

Both seemed to be silenced, however, by this intelligence; and while the remainder of the punch lasted the conversation was wholly engrossed by the gentleman with the fine waistcoat, who told a great many "immense comical stories" and "confounded smart things," as he termed them, acted and spoken by lords, ladies, and young bucks of quality, of his acquaintance. At last, the grazier, pulling out a watch, of a very unusual size, and telling the hour, said that he had an appointment. "Is it so late?" said the young gentleman; "then I am afraid I have missed an appointment already; but the truth is, I am cursedly given to missing of appointments."

When the grazier and he were gone, Harley turned to the remaining personage, and asked him if he knew that young gentleman. "A gentleman!" said he; "ay, he is one of your gentlemen at the top of an affidavit. I knew him, some years ago, in the quality of a footman; and I believe he had some times the honour to be a pimp. At last, some of the great folks, to whom he had been serviceable in both capacities, had him made a gauger; in which station he remains, and has the assurance to pretend an acquaintance with men of quality. The impudent dog! with a few shillings in his pocket, he will talk you three times as much as my friend Mundy there, who is worth nine thousand if he's worth a farthing. But I know the rascal, and despise him, as he deserves."

Harley began to despise him too, and to conceive some indignation at having sat with patience to hear such a fellow speak nonsense. But he corrected himself, by reflecting, that he was perhaps as well entertained, and instructed too, by this same modest gauger, as he should have been by such a man as he had thought proper to personate. And surely the fault may more properly be imputed to that rank where the futility is real, than where it is feigned: to that rank whose opportunities for nobler accomplishments have only served to rear a fabric of folly, which the untutored hand of affectation, even among the meanest of mankind, can imitate with success.

CHAPTER XX

He Visits Bedlam—the Distresses of a Daughter

Of those things called Sights in London, which every stranger is supposed desirous to see, Bedlam is one. To that place, therefore, an acquaintance of Harley's, after having accompanied him to several other shows, proposed a visit. Harley objected to it, "because," said he, "I think it an inhuman practice to expose the greatest misery with which our nature is afflicted to every idle visitant who can afford a trifling perquisite to the keeper; especially as it is a distress which the humane must see, with the painful reflection, that it is not in their power to alleviate it." He was overpowered, however, by the solicitations of his friend and the other persons of the party (amongst whom were several ladies); and they went in a body to Moorfields.

Their conductor led them first to the dismal mansions of those who are in the most horrid state of incurable madness. The clanking of chains, the wildness of their cries, and the imprecations which some of them uttered, formed a scene inexpressibly shocking. Harley and his companions, especially the female part of them, begged their guide to return; he seemed surprised at their uneasiness, and was with difficulty prevailed on to leave that part of the house without showing them some others: who, as he expressed it in the phrase of those that keep wild beasts for show, were much better worth seeing than any they had passed, being ten times more fierce and unmanageable.

He led them next to that quarter where those reside who, as they are not dangerous to themselves or others, enjoy a certain degree of freedom, according to the state of their distemper.

Harley had fallen behind his companions, looking at a man who was making pendulums with bits of thread and little balls of clay. He had delineated a segment of a circle on the wall with chalk, and marked their different vibrations by intersecting it with cross lines. A decent-looking man came up, and smiling at the maniac, turned to Harley, and told him that gentleman had once been a very celebrated mathematician. "He fell a sacrifice," said he, "to the theory of comets; for having, with infinite labour, formed a table on the conjectures of Sir Isaac Newton, he was disappointed in the return of one of those luminaries, and was very soon after obliged to be placed here by his friends. If you please to follow me, sir," continued the stranger, "I believe I shall be able to give a more satisfactory account of the unfortunate people you see here than the man who attends your companions." Harley bowed, and accepted his offer.

The next person they came up to had scrawled a variety of figures on a piece of slate. Harley had the curiosity to take a nearer view of them. They consisted of different columns, on the top of which were marked South-sea annuities, India-stock, and Three per cent annuities consol. "This," said Harley's instructor, "was a gentleman well known in Change Alley. He was once worth fifty thousand pounds, and had actually agreed for the purchase of an estate in the West, in order to realise his money; but he quarrelled with the proprietor about the repairs of the garden wall, and so returned to town to follow his old trade of stock-jobbing a little longer; when an unlucky fluctuation of stock, in which he was engaged to an immense extent, reduced him at once to poverty and to madness. Poor wretch! he told me t'other day that against the next payment of differences he should be some hundreds above a plum."—

"It is a spondee, and I will maintain it," interrupted a voice on his left hand. This assertion was followed by a very rapid recital of some verses from Homer. "That figure," said the gentleman, "whose clothes are so bedaubed with snuff, was a schoolmaster of some reputation: he came hither to be resolved of some doubts he entertained concerning the genuine pronunciation of the Greek vowels. In his highest fits, he makes frequent mention of one Mr. Bentley.[3]

"But delusive ideas, sir, are the motives of the greatest part of mankind, and a heated imagination the power by which their actions are incited: the world, in the eye of a philosopher, may be said to be a large madhouse."—"It is true," answered Harley, "the passions of men are temporary madnesses; and sometimes very fatal in their effects,

"From Macedonia's madman to the Swede."

"It was, indeed," said the stranger, "a very mad thing in Charles to think of adding so vast a country as Russia to his dominions: that would have been fatal indeed; the balance of the North would then have been lost; but the Sultan and I would never have allowed it."——"Sir!" said Harley, with no small surprise on his countenance.—"Why, yes," answered the other, "the Sultan and I; do you know me? I am the Chan of Tartary."

Harley was a good deal struck by this discovery; he had prudence enough, however, to conceal his amazement, and bowing as low to the monarch as his dignity required, left him immediately, and joined his companions.

He found them in a quarter of the house set apart for the insane of the other sex, several of whom had gathered about the female visitors, and were examining, with rather more accuracy than might have been expected, the particulars of their dress.

Separate from the rest stood one whose appearance had something of superior dignity. Her face, though pale and wasted, was less squalid than those of the others, and showed a dejection of that decent kind, which moves our pity unmixed with horror: upon her, therefore, the eyes of all were immediately turned. The keeper who accompanied them observed it: "This," said he, "is a young lady who was born to ride in her coach and six. She was beloved, if the story I have heard is true, by a young gentleman, her equal in birth, though by no means her match in fortune: but love, they say, is blind, and so she fancied him as much as he did her. Her father, it seems, would not hear of their marriage, and threatened to turn her out of doors, if ever she saw him again. Upon this the young gentleman took a voyage to the West Indies, in hopes of bettering his fortune, and obtaining his mistress; but he was scarce landed, when he was seized with one of the fevers which are common in those islands, and died in a few days, lamented by everyone that knew him. This news soon reached his mistress, who was at the same time pressed by her father to marry a rich miserly fellow, who was old enough to be her grandfather. The death of her lover had no effect on her inhuman parent: he was only the more earnest for her marriage with the man he had provided for her; and what between her despair at the death of the one, and her aversion to the other, the poor young lady was reduced to the condition you see her in. But God would not prosper such cruelty; her father's affairs soon after went to wreck, and he died almost a beggar."

Though this story was told in very plain language, it had particularly attracted Harley's notice; he had given it the tribute of some tears. The unfortunate young lady had till now seemed entranced in thought, with her eyes fixed on a little garnet ring she wore on her finger; she turned them now upon Harley. "My Billy is no more!" said she; "do you weep for my Billy? Blessings on your tears! I would weep too, but my brain is dry; and it burns, it burns, it burns!"—She drew nearer to Harley.—"Be comforted, young lady," said he, "your Billy is in heaven."—"Is he, indeed? and shall we meet again? and shall that frightful man (pointing to the keeper) not be there?—Alas! I am grown naughty of late; I have almost forgotten to think of heaven: yet I pray sometimes; when I can, I pray; and sometimes I sing; when I am saddest, I sing:—You shall hear me, hush!

"Light be the earth on Billy's breast,
And green the sod that wraps his grave!"

There was a plaintive wildness in the air not to be withstood; and, except the keeper's, there was not an unmoistened eye around her.

"Do you weep again?" said she. "I would not have you weep: you are like my Billy; you are, believe me; just so he looked when he gave me this ring; poor Billy! 'twas the last time ever we met!—

" 'Twas when the seas were roaring—I love you for re-sembling my Billy; but I shall never love any man like him." —She stretched out her hand to Harley; he pressed it between both of his, and bathed it with his tears.—"Nay, that is Billy's ring," said she, "you cannot have it, indeed; but here is an-other, look here, which I plaited to-day of some gold-thread from this bit of stuff; will you keep it for my sake? I am a strange girl;—but my heart is harmless: my poor heart; it will burst some day; feel how it beats!" She pressed his hand to her bosom, then holding her head in the attitude of listening —"Hark! one, two, three! be quiet, thou little trembler; my Billy is cold!—but I had forgotten the ring."—She put it on his finger.—"Farewell! I must leave you now."—She would have withdrawn her hand; Harley held it to his lips.—"I dare not stay longer; my head throbs sadly: farewell!"——She walked with a hurried step to a little apartment at some distance. Harley stood fixed in astonishment and pity; his friend gave money to the keeper.—Harley looked on his ring. —He put a couple of guineas into the man's hand: "Be kind to that unfortunate"—He burst into tears, and left them.

CHAPTER XXI

The Misanthropist

The friend who had conducted him to Moorfields called upon him again the next evening. After some talk on the adventures of the preceding day: "I carried you yesterday," said he to Harley, "to visit the mad; let me introduce you to-night, at supper, to one of the wise: but you must not look for anything of the Socratic pleasantry about him; on the contrary, I warn you to expect the spirit of a Diogenes. That you may be a little prepared for his extraordinary manner, I will let you into some particulars of his history.

"He is the elder of the two sons of a gentleman of considerable estate in the country. Their father died when they were young: both were remarkable at school for quickness of parts and extent of genius; this had been bred to no profession, because his father's fortune, which descended to him, was thought sufficient to set him above it; the other was put apprentice to an eminent attorney. In this the expectations of his friends were more consulted than his own inclination; for both his brother and he had feelings of that warm kind that could ill brook a study so dry as the law, especially in that department of it which was allotted to him. But the difference of their tempers made the characteristical distinction between them. The younger, from the gentleness of his nature, bore with patience a situation entirely discordant to his genius and disposition. At times, indeed, his pride would suggest of how little importance those talents were which the partiality of his friends had often extolled: they were now encumbrances in a walk of life where the dull and the ignorant passed him at every turn; his fancy and his feeling were invincible obstacles to eminence in a situation where his fancy had no room for exertion, and his feeling experienced perpetual disgust. But these murmurings he never suffered to be heard; and that he might not offend the prudence of those who had been concerned in the choice of his profession, he continued to labour in it several years, till, by the death of a relation, he succeeded to an estate of a little better than £100 a year, with which, and the small patrimony left him, he retired into the country, and made a love-match with a young lady of a similar temper to his own, with whom the sagacious world pitied him for finding happiness.

"But his elder brother, whom you are to see at supper, if you will do us the favour of your company, was naturally impetuous, decisive, and overbearing. He entered into life with those ardent expectations by which young men are commonly deluded: in his friendships, warm to excess; and equally violent in his dislikes. He was on the brink of marriage with a young lady, when one of those friends, for whose honour he would have pawned his life, made an elopement with that very goddess, and left him besides deeply engaged for sums which that good friend's extravagance had squandered.

"The dreams he had formerly enjoyed were now changed for ideas of a very different nature. He abjured all confidence in anything of human form; sold his lands, which still produced him a very large reversion, came to town, and immured himself with a woman who had been his nurse, in little better than a garret; and has ever since applied his talents to the vilifying of his species. In one thing I must take the liberty to instruct you; however different your sentiments may be (and different they must be), you will suffer him to go on without contradiction; otherwise, he will be silent immediately, and we shall not get a word from him all the night after." Harley promised to remember this injunction, and accepted the invitation of his friend.

When they arrived at the house, they were informed that the gentleman was come, and had been shown into the parlour. They found him sitting with a daughter of his friend's, about three years old, on his knee, whom he was teaching the alphabet from a horn book: at a little distance stood a sister of hers, some years older. "Get you away, miss," said he to this last; "you are a pert gossip, and I will have nothing to do with you."—"Nay," answered she, "Nancy is your favourite; you are quite in love with Nancy."—"Take away that girl," said he to her father, whom he now observed to have entered the room; "she has woman about her already." The children were accordingly dismissed.

Betwixt that and supper-time he did not utter a syllable. When supper came, he quarrelled with every dish at table, but eat of them all; only exempting from his censures a salad, "which you have not spoiled," said he, "because you have not attempted to cook it."

When the wine was set upon the table, he took from his pocket a particular smoking apparatus, and filled his pipe, without taking any more notice of Harley, or his friend, than if no such persons had been in the room.

Harley could not help stealing a look of surprise at him; but his friend, who knew his humour, returned it by annihilating his presence in the like manner, and, leaving him to his own meditations, addressed himself entirely to Harley.

In their discourse some mention happened to be made of an amiable character, and the words *honour* and *politeness* were applied to it. Upon this, the gentleman, laying down his pipe, and changing the tone of his countenance, from an ironical grin to something more intently contemptuous: "Honour," said he: "Honour and Politeness! this is the coin of the world, and passes current with the fools of it. You have substituted the shadow Honour, instead of the substance Virtue; and have banished the reality of friendship for the fictitious semblance, which you have termed Politeness: politeness, which consists in a certain ceremonious jargon, more ridiculous to the ear of reason than the voice of a puppet. You have invented sounds, which you worship, though they tyrannize over your peace; and are surrounded with empty forms, which take from the honest emotions of joy, and add to the poignancy of misfortune." "Sir!" said Harley—His friend winked to him, to remind him of the caution he had received. He was silenced by the thought. The philosopher turned his eye upon him: he examined him from top to toe, with a sort of triumphant contempt. Harley's coat happened to be a new one; the other's was as shabby as could possibly be supposed to be on the back of a gentleman: there was much significance in his look with regard to this coat; it spoke of the sleekness of folly and the threadbareness of wisdom.

"Truth," continued he, "the most amiable, as well as the most natural of virtues, you are at pains to eradicate. Your very nurseries are seminaries of falsehood; and what is called Fashion in manhood completes the system of avowed insincerity. Mankind, in the gross, is a gaping monster, that loves to be deceived, and has seldom been disappointed: nor is their vanity less fallacious to your philosophers, who adopt modes of truth to follow them through the paths of error, and defend paradoxes merely to be singular in defending them. These are they whom ye term Ingenious; 'tis a phrase of commendation I detest: it implies an attempt to impose on my judgment, by flattering my imagination: yet these are they whose works are read by the old with delight, which the young are taught to look upon as the codes of knowledge and philosophy.

"Indeed, the education of your youth is every way preposterous; you waste at school years in improving talents, without having ever spent an hour in discovering them; one promiscuous line of instruction is followed, without regard to genius, capacity, or probable situation in the commonwealth. From this bear-garden of the pedagogue, a raw, unprincipled boy is turned loose upon the world to travel; without any ideas but those of improving his dress at Paris, or starting into taste by gazing on some paintings at Rome. Ask him of the manners of the people, and he will tell you that the skirt is worn much shorter in France, and that everybody eats macaroni in Italy. When he returns home, he buys a seat in parliament, and studies the constitution at Arthur's.[4]

"Nor are your females trained to any more useful purpose: they are taught, by the very rewards which their nurses propose for good behaviour, by the first thing like a jest which they hear from every male visitor of the family, that a young woman is a creature to be married; and when they are grown somewhat older, are instructed that it is the purpose of marriage to have the enjoyment of pin-money, and the expectation of a jointure."

* "These indeed are the effects of luxury, which is perhaps inseparable from a certain degree of power and grandeur in a nation. But it is not simply of the progress of luxury that we have to complain: did its votaries keep in their own sphere of thoughtless dissipation, we might despise them without emotion; but the frivolous pursuits of pleasure are mingled with the most important concerns of the state; and public enterprise shall sleep till he who should guide its operation has decided his bets at Newmarket, or fulfilled his engagement with a favourite mistress in the country. We want some man of acknowledged eminence to point our counsels with that firmness which the counsels of a great people require. We have hundreds of ministers, who press forward into office without having ever learned that art which is necessary for every business, the art of thinking; and mistake the petulance, which could give inspiration to smart sarcasms on an obnoxious measure in a popular assembly, for the ability which is to balance the interest of kingdoms, and investigate the latent sources of national superiority. With the administration of such men the people can never be satisfied; for besides that their confidence is gained only by the view of superior talents, there needs that depth of knowledge, which is not only acquainted with the just extent of power, but can also trace its connection with the

---

* Though the Curate could not remember having shown this chapter to anybody, I strongly suspect that these political observations are the work of a later pen than the rest of this performance. There seems to have been, by some accident, a gap in the manuscript, from the words, "Expectation of a jointure," to these, "In short, man is an animal," where the present blank ends; and some other person (for the hand is different, and the ink whiter) has filled part of it with sentiments of his own. Whoever he was, he seems to have caught some portion of the spirit of the man he personates.

expedient, to preserve its possessors from the contempt which attends irresolution, or the resentment which follows temerity."

   •   •   •   •   •   •

[Here a considerable part is wanting.]

* * "In short, man is an animal equally selfish and vain. Vanity, indeed, is but a modification of selfishness. From the latter, there are some who pretend to be free: they are generally such as declaim against the lust of wealth and power, because they have never been able to attain any high degree in either: they boast of generosity and feeling. They tell us (perhaps they tell us in rhyme) that the sensations of an honest heart, of a mind universally benevolent, make up the quiet bliss which they enjoy; but they will not, by this, be exempted from the charge of selfishness. Whence the luxurious happiness they describe in their little family-circles? Whence the pleasure which they feel, when they trim their evening fires, and listen to the howl of winter's wind? Whence, but from the secret reflection of what houseless wretches feel from it? Or do you administer comfort in affliction—the motive is at hand; I have had it preached to me in nineteen out of twenty of your consolatory discourses—the comparative littleness of our own misfortunes.

"With vanity your best virtues are grossly tainted: your benevolence, which ye deduce immediately from the natural impulse of the heart, squints to it for its reward. There are some, indeed, who tell us of the satisfaction which flows from a secret consciousness of good actions: this secret satisfaction is truly excellent—when we have some friend to whom we may discover its excellence."

He now paused a moment to re-light his pipe, when a clock, that stood at his back, struck eleven; he started up at the sound, took his hat and his cane, and nodding good night with his head, walked out of the room. The gentleman of the house called a servant to bring the stranger's surtout. "What sort of a night is it, fellow?" said he.—"It rains, sir," answered the servant, "with an easterly wind."—"Easterly for ever!"— He made no other reply; but shrugging up his shoulders till they almost touched his ears, wrapped himself tight in his great coat, and disappeared.

"This is a strange creature," said his friend to Harley. "I cannot say," answered he, "that his remarks are of the pleasant kind: it is curious to observe how the nature of truth may be changed by the garb it wears; softened to the admonition of friendship, or soured into the severity of reproof: yet this severity may be useful to some tempers; it somewhat resembles a file; disagreeable in its operation, but hard metals may be the brighter for it."

    •   •   •   •   •   •

CHAPTER XXV

His Skill in Physiognomy

The company at the baronet's removed to the play-house accordingly, and Harley took his usual route into the Park. He observed, as he entered, a fresh-looking elderly gentleman in conversation with a beggar, who, leaning on his crutch, was recounting the hardships he had undergone, and explaining the wretchedness of his present condition. This was a very interesting dialogue to Harley; he was rude enough therefore to slacken his pace as he approached, and at last to make a full stop at the gentleman's back, who was just then expressing his compassion for the beggar, and regretting that he had not a farthing of change about him. At saying this, he looked piteously on the fellow: there was something in his physiognomy which caught Harley's notice: indeed, physiognomy was one of Harley's foibles, for which he had been often rebuked by his aunt in the country; who used to tell him that when he was come to her years and experience, he would know that all's not gold that glisters: and it must be owned that his aunt was a very sensible, harsh-looking maiden lady of threescore and upwards. But he was too apt to forget this caution; and now, it seems, it had not occurred to him. Stepping up, therefore, to the gentleman, who was lamenting the want of silver, "Your intentions sir," said he, "are so good, that I cannot help lending you my assistance to carry them into execution," and gave the beggar a shilling. The other returned a suitable compliment, and extolled the benevolence of Harley. They kept walking together, and benevolence grew the topic of discourse.

The stranger was fluent on the subject. "There is no use of money," said he, "equal to that of beneficence:—with the profuse, it is lost; and even with those who lay it out according to the prudence of the world, the objects acquired by it pall on the sense, and have scarce become our own till they lose their value with the power of pleasing; but here the enjoyment grows on reflection, and our money is most truly ours when it ceases being in our possession."

"Yet I agree in some measure," answered Harley, "with those who think that charity to our common beggars is often misplaced; there are objects less obtrusive whose title is a better one."

"We cannot easily distinguish," said the stranger; "and even of the worthless, are there not many whose imprudence, or whose vice, may have been one dreadful consequence of misfortune?"

Harley looked again in his face, and blessed himself for his skill in physiognomy.

By this time they had reached the end of the walk, the old gentleman leaning on the rails to take breath, and in the meantime they were joined by a younger man, whose figure was much above the appearance of his dress, which was poor and shabby. Harley's former companion addressed him as an acquaintance, and they turned on the walk together.

The elder of the strangers complained of the closeness of the evening, and asked the other if he would go with him into a house hard by, and take one draught of excellent cider. "The man who keeps this house," said he to Harley, "was once a servant of mine. I could not think of turning loose upon the world a faithful old fellow, for no other reason but that his age had incapacitated him; so I gave him an annuity of ten pounds, with the help of which he has set up this little place here, and his daughter goes and sells milk in the city, while her father manages his tap-room, as he calls it, at home. I can't well ask a gentleman of your appearance to accompany me to so paltry a place." "Sir," replied Harley, interrupting him, "I would much rather enter it than the most celebrated tavern in town. To give to the necessitous may sometimes be a weakness in the man; to encourage industry is a duty in the citizen." They entered the house accordingly.

On a table at the corner of the room lay a pack of cards, loosely thrown together. The old gentleman reproved the man of the house for encouraging so idle an amusement. Harley attempted to defend him from the necessity of accommodating himself to the humour of his guests, and taking up the cards, began to shuffle them backwards and forwards in his hand. "Nay, I don't think cards so unpardonable an amusement as some do," replied the other; "and now and then, about this time of the evening, when my eyes begin to fail me for my book, I divert myself with a game at piquet, without finding my morals a bit relaxed by it. Do you play piquet, sir?" (to Harley.) Harley answered in the affirmative; upon which the other proposed playing a pool at a shilling the game, doubling the stakes; adding, that he never played higher with anybody.

Harley's good nature could not refuse the benevolent old man; and the younger stranger, though he at first pleaded prior engagements, yet being earnestly solicited by his friend, at last yielded to solicitation.

When they began to play, the old gentleman, somewhat to the surprise of Harley, produced ten shillings to serve for markers of his score. "He had no change for the beggar," said Harley to himself; "but I can easily account for it; it is curious to observe the affection that inanimate things will create in us by a long acquaintance: if I may judge from my own feelings, the old man would not part with one of these counters for ten times its intrinsic value; it even got the better of his benevolence! I, myself, have a pair of old brass sleeve buttons"—Here he was interrupted by being told that the old gentleman had beat the younger, and that it was his turn to take up the conqueror. "Your game has been short," said Harley. "I re-piqued him," answered the old man, with joy sparkling in his countenance. Harley wished to be re-piqued too, but he was disappointed; for he had the same good fortune against his opponent. Indeed, never did fortune, mutable as she is, delight in mutability so much as at that moment: the victory was so quick, and so constantly alternate, that the stake, in a short time, amounted to no less a sum than

£12, Harley's proportion of which was within half-a-guinea of the money he had in his pocket. He had before proposed a division, but the old gentleman opposed it with such a pleasant warmth in his manner, that it was always over-ruled. Now, however, he told them that he had an appointment with some gentlemen, and it was within a few minutes of his hour. The young stranger had gained one game, and was engaged in the second with the other; they agreed, therefore, that the stake should be divided, if the old gentleman won that: which was more than probable, as his score was 90 to 35, and he was elder hand; but a momentous re-pique decided it in favour of his adversary, who seemed to enjoy his victory mingled with regret, for having won too much, while his friend, with great ebullience of passion, many praises of his own good play, and many maledictions on the power of chance, took up the cards, and threw them into the fire.

CHAPTER XXVI

The Man of Feeling in a Brothel

The company he was engaged to meet were assembled in Fleet Street. He had walked some time along the Strand, amidst a crowd of those wretches who wait the uncertain wages of prostitution, with ideas of pity suitable to the scene around him and the feelings he possessed, and had got as far as Somerset House, when one of them laid hold of his arm, and, with a voice tremulous and faint, asked him for a pint of wine, in a manner more supplicatory than is usual with those whom the infamy of their profession has deprived of shame. He turned round at the demand, and looked steadfastly on the person who made it.

She was above the common size, and elegantly formed; her face was thin and hollow, and showed the remains of tarnished beauty. Her eyes were black, but had little of their lustre left; her cheeks had some paint laid on without art, and productive of no advantage to her complexion, which exhibited a deadly paleness on the other parts of her face.

Harley stood in the attitude of hesitation; which she interpreting to her advantage, repeated her request, and endeavoured to force a leer of invitation into her countenance. He took her arm, and they walked on to one of those obsequious taverns in the neighbourhood, where the dearness of the wine is a discharge in full for the character of the house. From what impulse he did this we do not mean to enquire; as it has ever been against our nature to search for motives where bad ones are to be found.—They entered, and a waiter showed them a room, and placed a bottle of wine on the table.

Harley filled the lady's glass; which she had no sooner

155

tasted, than dropping it on the floor, and eagerly catching his arm, her eye grew fixed, her lip assumed a clayey whiteness, and she fell back lifeless in her chair.

Harley started from his seat, and, catching her in his arms, supported her from falling to the ground, looking wildly at the door, as if he wanted to run for assistance, but durst not leave the miserable creature. It was not till some minutes after that it occurred to him to ring the bell, which at last, however, he thought of, and rung with repeated violence even after the waiter appeared. Luckily the waiter had his senses somewhat more about him; and snatching up a bottle of water, which stood on a buffet at the end of the room, he sprinkled it over the hands and face of the dying figure before him. She began to revive, and, with the assistance of some harts-horn drops, which Harley now for the first time drew from his pocket, was able to desire the waiter to bring her a crust of bread, of which she swallowed some mouthfuls with the appearance of the keenest hunger. The waiter withdrew: when turning to Harley, sobbing at the same time, and shedding tears, "I am sorry, sir," said she, "that I should have given you so much trouble; but you will pity me when I tell you that till now I have not tasted a morsel these two days past."—He fixed his eyes on hers—every circumstance but the last was forgotten; and he took her hand with as much respect as if she had been a duchess. It was ever the privilege of misfortune to be revered by him.—"Two days!" said he; "and I have fared sumptuously every day!"—He was reaching to the bell; she understood his meaning, and prevented him. "I beg, sir," said she, "that you would give yourself no more trouble about a wretch who does not wish to live; but, at present, I could not eat a bit; my stomach even rose at the last mouthful of that crust."—He offered to call a chair, saying that he hoped a little rest would relieve her.—He had one half-guinea left. "I am sorry," he said, "that at present I should be able to make you an offer of no more than this paltry sum."—She burst into tears: "Your generosity, sir, is abused; to bestow it on me is to take it from the virtuous. I have no title but misery to plead; misery of my own procuring." "No more of that," answered Harley; "there is virtue in these tears; let the fruit of them be virtue."—He rung, and ordered a chair.—"Though I am the vilest of beings," said she, "I have not forgotten every virtue; gratitude, I hope, I shall still have left, did I but know who is my benefactor."—"My name is Harley."—"Could I ever have an opportunity"—"You shall, and a glorious one too! your future conduct—but I do not mean to reproach you—if, I say—it will be the noblest reward —I will do myself the pleasure of seeing you again."—Here the waiter entered, and told them the chair was at the door; the lady informed Harley of her lodgings, and he promised to wait on her at ten next morning.

He led her to the chair, and returned to clear with the waiter, without ever once reflecting that he had no money in his pocket. He was ashamed to make an excuse; yet an excuse must be made: he was beginning to frame one, when the waiter cut him short by telling him that he could not run scores; but that, if he would leave his watch, or any other pledge, it would be as safe as if it lay in his pocket. Harley jumped at the proposal, and pulling out his watch, delivered it into his hands immediately; and having, for once, had the precaution to take a note of the lodging he intended to visit next morning, sallied forth with a blush of triumph on his face, without taking notice of the sneer of the waiter, who, twirling the watch in his hand, made him a profound bow at the door, and whispered to a girl, who stood in the passage, something, in which the word CULLY[5] was honoured with a particular emphasis.

CHAPTER XXVII

His Skill in Physiognomy Is Doubted

After he had been some time with the company he had appointed to meet, and the last bottle was called for, he first recollected that he would be again at a loss how to discharge his share of the reckoning. He applied, therefore, to one of them, with whom he was most intimate, acknowledging that he had not a farthing of money about him; and, upon being jocularly asked the reason, acquainted them with the two adventures we have just now related. One of the company asked him if the old man in Hyde Park did not wear a brownish coat, with a narrow gold edging, and his companion an old green frock, with a buff-coloured waistcoat. Upon Harley's recollecting that they did, "Then," said he, "you may be thankful you have come off so well; they are two as noted sharpers, in their way, as any in town, and but t'other night took me in for a much larger sum: I had some thoughts of applying to a justice, but one does not like to be seen in those matters."

Harley answered, "That he could not but fancy the gentleman was mistaken, as he never saw a face promise more honesty than that of the old man he had met with."—"His face!" said a grave-looking man, who sat opposite to him, squirting the juice of his tobacco obliquely into the grate. There was something very emphatical in the action: for it was followed by a burst of laughter round the table. "Gentlemen," said Harley, "you are disposed to be merry; it may be as you imagine, for I confess myself ignorant of the town: but there is one thing which makes me bear the loss of my money with temper: the young fellow who won it must have been miserably poor; I observed him borrow money for the stake from his friend: he had distress and hunger in his countenance: be his character what it may, his necessities at least plead for him."—At this there was a louder laugh than before. "Gentlemen," said the lawyer, one of whose conversations with Harley we have already recorded, "here's a very pretty fellow for you: to have heard him talk some nights ago, as I did, you might have sworn he was a saint; yet now he games with sharpers, and loses his money, and is bubbled by a fine story invented by a whore, and pawns his watch; here are sanctified doings with a witness!"

"Young gentleman," said his friend on the other side of the table, "let me advise you to be a little more cautious for the future; and as for faces—you may look into them to know whether a man's nose be a long or a short one."

CHAPTER XXVIII

He Keeps His Appointment

The last night's raillery of his companions was recalled to his remembrance when he awoke, and the colder homilies of prudence began to suggest some things which were nowise favourable for a performance of his promise to the unfortunate female he had met with before. He rose uncertain of his purpose; but the torpor of such considerations was seldom prevalent over the warmth of his nature. He walked some turns backwards and forwards in his room; he recalled the languid form of the fainting wretch to his mind; he wept at the recollection of her tears. "Though I am the vilest of beings, I have not forgotten every virtue; gratitude, I hope, I shall still have left."—He took a larger stride—"Powers of mercy that surround me!" cried he, "do ye not smile upon deeds like these? to calculate the chances of deception is too tedious a business for the life of man!"—The clock struck ten.—When he had got down-stairs, he found that he had forgot the note of her lodgings; he gnawed his lips at the delay: he was fairly on the pavement, when he recollected having left his purse; he did but just prevent himself from articulating an imprecation. He rushed a second time up into his chamber. "What a wretch I am!" said he; "ere this time, perhaps——" 'Twas a perhaps not to be borne;—two vibrations of a pendulum would have served him to lock his bureau; but they could not be spared.

When he reached the house, and enquired for Miss Atkins (for that was the lady's name), he was shown up three pair of stairs, into a small room lighted by one narrow lattice, and patched round with shreds of different-coloured paper. In the darkest corner stood something like a bed, before which a

160

tattered coverlet hung by way of curtain. He had not waited long when she appeared. Her face had the glister of new-washed tears on it. "I am ashamed, sir," said she, "that you should have taken this fresh piece of trouble about one so little worthy of it; but, to the humane, I know there is a pleasure in goodness for its own sake: if you have patience for the recital of my story, it may palliate, though it cannot excuse, my faults." Harley bowed, as a sign of assent; and she began as follows:

"I am the daughter of an officer, whom a service of forty years had advanced no higher than the rank of captain. I have had hints from himself, and been informed by others, that it was in some measure owing to those principles of rigid honour, which it was his boast to possess, and which he early inculcated on me, that he had been able to arrive at no better station. My mother died when I was a child; old enough to grieve for her death, but incapable of remembering her precepts. Though my father was dotingly fond of her, yet there were some sentiments in which they materially differed: she had been bred from her infancy in the strictest principles of religion, and took the morality of her conduct from the motives which an adherence to those principles suggested. My father, who had been in the army from his youth, affixed an idea of pusillanimity to that virtue, which was formed by the doctrines, excited by the rewards, or guarded by the terrors of revelation; his darling idol was the honour of a soldier: a term which he held in such reverence, that he used it for his most sacred asseveration. When my mother died, I was some time suffered to continue in those sentiments which her instructions had produced; but soon after, though, from respect to her memory, my father did not absolutely ridicule them, yet he showed, in his discourse to others, so little regard to them, and at times suggested to me motives of action so different, that I was soon weaned from opinions which I began to consider as the dreams of superstition, or the artful inventions of designing hypocrisy. My mother's books were left behind at the different quarters we removed to, and my reading was principally confined to plays, novels, and those poetical descriptions of the beauty of virtue and honour, which the circulating libraries easily afforded.

"As I was generally reckoned handsome, and the quickness of my parts extolled by all our visitors, my father had a pride in showing me to the world. I was young, giddy, open to adulation, and vain of those talents which acquired it.

"After the last war, my father was reduced to half-pay; with which we retired to a village in the country, which the acquaintance of some genteel families who resided in it, and the cheapness of living, particularly recommended. My father rented a small house, with a piece of ground sufficient to keep a horse for him, and a cow for the benefit of his family. An old man servant managed his ground; while a maid, who had formerly been my mother's, and had since been mine, under-took the care of our little dairy: they were assisted in each of their provinces by my father and me; and we passed our time in a state of tranquillity, which he had always talked of with delight, and which my train of reading had taught me to admire.

"Though I had never seen the polite circles of the metrop-olis, the company my father had introduced me into had given me a degree of good breeding, which soon discovered a supe-riority over the young ladies of our village. I was quoted as an example of politeness, and my company courted by most of the considerable families in the neighbourhood.

"Amongst the houses to which I was frequently invited, was Sir George Winbrooke's. He had two daughters nearly of my age, with whom, though they had been bred up in those maxims of vulgar doctrine which my superior understanding could not but despise, yet as their good nature led them to an imitation of my manners in everything else, I cultivated a particular friendship.

"Some months after our first acquaintance, Sir George's eldest son came home from his travels. His figure, his ad-dress, and conversation, were not unlike those warm ideas of an accomplished man which my favourite novels had taught me to form; and his sentiments on the article of religion were as liberal as my own: when any of these happened to be the topic of our discourse, I, who before had been silent, from a fear of being single in opposition, now kindled at the fire he raised, and defended our mutual opinions with all the eloquence I was mistress of. He would be respectfully attentive all the while; and when I had ended, would raise his eyes from the ground, look at me with a gaze of admiration, and express his applause in the highest strain of encomium. This was an incense the more pleasing, as I seldom or never had met with it before; for the young gentlemen who visited Sir George were for the most part of that common race of country squires, the pleasure of whose lives is derived from fox-hunting: these are seldom solicitous to please the women at all; or if they were, would never think of applying their flattery to the mind.

"Mr. Winbrooke observed the weakness of my soul, and took every occasion of improving the esteem he had gained. He asked my opinion of every author, of every sentiment, with that submissive diffidence, which showed an unlimited confidence in my understanding. I saw myself revered, as a superior being, by one whose judgment my vanity told me was not likely to err: preferred by him to all the other visitors of my sex, whose fortunes and rank should have entitled them to a much higher degree of notice: I saw their little jealousies at the distinguished attention he paid me; it was gratitude, it was pride, it was love! Love which had made too fatal a progress in my heart, before any declaration on his part should have warranted a return: but I interpreted every look of attention, every expression of compliment, to the passion I imagined him inspired with, and imputed to his sensibility that silence which was the effect of art and design. At length, however, he took an opportunity of declaring his love: he now expressed himself in such ardent terms, that prudence might have suspected their sincerity: but prudence is rarely found in the situation I had been unguardedly led into; besides, that the course of reading to which I had been accustomed, did not lead me to conclude, that his expressions could be too warm to be sincere: nor was I even alarmed at the manner in which he talked of marriage, a subjection, he often hinted, to which genuine love should scorn to be confined. The woman, he would often say, who had merit like mine to fix his affection, could easily command it for ever. That honour too which I revered, was often called in to enforce his sentiments. I did not, however, absolutely assent to them; but I found my regard for their opposites diminish by degrees. If it is dangerous to be convinced, it is dangerous to listen; for our reason is so much of a machine, that it will not always be able to resist, when the ear is perpetually assailed.

"In short, Mr. Harley, (for I tire you with a relation, the catastrophe of which you will already have imagined), I fell a prey to his artifices. He had not been able so thoroughly to convert me, that my conscience was silent on the subject; but he was so assiduous to give repeated proofs of unabated affection, that I hushed its suggestions as they rose. The world, however, I knew, was not to be silenced; and therefore I took occasion to express my uneasiness to my seducer, and entreat him, as he valued the peace of one to whom he professed such attachment, to remove it by a marriage. He made excuses from his dependence on the will of his father, but quieted my fears by the promise of endeavouring to win his assent.

"My father had been some days absent on a visit to a dying relation, from whom he had considerable expectations. I was left at home, with no other company than my books: my books I found were not now such companions as they used to be; I was restless, melancholy, unsatisfied with myself. But judge my situation when I received a billet from Mr. Winbrooke informing me, that he had sounded Sir George on the subject we had talked of, and found him so averse to any match so unequal to his own rank and fortune, that he was obliged, with whatever reluctance, to bid adieu to a place, the remembrance of which should ever be dear to him.

"I read this letter a hundred times over. Alone, helpless, conscious of guilt, and abandoned by every better thought, my mind was one motley scene of terror, confusion, and remorse. A thousand expedients suggested themselves, and a thousand fears told me they would be vain: at last, in an agony of despair, I packed up a few clothes, took what money and trinkets were in the house, and set out for London, whither I understood he was gone, pretending to my maid, that I had received letters from my father requiring my immediate attend-ance. I had no other companion than a boy, a servant to the man from whom I hired my horses. I arrived in London within an hour of Mr. Winbrooke, and accidentally alighted at the very inn where he was.

"He started and turned pale when he saw me; but recov-ered himself in time enough to make many new protestations of regard, and beg me to make myself easy under a disappoint-ment which was equally afflicting to him. He procured me lodgings, where I slept, or rather endeavoured to sleep, for that night. Next morning I saw him again; he then mildly observed on the imprudence of my precipitate flight from the country, and proposed my removing to lodgings at another end of the town, to elude the search of my father, till he should fall upon some method of excusing my conduct to him, and reconciling him to my return. We took a hackney-coach, and drove to the house he mentioned.

"It was situated in a dirty lane, furnished with a tawdry affectation of finery, with some old family pictures hanging on walls which their own cobwebs would better have suited. I was struck with a secret dread at entering; nor was it lessened by the appearance of the landlady, who had that look of selfish shrewdness, which, of all others, is the most hateful to those whose feelings are untinctured with the world. A girl, who she told us was her niece, sat by her, playing on a guitar, while herself was at work, with the assistance of spectacles, and had a prayer-book, with the leaves folded down in several places, lying on the table before her. Perhaps, sir, I tire you with my minuteness; but the place, and every circumstance about it, is so impressed on my mind, that I shall never forget it.

"I dined that day with Mr. Winbrooke alone. He lost by degrees that restraint which I perceived too well to hang about him before, and, with his former gaiety and good humour, repeated the flattering things which, though they had once been fatal, I durst not now distrust. At last, taking my hand and kissing it, 'It is thus,' said he, 'that love will last, while freedom is preserved; thus let us ever be blessed, without the galling thought that we are tied to a condition where we may cease to be so.'

"I answered, 'That the world thought otherwise: that it had certain ideas of good fame, which it was impossible not to wish to maintain.'

" 'The world,' said he, 'is a tyrant; they are slaves who obey it: let us be happy without the pale of the world. To-morrow I shall leave this quarter of it, for one where the talkers of the world shall be foiled, and lose us. Could not my Emily accompany me? my friend, my companion, the mistress of my soul! Nay, do not look so, Emily! Your father may grieve for a while, but your father shall be taken care of; this bank-bill I intend as the comfort for his daughter.'

"I could contain myself no longer: 'Wretch,' I exclaimed, 'dost thou imagine that my father's heart could brook dependence on the destroyer of his child, and tamely accept of a base equivalent for her honour and his own!'

" 'Honour, my Emily,' said he, 'is the word of fools, or of those wiser men who cheat them. 'Tis a fantastic bauble that does not suit the gravity of your father's age; but, whatever it is, I am afraid it can never be perfectly restored to you: exchange the word then, and let pleasure be your object now.'

"At these words he clasped me in his arms, and pressed his lips rudely to my bosom. I started from my seat. 'Perfidious villain!' said I, 'who dar'st insult the weakness thou hast undone; were that father here, thy coward soul would shrink from the vengeance of his honour! Cursed be that wretch who has deprived him of it! oh! doubly cursed, who has dragged on his hoary head the infamy which should have crushed her own!' I snatched a knife which lay beside me, and would have plunged it in my breast; but the monster prevented my purpose, and smiling with a grin of barbarous insult—

" 'Madam,' said he, 'I confess you are too much in heroics for me: I am sorry we should differ about trifles: but as I seem somehow to have offended you, I would willingly remedy it by taking my leave. You have been put to some foolish expense in this journey on my account; allow me to reimburse you.'

"So saying he laid a bank-bill, of what amount I had no

patience to see, upon the table. Shame, grief, and indignation choked my utterance; unable to speak my wrongs, and unable to bear them in silence, I fell in a swoon at his feet.

"What happened in the interval I cannot tell, but when I came to myself I was in the arms of the landlady, with her niece chafing my temples, and doing all in her power for my recovery. She had much compassion in her countenance: the old woman assumed the softest look she was capable of, and both endeavoured to bring me comfort. They continued to show me many civilities, and even the aunt began to be less disagreeable in my sight. To the wretched, to the forlorn, as I was, small offices of kindness are endearing.

"Meantime my money was far spent, nor did I attempt to conceal my wants from their knowledge. I had frequent thoughts of returning to my father; but the dread of a life of scorn is insurmountable. I avoided, therefore, going abroad when I had a chance of being seen by any former acquaintance, nor indeed did my health for a great while permit it; and suffered the old woman, at her own suggestion, to call me niece at home, where we now and then saw (when they could prevail on me to leave my room) one or two other elderly women, and sometimes a grave business-like man, who showed great compassion for my indisposition, and made me very obligingly an offer of a room at his country-house for the recovery of my health. This offer I did not choose to accept, but told my landlady, 'that I should be glad to be employed in any way of business which my skill in needle-work could recommend me to, confessing, at the same time, that I was afraid I should scarce be able to pay her what I already owed for board and lodging, and that for her other good offices, I had nothing but thanks to give her.'

" 'My dear child,' said she, 'do not talk of paying; since I lost my own sweet girl' (here she wept), 'your very picture she was, Miss Emily, I have nobody, except my niece, to whom I should leave any little thing I have been able to save: you shall live with me, my dear; and I have sometimes a little millinery work, in which, when you are inclined to it, you may assist us. By the way, here are a pair of ruffles we have just finished for that gentleman you saw here at tea; a distant relation of mine, and a worthy man he is. 'Twas pity you refused the offer of an apartment at his country house; my niece, you know, was to have accompanied you, and you might have fancied yourself at home; a most sweet place it is, and but a short mile beyond Hampstead. Who knows, Miss Emily, what effect such a visit might have had! if I had half your beauty I should not waste it pining after e'er a worthless fellow of them all.'

"I felt my heart swell at her words; I would have been angry if I could; but I was in that stupid state which is not easily awakened to anger: when I would have chid her the reproof stuck in my throat; I could only weep!

"Her want of respect increased, as I had not spirit to assert it. My work was now rather imposed than offered, and I became a drudge for the bread I ate: but my dependence and servility grew in proportion, and I was now in a situation which could not make any extraordinary exertions to disengage itself from either—I found myself with child.

"At last the wretch, who had thus trained me to destruction, hinted the purpose for which those means had been used. I discovered her to be an artful procuress for the pleasures of those, who are men of decency to the world in the midst of debauchery.

"I roused every spark of courage within me at the horrid proposal. She treated my passion at first somewhat mildly; but when I continued to exert it she resented it with insult, and told me plainly that if I did not soon comply with her desires I should pay her every farthing I owed, or rot in a jail for life. I trembled at the thought; still, however, I resisted her importunities, and she put her threats in execution. I was conveyed to prison, weak from my condition, weaker from that struggle of grief and misery which for some time I had suffered. A miscarriage was the consequence.

"Amidst all the horrors of such a state, surrounded with wretches totally callous, lost alike to humanity and to shame, think, Mr. Harley, think what I endured: nor wonder that I at last yielded to the solicitations of that miscreant I had seen at her house, and sunk to the prostitution which he tempted. But that was happiness compared to what I have suffered since. He soon abandoned me to the common use of the town, and I was cast among those miserable beings in whose society I have since remained.

"Oh! did the daughters of virtue know our sufferings; did they see our hearts torn with anguish amidst the affectation of gaiety which our faces are obliged to assume! our bodies tortured by disease, our minds with that consciousness which they cannot lose! Did they know, did they think of this, Mr. Harley! —their censures are just; but their pity perhaps might spare the wretches whom their justice should condemn.

"Last night, but for an exertion of benevolence which the infection of our infamy prevents even in the humane, had I been thrust out from this miserable place which misfortune has yet left me; exposed to the brutal insults of drunkenness, or dragged by that justice which I could not bribe, to the punishment which may correct, but, alas! can never amend the abandoned objects of its terrors. From that, Mr. Harley, your goodness has relieved me."

He beckoned with his hand: he would have stopped the mention of his favours; but he could not speak, had it been to beg a diadem.

She saw his tears; her fortitude began to fail at the sight, when the voice of some stranger on the stairs awakened her attention. She listened for a moment, then starting up, exclaimed, "Merciful God! my father's voice!"

She had scarce uttered the word, when the door burst open, and a man entered in the garb of an officer. When he discovered his daughter and Harley, he started back a few paces; his look assumed a furious wildness! he laid his hand on his sword. The two objects of his wrath did not utter a syllable.

"Villain," he cried, "thou seest a father who had once a daughter's honour to preserve; blasted as it now is, behold him ready to avenge its loss!"

Harley had by this time some power of utterance. "Sir," said he, "if you will be a moment calm—"

"Infamous coward!" interrupted the other, "dost thou preach calmness to wrongs like mine?"

He drew his sword.

"Sir," said Harley, "let me tell you"—the blood ran quicker to his cheek—his pulse beat one—no more—and regained the temperament of humanity—"You are deceived, sir," said he, "you are much deceived; but I forgive suspicions which your misfortunes have justified: I would not wrong you, upon my soul I would not, for the dearest gratification of a thousand worlds; my heart bleeds for you!"

His daughter was now prostrate at his feet. "Strike," said she "strike here a wretch, whose misery cannot end but with that death she deserves."

Her hair had fallen on her shoulders! her look had the horrid calmness of out-breathed despair! Her father would have spoken; his lip quivered, his cheek grew pale; his eyes lost the lightning of their fury! there was a reproach in them, but with a mingling of pity! He turned them up to heaven—then on his daughter.—He laid his left hand on his heart—the sword dropped from his right—he burst into tears.

CHAPTER XXIX

The Distresses of a Father

Harley kneeled also at the side of the unfortunate daughter:

"Allow me, sir," said he, "to entreat your pardon for one whose offences have been already so signally punished. I know, I feel, that those tears, wrung from the heart of a father, are more dreadful to her than all the punishments your sword could have inflicted: accept the contrition of a child whom heaven has restored to you."

"Is she not lost," answered he, "irrecoverably lost? Damnation! a common prostitute to the meanest ruffian!"

"Calmly, my dear sir," said Harley, "did you know by what complicated misfortunes she has fallen to that miserable state in which you now behold her, I should have no need of words to excite your compassion. Think, sir, of what once she was. Would you abandon her to the insults of an unfeeling world, deny her opportunity of penitence, and cut off the little comfort that still remains for your afflictions and her own!"

"Speak," said he, addressing himself to his daughter; "speak; I will hear thee."

The desperation that supported her was lost; she fell to the ground, and bathed his feet with her tears!

Harley undertook her cause: he related the treacheries to which she had fallen a sacrifice, and again solicited the forgiveness of her father. He looked on her for some time in silence; the pride of a soldier's honour checked for a while the yearnings of his heart; but nature at last prevailed, he fell on her neck and mingled his tears with hers.

Harley, who discovered from the dress of the stranger

171

that he was just arrived from a journey, begged that they would both remove to his lodgings, till he could procure others for them. Atkins looked at him with some marks of surprise. His daughter now first recovered the power of speech.

"Wretch as I am," said she, " yet there is some gratitude due to the preserver of your child. See him now before you. To him I owe my life, or at least the comfort of imploring your forgiveness before I die."

"Pardon me, young gentleman," said Atkins, "I fear my passion wronged you."

"Never, never, sir," said Harley; "if it had, your reconciliation to your daughter were an atonement a thousand fold." He then repeated his request that he might be allowed to conduct them to his lodgings, to which Mr. Atkins at last consented. He took his daughter's arm. "Come, my Emily," said he, "we can never, never recover that happiness we have lost! but time may teach us to remember our misfortunes with patience."

When they arrived at the house where Harley lodged, he was informed that the first floor was then vacant, and that the gentleman and his daughter might be accommodated there. While he was upon his enquiry, Miss Atkins informed her father more particularly what she owed to his benevolence. When he returned into the room where they were Atkins ran and embraced him; begged him again to forgive the offence he had given him, and made the warmest protestations of gratitude for his favours. We would attempt to describe the joy which Harley felt on this occasion, did it not occur to us that one half of the world could not understand it though we did; and the other half will, by this time, have understood it without any description at all.

Miss Atkins now retired to her chamber, to take some rest from the violence of the emotions she had suffered. When she was gone, her father, addressing himself to Harley, said, "You have a right, sir, to be informed of the present situation of one who owes so much to your compassion for his misfortunes. My daughter I find has informed you what that was at the fatal juncture when they began. Her distresses you have heard, you have pitied as they deserved; with mine, perhaps, I cannot so easily make you acquainted. You have a feeling heart, Mr. Harley; I bless it that it has saved my child; but you never were a father, a father torn by that most dreadful of calamities, the dishonour of a child he doted on! You have been already informed of some of the circumstances of her elopement. I was then from home, called by the death of a relation, who, though he would never advance me a shilling on the utmost exigency in his life-time, left me all the gleanings of his frugality at his death. I would not write this intelligence to my daughter, because I intended to be the bearer myself; and as soon as my business would allow me, I set out on my return, winged with all the haste of paternal affection. I fondly built those schemes of future happiness, which present prosperity is ever busy to suggest: my Emily was concerned in them all. As I approached our little dwelling my heart throbbed with the anticipation of joy and welcome. I imagined the cheering fire, the blissful contentment of a frugal meal, made luxurious by a daughter's smile: I painted to myself her surprise at the tidings of our new-acquired riches, our fond disputes about the disposal of them.

"The road was shortened by the dreams of happiness I enjoyed, and it began to be dark as I reached the house: I alighted from my horse, and walked softly upstairs to the room we commonly sat in. I was somewhat disappointed at not finding my daughter there. I rung the bell; her maid appeared, and showed no small signs of wonder at the summons. She blessed herself as she entered the room: I smiled at her surprise. 'Where is Miss Emily, sir?' said she.

" 'Emily!'

" 'Yes, sir; she has been gone hence some days, upon receipt of those letters you sent her.'

" 'Letters!' said I.

" 'Yes, sir, so she told me, and went off in all haste that very night.'

"I stood aghast as she spoke, but was able so far to

recollect myself, as to put on the affectation of calmness, and telling her there was certainly some mistake in the affair, desired her to leave me.

"When she was gone, I threw myself into a chair, in that state of uncertainty which is, of all others, the most dreadful. The gay visions with which I had delighted myself, vanished in an instant: I was tortured with tracing back the same circle of doubt and disappointment. My head grew dizzy as I thought: I called the servant again, and asked her a hundred questions, to no purpose; there was not room even for conjecture.

"Something at last arose in my mind, which we call Hope, without knowing what it is. I wished myself deluded by it; but it could not prevail over my returning fears. I arose and walked through the room. My Emily's spinet stood at the end of it, open, with a book of music folded down at some of my favourite lessons. I touched the keys; there was a vibration in the sound that froze my blood; I looked around, and methought the family pictures on the walls gazed on me with compassion in their faces. I sat down again with an attempt at more composure; I started at every creaking of the door, and my ears rung with imaginary noises!

"I had not remained long in this situation, when the arrival of a friend, who had accidentally heard of my return, put an end to my doubts, by the recital of my daughter's dishonour. He told me he had his information from a young gentleman, to whom Winbrooke had boasted of having seduced her.

"I started from my seat, with broken curses on my lips, and without knowing whither I should pursue them, ordered my servant to load my pistols, and saddle my horses. My friend, however, with great difficulty, persuaded me to compose myself for that night, promising to accompany me on the morrow, to Sir George Winbrooke's in quest of his son.

"The morrow came, after a night spent in a state little distant from madness. We went as early as decency would allow to Sir George's; he received me with politeness, and indeed compassion; protested his abhorrence of his son's conduct, and told me that he had set out some days before for London, on which place he had procured a draft for a large sum, on pretence of finishing his travels; but that he had not heard from him since his departure.

"I did not wait for any more, either of information or comfort, but against the united remonstrances of Sir George and my friend, set out instantly for London, with a frantic uncertainty of purpose; but there, all manner of search was in vain. I could trace neither of them any farther than the inn where they first put up on their arrival; and after some days' fruitless enquiry, returned home destitute of every little hope that had hitherto supported me. The journeys I had made, the restless nights I had spent, above all, the perturbation of my mind, had the effect which naturally might be expected; a very dangerous fever was the consequence. From this, however, contrary to the expectation of my physicians, I recovered. It was now that I first felt something like calmness of mind; probably from being reduced to a state which could not produce the exertions of anguish or despair. A stupid melancholy settled on my soul; I could endure to live with an apathy of life; at times I forgot my resentment, and wept at the remembrance of my child.

"Such has been the tenor of my days since that fatal moment when these misfortunes began, till yesterday, that I received a letter from a friend in town, acquainting me of her present situation. Could such tales as mine, Mr. Harley, be sometimes suggested to the daughters of levity, did they but know with what anxiety the heart of a parent flutters round the child he loves, they would be less apt to construe into harshness that delicate concern for their conduct, which they often complain of as laying restraint upon things, to the young, the gay, and the thoughtless, seemingly harmless and indifferent. Alas! I fondly imagined that I needed not even these common cautions! my Emily was the joy of my age, and the pride of my soul!—Those things are now no more, they are lost for ever! Her death I could have borne! but the death of her honour has added obloquy and shame to that sorrow which bends my grey hairs to the dust!"

As he spoke these last words, his voice trembled in his throat; it was now lost in his tears! He sat with his face half turned from Harley, as if he would have hid the sorrow which he felt. Harley was in the same attitude himself; he durst not meet Atkins' eye with a tear; but gathering his stifled breath, "Let me entreat you, sir," said he, "to hope better things. The world is ever tyrannical; it warps our sorrows to edge them with keener affliction: let us not be slaves to the names it affixes to motive or to action. I know an ingenuous mind cannot help feeling when they sting: but there are considerations by which it may be overcome. Its fantastic ideas vanish as they rise; they teach us—to look beyond it."

•   •   •   •   •   •

A FRAGMENT

Showing His Success with the Baronet

· · · The card he received was in the politest style in which disappointment could be communicated: the baronet "was under a necessity of giving up his application for Mr. Harley, as he was informed that the lease was engaged for a gentleman who had long served His Majesty in another capacity, and whose merit had entitled him to the first lucrative thing that should be vacant." Even Harley could not murmur at such a disposal.—"Perhaps," said he to himself, "some war-worn officer, who, like poor Atkins, had been neglected from reasons which merited the highest advancement; whose honour could not stoop to solicit the preferment he deserved; perhaps, with a family, taught the principles of delicacy, without the means of supporting it; a wife and children—gracious heaven! whom my wishes would have deprived of bread——."

He was interrupted in his reverie by someone tapping him on the shoulder, and, on turning round, he discovered it to be the very man who had explained to him the condition of his gay companion at Hyde Park Corner. "I am glad to see you, sir," said he; "I believe we are fellows in disappointment." Harley started, and said that he was at a loss to understand him. "Poh! you need not be so shy," answered the other; "everyone for himself is but fair, and I had much rather you had got it than the rascally gauger." Harley still protested his ignorance of what he meant. "Why, the lease of Bancroft Manor; had not you been applying for it?" "I confess I was," replied Harley; "but I cannot conceive how you should be interested in the matter."—"Why, I was making interest for it myself," said he, "and I think I had some title. I voted for this same baronet

177

at the last election, and made some of my friends do so too; though I would not have you imagine that I sold my vote. No, I scorn it, let me tell you I scorn it; but I thought as how this man was staunch and true, and I find he's but a double-faced fellow after all, and speechifies in the House for any side he hopes to make most by. Oh, how many fine speeches and squeezings by the hand we had of him on the canvass! 'And if ever I shall be so happy as to have an opportunity of serving you'—A murrain on the smooth-tongued knave! and after all to get it for this pimp of a gauger."—"The gauger! there must be some mistake," said Harley. "He writes me, that it was engaged for one whose long services——" "Services!" interrupted the other; "you shall hear. Services! Yes, his sister arrived in town a few days ago, and is now sempstress to the baronet. A plague on all rogues! says honest Sam Wrightson. I shall but just drink damnation to them to-night, in a crown's worth of Ashley's, and leave London to-morrow by sun-rise."— "I shall leave it too!" said Harley, and so he accordingly did.

In passing through Piccadilly, he had observed, on the window of an inn, a notification of the departure of a stage-coach for a place in his road homewards; in the way back to his lodgings he took a seat in it for his return.

CHAPTER XXXIII

He Leaves London—Characters in a Stage-Coach

The company in the stage-coach consisted of a grocer and his wife, who were going to pay a visit to some of their country friends; a young officer, who took this way of marching to quarters; a middle-aged gentlewoman, who had been hired as housekeeper to some family in the country; and an elderly, well-looking man, with a remarkable old-fashioned periwig.

Harley, upon entering, discovered but one vacant seat, next the grocer's wife, which, from his natural shyness of temper, he made no scruple to occupy, however aware that riding backwards always disagreed with him.

Though his inclination to physiognomy had met with some rubs in the metropolis, he had not yet lost his attachment to that science: he set himself, therefore, to examine, as usual, the countenances of his companions. Here, indeed, he was not long in doubt as to the preference; for besides that the elderly gentleman, who sat opposite to him, had features by nature more expressive of good dispositions, there was something in that periwig we mentioned, peculiarly attractive of Harley's regard.

He had not been long employed in these speculations, when he found himself attacked with that faintish sickness, which was the natural consequence of his situation in the coach. The paleness of his countenance was first observed by the housekeeper, who immediately made offer of her smelling bottle, which Harley, however, declined, telling at the same time the cause of his uneasiness. The gentleman, on the opposite side of the coach, now first turned his eye from the side direction in which it had been fixed, and begged Harley to exchange places with him, expressing his regret that he had not made the proposal before. Harley thanked him, and, upon being assured that both seats were alike to him, was about to accept of his offer, when the young gentleman of the sword, putting on an arch look, laid hold of the other's arm. "So, my old boy," said he, "I find you have still some youthful blood about you, but, with your leave, I will do myself the honour of sitting by this lady;" and took his place accordingly. The grocer stared him as full in the face as his own short neck would allow, and his wife, who was a little, roundfaced woman, with a great deal of colour in her cheeks, drew up at the compliment that was paid her, looking first at the officer, and then at the house-keeper.

This incident was productive of some discourse; for before, though there was sometimes a cough or a hem from the grocer, and the officer now and then humm'd a few notes of a song, there had not a single word passed the lips of any of the company.

Mrs. Grocer observed, how ill-convenient it was for people, who could not bear to ride backwards, to travel in a stage. This brought on a dissertation on stage-coaches in general, and the pleasure of keeping a chay of one's own; which led to another, on the great riches of Mr. Deputy Bearskin, who, according to her, had once been of that industrious order of youths who sweep the crossings of the streets for the con-veniency of passengers, but, by various fortunate accidents, had now acquired an immense fortune, and kept his coach and a dozen livery servants. All this afforded ample fund for conversation, if conversation it might be called, that was car-ried on solely by the before-mentioned lady, nobody offering to interrupt her, except that the officer sometimes signified his approbation by a variety of oaths, a sort of phraseology in which he seemed extremely conversant. She appealed indeed frequently to her husband for the authenticity of certain facts, of which the good man as often protested his total ignorance; but as he was always called fool, or something very like it, for his pains, he at last contrived to support the credit of his wife without prejudice to his conscience, and signified his assent by a noise not unlike the grunting of that animal which in shape and fatness he somewhat resembled.

The housekeeper, and the old gentleman who sat next to Harley, were now observed to be fast asleep; at which the lady, who had been at such pains to entertain them, muttered some words of displeasure, and, upon the officer's whispering to smoke the old put, both she and her husband pursed up their mouths into a contemptuous smile. Harley looked sternly on the grocer: "You are come, sir," said he, "to those years when you might have learned some reverence for age: as for this young man, who has so lately escaped from the nursery, he may be allowed to divert himself." "Damme, sir!" said the officer, "do you call me young?" striking up the front of his hat, and stretching forward on his seat, till his face almost touched Harley's. It is probable, however, that he discovered something there which tended to pacify him, for, on the ladies' entreating them not to quarrel, he very soon resumed his posture and calmness together, and was rather less profuse of his oaths during the rest of the journey.

It is possible the old gentleman had waked time enough to hear the last part of this discourse; at least (whether from that cause, or that he too was a physiognomist) he wore a look remarkably complacent to Harley, who, on his part, showed a particular observance of him: indeed, they had soon a better opportunity of making their acquaintance, as the coach arrived that night at the town where the officer's regiment lay, and the places of destination of their other fellow-travellers, it seems, were at no great distance; for next morning the old gentleman and Harley were the only passengers remaining.

When they left the inn in the morning, Harley, pulling out a little pocket-book, began to examine the contents, and make some corrections with a pencil. "This," said he, turning to his companion, "is an amusement with which I sometimes pass idle hours at an inn: these are quotations from those humble poets, who trust their fame to the brittle tenure of windows and drinking-glasses." "From our inns," returned the gentleman, "a stranger might imagine that we were a nation of poets: machines, at least, containing poetry, which the motion of a journey emptied of their contents. Is it from the vanity of being thought geniuses, or a mere mechanical imitation of the custom of others, that we are tempted to scrawl rhyme upon such places?"

"Whether vanity is the cause of our becoming rhymesters or not," answered Harley, "it is a pretty certain effect of it. An old man of my acquaintance, who dealt in apophthegms, used to say that he had known few men without envy, few wits without ill-nature, and no poet without vanity; and I believe his remark is a pretty just one: vanity has been immemorially the charter of poets. In this, the ancients were more honest than we are: the old poets frequently make boastful predictions of the immortality their works will obtain for them; ours, in their dedications and prefatory discourses, employ much eloquence to praise their patrons, and much seeming honesty to condemn themselves, or at least to apologize for their productions to the world. But this, in my opinion, is the more assuming manner of the two; for of all the garbs I ever saw Pride put on, that of her humility is to me the most disgusting."

"It is natural enough for a poet to be vain," said the stranger: "the little worlds which he raises, the inspiration which he claims, may easily be productive of self-importance; though that inspiration is fabulous, it brings on egotism, which is always the parent of vanity."

"It may be supposed," answered Harley, "that inspiration of old was an article of religious faith; in modern times it may be translated a propensity to compose; and I believe it is not always most readily found where the poets have fixed its residence, amidst groves and plains, and the scenes of pastoral retirement. The mind may be there unbent from the cares of the world; but it will frequently, at the same time, be unnerved from any great exertion: it will feel the languor of indolence, and wander without effort over the regions of reflection."

"There is at least," said the stranger, "one advantage in the poetical inclination, that it is an incentive to philanthropy. There is a certain poetic ground, on which a man cannot tread without feelings that enlarge the heart: the causes of human depravity vanish before the romantic enthusiasm he professes, and many who are not able to reach the Parnassian heights, may yet approach so near as to be bettered by the air of the climate."

"I have always thought so," replied Harley; "but this is an argument with the prudent against it: they urge the danger of unfitness for the world."

"I allow it," returned the other; "but I believe it is not always rightfully imputed to the bent for poetry: that is only one effect of the common cause.—Jack, says his father, is indeed no scholar; nor could all the drubbings from his master ever bring him one step forward in his accidence or syntax: but I intend him for a merchant.—Allow the same indulgence to Tom.—Tom reads Virgil and Horace when he should be casting accounts; and but t'other day he pawned his great-coat for an edition of Shakespeare.—But Tom would have been as he is, though Virgil and Horace had never been born, though Shakespeare had died a link-boy; for his nurse will tell you, that when he was a child, he broke his rattle, to discover what it was that sounded within it; and burnt the sticks of his go-cart, because he liked to see the sparkling of timber in the fire.—'Tis a sad case; but what is to be done?—Why, Jack shall make a fortune, dine on vension, and drink claret.—Ay, but Tom—Tom shall dine with his brother, when his pride will let him; at other times, he shall bless God over a half-pint of ale and a Welsh-rabbit; and both shall go to heaven as they may.—That's a poor prospect for Tom, says the father.—To go to heaven! I cannot agree with him."

"Perhaps," said Harley, "we now-a-days discourage the romantic turn a little too much. Our boys are prudent too soon. Mistake me not, I do not mean to blame them for want of levity or dissipation; but their pleasures are those of hackneyed vice, blunted to every finer emotion by the repetition of de-bauch; and their desire of pleasure is warped to the desire of wealth, as the means of procuring it. The immense riches acquired by individuals have erected a standard of ambition, destructive of private morals, and of public virtue. The weaknesses of vice are left us; but the most allowable of our failings we are taught to despise. Love, the passion most natural to the sensibility of youth, has lost the plaintive dignity it once possessed, for the unmeaning simper of a dangling coxcomb; and the only serious concern, that of a dowry, is settled, even amongst the beardless leaders of the dancing-school. The Frivolous and the Interested (might a satirist say) are the characteristical features of the age; they are visible even in the essays of our philosophers. They laugh at the pedantry of our fathers, who complained of the times in which they lived; they are at pains to persuade us how much those were deceived; they pride themselves in defending things as they find them, and in exploding the barren sounds which had been reared into motives for action. To this their style is suited; and the manly tone of reason is exchanged for perpetual efforts at sneer and ridicule. This I hold to be an alarming crisis in the corruption of a state; when not only is virtue declined, and vice prevailing, but when the praises of virtue are forgotten, and the infamy of vice unfelt."

They soon after arrived at the next inn upon the route of the stage-coach, when the stranger told Harley, that his brother's house, to which he was returning, lay at no great dis-tance, and he must therefore unwillingly bid him adieu.

"I should like," said Harley, taking his hand, "to have some word to remember so much seeming worth by: my name is Harley."

"I shall remember it," answered the old gentleman, "in my prayers; mine is Silton."

And Silton indeed it was! Ben Silton himself! Once more, my honoured friend, farewell!——Born to be happy without the world, to that peaceful happiness which the world has not to bestow! Envy never scowled on thy life, nor hatred smiled on thy grave.

CHAPTER XXXIV

He Meets an Old Acquaintance

When the stage-coach arrived at the place of its destination, Harley began to consider how he should proceed the remaining part of his journey. He was very civilly accosted by the master of the inn, who offered to accommodate him either with a post-chaise or horses, to any distance he had a mind: but as he did things frequently in a way different from what other people call natural, he refused these offers, and set out immediately a-foot, having first put a spare shirt in his pocket, and given directions for the forwarding of his portmanteau. This was a method of travelling which he was accustomed to take; it saved the trouble of provision for any animal but himself, and left him at liberty to choose his quarters, either at an inn, or at the first cottage in which he saw a face he liked: nay, when he was not peculiarly attracted by the reasonable creation, he would sometimes consort with a species of inferior rank, and lay himself down to sleep by the side of a rock, or on the banks of a rivulet. He did few things without a motive, but his motives were rather eccentric: and the usual and expedient were terms which he held to be very indefinite, and which therefore he did not always apply to the sense in which they are commonly understood.

The sun was now in his decline, and the evening remarkably serene, when he entered a hollow part of the road, which winded between the surrounding banks, and seamed the sward in different lines, as the choice of travellers had directed them to tread it. It seemed to be little frequented now, for some of those had partly recovered their former verdure. The scene was such as induced Harley to stand and enjoy it; when, turning

185

round, his notice was attracted by an object, which the fixture of his eye on the spot he walked had before prevented him from observing.

An old man, who from his dress seemed to have been a soldier, lay fast asleep on the ground; a knapsack rested on a stone at his right hand, while his staff and brass-hilted sword were crossed at his left.

Harley looked on him with the most earnest attention. He was one of those figures which Salvator[6] would have drawn; nor was the surrounding scenery unlike the wildness of that painter's back-grounds. The banks on each side were covered with fantastic shrub-wood, and at a little distance, on the top of one of them, stood a finger-post, to mark the directions of two roads which diverged from the point where it was placed. A rock, with some dangling wild flowers, jutted out above where the soldier lay; on which grew the stump of a large tree, white with age, and a single twisted branch shaded his face as he slept. His face had the marks of manly comeliness impaired by time; his forehead was not altogether bald, but its hairs might have been numbered; while a few white locks behind crossed the brown of his neck with a contrast the most venerable to a mind like Harley's. "Thou art old," said he to himself; "but age has not brought thee rest for its infirmities: I fear those silver hairs have not found shelter from thy country, though that neck has been bronzed in its service." The stranger waked. He looked at Harley with the appearance of some confusion: it was a pain the latter knew too well to think of causing in another; he turned and went on. The old man re-adjusted his knapsack, and followed in one of the tracks on the opposite side of the road.

When Harley heard the tread of his feet behind him, he could not help stealing back a glance at his fellow-traveller. He seemed to bend under the weight of his knapsack; he halted in his walk, and one of his arms was supported by a sling, and lay motionless across his breast. He had that steady look of sorrow, which indicates that its owner has gazed upon his griefs till he has forgotten to lament them; yet not without those streaks of complacency, which a good mind will sometimes throw into the countenance, through all the incumbent load of its depression.

He had now advanced nearer to Harley, and, with an uncertain sort of voice, begged to know what it was o'clock; "I fear," said he, "sleep has beguiled me of my time, and I shall hardly have light enough left to carry me to the end of my journey."

"Father!" said Harley (who by this time found the romantic enthusiasm rising within him) "how far do you mean to go?"

"But a little way, sir," returned the other; "and indeed it is but a little way I can manage now: 'tis just four miles from the height to the village, thither I am going."

"I am going there too," said Harley; "we may make the road shorter to each other. You seem to have served your country, sir, to have served it hardly too; 'tis a character I have the highest esteem for.—I would not be impertinently inquisitive; but there is that in your appearance which excites my curiosity to know something more of you: in the meantime, suffer me to carry that knapsack."

The old man gazed on him; a tear stood in his eye! "Young gentleman," said he, "you are too good; may Heaven bless you for an old man's sake, who has nothing but his blessing to give! but my knapsack is so familiar to my shoulders, that I should walk the worse for wanting it; and it would be troublesome to you, who have not been used to its weight."

"Far from it," answered Harley, "I should tread the lighter; it would be the most honourable badge I ever wore."

"Sir," said the stranger, who had looked earnestly in Harley's face during the last part of his discourse, "is not your name Harley?"

"It is," replied he; "I am ashamed to say I have forgotten yours."

"You may well have forgotten my face," said the stranger; —'tis a long time since you saw it; but possibly you may remember something of old Edwards."

"Edwards!" cried Harley, "oh! heavens!" and sprung to embrace him; "let me clasp those knees on which I have sat so often: Edwards!—I shall never forget that fire-side, round which I have been so happy! But where, where have you been? where is Jack? where is your daughter? How has it fared with them, when fortune, I fear, has been so unkind to you?"

"'Tis a long tale," replied Edwards; "but I will try to tell it you as we walk.

"When you were at school in the neighbourhood, you remember me at South-hill: that farm had been possessed by my father, grandfather, and great-grandfather, which last was a younger brother of that very man's ancestor, who is now lord of the manor. I thought I managed it, as they had done, with prudence; I paid my rent regularly as it became due, and had always as much behind as gave bread to me and my children. But my last lease was out soon after you left that part of the country; and the squire, who had lately got a London-attorney for his steward, would not renew it, because, he said, he did not choose to have any farm under £300 a year value on his estate; but offered to give me the preference on the same terms with another, if I chose to take the one he had marked out, of which mine was a part.

"What could I do, Mr. Harley? I feared the undertaking was too great for me; yet to leave, at my age, the house I had lived in from my cradle! I could not, Mr. Harley, I could not; there was not a tree about it that I did not look on as my father, my brother, or my child: so I even ran the risk, and took the squire's offer of the whole. But I had soon reason to repent of my bargain; the steward had taken care that my former farm should be the best land of the division: I was obliged to hire more servants, and I could not have my eye over them all; some unfavourable seasons followed one another, and I found my affairs entangling on my hands. To add to my distress, a considerable corn-factor turned bankrupt with a sum of mine in his possession: I failed paying my rent so punctually as I was wont to do, and the same steward had my stock taken in execution in a few days after. So, Mr. Harley, there was an end of my prosperity. However, there was as much produced from the sale of my effects as paid my debts and saved me from a jail: I thank God I wronged no man, and the world could never charge me with dishonesty.

"Had you seen us, Mr. Harley, when we were turned out of South-hill, I am sure you would have wept at the sight. You remember old Trusty, my shag house-dog; I shall never forget it while I live; the poor creature was blind with age, and could scarce crawl after us to the door; he went however as far as the gooseberry-bush; which you may remember stood on the left side of the yard; he was wont to bask in the sun there; when he had reached that spot, he stopped; we went on: I called to him; he wagged his tail, but did not stir: I called again; he lay down: I whistled, and cried Trusty; he gave a short howl, and died! I could have lain down and died too; but God gave me strength to live for my children."

The old man now paused a moment to take breath. He eyed Harley's face; it was bathed with tears: the story was grown familiar to himself; he dropped one tear, and no more.

"Though I was poor," continued he, " I was not altogether without credit. A gentleman in the neighbourhood, who had a small farm unoccupied at the time, offered to let me have it, on giving security for the rent; which I made shift to procure. It was a piece of ground which required management to make anything of; but it was nearly within the compass of my son's labour and my own. We exerted all our industry to bring it into some heart. We began to succeed tolerably, and lived contented on its produce, when an unlucky accident brought us under the displeasure of a neighbouring justice of the peace, and broke all our family happiness again.

"My son was a remarkable good shooter; he had always kept a pointer on our former farm, and thought no harm in doing so now; when one day, having sprung a covey of part-ridges in our own ground, the dog, of his own accord, followed them into the justice's. My son laid down his gun, and went after his dog to bring him back: the game-keeper, who had marked the birds, came up, and seeing the pointer, shot him just as my son approached. The creature fell; my son ran up to him: he died with a complaining sort of cry at his master's feet.

Jack could bear it no longer; but, flying at the game-keeper, wrenched his gun out of his hand, and with the butt end of it, felled him to the ground.

"He had scarce got home, when a constable came with a warrant, and dragged him to prison; there he lay, for the justices would not take bail, till he was tried at the quarter-sessions for the assault and battery. His fine was hard upon us to pay; we contrived however to live the worse for it, and make up the loss by our frugality: but the justice was not content with that punishment, and soon after had an opportunity of punishing us indeed.

"An officer with press-orders came down to our county and having met with the justices, agreed that they should pitch on a certain number, who could most easily be spared from the county, of whom he would take care to clear it: my son's name was in the justices' list.

" 'Twas on a Christmas eve, and the birth-day too of my son's little boy. The night was piercing cold, and it blew a storm, with showers of hail and snow. We had made up a cheering fire in an inner room; I sat before it in my wicker-chair, blessing Providence, that had still left a shelter for me and my children. My son's two little ones were holding their gambols around us; my heart warmed at the sight: I brought a bottle of my best ale, and all our misfortunes were forgotten.

"It had long been our custom to play a game at blind man's buff on that night, and it was not omitted now; so to it we fell, I, and my son, and his wife, the daughter of a neigh-bouring farmer, who happened to be with us at the time, the two children, and an old maid servant, who had lived with me from a child. The lot fell on my son to be blindfolded: we had continued some time at our game, when he groped his way into an outer room in pursuit of some of us, who, he imagined, had taken shelter there; we kept snug in our places, and en-joyed his mistake. He had not been long there, when he was suddenly seized from behind; 'I shall have you now,' said he, and turned about. 'Shall you so, master?' answered the ruffian, who had laid hold of him; 'we shall make you play at another sort of game by and by.' "—At these words Harley started with a convulsive sort of motion, and grasping Edwards's sword, drew it half out of the scabbard, with a look of the most frantic wildness. Edwards gently replaced it in its sheath, and went on with his relation.

"On hearing these words in a strange voice, we all rushed out to discover the cause; the room by this time was almost full of the gang. My daughter-in-law fainted at the sight; the maid and I ran to assist her, while my poor son remained motionless, gazing by turns on his children and their mother. We soon recovered her to life, and begged her to retire and wait the issue of the affair; but she flew to her husband, and clung round him in an agony of terror and grief.

"In the gang was one of a smoother aspect, whom, by his dress, we discovered to be a serjeant of foot: he came up to me, and told me, that my son had his choice of the sea or land service, whispering at the same time that, if he chose the land, he might get off, on procuring him another man, and paying a certain sum for his freedom. The money we could just muster up in the house, by the assistance of the maid, who produced, in a green bag, all the little savings of her service; but the man we could not expect to find. My daughter-in-law gazed upon her children with a look of the wildest despair: 'My poor infants!' said she, 'your father is forced from you; who shall now labour for your bread? or must your mother beg for herself and you?' I prayed her to be patient; but comfort I had none to give her. At last, calling the serjeant aside, I asked him, 'If I was too old to be accepted in place of my son?'

" 'Why, I don't know,' said he; 'you are rather old to be sure, but yet the money may do much.'

"I put the money in his hand, and coming back to my children, 'Jack,' said I, 'you are free; live to give your wife and these little ones bread; I will go, my child, in your stead; I have but little life to lose, and if I stayed, I should add to the wretches you left behind.'

" 'No,' replied my son, 'I am not that coward you imagine me; heaven forbid that my father's grey hairs should be so exposed, while I sat idle at home; I am young and able to endure much, and God will take care of you and my family.'

"'Jack,' said I, 'I will put an end to this matter; you have never hitherto disobeyed me; I will not be contradicted in this; stay at home, I charge you, and, for my sake, be kind to my children.'

"Our parting, Mr. Harley, I cannot describe to you; it was the first time we ever had parted: the very press-gang could scarce keep from tears; but the serjeant, who had seemed the softest before, was now the least moved of them all. He conducted me to a party of new-raised recruits, who lay at a village in the neighbourhood; and we soon after joined the regiment. I had not been long with it when we were ordered to the East Indies, where I was soon made a serjeant, and might have picked up some money, if my heart had been as hard as some others were; but my nature was never of that kind, that could think of getting rich at the expense of my conscience.

"Amongst our prisoners was an old Indian, whom some of our officers supposed to have a treasure hidden somewhere; which is no uncommon practice in that country. They pressed him to discover it. He declared he had none; but that would not satisfy them: so they ordered him to be tied to a stake, and suffer fifty lashes every morning till he should learn to speak out, as they said. Oh! Mr. Harley, had you seen him, as I did, with his hands bound behind him, suffering in silence, while the big drops trickled down his shrivelled cheeks and wet his gray beard, which some of the inhuman soldiers plucked in scorn! I could not bear it, I could not for my soul; and one morning, when the rest of the guard were out of the way, I found means to let him escape. I was tried by a court-martial for negligence on my post, and ordered, in compassion of my age, and having got this wound in my arm and that in my leg, in the service, only to suffer three hundred lashes, and be turned out of the regiment; but my sentence was mitigated as to the lashes, and I had only two hundred. When I had suffered these I was turned out of the camp, and had betwixt three and four hundred miles to travel before I could reach a sea-port, without guide to conduct me, or money to buy me provisions by the way. I set out, however, resolved to walk as far as I could, and then to lay myself down and die. But I had scarce gone a mile when I was met by the Indian whom I had delivered. He pressed me in his arms, and kissed the marks of the lashes on my back a thousand times; he led me to a little hut, where some friend of his dwelt, and after I was recovered of my wounds conducted me so far on my journey himself, and sent another Indian to guide me through the rest. When we parted, he pulled out a purse with two hundred pieces of gold in it: 'Take this,' said he, 'my dear preserver, it is all I have been able to procure.'

"I begged him not to bring himself to poverty for my sake, who should probably have no need of it long, but he insisted on my accepting it. He embraced me: 'You are an Englishman,' said he, 'but the Great Spirit has given you an Indian heart; may He bear up the weight of your old age, and blunt the arrow that brings it rest!'

"We parted; and not long after I made shift to get my passage to England. 'Tis but about a week since I landed, and I am going to end my days in the arms of my son. This sum may be of use to him and his children; 'tis all the value I put upon it. I thank Heaven I never was covetous of wealth; I never had much, but was always so happy as to be content with my little."

When Edwards had ended his relation, Harley stood a while looking at him in silence; at last he pressed him in his arms, and when he had given vent to the fulness of his heart by a shower of tears, "Edwards," said he, "let me hold thee to my bosom; let me imprint the virtue of thy sufferings on my soul. Come, my honoured veteran! let me endeavour to soften the last days of a life, worn out in the service of humanity: call me also thy son, and let me cherish thee as a father."

Edwards, from whom the recollection of his own sufferings had scarce forced a tear, now blubbered like a boy; he could not speak his gratitude, but by some short exclamations of blessings upon Harley.

CHAPTER XXXV

He Misses an Old Acquaintance—an Adventure Consequent Upon It

When they had arrived within a little way of the village they journeyed to, Harley stopped short, and looked steadfastly on the mouldering walls of a ruined house that stood on the road side. "Oh, heavens!" he cried, "what do I see: silent, unroofed, and desolate! Are all the gay tenants gone? do I hear their hum no more? Edwards, look there, look there! the scene of my infant joys, my earliest friendships, laid waste and ruinous! That was the very school where I was boarded when you were at South-hill; 'tis but a twelve-month since I saw it standing, and its benches filled with little cherubs: that opposite side of the road was the green on which they sported; see it now ploughed up! I would have given fifty times its value to have saved it from the sacrilege of that plough."

"Dear sir," replied Edwards, "perhaps they have left it from choice, and may have got another spot as good."

"They cannot," said Harley, "they cannot; I shall never see the sward covered with its daisies, nor pressed by the dance of the dear innocents: I shall never see that stump decked with the garlands which their little hands had gathered. These two long stones, which now lie at the foot of it, were once the supports of a hut I myself assisted to rear: I have sat on the sods within it, when we had spread our banquet of apples before us, and been more blessed—Oh! Edwards, infinitely more blessed, than ever I shall be again."

Just then a woman passed them on the road, and discovered some signs of wonder at the attitude of Harley, who stood, with his hands folded together, looking with a moistened eye on the fallen pillars of the hut. He was too much entranced in thought to observe her at all; but Edwards, civilly accosting her, desired to know if that had not been the school-house, and how it came into the condition in which they now saw it.

"Alack a day!" said she, "it was the school-house indeed; but to be sure, sir, the squire has pulled it down because it stood in the way of his prospects."

"What! how! prospects! pulled down!" cried Harley.

"Yes, to be sure, sir; and the green, where the children used to play, he has ploughed up, because, he said, they hurt his fence on the other side of it.——"

"Curses on his narrow heart," cried Harley, "that could violate a right so sacred! Heaven blast the wretch!

"And from his derogate body never spring
A babe to honour him!"——

But I need not, Edwards, I need not" (recovering himself a little), "he is cursed enough already: to him the noblest source of happiness is denied; and the cares of his sordid soul shall gnaw it, while thou sittest over a brown crust, smiling on those mangled limbs that have saved thy son and his children!"

"If you want anything with the school-mistress, sir," said the woman, "I can show you the way to her house." He followed her without knowing whither he went.

They stopped at the door of a snug habitation, where sat an elderly woman with a boy and a girl before her, each of whom held a supper of bread and milk in their hands.

"There, sir, is the school-mistress."

"Madam," said Harley, "was not an old venerable man school-master here some time ago?"

"Yes, sir, he was, poor man; the loss of his former school-house, I believe, broke his heart, for he died soon after it was taken down; and as another has not yet been found, I have that charge in the meantime."

"And this boy and girl, I presume, are your pupils?"

"Ay, sir; they are poor orphans, put under my care by the parish, and more promising children I never saw."

"Orphans?" said Harley.

"Yes, sir, of honest creditable parents as any in the parish; and it is a shame for some folks to forget their relations at a time when they have most need to remember them."

"Madame," said Harley, "let us never forget that we are all relations."

He kissed the children.

"Their father, sir," continued she, "was a farmer here in the neighbourhood, and a sober industrious man he was; but nobody can help misfortunes: what with bad crops, and bad debts, which are worse, his affairs went to wreck, and both he and his wife died of broken hearts. And a sweet couple they were, sir; there was not a properer man to look on in the county than John Edwards, and so indeed were all the Edwardses."

"What Edwardses?" cried the old soldier hastily.

"The Edwardses of South-hill; and a worthy family they were."

"South-hill!" said he, in a languid voice, and fell back into the arms of the astonished Harley. The school-mistress ran for some water and a smelling-bottle, with the assistance of which they soon recovered the unfortunate Edwards. He stared wildly for some time, then folding his orphan grand-children in his arms,

"Oh! my children, my children," he cried, "have I found you thus? My poor Jack, art thou gone? I thought thou shouldst have carried thy father's grey hairs to the grave! and these little ones"—his tears choked his utterance, and he fell again on the necks of the children.

"My dear old man!" said Harley, "Providence has sent you to relieve them; it will bless me if I can be the means of assisting you."

"Yes, indeed, sir," answered the boy; "father, when he was a-dying, bade God bless us; and prayed that if grandfather lived he might send him to support us."

"Where did they lay my boy?" said Edwards.

"In the Old Churchyard," replied the woman, "hard by his mother."

"I will show it you," answered the boy; "for I have wept over it many a time when first I came among strange folks."

He took the old man's hand, Harley laid hold of his sister's, and they walked in silence to the churchyard.

There was an old stone, with the corner broken off, and some letters, half-covered with moss, to denote the names of the dead: there was a cyphered R. E. plainer than the rest; it was the tomb they sought.

"Here it is, grandfather," said the boy.

Edwards gazed upon it without uttering a word: the girl, who had only sighed before, now wept outright: her brother sobbed, but he stifled his sobbing.

"I have told sister," said he, "that she should not take it so to heart; she can knit already, and I shall soon be able to dig: we shall not starve, sister, indeed we shall not, nor shall grandfather neither."

The girl cried afresh; Harley kissed off her tears as they flowed, and wept between every kiss.

CHAPTER XXXVI

He Returns Home—A Description of His Retinue

It was with some difficulty that Harley prevailed on the old man to leave the spot where the remains of his son were laid. At last, with the assistance of the school-mistress, he prevailed; and she accommodated Edwards and him with beds in her house, there being nothing like an inn nearer than the distance of some miles.

In the morning, Harley persuaded Edwards to come with the children to his house, which was distant but a short day's journey. The boy walked in his grandfather's hand; and the name of Edwards procured him a neighbouring farmer's horse, on which a servant mounted, with the girl on a pillow before him.

With this train Harley returned to the abode of his fathers: and we cannot but think, that his enjoyment was as great as if he had arrived from the tour of Europe with a Swiss valet for his companion, and half a dozen snuff-boxes, with invisible hinges, in his pocket. But we take our ideas from sounds which folly has invented; Fashion, Bon ton, and Vertù, are the names of certain idols, to which we sacrifice the genuine pleasures of the soul: in this world of semblance, we are contented with personating happiness; to feel it is an art beyond us.

It was otherwise with Harley; he ran upstairs to his aunt with the history of his fellow-travellers glowing on his lips. His aunt was an economist; but she knew the pleasure of doing charitable things, and withal was fond of her nephew, and solicitous to oblige him. She received old Edwards therefore with a look of more complacency than is perhaps natural to maiden ladies of three-score, and was remarkably attentive to his grandchildren: she roasted apples with her own hands for their supper, and made up a little bed beside her own for the girl. Edwards made some attempts towards an acknowledgment for these favours; but his young friend stopped them in their beginnings.

"Whosoever receiveth any of these children"—said his aunt; for her acquaintance with her Bible was habitual.

Early next morning Harley stole into the room where Edwards lay: he expected to have found him a-bed, but in this he was mistaken: the old man had risen, and was leaning over his sleeping grandson, with the tears flowing down his cheeks. At first he did not perceive Harley; when he did, he endeavoured to hide his grief, and crossing his eyes with his hand expressed his surprise at seeing him so early astir.

"I was thinking of you," said Harley, "and your children: I learned last night that a small farm of mine in the neighbourhood is now vacant: if you will occupy it I shall gain a good neighbour and be able in some measure to repay the notice you took of me when a boy, and as the furniture of the house is mine, it will be so much trouble saved."

Edwards' tears gushed afresh, and Harley led him to see the place he intended for him.

The house upon this farm was indeed little better than a hut; its situation, however, was pleasant, and Edwards, assisted by the beneficence of Harley, set about improving its neatness and convenience. He staked out a piece of the green before for a garden, and Peter, who acted in Harley's family as valet, butler, and gardener, had orders to furnish him with parcels of the different seeds he chose to sow in it. I have seen his master at work in this little spot with his coat off, and his dibble in his hand: it was a scene of tranquil virtue to have stopped an angel on his errands of mercy! Harley had contrived to lead a little bubbling brook through a green walk in the middle of the ground, upon which he had erected a mill in miniature for the diversion of Edwards' infant grandson, and made shift in its construction to introduce a pliant bit of wood that answered with its fairy clack to the murmuring of the rill that turned it. I have seen him stand, listening to these mingled sounds, with his eye fixed on the boy, and the smile of conscious satisfaction on his cheek; while the old man, with a look half turned to Harley and half to Heaven, breathed an ejaculation of gratitude and piety.

Father of mercies! I also would thank thee that not only hast thou assigned eternal rewards to virtue, but that, even in this bad world, the lines of our duty and our happiness are so frequently woven together.

.   .   .   .   .   .

A FRAGMENT

The Man of Feeling Talks of What He Does Not Understand—An Incident

· · · "Edwards," said he, "I have a proper regard for the prosperity of my country: every native of it appropriates to himself some share of the power, or the fame, which, as a nation, it acquires, but I cannot throw off the man so much as to rejoice at our conquests in India. You tell me of immense territories subject to the English: I cannot think of their possessions without being led to enquire by what right they possess them. They came there as traders, bartering the commodities they brought for others which their purchasers could spare; and however great their profits were, they were then equitable. But what title have the subjects of another kingdom to establish an empire in India? to give laws to a country where the inhabitants received them on the terms of friendly commerce? You say they are happier under our regulations than under the tyranny of their own petty princes. I must doubt it, from the conduct of those by whom these regulations have been made. They have drained the treasuries of Nabobs, who must fill them by oppressing the industry of their subjects. Nor is this to be wondered at, when we consider the motive upon which those gentlemen do not deny their going to India. The fame of conquest, barbarous as that motive is, is but a secondary consideration: there are certain stations in wealth, as well as in rank and honour, to which the warriors of the East aspire. It is there, indeed, where the wishes of their friends assign them eminence, and to that object the question of their country is pointed at their return. When shall I see a commander return from India in the pride of honourable poverty?—You describe the victories they have gained; they are sullied by the cause in which they fought: you enumerate the spoils of those victories; they are covered with the blood of the vanquished!

"Could you tell me of some conqueror giving peace and happiness to the conquered? did he accept the gifts of their princes to use them for the comfort of those whose fathers, sons, or husbands, fell in battle? did he use his power to gain security and freedom to the regions of oppression and slavery? did he endear the British name by examples of generosity, which the most barbarous or most depraved are rarely able to resist? did he return with the consciousness of duty discharged to his country, and humanity to his fellow-creatures? did he return with no lace on his coat, no slaves in his retinue, no chariot at his door, and no burgundy at his table?—these were laurels which princes might envy—which an honest man would not condemn!"

"Your maxims, Mr. Harley, are certainly right," said Edwards. "I am not capable of arguing with you; but I imagine there are great temptations in a great degree of riches, which it is no easy matter to resist: those a poor man like me cannot describe, because he never knew them; and perhaps I have reason to bless God that I never did; for then, it is likely, I should have withstood them no better than my neighbours. For you know, sir, that it is not the fashion now, as it was in former times, that I have read of in books, when your great generals died so poor, that they did not leave wherewithal to buy them a coffin; and people thought the better of their memories for it: if they did so now-a-days, I question if any body, except yourself, and some few like you, would thank them."

"I am sorry," replied Harley, "that there is so much truth in what you say; but however the general current of opinion may point, the feelings are not yet lost that applaud benevolence, and censure inhumanity. Let us endeavour to strengthen them in ourselves; and we, who live sequestered from the noise of the multitude, have better opportunities of listening undisturbed to their voices."

They now approached the little dwelling of Edwards. A maid-servant, whom he had hired to assist him in the care of his grandchildren, met them a little way from the house: "There is a young lady within with the children," said she. Edwards expressed his surprise at the visit: it was however not the less true; and we mean to account for it.

This young lady then was no other than Miss Walton. She had heard the old man's history from Harley, as we have already related it. Curiosity, or some other motive, made her desirous to see his grandchildren; this she had an opportunity of gratifying soon, the children, in some of their walks, having strolled as far as her father's avenue. She put several questions to both; she was delighted with the simplicity of their answers, and promised, that if they continued to be good children, and do as their grandfather bid them, she would soon see them again, and bring some present or other for their reward. This promise she had performed now: she came attended only by her maid, and brought with her a complete suit of green for the boy, and a chintz gown, a cap, and a suit of ribands, for his sister. She had time enough, with her maid's assistance, to equip them in their new habiliments before Harley and Edwards returned. The boy heard his grandfather's voice; and, with that silent joy which his present finery inspired, ran to the door to meet him: putting one hand in his, with the other pointing to his sister, "See," said he, "what Miss Walton has brought us?" —Edwards gazed on them. Harley fixed his eyes on Miss Walton; hers were turned to the ground;—in Edwards' was a beamy moisture.—He folded his hands together—"I cannot speak, young lady," he said, "to thank you." Neither could Harley. There were a thousand sentiments; but they gushed so impetuously on his heart, that he could not utter a syllable.

·　　·　　·　　·　　·　　·　　·

CHAPTER XL

The Man of Feeling Jealous

The desire of communicating knowledge or intelligence, is an argument with those who hold that man is naturally a social animal. It is indeed one of the earliest propensities we discover; but it may be doubted whether the pleasure (for pleasure there certainly is) arising from it be not often more selfish than social: for we frequently observe the tidings of Ill communicated as eagerly as the annunciation of Good. Is it that we delight in observing the effects of the stronger passions? for we are all philosophers in this respect; and it is perhaps amongst the spectators at Tyburn that the most genuine are to be found.

Was it from this motive that Peter came one morning into his master's room with a meaning face of recital? His master indeed did not at first observe it; for he was sitting with one shoe buckled, delineating portraits in the fire. "I have brushed those clothes, sir, as you ordered me."—Harley nodded his head; but Peter observed that his hat wanted brushing too: his master nodded again. At last Peter bethought him that the fire needed stirring; and taking up the poker, demolished the turban'd head of a Saracen, while his master was seeking out a body for it. "The morning is main cold, sir," said Peter. "Is it?" said Harley. "Yes, sir; I have been as far as Tom Dowson's to fetch some barberries he had picked for Mrs. Margery. There was a rare junketting last night at Thomas's among Sir Harry Benson's servants; he lay at Squire Walton's, but he would not suffer his servants to trouble the family: so, to be sure, they were all at Tom's, and had a fiddle, and a hot supper in the big room where the justices meet about the destroying of hares and partridges, and them things; and Tom's eyes looked so red and so bleared when I called him to get the barberries:—And I hear as how Sir Harry is going to be married to Miss Walton."—"How! Miss Walton married!" said Harley. "Why, it mayn't be true, sir, for all that: but Tom's wife told it me, and to be sure the servants told her, and their master told them, as I guess, sir; but it mayn't be true for all that, as I said before."—Have done with your idle information," said Harley:—"Is my aunt come down into the parlour to breakfast?"—"Yes, sir."—"Tell her I'll be with her immediately."

When Peter was gone, he stood with his eyes fixed on the ground, and the last words of his intelligence vibrating in his ears. "Miss Walton married!" he sighed—and walked down stairs, with his shoe as it was, and the buckle in his hand. His aunt, however, was pretty well accustomed to those appearances of absence; besides, that the natural gravity of her temper, which was commonly called into exertion by the care of her household concerns, was such as not easily to be discomposed by any circumstance of accidental impropriety. She too had been informed of the intended match between Sir Harry Benson and Miss Walton. "I have been thinking," said she, "that they are distant relations: for the great grandfather of this Sir Harry Benson, who was knight of the shire in the reign of Charles the First, and one of the cavaliers of those times, was married to a daughter of the Walton family." Harley answered drily, that it might be so; but that he never troubled himself about those matters. "Indeed," said she, "you are to blame, nephew, for not knowing a little more of them: before I was near your age I had sewed the pedigree of our family in a set of chair-bottoms, that were made a present of to my grandmother, who was a very notable woman, and had a proper regard for gentility, I'll assure you; but now-a-days it is money, not birth, that makes people respected; the more shame for the times."

Harley was in no very good humour for entering into a discussion of this question; but he always entertained so much filial respect for his aunt, as to attend to her discourse.

"We blame the pride of the rich," said he, "but are not we ashamed of our poverty?"

"Why, one would not choose," replied his aunt, "to make a much worse figure than one's neighbours; but, as I was saying before, the times (as my friend, Mrs. Dorothy Walton, observes) are shamefully degenerated in this respect. There was but t'other day at Mr. Walton's, that fat fellow's daughter, the London merchant, as he calls himself, though I have heard that he was little better than the keeper of a chandler's shop: —We were leaving the gentlemen to go to tea. She had a hoop, forsooth, as large and as stiff—and it showed a pair of bandy legs, as thick as two——I was nearer the door by an apron's length, and the pert hussy brushed by me, as who should say, Make way for your betters, and with one of her London bobs— but Mrs. Dorothy did not let her pass with it; for all the time of drinking tea, she spoke of the precedency of family, and the disparity there is between people who are come of something and your mushroom gentry who wear their coats of arms in their purses."

Her indignation was interrupted by the arrival of her maid with a damask table-cloth, and a set of napkins, from the loom, which had been spun by her mistress's own hand. There was the family crest in each corner, and in the middle a view of the battle of Worcester, where one of her ancestors had been a captain in the king's forces; and with a sort of poetical licence in perspective, there was seen the Royal Oak, with more wig than leaves upon it.

On all this the good lady was very copious, and took up the remaining intervals of filling tea, to describe its excellencies to Harley; adding, that she intended this as a present for his wife, when he should get one. He sighed and looked foolish, and commending the serenity of the day, walked out into the garden.

He sat down on a little seat which commanded an extensive prospect round the house. He leaned on his hand, and scored the ground with his stick: "Miss Walton married!" said he; "but what is that to me? May she be happy! her virtues deserve it; to me her marriage is otherwise indifferent:—I had romantic dreams! they are fled!—it is perfectly indifferent."

Just at that moment he saw a servant with a knot of ribands in his hat, go into the house. His cheeks grew flushed at the sight! He kept his eye fixed for some time on the door by which he had entered, then starting to his feet, hastily followed him.

When he approached the door of the kitchen where he supposed the man had entered, his heart throbbed so violently, that when he would have called Peter, his voice failed in the attempt. He stood a moment listening in this breathless state of palpitation: Peter came out by chance. "Did your honour want any thing?"—"Where is the servant that came just now from Mr. Walton's?"——"From Mr. Walton's, sir! there is none of his servants here that I know of."—"Nor of Sir Harry Benson's?"—He did not wait for an answer; but having by this time observed the hat with its parti-coloured ornament hanging on a peg near the door, he pressed forwards into the kitchen, and addressing himself to a stranger whom he saw there, asked him, with no small tremor in his voice, "If he had any commands for him?" The man looked silly, and said, "That he had nothing to trouble his honour with."—"Are not you a servant of Sir Harry Benson's?"—"No, sir."—"You'll pardon me, young man; I judged by the favour in your hat."—"Sir, I'm his majesty's servant, God bless him! and these favours we always wear when we are recruiting."—"Recruiting!" his eyes glistened at the word: he seized the soldier's hand, and shaking it violently, ordered Peter to fetch a bottle of his aunt's best dram. The bottle was brought: "You shall drink the king's health," said Harley, "in a bumper."——"The king and your honour."—"Nay, you shall drink the king's health by itself; you may drink mine in another." Peter looked in his master's face, and filled with some little reluctance. "Now to your mistress," said Harley; "every soldier has a mistress." The man excused himself—"To your mistress! you cannot refuse it." 'Twas Mrs. Margery's best dram! Peter stood with the bottle a little inclined, but not so as to discharge a drop of its contents: "Fill it, Peter," said his master, "fill it to the brim."

Peter filled it; and the soldier having named Suky Simpson, dispatched it in a twinkling. "Thou art an honest fellow," said Harley, "and I love thee;" and shaking his hand again, desired Peter to make him his guest at dinner, and walked up into his room with a pace much quicker and more springy than usual.

This agreeable disappointment, however, he was not long suffered to enjoy. The curate happened that day to dine with him: his visits, indeed, were more properly to the aunt than the nephew; and many of the intelligent ladies in the parish, who, like some very great philosophers, have the happy knack at accounting for everything, gave out that there was a particular attachment between them, which wanted only to be matured by some more years of courtship to end in the tenderest con- nection. In this conclusion, indeed, supposing the premises to have been true, they were somewhat justified by the known opinion of the lady, who frequently declared herself a friend to the ceremonial of former times, when a lover might have sighed seven years at his mistress's feet before he was allowed the liberty of kissing her hand. 'Tis true Mrs. Margery was now about her grand climacteric;[7] no matter: that is just the age when we expect to grow younger. But I verily believe there was nothing in the report; the curate's connection was only that of a genealogist; for in that character he was no way inferior to Mrs. Margery herself. He dealt also in the present times; for he was a politician and a news-monger.

He had hardly said grace after dinner, when he told Mrs. Margery that she might soon expect a pair of white gloves, as Sir Harry Benson, he was very well informed, was just going to be married to Miss Walton. Harley spilt the wine he was carrying to his mouth: he had time, however, to recollect him- self before the curate had finished the different particulars of his intelligence, and summoning up all the heroism he was master of, filled a bumper, and drank to Miss Walton. "With all my heart," said the curate, "the bride that is to be." Harley would have said bride too; but the word bride stuck in his throat. His confusion, indeed, was manifest; but the curate began to enter on some point of descent with Mrs. Margery, and Harley had very soon after an opportunity of leaving them, while they were deeply engaged in a question, whether the name of some great man in the time of Henry the Seventh was Richard or Humphrey.

He did not see his aunt again till supper; the time between he spent in walking, like some troubled ghost, round the place where his treasure lay. He went as far as a little gate, that led into a copse near Mr. Walton's house, to which that gentleman had been so obliging as to let him have a key. He had just begun to open it when he saw, on a terrace below, Miss Walton walking with a gentleman in a riding-dress, whom he immediately guessed to be Sir Harry Benson. He stopped of a sudden; his hand shook so much that he could hardly turn the key; he opened the gate, however, and advanced a few paces. The lady's lap-dog pricked up its ears, and barked; he stopped again—

> ————"the little dogs and all,
> Tray, Blanch, and Sweetheart, see they bark at me!"

His resolution failed; he slunk back, and, locking the gate as softly as he could, stood on tiptoe looking over the wall till they were gone. At that instant a shepherd blew his horn: the romantic melancholy of the sound quite overcame him!—it was the very note that wanted to be touched—he sighed! he dropped a tear!—and returned.

At supper his aunt observed that he was graver than usual; but she did not suspect the cause: indeed, it may seem odd that she was the only person in the family who had no suspicion of his attachment to Miss Walton. It was frequently matter of discourse amongst the servants: perhaps her maiden coldness—but for those things we need not account.

In a day or two he was so much master of himself as to be able to rhyme upon the subject. The following pastoral he left, some time after, on the handle of a tea-kettle, at a neighbouring house where we were visiting; and as I filled the teapot after him, I happened to put it in my pocket by a similar act of forgetfulness. It is such as might be expected from a man who makes verses for amusement. I am pleased with somewhat of good nature that runs through it, because I have commonly

observed the writers of those complaints to bestow epithets on
their lost mistresses rather too harsh for the mere liberty of
choice, which led them to prefer another to the poet himself:
I do not doubt the vehemence of their passion; but, alas! the
sensations of love are something more than the returns of
gratitude.

Lavinia.

A PASTORAL.

Why steals from my bosom the sigh?
    Why fixed is my gaze on the ground?
Come, give me my pipe, and I'll try
    To banish my cares with the sound.

Erewhile were its notes of accord
    With the smile of the flow'r-footed Muse;
Ah! why by its master implored
    Shou'd it now the gay carol refuse?

'Twas taught by LAVINIA's sweet smile,
    In the mirth-loving chorus to join:
Ah me! how unweeting the while!
    LAVINIA——cannot be mine!

Another, more happy, the maid
    By fortune is destin'd to bless——
'Tho' the hope has forsook that betray'd,
    Yet why should I love her the less?

Her beauties are bright as the morn,
    With rapture I counted them o'er;
Such virtues these beauties adorn,
    I knew her, and prais'd them no more.

I term'd her no goddess of love,
    I call'd not her beauty divine:
These far other passions may prove,
    But they could not be figures of mine.

It ne'er was apparel'd with art,
    On words it could never rely;
It reign'd in the throb of my heart,
    It spoke in the glance of my eye.

Oh fool! in the circle to shine
    That Fashion's gay daughters approve,
You must speak as the fashions incline;—
    Alas! are there fashions in love?

Yet sure they are simple who prize
    The tongue that is smooth to deceive;
Yet sure she had sense to despise,
    The tinsel that Folly may weave.

When I talk'd, I have seen her recline,
    With an aspect so pensively sweet,—
Tho' I spoke what the shepherds opine,
    A fop were ashamed to repeat.

She is soft as the dew-drops that fall
    From the lip of the sweet-scented pea;
Perhaps when she smil'd upon all,
    I have thought that she smil'd upon me.

But why of her charms should I tell?
    Ah me! whom her charms have undone!
Yet I love the reflection too well,
    The painful reflection to shun.

Ye souls of more delicate kind,
    Who feast not on pleasure alone,
Who wear the soft sense of the mind,
    To the sons of the world still unknown.

Ye know, tho' I cannot express,
    Why I foolishly doat on my pain;
Nor will ye believe it the less
    That I have not the skill to complain.

I lean on my hand with a sigh,
    My friends the soft sadness condemn;

Yet, methinks, tho' I cannot tell why,
   I should hate to be merry like them.

When I walk'd in the pride of the dawn,
   Methought all the region look'd bright:
Has sweetness forsaken the lawn?
   For, methinks, I grow sad at the sight.

When I stood by the stream, I have thought
   There was mirth in the gurgling soft sound;
But now 'tis a sorrowful note,
   And the banks are all gloomy around!

I have laugh'd at the jest of a friend;
   Now they laugh, and I know not the cause,
Tho' I seem with my looks to attend,
   How silly! I ask what it was.

They sing the sweet song of the May,
   They sing it with mirth and with glee;
Sure I once thought the sonnet was gay,
   But now 'tis all sadness to me.

Oh! give me the dubious light
   That gleams thro' the quivering shade;
Oh! give me the horrors of night,
   By gloom and by silence array'd!

Let me walk where the soft-rising wave,
   Has pictur'd the moon on its breast:
Let me walk where the new cover'd grave
   Allows the pale lover to rest!

When shall I in its peaceable womb,
   Be laid with my sorrows asleep!
Should LAVINIA but chance on my tomb—
   I could die if I thought she would weep.

Perhaps, if the souls of the just
   Revisit these mansions of care,
It may be my favourite trust
   To watch o'er the fate of the fair.

Perhaps the soft thought of her breast,
    With rapture more favour'd to warm;
Perhaps, if with sorrow oppress'd,
    Her sorrow with patience to arm.

Then! then! in the tenderest part
    May I whisper, "Poor COLIN was true,"
And mark if a heave of her heart
    The thought of her COLIN pursue.

     •   •   •   •   •   •

THE PUPIL

A Fragment

· · · "But as to the higher part of education, Mr. Harley, the culture of the mind;—let the feelings be awakened, let the heart be brought forward to its object, placed in the light in which nature would have it stand, and its decisions will ever be just. The world

Will smile, and smile, and be a villain;

and the youth, who does not suspect its deceit, will be content to smile with it. His teachers will put on the most forbidding aspect in nature, and tell him of the beauty of virtue.

"I have not, under these grey hairs, forgotten that I was once a young man, warm in the pursuit of pleasure, but meaning to be honest as well as happy. I had ideas of virtue, of honour, of benevolence, which I had never been at the pains to define; but I felt my bosom heave at the thoughts of them, and I made the most delightful soliloquies.—It is impossible, said I, that there can be half so many rogues as are imagined.

"I travelled, because it is the fashion for young men of my fortune to travel. I had a travelling tutor, which is the fashion too; but my tutor was a gentleman, which it is not always the fashion for tutors to be. His gentility, indeed, was all he had from his father, whose prodigality had not left him a shilling to support it.

" 'I have a favor to ask of you, my dear Mountford,' said my father, 'which I will not be refused. You have travelled as became a man; neither France nor Italy have made anything of Mountford, which Mountford, before he left England, would

214

have been ashamed of. My son Edward goes abroad, would you take him under your protection?'

"He blushed—my father's face was scarlet.—He pressed his hand to his bosom, as if he had said,—my heart does not mean to offend you. Mountford sighed twice.

" 'I am a proud fool,' said he, 'and you will pardon it. There! (he sighed again) I can hear of dependence, since it is dependence on my Sedley.'

" 'Dependence!' answered my father; 'there can be no such word between us. What is there in £9,000 a year that should make me unworthy of Mountford's friendship?'

"They embraced; and soon after I set out on my travels, with Mountford for my guardian.

"We were at Milan, where my father happened to have an Italian friend, to whom he had been of some service in England. The count, for he was of quality, was solicitous to return the obligation by a particular attention to his son. We lived in his palace, visited with his family, were caressed by his friends, and I began to be so well pleased with my entertainment, that I thought of England as of some foreign country.

"The count had a son not much older than myself. At that age a friend is an easy acquisition: we were friends the first night of our acquaintance.

"He introduced me into the company of a set of young gentlemen, whose fortunes gave them the command of pleasure, and whose inclinations incited them to the purchase. After having spent some joyous evenings in their society, it became a sort of habit which I could not miss without uneasiness; and our meetings, which before were frequent, were now stated and regular.

"Sometimes, in the pauses of our mirth, gaming was introduced as an amusement: it was an art in which I was a novice. I received instruction, as other novices do, by losing pretty largely to my teachers. Nor was this the only evil which Mountford foresaw would arise from the connection I had formed; but a lecture of sour injunctions was not his method of reclaiming. He sometimes asked me questions about the company, but they were such as the curiosity of any indifferent man might have prompted. I told him of their wit, their eloquence, their warmth of friendship, and their sensibility of heart. 'And their honour,' said I, laying my hand on my breast, 'is unquestionable.' Mountford seemed to rejoice at my good fortune, and begged that I would introduce him to their acquaintance. At the next meeting I introduced him accordingly.

"The conversation was as animated as usual; they displayed all that sprightliness and good-humour which my praises had led Mountford to expect; subjects too of sentiment occurred, and their speeches, particularly those of our friend the son of Count Respino, glowed with the warmth of honour, and softened into the tenderness of feeling. Mountford was charmed with his companions; when we parted, he made the highest eulogiums upon them. 'When shall we see them again?' said he. I was delighted with the demand, and promised to reconduct him on the morrow.

"In going to their place of rendezvous, he took me a little out of the road, to see, as he told me, the performances of a young statuary. When we were near the house in which Mountford said he lived, a boy of about seven years old crossed us in the street. At sight of Mountford he stopped, and grasping his hand,

" 'My dearest sir,' said he, 'my father is likely to do well. He will live to pray for you, and to bless you. Yes, he will bless you, though you are an Englishman, and some other hard word that the monk talked of this morning, which I have forgot, but it meant that you should not go to heaven; but he shall go to heaven, said I, for he has saved my father. Come and see him, sir, that we may be happy.'

" 'My dear, I am engaged at present with this gentleman.'

" 'But he shall come along with you; he is an Englishman, too, I fancy. He shall come and learn how an Englishman may go to heaven.'

"Mountford smiled, and we followed the boy together.

"After crossing the next street, we arrived at the gate of a prison. I seemed surprised at the sight; our little conductor observed it.

" 'Are you afraid, sir?' said he. 'I was afraid once too, but my father and mother are here, and I am never afraid when I am with them.'

"He took my hand, and led me through a dark passage that fronted the gate. When we came to a little door at the end, he tapped. A boy, still younger than himself, opened it to receive us. Mountford entered with a look in which was pictured the benign assurance of a superior being. I followed in silence and amazement.

"On something like a bed, lay a man, with a face seemingly emaciated with sickness, and a look of patient dejection; a bundle of dirty shreds served him for a pillow, but he had a better support—the arm of a female who kneeled beside him, beautiful as an angel, but with a fading languor in her countenance, the still life of melancholy, that seemed to borrow its shade from the object on which she gazed. There was a tear in her eye!—the sick man kissed it off in its bud, smiling through the dimness of his own!—when she saw Mountford, she crawled forward on the ground, and clasped his knees. He raised her from the floor; she threw her arms round his neck, and sobbed out a speech of thankfulness, eloquent beyond the power of language.

" 'Compose yourself, my love,' said the man on the bed; 'but he, whose goodness has caused that emotion, will pardon its effects.'

" 'How is this, Mountford?' said I; 'what do I see? What must I do?'

" 'You see,' replied the stranger, 'a wretch, sunk in poverty, starving in prison, stretched on a sick bed! but that is little: there are his wife and children wanting the bread which he has not to give them! Yet you cannot easily imagine the conscious serenity of his mind; in the grip of affliction, his heart swells with the pride of virtue! it can even look down with pity on the man whose cruelty has wrung it almost to bursting. You are, I fancy, a friend of Mr. Mountford's. Come nearer, and I'll tell you, for, short as my story is, I can hardly command breath enough for a recital. The son of Count Respino (I started, as if I had trod on a viper) has long had a criminal passion for my wife; this her prudence had concealed from me; but he had lately the boldness to declare it to myself. He promised me affluence in exchange for honour, and threatened misery as its attendant if I kept it. I treated him with the contempt he deserved; the consequence was, that he hired a couple of bravoes (for I am persuaded they acted under his direction), who attempted to assassinate me in the street; but I made such a defence as obliged them to fly, after having given me two or three stabs, none of which however were mortal. But his revenge was not thus to be disappointed: in the little dealings of my trade I had contracted some debts, of which he had made himself master for my ruin; I was confined here at his suit, when not yet recovered from the wounds I had received; this dear woman, and these two boys, followed me, that we might starve together; but Providence interposed, and sent Mr. Mountford to our support: he has relieved my family from the gnawings of hunger, and rescued me from death, to which a fever, consequent on my wounds and increased by the want of every necessary, had almost reduced me."

" 'Inhuman villain!' I exclaimed, lifting up my eyes to heaven.

" 'Inhuman indeed!' said the lovely woman who stood at my side. 'Alas! sir, what had we done to offend him? what had these little ones done, that they should perish in the toils of his vengeance?'—

"I reached a pen which stood in the ink-standish at the bed-side—

" 'May I ask what is the amount of the sum for which you are imprisoned?'

" 'I was able,' he replied, 'to pay all but 500 crowns.'

"I wrote a draft on the banker with whom I had a credit from my father for 2,500, and presenting it to the stranger's wife,

" 'You will receive, madam, on presenting this note, a sum more than sufficient for your husband's discharge; the remainder I leave for his industry to improve.'

"I would have left the room. Each of them laid hold of one of my hands, the children clung to my coat. Oh! Mr. Harley, methinks I feel their gentle violence at this moment; it beats here with delight inexpressible!

" 'Stay, sir,' said he, 'I do not mean attempting to thank you' (he took a pocket-book from under his pillow), 'let me but know what name I shall place here next to Mr. Mountford?'

" 'Sedley.'

"He writ it down.

" 'An Englishman too, I presume.'

" 'He shall go to heaven, notwithstanding,' said the boy who had been our guide.

"It began to be too much for me; I squeezed his hand that was clasped in mine, his wife's I pressed to my lips, and burst from the place to give vent to the feelings that laboured within me.

" 'Oh, Mountford!' said I, when he had overtaken me at the door.

" 'It is time,' replied he, 'that we should think of our appointment; young Respino and his friends are waiting us.'

" 'Damn him, damn him!' said I. 'Let us leave Milan instantly; but soft—I will be calm; Mountford, your pencil.' I wrote on a slip of paper,

To Signor RESPINO,

" 'When you receive this, I am at a distance from Milan. Accept of my thanks for the civilities I have received from you and your family. As to the friendship with which you were pleased to honour me, the prison, which I have just left, has exhibited a scene to cancel it for ever. You may possibly be merry with your companions at my weakness, as I suppose you will term it. I give you leave for derision. You may affect a triumph; I shall feel it.

" 'EDWARD SEDLEY.'

" 'You may send this if you will,' said Mountford, coolly; 'but still Respino is *a man of honour;* the world will continue to call him so.'

" 'It is probable,' I answered, 'they may; I envy not the

appellation. If this is the world's honour, if these men are the guides of its manners——'

"'Tut!' said Mountford, 'do you eat macaroni——'"

.   .   .   .   .   .

[At this place had the greatest depredations of the curate begun. There were so very few connected passages of the subsequent chapters remaining, that even the partiality of an editor could not offer them to the public. I discovered, from some scattered sentences, that they were of much the same tenor with the preceding; recitals of little adventures, in which the dispositions of a man, sensible to judge, and still more warm to feel, had room to unfold themselves. Some instruction, and some example, I make no doubt they contained; but it is likely that many of those, whom chance has led to a perusal of what I have already presented, may have read it with little pleasure, and will feel no disappointment from the want of those parts which I have been unable to procure; to such as may have expected the intricacies of a novel, a few incidents in a life undistinguished, except by some features of the heart, cannot have afforded much entertainment.

Harley's own story, from the mutilated passages I have mentioned, as well as from some enquiries I was at the trouble of making in the country, I found to have been simple to excess. His mistress, I could perceive, was not married to Sir Harry Benson; but it would seem, by one of the following chapters, which is still entire, that Harley had not profited on the occasion by making any declaration of his own passion, after those of the other had been unsuccessful. The state of his health, for some part of this period, appears to have been such as to forbid any thoughts of that kind: he had been seized with a very dangerous fever, caught by attending old Edwards in one of an infectious kind. From this he had recovered but imperfectly, and though he had no formed complaint, his health was manifestly on the decline.

It appears that the sagacity of some friend had at length pointed out to his aunt a cause from which this might be supposed to proceed, to wit, his hopeless love for Miss Walton; for, according to the conceptions of the world, the love of a man of Harley's fortune for the heiress of £4,000 a year, is indeed desperate. Whether it was so in this case may be gathered from the next chapter, which, with the two subsequent, concluding the performance, have escaped those accidents that proved fatal to the rest.]

CHAPTER LV

He Sees Miss Walton, and Is Happy

Harley was one of those few friends whom the malevolence of fortune had yet left me: I could not therefore but be sensibly concerned for his present indisposition; there seldom passed a day on which I did not make enquiry about him.

The physician who attended him had informed me the evening before, that he thought him considerably better than he had been for some time past. I called next morning to be confirmed in a piece of intelligence so welcome to me.

When I entered his apartment, I found him sitting on a couch, leaning on his hand, with his eye turned upwards in the attitude of thoughtful inspiration. His look had always an open benignity, which commanded esteem; there was now something more—a gentle triumph in it.

He rose, and met me with his usual kindness. When I gave him the good accounts I had had from his physician, "I am foolish enough," said he, "to rely but little, in this instance, upon physic: my presentiment may be false; but I think I feel myself approaching to my end, by steps so easy, that they woo me to approach it.

"There is a certain dignity in retiring from life at a time, when the infirmities of age have not sapped our faculties. This world, my dear Charles, was a scene in which I never much delighted. I was not formed for the bustle of the busy, nor the dissipation of the gay; a thousand things occurred, where I blushed for the impropriety of my conduct when I thought on the world, though my reason told me I should have blushed to have done otherwise.—It was a scene of dissimulation, of restraint, of disappointment. I leave it to enter on that state which I have learned to believe is replete with the genuine happiness attendant upon virtue. I look back on the tenor of my life, with the consciousness of few great offences to account for. There are blemishes, I confess, which deform in some degree the picture. But I know the benignity of the Supreme Being, and rejoice at the thoughts of its exercises in my favour. My mind expands at the thought I shall enter into the society of the blessed, wise as angels, with the simplicity of children." He had by this time clasped my hand, and found it wet by a tear which had just fallen upon it.—His eye began to moisten too—we sat for some time silent.—At last, with an attempt to a look of more composure, "There are some remembrances," said Harley, "which rise involuntarily on my heart, and make me almost wish to live. I have been blessed with a few friends, who redeem my opinion of mankind. I recollect, with the tenderest emotion, the scenes of pleasure I have passed among them; but we shall meet again, my friend, never to be separated. There are some feelings which perhaps are too tender to be suffered by the world. The world is in general selfish, interested, and unthinking, and throws the imputation of romance or melancholy on every temper more susceptible than its own. I cannot think but in those regions which I contemplate, if there is anything of mortality left about us, that these feelings will subsist;—they are called,—perhaps they are—weaknesses here;—but there may be some better modifications of them in heaven, which may deserve the name of virtues." He sighed as he spoke these last words. He had scarcely finished them, when the door opened, and his aunt appeared, leading in Miss Walton.

"My dear," said she, "here is Miss Walton, who has been so kind as to come and enquire for you herself." I could observe a transient glow upon his face. He rose from his seat—"If to know Miss Walton's goodness," said he, "be a title to deserve it, I have some claim." She begged him to resume his seat, and placed herself on the sofa beside him. I took my leave. Mrs. Margery accompanied me to the door. He was left with Miss Walton alone. She enquired anxiously about his health. "I believe," said he, "from the accounts which my physicians unwillingly give me, that they have no great hopes of my recovery."—She started as he spoke; but recollecting herself immediately, endeavoured to flatter him into a belief that his apprehensions were groundless. "I know," said he, "that it is usual with persons at my time of life to have these hopes, which your kindness suggests; but I would not wish to be deceived. To meet death as becomes a man, is a privilege bestowed on few.—I would endeavour to make it mine;—nor do I think that I can ever be better prepared for it than now:—It is that chiefly which determines the fitness of its approach." "Those sentiments," answered Miss Walton, "are just; but your good sense, Mr. Harley, will own, that life has its proper value.—As the province of virtue, life is ennobled; as such, it is to be desired. —To virtue has the Supreme Director of all things assigned rewards enough even here to fix its attachment."

The subject began to overpower her.—Harley lifted his eyes from the ground—"There are," said he, in a very low voice, "there are attachments, Miss Walton"—His glance met hers.—They both betrayed a confusion, and were both instantly withdrawn.—He paused some moments—"I am in such a state as calls for sincerity, let that also excuse it—It is perhaps the last time we shall ever meet. I feel something particularly solemn in the acknowledgment, yet my heart swells to make it, awed as it is by a sense of my presumption, by a sense of your perfections"—He paused again—"Let it not offend you, to know their power over one so unworthy—It will, I believe, soon cease to beat, even with that feeling which it shall lose the latest.—To love Miss Walton could not be a crime;—if to declare it is one—the expiation will be made."—Her tears were now flowing without control.—"Let me entreat you," said she, "to have better hopes—Let not life be so indifferent to you; if my wishes can put any value on it—I will not pretend to misunderstand you—I know your worth—I have known it long —I have esteemed it—What would you have me say?—I have loved it as it deserved."— He seized her hand—a languid colour reddened his cheek—a smile brightened faintly in his eye. As he gazed on her, it grew dim, it fixed, it closed—He sighed and fell back on his seat—Miss Walton screamed at the sight—His aunt and the servants rushed into the room—They found them lying motionless together.—His physician happened to call at that instant. Every art was tried to recover them—With Miss Walton they succeeded—But Harley was gone for ever!

CHAPTER LVI

The Emotions of the Heart

I entered the room where his body lay; I approached it with reverence, not fear: I looked; the recollection of the past crowded upon me. I saw that form which, but a little before, was animated with a soul which did honour to humanity, stretched without sense or feeling before me. 'Tis a connection we cannot easily forget:—I took his hand in mine; I repeated his name involuntarily;—I felt a pulse in every vein at the sound. I looked earnestly in his face; his eye was closed, his lip pale and motionless. There is an enthusiasm in sorrow that forgets impossibility; I wondered that it was so. The sight drew a prayer from my heart: it was the voice of frailty and of man! the confusion of my mind began to subside into thought; I had time to weep!

I turned with the last farewell upon my lips, when I observed old Edwards standing behind me. I looked him full in the face; but his eye was fixed on another object: he pressed between me and the bed, and stood gazing on the breathless remains of his benefactor. I spoke to him I know not what; but he took no notice of what I said, and remained in the same attitude as before. He stood some minutes in that posture, then turned and walked towards the door. He paused as he went;— he returned a second time: I could observe his lips move as he looked: but the voice they would have uttered was lost. He attempted going again; and a third time he returned as before.— I saw him wipe his cheek: then covering his face with his hands, his breast heaving with the most convulsive throbs, he flung out of the room.

THE CONCLUSION

He had hinted that he should like to be buried in a certain spot near the grave of his mother. This is a weakness; but it is universally incident to humanity: 'tis at least a memorial for those who survive: for some indeed a slender memorial will serve; and the soft affections, when they are busy that way, will build their structures, were it but on the paring of a nail.

He was buried in the place he had desired. It was shaded by an old tree, the only one in the church-yard, in which was a cavity worn by time. I have sat with him in it, and counted the tombs. The last time we passed there, methought he looked wistfully on the tree: there was a branch of it that bent towards us waving in the wind; he waved his hand as if he mimicked its motion. There was something predictive in his look! perhaps it is foolish to remark it; but there are times and places when I am a child at those things.

I sometimes visit his grave; I sit in the hollow of the tree. It is worth a thousand homilies; every noble feeling rises within me! every beat of my heart awakens a virtue!—but it will make you hate the world——No: there is such an air of gentleness around, that I can hate nothing; but, as to the world—I pity the men of it.

THOMAS DAY

The History of Sandford and Merton

and Merton

(Abridged)

In the western part of England lived a gentleman of great fortune, whose name was Merton. He had a large estate in the island of Jamaica, where he had passed the greater part of his life, and was master of many servants, who cultivated sugar and other valuable things for his advantage. He had only one son, of whom he was excessively fond; and to educate this child properly was the reason of his determining to stay some years in England. Tommy Merton, who at the time he came from Jamaica, was only six years old, was naturally a very good-natured boy, but unfortunately had been spoiled by too much indulgence. While he lived in Jamaica, he had several black servants to wait upon him, who were forbidden upon any account to contradict him. If he walked, there always went two negroes with him, one of whom carried a large umbrella to keep the sun from him, and the other was to carry him in his arms, whenever he was tired. Besides this, he was always dressed in silk or laced clothes, and had a fine gilded carriage, which was borne upon men's shoulders, in which he made visits to his play-fellows. His mother was so excessively fond of him, that she gave him everything he cried for, and would never let him learn to read, because he complained that it made his head ache.

The consequence of this was, that, though Master Merton had everything he wanted, he became very fretful and unhappy. Sometimes he ate sweetmeats till he made himself sick, and then he suffered a great deal of pain, because he would not take bitter physic to make him well. Sometimes he cried for things that it was impossible to give him, and then, as he had never been used to be contradicted, it was many hours before he could be pacified. When any company came to dine at the house, he was always to be helped first, and to have the most delicate parts of the meat, otherwise he would make such a noise as disturbed the whole company. When his father and mother were sitting at the tea-table with their friends, instead of waiting till they were at leisure to attend to him, he would scramble upon the table, seize the cake and bread and butter, and frequently overset the tea-cups. By these pranks he not only made himself disagreeable to everybody, but often met with very dangerous accidents. Frequently has he cut himself with knives, at other times thrown heavy things upon his head, and once he narrowly escaped being scalded to death by a kettle of boiling water. He was also so delicately brought up, that he was perpetually ill; the least wind or rain gave him a cold, and the least sun was sure to throw him into a fever. Instead of playing about, and jumping, and running like other children, he was taught to sit still for fear of spoiling his clothes, and to stay in the house for fear of injuring his complection. By this kind of education, when Master Merton came over to England, he could neither write, nor read, nor cipher; he could use none of his limbs with ease, nor bear any degree of fatigue; but he was very proud, fretful, and impatient.

Very near to Mr. Merton's seat lived a plain, honest farmer, whose name was Sandford. This man had, like Mr. Merton, an only son, not much older than Master Merton, whose name was Harry. Harry, as he had been always accustomed to run about in the fields, to follow the labourers while they were ploughing, and to drive the sheep to their pasture, was active, strong, hardy, and fresh-coloured. He was neither so fair, nor so delicately shaped as Master Merton; but he had an honest, good-natured countenance, which made everybody love him; was never out of humour, and took the greatest pleasure in obliging everybody. If little Harry saw a poor wretch who wanted victuals, while he was eating his dinner, he was sure to give him half, and sometimes the whole: nay, so very good-natured was he to everything, that he would never go into the fields to take the eggs of poor birds, or their young ones, nor practice any other kind of sport which gave pain to poor animals, who are as capable of feeling as we ourselves, though they have no words to express their sufferings. Once, indeed,

Harry was caught twirling a cockchafer[1] round, which he had fastened by a crooked pin to a long piece of thread, but then this was through ignorance and want of thought: for as soon as his father told him that the poor helpless insect felt as much, or more than he would do, were a knife thrust through his hand, he burst into tears, and took the poor animal home, where he fed him during a fortnight upon fresh leaves; and when he was perfectly recovered, turned him out to enjoy liberty and the fresh air. Ever since that time, Harry was so careful and considerate, that he would step out of the way for fear of hurting a worm, and employed himself in doing kind offices to all the animals in the neighbourhood. He used to stroke the horses as they were at work, and fill his pockets with acorns for the pigs: if he walked in the fields, he was sure to gather green boughs for the sheep, who were so fond of him, that they followed him wherever he went. In the winter time, when the ground was covered with frost and snow, and the poor little birds could get at no food, he would often go supperless to bed, that he might feed the robin red-breasts. Even toads, and frogs, and spiders, and such kind of disagreeable animals, which most people destroy wherever they find them, were perfectly safe with Harry: he used to say they had a right to live as well as we, and that it was cruel and unjust to kill creatures only because we did not like them.

These sentiments made little Harry a great favourite with everybody; particularly with the clergyman of the parish, who became so fond of him, that he taught him to read and write, and had him almost always with him. Indeed, it was not surprising that Mr. Barlow showed so particular an affection for him; for, besides learning everything that he was taught with the greatest readiness, little Harry was the most honest, obliging creature in the world. He was never discontented, nor did he ever grumble, whatever he was desired to do. And then you might believe Harry in everything he said; for though he could have gained a plumcake by telling an untruth, and was sure that speaking the truth would expose him to a severe whipping, he never hesitated in declaring it. Nor was he like many other children, who place their whole happiness in eating:

for give him but a morsel of dry bread for his dinner, and he would be satisfied, though you placed sweetmeats and fruit, and every other nicety, in his way.

With this little boy did Master Merton become acquainted in the following manner:—As he and the maid were once walking in the fields upon a fine summer's morning, diverting themselves with gathering different kinds of wild flowers, and running after butterflies, a large snake, on a sudden, started up from among some long grass, and coiled itself round little Tommy's leg. You may imagine the fright they were both in at this accident: the maid ran away shrieking for help, while the child, who was in an agony of terror, did not dare to stir from the place where he was standing. Harry, who happened to be walking near the place, came running up, and asked what was the matter? Tommy, who was sobbing most piteously, could not find words to tell him, but pointed to his leg, and made Harry sensible of what had happened. Harry, who though young, was a boy of a most courageous spirit, told him not to be frightened, and instantly seizing the snake by the neck with as much dexterity as resolution, tore him from Tommy's leg, and threw him to a great distance off. Just as this happened, Mrs. Merton and all the family, alarmed by the servant's cries, came running breathless to the place, as Tommy was recovering his spirits, and thanking his brave little deliverer. Her first emotions were to catch her darling up in her arms, and, after giving him a thousand kisses, to ask him whether he had received any hurt? "No," says Tommy, "indeed I have not, mamma; but I believe that nasty, ugly beast would have bitten me, if that little boy had not come and pulled him off." "And who are you, my dear," says she, "to whom we are all so obliged?" "Harry Sandford, madam." "Well, my child, you are a dear, brave little creature, and you shall go home and dine with us." "No, thank you, madam; my father will want me." "And who is your father, my sweet boy?" "Farmer Sandford, madam, that lives at the bottom of the hill." "Well, my dear, you shall be my child henceforth, will you?" "If you please, madam, if I may have my own father and mother too."

Mrs. Merton instantly dispatched a servant to the farmer's, and taking little Harry by the hand, she led him to the mansion-house, where she found Mr. Merton, whom she entertained with a long account of Tommy's danger and Harry's bravery. Harry was now in a new scene of life. He was carried through costly apartments, where everything that could please the eye, or contribute to convenience, was assembled. He saw large looking-glasses in gilded frames, carved tables and chairs, curtains made of the finest silk, and the very plates and knives and forks were silver. At dinner he was placed close to Mrs. Merton, who took care to supply him with the choicest bits, and engaged him to eat with the most endearing kindness. But, to the astonishment of everybody, he neither appeared pleased or surprised at anything he saw. Mrs. Merton could not conceal her disappointment; for as she had always been used to a great degree of finery herself, she had expected it should make the same impression upon everybody else. At last, seeing him eye a small silver cup, with great attention, out of which he had been drinking, she asked him, whether he should not like to have such a fine thing to drink out of? and added, that, though it was Tommy's cup, she was sure he would give it with great pleasure to his little friend. "Yes, that I will," says Tommy; "for you know, mamma, I have a much finer than that, made of gold, besides two large ones made of silver." "Thank you with all my heart," says little Harry; "but I will not rob you of it, for I have a much better one at home." "How!" says Mrs. Merton, "what! does your father eat and drink out of silver?" "I don't know, madam, what you call this, but we drink at home out of long things made of horn, just such as the cows wear upon their heads." "The child is a simpleton, I think," says Mrs. Merton;—"and why is that better than silver ones?" "Because," says Harry, "they never make us uneasy." "Make you uneasy, my child," says Mrs. Merton; "what do you mean?" "Why, madam, when the man threw that great thing down, which looks just like this, I saw that you were very sorry about it, and looked as if you had been just ready to drop. Now, ours at home are thrown about by all the family, and nobody minds it."

"I protest," says Mrs. Merton to her husband, "I do not know what to say to this boy, he makes such strange observations." The fact was, that during dinner one of the servants had thrown down a large piece of plate, which, as it was very valuable, had made Mrs. Merton not only look very uneasy, but give the man a very severe scolding for his carelessness.

After dinner, Mrs. Merton filled a large glass with wine, and, giving it to Harry, bade him drink it up; but he thanked her, and said he was not dry. "But, my dear," says she, "this is very sweet and pleasant, and, as you are a good boy, you may drink it up." "Ay! but, madam, Mr. Barlow says, that we must only eat when we are hungry, and drink when we are dry; and that we must only eat and drink such things as are easily met with, otherwise we shall grow peevish and vexed when we can't get them. And this was the way that the apostles did, who were all very good men." Mr. Merton laughed at this: "And pray," says he, "little man, do you know who the apostles were?" "Oh! yes, to be sure I do." "And who were they?"

"Why, sir, there was a time when people were grown so very wicked that they did not care what they did, and the great folks were all proud, and minded nothing but eating and drinking, and sleeping, and amusing themselves, and took no care of the poor, and would not give a morsel of bread to hinder a beggar from starving; and the poor were all lazy, and loved to be idle better than to work; and little boys were disobedient to their parents, and their parents took no care to teach them anything that was good, and all the world was very bad, very bad indeed:—and then there came a very good man indeed, whose name was Christ; and he went about doing good to everybody, and curing people of all sorts of diseases, and taught them what they ought to do—and he chose out twelve other very good men, and called them the apostles, and these apostles went about the world, doing as he did, and teaching people as he taught them. And they never minded what they ate or drank, but lived upon dry bread and water; and when anybody offered them money, they would not take it, but told him to be good, and give it to the poor and the sick: and so they made the world a great deal better—and therefore it is not fit to mind what we live upon, but we should take what we can get and be contented; just as the beasts and birds do, who lodge in the open air, and live upon herbs, and drink nothing but water, and yet they are strong, and active, and healthy."

"Upon my word," says Mr. Merton, "this little man is a great philosopher, and we should be much obliged to Mr. Barlow if he would take our Tommy under his care; for he grows a great boy, and it is time that he should know something. What say you, Tommy, should you like to be a philosopher?" "Indeed, papa, I don't know what a philosopher is, but I should like to be a king; because he's finer and richer than anybody else, and has nothing to do, and everybody waits upon him, and is afraid of him." "Well said, my dear," says Mrs. Merton, and rose and kissed him; "and a king you deserve to be with such a spirit, and here's a glass of wine for you for making such a pretty answer. And should not you like to be a king too, little Harry?" "Indeed, madam, I don't know what that is; but I hope I shall soon be big enough to go to plough, and get my own living; and then I shall want nobody to wait upon me." "What a difference there is between the children of farmers and gentlemen!" whispered Mrs. Merton to her husband, looking rather contemptuously upon Harry. "I am not sure," said Mr. Merton, "that for this time the advantage is on the side of our son. But should not you like to be rich, my dear," says he to Harry? "No, indeed, Sir." "No, simpleton," says Mrs. Merton, "and why not?" "Because the only rich man I ever saw is 'squire Chace, who lives hard by, and he rides among people's corn, and breaks down their hedges, and shoots their poultry, and kills their dogs, and lames their cattle, and abuses the poor, and they say he does all this because he's rich; but everybody hates him, though they dare not tell him so to his face—and I would not be hated for anything in the world." "But should not you like to have a fine laced coat, and a coach to carry you about, and servants to wait upon you?" "As to that, madam, one coat is as good as another, if it will but keep one warm; and I don't want to ride, because I can walk wherever I choose; and, as to servants, I should have nothing for them to do, if I had an hundred of them." Mrs. Merton continued to look at him with a sort of contemptuous astonishment, but did not ask him any more questions.

—In the evening little Harry was sent home to his father, who asked him what he had seen at the great house, and how he liked being there? "Why," says Harry, "they were all very kind to me, for which I'm much obliged to them; but I had rather have been at home, for I never was so troubled in all my life to get a dinner.—There was one man to take away my plate, and another to give me drink, and another to stand behind my chair, just as if I had been lame or blind, and could not have waited upon myself. And, then, there was so much to do with putting this thing on, and taking another off, I thought it would never have been over. And after dinner I was obliged to sit two whole hours without ever stirring, while the lady was talking to me, not as Mr. Barlow does, but wanting me to love fine clothes, and to be a king, and to be rich, that I may be hated like 'squire Chace."

But, at the mansion-house, much of the conversation, in the meantime, was employed in examining the merits of little Harry. Mrs. Merton acknowledged his bravery and openness of temper; she was also struck with the general good-nature and benevolence of his character; but she contended there were a certain grossness and indelicacy in his ideas which distinguish the children of the lower and middling classes of people from those of persons of fashion. Mr. Merton, on the contrary, contended that he had never before seen a child whose sentiments and dispositions would do so much honour even to the most elevated situations. Nothing, he affirmed, was more easily acquired than those external manners, and that superficial address, upon which too many of the higher classes pride themselves as their greatest, or even as their only accomplishment: "nay, so easily are they picked up," said he, "that we frequently see them descend with the cast clothes to maids and valets; between whom and their masters and mistresses there is frequently little other difference that what results from the former wearing soiled clothes and healthier countenances. Indeed, the real seat of all superiority, even of manners, must be placed in the mind: dignified sentiments, superior courage, accompanied with genuine and universal courtesy, are always necessary to constitute the real gentleman; and where these are wanting, it is the greatest absurdity to think they can be supplied by affected tones of voice, particular grimaces, or extravagant and un-natural modes of dress; which, far from being the real test of gentility, have in general no higher origin than the caprice of barbers, tailors, actors, opera-dancers, milliners, fiddlers, and French servants of both sexes. I cannot help, therefore, assert-ing," said he very seriously, "that this little peasant has within his mind the seeds of true gentility and dignity of character; and, though I shall also wish that our son may possess all the common accomplishments of his rank, nothing would give me more pleasure than a certainty that he would never in any re-spect fall below the son of farmer Sandford."

Whether Mrs. Merton fully acceded to these observations of her husband I cannot decide; but without waiting to hear her particular sentiments, he thus went on:—"Should I appear more warm than usual upon this subject, you must pardon me, my dear, and attribute it to the interest I feel in the welfare of our little Tommy. I am too sensible, that our mutual fondness has hitherto treated him with rather too much indulgence. While we have been over solicitous to remove from him every painful and disagreeable impression, we have made him too delicate and fretful; our desire of constantly consulting his in-clinations has made us gratify even his caprices and humours; and, while we have been too studious to preserve him from restraint and opposition, we have in reality been the cause why he has not acquired even the common acquisitions of his age and situation. All this I have long observed in silence; but have hitherto concealed, both from my fondness for our child, and my fear of offending you. But at length a consideration of his real interests has prevailed over every other motive, and has compelled me to embrace a resolution which I hope will not be disagreeable to you, that of sending him directly to Mr. Barlow, provided he will take the care of him: and I think this acci-dental acquaintance with young Sandford may prove the luck-iest thing in the world, as he is so nearly of the age and size of our Tommy. I will therefore propose to the farmer that I will for some years pay for the board and education of his little boy, that he may be a constant companion to our son."

As Mr. Merton said this with a certain degree of firmness, and the proposal was in itself so reasonable and necessary, Mrs. Merton did not make any objection to it, but consented, although very reluctantly, to part with her son. Mr. Barlow was accordingly invited to dinner the next Sunday, and Mr. Merton took an opportunity of introducing the subject, and making the proposal to him; assuring him, at the same time, that, though there was no return within the bounds of his fortune which he would not willingly make, yet the education and improvement of his son were objects of so much importance to him, that he should always consider himself as the obliged party.

To this Mr. Barlow, after thanking Mr. Merton for the confidence and liberality with which he treated him, answered in the following manner:—"I should be little worthy of the distinguished regard with which you treat me, did I not with the greatest sincerity assure you, that I feel myself totally unqualified for such a task. I am, Sir, a Minister of the Gospel, and I would not exchange that character, and the severe duties it enjoins, for any other situation in life. But you must be sensible that the retired manner of life which I have led for these twenty years, in consequence of my profession, at a distance from the gaieties of the capital and the refinements of polite life, is little adapted to form such a tutor as the manners and opinions of the world require for your son. Gentlemen in your situation of life are accustomed to divide the world into two general classes; those that are persons of fashion, and those that are not. The first class contains everything that is valuable in life; and therefore their manners, their prejudices, their very vices, must be inculcated upon the minds of children from the earliest period of infancy: the second comprehends the great body of mankind, who, under the general name of the vulgar, are represented as being only objects of contempt and disgust, and scarcely worthy to be put upon a footing with the very beasts that contribute to the pleasures and convenience of their superiors."

Mr. Merton could not help interrupting Mr. Barlow here, to assure him, that, though there was too much truth in the observation, yet he must not think that either he, or Mrs. Merton, carried things to that extravagant length; and that, although they wished their son to have the manners of a man of fashion, they thought his morals and religion of infinitely more consequence.

"If you think so," said Mr. Barlow, "Sir, it is more than a noble Lord did, whose written opinions are now considered as the oracles of polite life, and more than I believe most of his admirers do at this time.[2] But if you allow what I have just mentioned to be the common distinctions of genteel people, you must at one glance perceive how little I must be qualified to educate a young gentleman intended to move in that sphere; I, whose temper, reason, and religion, equally combine to make me reject the principles upon which those distinctions are founded.

"The Christian religion, though not exclusively, is, emphatically speaking, the religion of the poor.—Its first ministers were taken from the lower orders of mankind, and to the lower orders of mankind was it first proposed; and in this, instead of feeling myself mortified or ashamed, I am the more inclined to adore the wisdom and benevolence of that Power by whose command it was first promulgated. Those, who engross the riches and advantages of this world, are too much employed with their pleasures and ambition to be much interested about any system, either of religion, or of morals. They too frequently feel a species of habitual intoxication which excludes every serious thought, and makes them view with indifference everything but the present moment. Those, on the contrary, to whom all the hardships and miseries of this world are allotted as their natural portion,—those who eat the bread of bitterness, and drink the waters of affliction, have more interest in futurity, and are therefore more prepared to receive the promises of the Gospel.—Yes, Sir; mark the disingenuousness of many of our modern philosophers—they quarrel with the Christian religion, because it has not yet penetrated the deserts of Africa, or arrested the wandering hordes of Tartary; yet they ridicule it for the meanness of its origin, and because it is the Gospel of the poor!—that is to say, because it is expressly calculated to inform the judgments, and alleviate the miseries, of that vast promiscuous body which constitutes the majestic species of man.

"But for whom would these philosophers have Heaven itself interested, if not for the mighty whole which it has created? Poverty, that is to say, a state of labour and frequent self-denial, is the natural state of man—it is the state of all in the happiest and most equal governments, the state of nearly all in every country:—it is a state in which all the faculties both of body and mind are always found to develop themselves with the most advantage, and in which the moral feelings have generally the greatest influence. The accumulation of riches, on the contrary, can never increase, but by the increasing poverty and degradation of those whom Heaven has created equal; a thousand cottages are thrown down to afford space for a single palace.

"How benevolently therefore has Heaven acted, in thus extending its blessings to all who do not disqualify themselves for their reception by voluntary hardness of heart! how wisely, in thus opposing a continual boundary to human pride and sensuality, two passions the most fatal in their effects, and the most apt to desolate the world!—And shall a Minister of that Gospel, conscious of these great truths, and professing to govern himself by their influence, dare to preach a different doctrine, and flatter those excesses which he must know are equally contrary both to reason and religion? Shall he become the abject sycophant of human greatness, and assist it in trampling all relations of humanity beneath its feet, instead of setting before it the severe duties of its station, and the account which will one day be expected of all the opportunities of doing good, so idly, so irretrievably lost and squandered?—But I beg pardon, sir, for that warmth which has transported me so far, and made me engross so much of the conversation. But it will at least have this good effect, that it will demonstrate the truth of what I have been saying; and show, that, though I might undertake the education of a farmer, or a mechanic, I shall never succeed in that of a modern gentleman."

"Sir," replied Mr. Merton, "there is nothing which I now hear from you which does not increase my esteem of your character and my desire to engage your assistance. Permit me only to ask, whether, in the present state of things, a difference of conditions and an inequality of fortune are not necessary, and, if necessary, I should infer, not contrary to the spirit of Christianity?"

"So it is declared, sir, that offences must come; but that does not prevent a severe denunciation against the offenders. But if you wish to know, whether I am one of those enthusiasts who are continually preaching up an ideal state of perfection, totally inconsistent with human affairs, I will endeavour to give you every satisfaction upon the subject. If you mean by difference of conditions and inequality of fortunes, that the present state of human affairs, in every society we are acquainted with, does not admit that perfect equality which the purer interpretations of the Gospel inculcate, I certainly shall not disagree with you in opinion. He that formed the human heart, certainly must be acquainted with all the passions to which it would be subject; and if, under the immediate dispensation of Christ himself, it was found impossible for a rich man to give his possessions to the poor, that degree of purity will hardly be expected now, which was not found in the origin.

"But here, sir, permit me to remark, how widely the principles of genuine Christianity differ from that imaginary scheme of ideal perfection, equally inconsistent with human affairs and human characters, which many of its pretended friends would persuade us to believe it; and as comparisons sometimes throw a new and sudden light upon a subject, give me leave to use one here, which I think bears the closest analogy to what we are now considering. Were some physician to arise, who, to a perfect knowledge of all preceding medical facts, had added, by a more than human skill, a knowledge of the most secret principles of the human frame; could he calculate, with an accuracy that never was deceived, the effect of every cause that could act upon our constitutions; and were he inclined, as the result of all his science and observation, to leave a rule of life that might remain unimpeached to the latest posterity; I ask, what kind of one he would form?"—"I suppose one," said Mr. Merton, "that was the most adapted to the general circumstances of the human species, and which observed, would confer the greatest degree of health and vigour."

"Right," said Mr. Barlow.—"I ask again, whether, observing the common luxury and intemperance of the rich, he would take his directions from the usages of a polite table, and recommend that heterogeneous assemblage of contrary mixtures, high seasonings, poignant sauces, fermented and distilled poisons, which is continually breeding diseases in their veins, as the best means of preserving, or regaining health?"

"Certainly not—That were to debase his art, and sanctify abuses, instead of reforming them."

"Would he not, then, recommend simplicity of diet, light repasts, early slumbers, and moderate exercise in the open air, if he judged them salutary to human nature, even though fashionable prejudice had stamped all these particulars with the mark of extreme vulgarity?"

"Were he to act otherwise, he must forfeit all pretensions either to honesty or skill."

"Let us then apply all this to the mind, instead of the body, and suppose, for an instant, that some legislator, either human or divine, who comprehended all the secret springs that govern the mind, was preparing an universal code for all mankind;—must he not imitate the physician, and deliver general truths, however unpalatable, however repugnant to particular prejudices, since upon the observance of these truths alone the happiness of the species must depend?"

"I think so indeed."

"Should such a person observe, that an immoderate desire and accumulation of riches, a love of ostentatious trifles, and unnecessary splendor in all that relates to human life, and habitual indulgence of sensuality, tended not only to produce evil in all around, but even in the individual himself who suffered the tyranny of these vices, how would you have the legislator act?—Should he be silent?"

"No, certainly—he should arraign these pernicious habitudes by every means within his power; by precept, by example."

"Should he also observe, that riches employed in another manner, in removing the real miseries of humanity, in cherishing, comforting, and supporting all around, produced a contrary effect, and tended equally to make the obliged and obliger happy; should he conceal this great, eternal truth, or should he divulge it with all the authority he possessed,—conscious, that, in whatever degree it became the rule of human life, in the same degree would it tend to the advantage of all the world?"

"There cannot be a doubt upon the subject."

"But, should he know, either by the spirit of prophecy, or by intuitive penetration, that the majority of mankind would never observe these rules to any great degree, but would be blindly precipitated by their passions into every excess against which he so benevolently cautioned them; should this be a reason for his withdrawing his precepts and admonitions, or for seeming to approve what was in its own nature most pernicious?"

"As prudent would it be to pull off the bridle when we mounted an impetuous horse, because we doubted of our power to hold him in—or to increase his madness by the spur, when it was already too great before."

"Thus, sir, you will perceive, that the precepts of the Christian religion are founded upon the most perfect knowledge of the human heart, as they furnish a continual barrier against the most destructive passions, and the most subversive of human happiness. Your own concessions sufficiently prove, that it would have been equally derogatory to truth, and the common interests of the species, to have made the slightest concessions in favour either of human pride or sensuality. Your extensive acquaintance with mankind will sufficiently convince you, how prone the generality are to give an unbounded loose to these two passions: neither the continual experience of their own weakness, nor of the fatal effects which are produced by vicious indulgences, has yet been capable of teaching them either humility, or moderation. What then could the wisest legislator do, more useful, more benevolent, more necessary, than to establish general rules of conduct, which have a continual tendency to restore moral and natural order, and to diminish the wild inequality produced by pride and avarice? Nor is there any greater danger that these precepts should be too rigidly observed, than that the bulk of mankind should injure themselves by too abstemious a temperance. All that can be expected from human weakness, even in working after the most perfect model, is barely to arrive at mediocrity; and were the model less perfect, or the duties less severe, there is the greatest reason to think that even that mediocrity would never be attained. Examine the conduct of those who are placed at a distance from all labour and fatigue, and you will find the most trifling exertions act upon their imaginations with the same force as the most insuperable difficulties.

"If I have now succeeded in laying down the genuine principles of Christian morality, I apprehend it will not be difficult to deduce the duty of one who takes upon him the office of its minister and interpreter. He can no more have a right to alter the slightest of its principles, than a magistrate can be justified in giving false interpretations to the laws. The more the corruptions of the world increase, the greater the obligation that he should oppose himself to their course; and he can no more relax in his opposition, than the pilot can abandon the helm, because the winds and the waves begin to augment their fury. Should he be despised, or neglected by all the rest of the human species, let him still persist in bearing testimony to the truth, both in his precepts and example: the cause of virtue is not desperate, while it retains a single friend; should it even sink forever, it is enough for him to have discharged his duty.

"But, although he is thus restricted as to what he shall teach, I do not assert, that it is improper for him to use his understanding and experience as to the manner of his instructions. He is strictly bound never to teach anything contrary to the purest morality; but he is not bound always to teach that morality in its greatest extent. In that respect, he may use the wisdom of the serpent, though guided by the innocence of the dove. If, therefore, he sees the reign of prejudice and corruption so firmly established, that men would be offended with the genuine simplicity of the Gospel and the purity of its primeval doctrines, he may so far moderate their rigour, as to prevent them from entirely disgusting weak and luxurious minds. If we cannot effect the greatest possible perfection, it is still a material point to preserve from the grossest vices. A physician that practices amongst the great, may certainly be excused, though he should not be continually advising the exercise and regimen of the poor; not, that the doctrine is not true, but that there would not be the smallest probability of its ever being adopted. But, although he never assents to that luxurious method of life which he is continually obliged to see, he may content himself with only inculcating those restrictions which even the luxurious may submit to, if they possess the smallest portion of understanding. Should he succeed thus far, there is no reason for his stopping in his career, or not enforcing a superior degree of temperance; but, should it be difficult to persuade even so slight a restriction, he could hope for no success, were he to preach up a Spartan or a Roman diet. Thus the Christian Minister may certainly use his own discretion in the mode of conveying his instructions; and it is permitted him to employ all his knowledge of the human heart in reclaiming men from their vices, and winning them over to the cause of virtue. By the severity of his own manners he may sufficiently evince the motives of his conduct; nor can he, by any means, hope for more success, than if he shows that he practices more than he preaches, and uses a greater degree of indulgence to the failings of others than he requires for his own."

"Nothing," said Mr. Merton, "can be more rational or moderate than these sentiments; why, then, do you persist in pleading your incapacity for an employment which you can so well discharge?"

"Because," said Mr. Barlow, "he that undertakes the education of a child, undertakes the most important duty in society, and is severely answerable for every voluntary omission. The same mode of reasoning which I have just been using is not applicable here. It is out of the power of any individual, however strenuous may be his endeavours, to prevent the mass of mankind from acquiring prejudices and corruptions; and when he finds them in that state, he certainly may use all the wisdom he possesses for their reformation. But this rule will never justify him, for an instant, in giving false impressions where he is at liberty to instill truth, and in losing the only opportunity which he perhaps may ever possess, of teaching pure morality and religion.

"How will such a man, if he has the least feeling, bear to see his pupil become a slave, perhaps, to the grossest vices; and to reflect, with a great degree of probability, that this catastrophe has been owing to his own inactivity and improper indulgence? May not all human characters frequently be traced back to impressions made at so early a period, that none but discerning eyes would ever suspect their existence? Yet nothing is more certain; what we are at twenty, depends upon what we were at fifteen; what we are at fifteen, upon what we were at ten; where shall we then place the beginning of the series?

"Besides, sir, the very prejudices and manners of society, which seem to be an excuse for the present negligence in the early education of children, act upon my mind with a contrary effect. Need we fear that, after every possible precaution has been taken, our pupil should not give a sufficient loose to his passions, or should be in danger of being too severely virtuous? How glorious would be such a distinction, how much to be wished for, and yet how little to be expected by anyone who is moderately acquainted with the world! The instant he makes his entrance there, he will find an universal relaxation and indifference to everything that is serious; everything will conspire to represent pleasure and sensuality as the only business of human beings, and to throw a ridicule upon every pretence to principle or restraint. This will be the doctrine that he will learn at theatres, from his companions, from the polite circles into which he is introduced. The ladies too will have their share in the improvement of his character: they will criticise the colour of his clothes, his method of making a bow, and of entering a room. They will teach him that the great object of human life is to please the fair; and that the only method of doing it is to acquire the graces. Need we fear that, thus beset on every side, he should not attach a sufficient importance to trifles, or grow fashionably languid in the discharge of all his duties?—Alas! sir, it seems to me, that this will unavoidably happen, in spite of all our endeavours. Let us then not lose the important moment of human life, when it is possible to flatter ourselves with some hopes of success in giving good impressions; they may succeed; they may either preserve a young man from gross immorality, or may have a tendency to reform him, when the first ardour of youth is past. If we neglect this awful moment, which can never return; with the view which, I must confess, I have of modern manners, it appears to me like launching a vessel into the midst of a storm, without a compass and without a pilot."

"Sir," said Mr. Merton, "I will make no other answer to what you have now been saying than to tell you, it adds, if possible, to my esteem of your character, and that I will deliver my son into your hands, upon your own conditions. And as to the terms—"

"Pardon me," replied Mr. Barlow, "if I interrupt you here, and give you another specimen of the singularity of my opinions. I am contented to take your son for some months under my care, and to endeavour by every means within my power, to improve him. But there is one circumstance which is indispensable; that you permit me to have the pleasure of serving you as a friend. If you approve of my ideas and conduct, I will keep him as long as you desire. In the meantime, as there are, I fear, some little circumstances, which have grown up by too much tenderness and indulgence, to be altered in his character, I think that I shall possess more of the necessary influence and authority, if I for the present appear to him and your whole family, rather in the light of a friend than that of a schoolmaster."

However disagreeable this proposal was to the generosity of Mr. Merton, he was obliged to consent to it; and little Tommy was accordingly sent the next day to the vicarage, which was at the distance of about two miles from his father's house.

The day after Tommy came to Mr. Barlow's, as soon as breakfast was over, he took him and Harry into the garden: when he was there, he took a spade into his own hand, and giving Harry a hoe, they both began to work with great eagerness. "Everybody that eats," says Mr. Barlow, "ought to assist in procuring food, and therefore little Harry and I begin our daily work; this is my bed, and that other is his; we work upon it every day, and he that raises the most out of it, will deserve to fare the best. Now, Tommy, if you choose to join us, I will mark you out a piece of ground, which you shall have to yourself, and all the produce shall be your own." "No, indeed," says Tommy, very sulkily, "I am a gentleman, and don't choose to slave like a ploughboy." "Just as you please, Mr. Gentleman," said Mr. Barlow; "but Harry and I, who are not above being useful, will mind our work."

In about two hours Mr. Barlow said it was time to leave off, and, taking Harry by the hand, he led him into a very pleasant summer-house, where they sat down, and Mr. Barlow, taking out a plate of very fine ripe cherries, divided them between Harry and himself. Tommy, who had followed, and expected his share, when he saw them both eating without taking any notice of him, could no longer restrain his passion, but burst into a violent fit of sobbing and crying. "What is the matter?" said Mr. Barlow very coolly to him. Tommy looked upon him very sulkily, but returned no answer. "Oh! sir, if you don't choose to give me an answer, you may be silent; nobody is obliged to speak here." Tommy became still more disconcerted at this, and, being unable to conceal his anger, ran out of the summer-house, and wandered very disconsolately about the garden; equally surprised and vexed to find that he was now in a place where nobody felt any concern whether he was pleased or the contrary. When all the cherries were eaten, little Harry said, "You promised to be so good as to hear me read when we had done working in the garden; and if it is agreeable to you, I will now read the story of the Flies and the Ants." "With all my heart," said Mr. Barlow: "remember to read it slowly and distinctly, without hesitating, or pronouncing the words wrong; and be sure to read it in such a manner as to show that you understand it." Harry then took up the book and read as follows:

The Flies and the Ants

In a corner of a farmer's garden, there once happened to be a nest of ants, who, during all the fine weather of the summer, were employed all day long in drawing little seeds and grains of corn into their hole. Near them there happened to be a bed of flowers, upon which a great quantity of flies used to be always sporting, and humming, and diverting themselves by flying from one flower to another. A little boy, who was the farmer's son, used frequently to observe the different employments of the animals; and, as he was very young and ignorant, he one day thus expressed himself:—"Can any creature be so simple as these ants? All day long they are working and toiling, instead of enjoying the fine weather, and diverting themselves like these flies, who are the happiest creatures in the world."—Some time after he had made this observation, the weather grew extremely cold, the sun was scarcely seen to shine, and the nights were chill and frosty. The same little boy, walking then in the garden with his father, did not see a single ant, but all the flies lay scattered up and down either dead or dying. As he was very good-natured, he could not help pitying the unfortunate animals, and asking, at the same time, what had happened to the ants that he used to see in the same place? The father said, "The flies are all dead, because they were careless animals, who gave themselves no trouble about laying up provisions, and were too idle to work: but the ants, who have been busy all the summer, in providing for their maintenance during the winter, are all alive and well; and you will see them again, as soon as the warm weather returns."

"Very well, Harry," says Mr. Barlow; "we will now take a walk." They accordingly rambled out into the fields, where Mr. Barlow made Harry take notice of several kinds of plants, and told him the names and nature of them. At last, Harry, who had observed some very pretty purple berries upon a plant that bore a purple flower and grew in the hedges, brought them to Mr. Barlow, and asked whether they were good to eat. "It is very lucky," said Mr. Barlow, "young man, that you asked the question before you put them into your mouth; for had you tasted them they would have given you violent pains in your head and stomach, and perhaps have killed you; as they grow upon a plant called night-shade, which is a rank poison." "Sir," says Harry, "I take care never to eat any thing without knowing what is is; and I hope, if you will be so good as to continue to teach me, I shall very soon know the names and qualities of all the herbs which grow." As they were returning home, Harry saw a very large bird, called a kite, upon the ground, who seemed to have something in his claws, which he was tearing to pieces. Harry, who knew him to be one of those ravenous creatures which prey upon others, ran up to him, shouting as loud as he could, and the bird being frightened flew away, and left a chicken behind him, very much hurt indeed, but still alive. "Look, sir," said Harry, "if that cruel creature has not almost killed this poor chicken! See how he bleeds, and hangs his wings!—I will put him into my bosom, to recover him, and carry him home; and he shall have part of my dinner every day, till he is well, and able to shift for himself."

As soon as they came home, the first care of little Harry was to put his wounded chicken into a basket with some fresh straw, some water, and some bread: after that, Mr. Barlow and he went to dinner. In the meantime, Tommy, who had been skulking about all day, very much mortified and uneasy, came in, and, being very hungry, was going to sit down to the table with the rest; but Mr. Barlow stopped him, and said, "No, sir, as you are too much a gentleman to work, we, who are not so, do not choose to work for the idle." Upon this, Tommy retired into a corner, crying as if his heart would break, but more from grief than passion, as he began to perceive that nobody minded his ill temper. But little Harry, who could not bear to see his friend so unhappy, looked up half crying into Mr. Barlow's face, and said, "Pray, sir, may I do as I please with my share of the dinner?" "Yes, to be sure, child." "Why then," said he, getting up, "I will give it all to poor Tommy, that wants it more than I do." Saying this, he gave it to him as he sat in the corner; and Tommy took it, and thanked him, without ever turning his eyes from off the ground. "I see," says Mr. Barlow, "that, though gentlemen are above being of any use themselves, they are not above taking the bread that other people have been working hard for." At this Tommy cried still more bitterly than before.

The next day Mr. Barlow and Harry went to work as before; but they had scarcely begun before Tommy came to them, and desired that he might have an hoe too, which Mr. Barlow gave him: but as he had never before learned to handle one, he was very awkward in the use of it, and hit himself several strokes upon the legs. Mr. Barlow then laid down his own spade, and showed him how to hold and use it, by which means, in a very short time, he became very expert, and worked with the greatest pleasure. When their work was over, they retired all three to the summer-house; and Tommy felt the greatest joy imaginable when the fruit was produced, and he was invited to take his share, which seemed to him the most delicious he had ever tasted, because working in the air had given him an appetite. As soon as they had done eating, Mr. Barlow took up a book, and asked Tommy whether he would read them a story out of it; but he, looking a little ashamed, said, he had never learned to read. "I am very sorry for it," said Mr. Barlow, "because you lose a very great pleasure; then Harry shall read to you." Harry accordingly took up the book, and read the following story.

[*Here a series of stories is omitted, two of which are The Good-Natured Little Boy and The Bad-Natured Little Boy.*]

When the story was ended, Tommy said it was very surprising to see how differently the two little boys fared. The one little boy was good-natured, and therefore everything he met became his friend, and assisted him in return: the other, who was ill-natured, made everything his enemy, and therefore he met with nothing but misfortunes and vexations, and nobody seemed to feel any compassion for him, excepting the poor little girl that assisted him at last, which was very kind indeed of her, considering how ill she had been used. "That is very true, indeed," said Mr. Barlow: "nobody is loved in this world, unless he loves others and does good to them; and nobody can tell but one time or other he may want the assistance of the meanest and lowest. Therefore every sensible man will behave well to everything around him; he will behave well, because it is his duty to do it, because every benevolent person feels the greatest pleasure in doing good, and even because it is his own interest to make as many friends as possible. No one can tell, however secure his present situation may appear, how soon it may alter, and he may have occasion for the compassion of those who are now infinitely below him. I could show you a story to that purpose, but you have read enough, and therefore you must now go out and use some exercise."

"Oh! pray, sir," said Tommy, "do let me hear the story. I think I could now read forever, without being tired." "No," said Mr. Barlow; "everything has its turn. Tomorrow you shall read, but now we must work in the garden." "Then pray, sir," said Tommy, "may I ask a favour of you?" "Surely," answered Mr. Barlow: "if it is proper for you to have, there is nothing can give me a greater pleasure than to grant it." "Why then," said Tommy, "I have been thinking that a man should know how to do everything in this world." Mr. B. "Very right: the more knowledge he acquires, the better." T. "And therefore Harry and I are going to build an house." Mr. B. "To build an house!——Well, and have you laid in a sufficient quantity of brick and mortar?" "No, no," said Tommy, smiling, "Harry and I can build houses without brick and mortar." Mr. B. "What are they to be made of then, cards?" "Dear sir," answered Tommy, "do you think we are such little children as to want card-houses? No, we are going to build real houses, fit for people to live in. And then you know if ever we should be thrown upon a desert coast, as the poor men were, we shall be able to supply ourselves with necessaries, till some ship comes to take us away." Mr. B. "And if no ship should come, what then?" T. "Why then we must stay there all our lives, I am afraid." Mr. B. "If you wish to prepare yourself against that event, I think you are much in the right, for nobody knows what may happen to him in this world. What is it then you want, to make your house?" T. "The first thing we want, sir, is wood, and an hatchet." Mr. B. "Wood you shall have in plenty;—but did you ever use an hatchet?" T. "No, sir." Mr. B. "Then I am afraid to let you have one, because it is a very dangerous kind of tool; and if you are not expert in the use of it, you may wound yourself severely. But if you will let me know what you want, I, who am more strong and expert, will take the hatchet and cut down the wood for you." "Thank you, sir," said Tommy; "you are very good to me indeed."—

And away Harry and he ran to the copse at the bottom of the garden. Mr. Barlow went to work, and presently, by Harry's direction, cut down several poles about as thick as a man's wrist, and about eight feet long: these he sharpened at the end, in order to run into the ground; and so eager were the two little boys at the business, that in a very short time they had transported them all to the bottom of the garden, and Tommy entirely forgot he was a gentleman, and worked with the greatest eagerness. "Now, said Mr. Barlow, "where will you fix your house?" "Here," answered Tommy, "I think, just at the bottom of this hill, because it will be warm and sheltered." So Harry took the stakes, and began to thrust them into the ground at about the difference of a foot; and in this manner he enclosed a bit of ground which was about ten feet long and eight feet wide, leaving an opening in the middle, of three feet wide, for a door. After this was done, they gathered up the brush-wood that was cut off, and by Harry's direction they interwove it between the poles, in such a manner as to form a compact kind of fence. This labour, as may be imagined, took them up several days: however, they worked at it very hard every day, and every day the work advanced, which filled Tommy's heart with so much pleasure, that he thought himself the happiest little boy in the universe.

[A long narrative is omitted here.]

It happened about this time, that Tommy and Harry rose early one morning, and went to take a long walk before break-fast, as they used frequently to do: they rambled so far, that at last they both found themselves tired, and sat down under an hedge to rest. While they were here, a very clean and decently dressed woman passed by, who seeing two little boys sitting by themselves, stopped to look at them; and after considering them attentively, she said, "You seem, my little dears, to be either tired, or to have lost your way." "No," said Harry, "madam, we have not lost our way; but we have walked farther than usual this morning, and we wait here a little while to rest ourselves." "Well," said the woman, "if you will come into my little house that you see a few yards farther on, you may sit more comfortably; and as my daughter has by this time milked the cows, she shall give you a mess of bread and milk."

Tommy, who was by this time extremely hungry as well as tired, told Harry that he should like to accept the good woman's invitation; so they both followed her to a small but clean-looking farm-house which stood at a little distance. Here they entered a very clean kitchen, furnished with plain but convenient furniture, and were desired to sit down by a warm and comfortable fire, which was made of turf. Tommy, who had never seen such a fire, could not help enquiring about it: and the good woman told him, that poor people, like her, were unable to purchase coals; "therefore," said she, "we go and pare the surface of the commons, which is full of grass, and heath, and other vegetables, together with their roots all matted together; these we dry in small pieces, by leaving them exposed to the summer's sun, and then we bring them home and put them under the cover of a shed, and use them for our fires." "But," said Tommy, "I should think that you would hardly have fire enough by these means to dress your dinner; for I have by accident been in my father's kitchen when they were dressing the dinner, and I saw a fire that blazed up to the very top of the chimney." The poor woman smiled at this, and said, "Your father, I suppose, master, is some rich man that has a great deal of victuals to dress; but we poor people must be more easily contented." "Why," said Tommy, "you must at least want to roast meat every day." "No," said the poor woman, "we seldom see roast meat in our house; but we are very well contented, if we can have a bit of fat pork every day, boiled in a pot with turnips: and we bless God that we fare so well; for there are many poor souls, that are as good as we, that can scarcely get a morsel of dry bread."

As they were conversing in this manner, Tommy happened to cast his eyes on one side, and saw a room that was almost filled with apples. "Pray," said he, "what can you do with all these apples? I should think you would never be able to eat them, though you were to eat nothing else." "That is very true," said the woman; "but we make cider of them." "What," cried Tommy, "are you able to make that sweet pleasant liquor that they call cider, and is it made of apples?" The woman. "Yes, indeed it is." Tommy. "And pray how is it made?" The woman. "We take the apples when they are ripe, and squeeze them in a machine we have for that purpose. Then we take this pulp and put it into large hair bags, which we press in a great press, till all the juice runs out." Tommy. "And is this juice cider?" The woman. "You shall taste, little master, as you seem so curious." She then led him into another room, where there was a great tub full of the juice of apples, and taking some up in a cup, she desired him to taste whether it was cider. Tommy tasted, and said it was very sweet and pleasant, but not cider. "Well," said the woman, "let us try another cask." She then took some liquor out of another barrel, which she gave him; and Tommy, when he had tasted it, said that it really was cider. "But pray," said he, "what do you do to the apple-juice to make it into cider?" The woman. "Nothing at all." Tommy. "How then should it become cider? for I am sure what you gave me at first is not cider." The woman. "Why, we put the juice into a large cask, and let it stand in some warm place, where it soon begins to ferment." Tommy. "Ferment! pray what is that?" The woman. "You shall see."

She then showed him another cask, and bid him observe the liquor that was in it. This he did, and saw it was covered all over with a thick scum and froth. Tommy. "And is this what you call fermentation?" The woman. "Yes, master." Tommy. "And what is the reason of it?" The woman. "That I do not know indeed; but when we have pressed the juice out, as I told you, we put it into a cask, and let it stand in some warm place, and in a short time it begins to work or ferment of itself, as you see; and after this fermentation has continued some time, it acquires the taste and properties of cider; and then we draw it off into casks and sell it, or else keep it for our own use. And I am told this is the manner in which they make wine in other countries." Tommy. "What is wine made of, apples then?" The woman. "No, master; wine is made of grapes, but they squeeze the juice out and treat it in the same manner as we do the juice of the apples." Tommy. "I declare this is very curious indeed. Then cider is nothing but wine made of apples." While they were conversing in this manner, a little clean girl came and brought Tommy an earthen porringer full of new milk, with a large slice of brown bread. Tommy took it, and ate it with so good a relish that he thought he had never made a better breakfast in his life.

When Harry and he had eaten their breakfast, Tommy told him it was time they should go home: so he thanked the good woman for her kindness, and putting his hand into his pocket, pulled out a shilling, which he desired her to accept. "No, God bless you, my little dear," said the woman; "I will not take a farthing of you for the world. What, though my husband and I are poor; yet we are able to get a living by our labour, and give a mess of milk to a traveller, without hurting ourselves."

Tommy thanked her again, and was just going away, when a couple of surly looking men came in, and asked the woman if her name was Toffet. "Yes, it is," said the woman; "I have never been ashamed of it." "Why then," said one of the men, pulling a paper out of his pocket, "here is an execution against you, on the part of Mr. Richard Gruff; and if your husband does not instantly discharge the debt with interest and all costs, amounting altogether to the sum of thirty-nine pounds ten shillings, we shall take an inventory of all you have, and proceed to sell it by auction for the discharge of the debt." "Indeed," said the poor woman, looking a little confused, "this must certainly be a mistake; for I never heard of Mr. Richard Gruff in all my life, nor do I believe that my husband owes a farthing in the world, unless to his landlord; and I know that he has almost made up half a year's rent for him: so that I do not think he would go to trouble a poor man." "No, no mistress," said the man, shaking his head; "we know our business too well to make these kind of mistakes: but when your husband comes in we'll talk with him; in the meantime we must go on with our inventory."

The two men then went into the next room, and, immediately after, a stout, comely-looking man, of about the age of forty, came in, with a good-humoured countenance, and asked if his breakfast was ready. "Oh! my poor dear William," said the woman, "here is a sad breakfast for you; but I think it cannot be true that you owe anything; so what the fellows told me must be false, about Richard Gruff."—At this name the man instantly started, and his countenance, which was before ruddy, became pale as a sheet. "Surely," said the woman, "it cannot be true, that you owe forty pounds to Richard Gruff." "Alas," answered the man, "I do not know the exact sum; but when your brother Peter failed, and his creditors seized all that he had, this Richard Gruff was going to send him to a jail, had not I agreed to be bound for him, which enabled him to go to sea: he indeed promised to remit his wages to me, to prevent my getting into any trouble upon that account; but you know it is now three years since he went, and in all that time we have heard nothing about him." "Then," said the woman, bursting into tears, "you and all your poor dear children are ruined for my ungrateful brother; for here are two bailiffs in the house, who are come to take possession of all you have, and to sell it."

At this the man's face became red as scarlet; and seizing an old sword which hung over the chimney, he cried out, "No, it shall not be—I will die first—I will make these villains know what it is to make honest men desperate." He then drew the sword, and was going out in a fit of madness which might have proved fatal either to himself or to the bailiffs; but his wife flung herself upon her knees before him, and, catching hold of his legs, besought him to be more composed. "Oh! for Heaven's sake," said she, "my dear, dear husband, consider what you are doing! You can do neither me nor your children any service by this violence; instead of that, should you be so unfortunate as to kill either of these men, would it not be murder? And would not our lot be a thousand times harder than it is at present?" This remonstrance seemed to have some effect upon the farmer: his children too, although too young to understand the cause of all this confusion, gathered round him, and hung about him, sobbing in concert with their mother. Little Harry too, although a stranger to the poor man before, yet with the tenderest sympathy took him by the hand, and bathed it with his tears. At length, softened and overcome by the sorrows of those he loved so well, and by his own cooler reflections, he resigned the fatal instrument, and sat himself down upon a chair, covering his face with his hands, and only saying, "The will of God be done!"

——Tommy had beheld this affecting scene with the greatest attention, although he had not said a word; and now beckoning Harry away, he went silently out of the house, and took the road which led to Mr. Barlow's. While he was upon the way, he seemed to be so full of the scene which he had just passed, that he did not open his lips; but when he came home, he instantly went to Mr. Barlow, and desired that he would directly send him to his father's. Mr. Barlow stared at the request, and asked him what was the occasion of his being so suddenly tired with his residence at the vicarage? "Sir," answered Tommy, "I am not the least tired, I assure you; you have been extremely kind to me, and I shall always remember it with the greatest gratitude; but I want to see my father immediately, and I am sure, when you come to know the occasion, you will not disapprove it." Mr. Barlow did not press him any farther, but ordered a careful servant to saddle an horse directly and take Tommy home before him.

Mr. and Mrs. Merton were extremely surprised and overjoyed at the sight of their son, who thus unexpectedly arrived at home; but Tommy, whose mind was full of the project which he had formed, as soon as he had answered their first questions, accosted his father thus: "Pray, sir, will you be angry with me, if I ask you for a great favour?" "No surely," said Mr. Merton, "that I will not." "Why then," said Tommy, "as I have often heard you say that you were very rich, and that, if

I was good, I should be rich too, will you give me some money?" "Money," said Mr. Merton, "yes, to be sure: how much do you want?" "Why, sir," said Tommy, "I want a very large sum, indeed." "Perhaps a guinea," answered Mr. Merton. Tommy. "No, sir, a great deal more—a great many guineas." Mr. Merton. "Let us however see." T. "Why, sir, I want at least forty pounds." "God bless the boy!" answered Mrs. Merton; "surely Mr. Barlow must have taught him to be ten times more extravagant than he was before." Tommy. "Indeed, madam, Mr. Barlow knows nothing about the matter." "But," said Mr. Merton, "what can such an urchin as you want with such a large sum of money?" "Sir," answered Tommy, "that is a secret; but I am sure, when you come to hear it, you will approve of the use I intend to make of it." Mr. Merton. "That I very much doubt." "But," replied Tommy, "sir, if you please, you may let me have this money, and I will pay you again by degrees." Mr. Merton. "How will you ever be able to pay me such a sum?" T. "Why, sir, you know you are so kind as frequently to give me new clothes and pocket money; now, if you will only let me have this money, I will neither want new clothes, nor anything else, till you have made it up." Mr. Merton. "But what can such a child as you want with all this money?" T. "Pray, sir, wait a few days, and you shall know, and if I make a bad use of it, never believe me again as long as I live."

Mr. Merton was extremely struck with the earnestness with which his son persevered in his demand; and as he was both very rich and very liberal, he determined to hazard the experiment, and comply with his request. He accordingly went and fetched him the money which he asked, and put it into his hands, telling him at the same time, that he expected to be acquainted with the use he put it to, and that if he was not satisfied with the account, he would never trust him again. Tommy appeared in ecstasies at the confidence which was reposed in him, and after thanking his father for his extraordinary goodness, he desired leave to go back again with Mr. Barlow's servant. When he arrived at Mr. Barlow's, his first care was to desire Harry to accompany him again to the farmer's house.

Thither the two little boys went with the greatest expedition, and, upon their entering the house, found the unhappy family in the same situation as before.

But Tommy, who had hitherto suppressed his feelings, finding himself now enabled to execute the project he had formed, went up to the good woman of the house, who sat sobbing in a corner of the room, and taking her gently by the hand, said, "My good woman, you were very kind to me in the morning, and therefore I am determined to be kind to you in return." "God bless you, my little master," said the woman, "you were very welcome to what you had; but you are not able to do anything to relieve our distress." "How do you know that?" said Tommy; "perhaps I can do more for you than you imagine." "Alas!" answered the woman, "I believe you would do all you could; but all our goods will be seized and sold, unless we can immediately raise the sum of forty pounds; and that is impossible, for we have no earthly friend to assist us: therefore, my poor babes and I must soon be turned out of doors, and God alone can keep them from starving." Tommy's little heart was too much affected to keep the woman longer in suspense; therefore pulling out his bag of money, he poured it into her lap, saying, "Here, my good woman, take this, and pay your debts, and God bless you and your children!" It is impossible to express the surprise of the poor woman at the sight; she stared wildly round her, and upon her little benefactor, and clasping her hands together in an agony of gratitude and feeling, she fell back in her chair with a kind of convulsive motion. Her husband, who was in the next room, seeing her in this condition, ran up to her, and catching her in his arms, asked her, with the greatest tenderness, what was the matter: but she, springing on a sudden from his embraces, threw herself upon her knees before the little boy, sobbing and blessing with a broken, inarticulate voice, embracing his knees and kissing his feet.

The husband, who did not know what had happened, imagined that his wife had lost her senses, and the little children that had before been skulking about the room, ran up to their mother, pulling her by the gown, and hiding their faces in her bosom. But the woman, at sight of them, seemed to recollect herself, and cried out, "Little wretches, that must all have been starved without the assistance of this little angel, why do you not fall down and join with me to worship him?" At this the husband said, "Surely, Mary, you must have lost your senses. What can this young gentleman do for us, or to prevent our wretched babes from perishing?" "Oh!" said the woman, "William, I am not mad, though I may appear so: but look here, William, look what Providence has sent us by the hands of this little angel, and then wonder that I should be wild." Saying this, she held up the money, and at the sight her husband looked as wild and astonished as she. But Tommy went up to the man, and taking him by the hand, said, "My good friend, you are very welcome to this; I freely give it you, and I hope it will enable you to pay what you owe, and to preserve these poor little children." But the man, who had before appeared to bear his misfortunes with silent dignity, now burst into tears, and sobbed like his wife and children. But Tommy, who now began to be pained with this excess of gratitude, went silently out of the house, followed by Harry, and before the poor family perceived what was become of him, was out of sight.

When he came back to Mr. Barlow's, that gentleman received him with the greatest affection, and when he had enquired after the health of Mr. and Mrs. Merton, asked Tommy whether he had forgotten the story of the grateful Turk. Tommy told him he had not, and should now be very glad to hear the remainder, which Mr. Barlow gave him to read, and was as follows: [*story omitted*].

When this story was concluded, Mr. Barlow and his two pupils went out to walk upon the high road; but they had not gone far, before they discovered three men that seemed each to lead a large and shaggy beast by a string, followed by a crowd of boys and women, whom the novelty of the sight had drawn together. When they approached more near, Mr. Barlow discovered that the beasts were three tame bears led by as many Savoyards, who got their living by exhibiting them. Upon the head of each of these formidable animals was seated a monkey, who grinned and chattered, and, by his strange grimaces, excited the mirth of the whole assembly. Tommy, who had never before seen one of these creatures, was very much surprised and entertained; but still more so, when he saw the animal rise upon his hind legs at the word of command, and dance about in a strange, uncouth manner, to the sound of music. After having satisfied themselves with this spectacle, they proceeded upon their way, and Tommy asked Mr. Barlow, whether a bear was an animal easily tamed, and that did mischief in those places where he was wild.

"The bear," replied Mr. Barlow, "is not an animal quite so formidable or destructive as a lion or a tiger; he is however sufficiently dangerous, and will frequently devour women and children, and even men, when he has an opportunity. These creatures are generally found in cold countries; and it is observed that the colder is the climate, the greater size and fierceness do they attain to. You may remember, in the account of those poor men who were obliged to live so long upon a dreary and uninhabited country, that they were frequently in danger of being devoured by the bears that abounded in that place. In those northern countries which are perpetually covered with snow and ice, a species of bear is found, that is white in colour, and of amazing strength as well as fierceness. These animals are often seen clambering over the huge pieces of ice which almost cover those seas, and preying upon fish and other sea animals.

"I remember reading an account of one that came unexpectedly upon some sailors who were boiling their dinners upon the shore. This creature had two young ones with her, and the sailors, as you may easily imagine, did not like such dangerous guests, but made their escape immediately to the ship. The old bear then seized upon the flesh which the sailors had left, and set it before her cubs, reserving a very small portion for herself; showing by this, that she took a much greater interest in their welfare than in her own. But the sailors, enraged at the loss of their dinners, levelled their muskets at the cubs, and, from the ship, shot them both dead. They also wounded the dam, who was fetching away another piece of flesh, but not mortally, so that she was still able to move. But it would have affected anyone with pity, but a brutal mind, (says the relation,) to see the behaviour of this poor beast, all wounded as she was and bleeding, to her young ones. Though she was sorely hurt, and could but just crawl to the place where they lay, she carried the lump of flesh she had in her mouth, as she had done the preceding ones, and laid it down before them; and when she observed that they did not eat, she laid her paws first upon one, and then upon another, and endeavoured to raise them up, all this while making the most pitiful moans. When she found that they did not stir, she went away to a little distance, and then looked back and moaned, as if to entice them to her; but finding them still immoveable, she returned, and smelling round them began to lick their wounds. She then went off a second time as before; and after crawling a few yards, turned back and moaned, as if to entreat them not to desert their mother. But her cubs not yet rising to follow her, she returned to them again, and with signs of inexpressible fondness went round first one, and then the other, pawing them, and moaning all the time. Finding them at last cold and lifeless, she raised her head towards the ship, and began to growl in an indignant manner, as if she were denouncing vengeance against the murderers of her young: but the sailors levelled their muskets again, and wounded her in so many places, that she dropped down between her young ones; yet even while she was expiring, she seemed only sensible to their fate, and died licking their wounds."

"And is it possible," said Harry, "that men can be so cruel towards poor, unfortunate animals?" "It is too true," answered Mr. Barlow, "that men are frequently guilty of very wanton and unnecessary acts of barbarity. But in this case, it is probable, that the fear of these animals contributed to render the sailors more unpitying than they would otherwise have been. They had often seen themselves in danger of being devoured, and that inspired them with a great degree of hatred against them, which they took every opportunity of gratifying."

"But would it not be enough," answered Harry, "if they carried arms to defend themselves when they were attacked, without unnecessarily destroying other creatures, who did not meddle with them?" "To be sure it would," replied Mr. Barlow, "and a generous mind would at any time rather spare an enemy than destroy him."

While they were conversing in this manner, they beheld a crowd of women and children running away, in the greatest trepidation, and looking behind them, saw that one of the bears had broken his chain, and was running after them, growling all the time in a very disagreeable manner. Mr. Barlow, who had a good stick in his hand, and was a man of an intrepid character, perceiving this, bade his pupils remain quiet, and instantly ran up to the bear, who stopped in the middle of his career, and seemed inclined to attack Mr. Barlow for his interference. But this gentleman struck him two or three blows, rating him at the same time in a loud and severe tone of voice, and seizing the end of the chain with equal boldness and dexterity, the animal quietly submitted, and suffered himself to be taken prisoner. Presently, the keeper of the bear came up, into whose hands Mr. Barlow consigned him, charging him for the future to be more careful in guarding so dangerous a creature.

While this was doing, the boys had remained quiet spectators at a distance; but by accident, the monkey who used to be perched upon the head of the bear, and was shaken off when the beast broke loose, came running that way, playing a thousand antic grimaces as he passed. Tommy, who was determined not to be outdone by Mr. Barlow, ran very resolutely up, and seized a string, which was tied round the loins of the animal; but he not choosing to be taken prisoner, instantly snapped at Tommy's arm, and almost made his teeth meet in the fleshy part of it. But Tommy, who was now greatly improved in courage and the use of his limbs, instead of letting his enemy escape, began threshing him very severely with a stick which he had in his hand; till the monkey, seeing he had so resolute an antagonist to deal with, desisted from opposition, and suffered himself to be led captive like his friend the bear.

As they were returning home, Tommy asked Mr. Barlow whether he did not think it very dangerous to meddle with such an animal when he was loose. Mr. Barlow told him it was not without danger, but that it was much less so than most people would imagine. "Most animals," said he, "are easily awed by the appearance of intrepidity, while they are invited to pursue by marks of fear and apprehension." "That, I believe, is very true," answered Harry; "for I have very often observed the behaviour of dogs to each other. When two strange dogs meet, they generally approach with caution, as if they were mutually afraid; but as sure as either of them runs away, the other will pursue him with the greatest insolence and fury." "This is not confined to dogs," replied Mr. Barlow; "almost all wild beasts are subject to receive the sudden impressions of terror; and therefore men that have been obliged to travel without arms through forests that abound with dangerous animals, have frequently escaped unhurt by shouting aloud whenever they have met with any of them upon their way. But what I chiefly depended upon, was the education which the bear had received since he left his own country."

Tommy laughed heartily at this idea, and Mr. Barlow went on:—"Whenever an animal is taught anything which is not natural to him, that is properly receiving an education. Did you ever observe colts running about wild upon the common?" Tommy. "Yes, sir, very often." Mr. Barlow. "And do you think it would be an easy matter for any one to mount upon their backs, or ride them?" Tommy. "By no means. I think that they would kick and prance to that degree, that they would throw any person down." Mr. Barlow. "And yet your little horse very frequently takes you upon his back, and carries you very safely between this and your father's house." Tommy. "That is because he is used to it." Mr. Barlow. "But he was not always used to it: he was once a colt, and then he ran about as wild and unrestrained as any of those upon the common." Tommy. "Yes, sir." Mr. Barlow. "How came he then to be so altered as to submit to bear you about upon his back?" Tommy. "I do not know; unless it was by feeding him." Mr. Barlow. "That is one method, but that is not all. They first accustom the colt, who naturally follows his mother, to come into the stable with her. Then they stroke him and feed him, till he gradually becomes gentle, and will suffer himself to be handled. Then they take an opportunity of putting an halter upon his head, and accustom him to stand quietly in the stable, and be tied to the manger. Thus, they gradually proceed from one thing to another, till they teach him to bear the bridle and the saddle, and to be commanded by his rider. This may very properly be called the education of an animal, since by these means he is obliged to acquire habits, which he would never have learned had he been left to himself.[3] Now, I knew that the poor bear had been frequently beaten and very ill used, in order to make him submit to be led about with a string, and exhibited as a sight. I knew that he had been accustomed to submit to man, and to tremble at the sound of the human voice; and I depended upon the force of these impressions, for making him submit without resistance to the authority I assumed over him. You see I was not deceived in my opinion; and by these means I probably prevented the mischief which he might otherwise have done to some of those women or children."

As Mr. Barlow was talking in this manner, he perceived that Tommy's arm was bloody, and enquiring into the reason, he heard the history of his adventure with the monkey. Mr. Barlow then looked at the wound, which he found of no great consequence; and told Tommy that he was sorry for his accident, but imagined that he was now too courageous to be daunted by a trifling hurt. Tommy assured him he was, and proceeded to ask some questions concerning the nature of the monkey; which Mr. Barlow answered in the following manner. "The monkey is a very extraordinary animal, which closely resembles a man in his shape and appearance, as perhaps you may have observed. He is always found to inhabit hot countries, the forests of which in many parts of the world are filled with innumerable bands of these animals. He is extremely active, and his fore legs exactly resemble the arms of a man; so that he not only uses them to walk upon, but frequently to climb trees, to hang by the branches, and to take hold of his food with. He supports himself upon almost every species of wild fruit which is found in those countries, so that it is necessary he should be continually scrambling up and down the highest trees in order to procure himself a subsistence.

"Nor is he contented always with the diet which he finds in the forest where he makes his residence. Large bands of these creatures will frequently sally out to plunder the gardens in the neighbourhood; and many wonderful stories are told of their ingenuity and contrivance." "What are these?" said Tommy. "It is said," answered Mr. Barlow, "that they proceed with all the caution and regularity which could be found in men themselves. Some of these animals are placed as spies to give notice to the rest, in case any human being should approach the garden; and should that happen, one of the sentinels informs them by a peculiar chattering, and they all escape in an instant." "I can easily believe that," answered Harry; "for I have observed, that when a flock of rooks alight upon a farmer's field of corn, two or three of them always take their station upon the highest tree they can find; and if anyone approaches, they instantly give notice by their cawing, and all the rest take wing directly and fly away." "But," answered Mr. Barlow, "the monkeys are said to be yet more ingenious in their thefts; for they station some of their body at a small distance from each other, in a line that reaches quite from the forest they inhabit to the particular garden they wish to plunder. When this is done, several of them mount the fairest fruit-trees, and picking the fruit, throw it down to their companions who stand below; these again chuck it to others at a little distance; and thus it flies from hand to hand, till it is safely deposited in the woods or mountains whence they came.

"When they are taken very young, they are easily tamed, but always retain a great disposition to mischief, as well as to imitate every thing they see done by men. Many ridiculous stories are told of them in this respect. I have heard of a monkey, that resided in a gentleman's family, and that frequently observed his master undergo the operation of shaving. The imitative animal one day took it into his head to turn barber, and seizing a cat that lived in the same house, in one hand, and a bottle of ink in the other, he carried her up to the

top of a very fine marble stair-case. The servants were all attracted by the screams of the cat, who did not relish the
operation which was going forward; and, running out, were
equally surprised and diverted, to see the monkey gravely
seated upon the landing-place of the stairs, and holding the
cat fast in one of his paws; while with the other he continually
applied ink to puss's face, rubbing it all over just as he had
observed the barber do to his master. Whenever the cat strug-
gled to escape, the monkey gave her a pat with his paw,
chattering all the time, and making the most ridiculous grimaces; and when she was quiet, he applied himself to his bottle,
and continued the operation.

"But I have heard a more tragic story of the imitative
genius of these animals. One of them lived in a fortified town,
and used frequently to run up and down upon the ramparts,
where he had observed the gunner discharge the great guns
that defended the town. One day he got possession of the
lighted match with which this man used to perform his business,
and applying it to the touch-hole of a gun, he ran to the mouth
of it to see the explosion; but the cannon, which happened to
be loaded, instantly went off and blew the poor monkey into
a thousand pieces."

When they came back to Mr. Barlow's, they found Master
Merton's servant and horses waiting to bring him home. When
he arrived there, he was received with the greatest joy and
tenderness by his parents; but though he gave them an account
of everything else that had happened, he did not say a word
about the money he had given to the farmer. But the next day
being Sunday, Mr. and Mrs. Merton and Tommy went together
to the parish-church; which they had scarcely entered, when
a general whisper ran through the whole congregation, and
all eyes were in an instant turned upon the little boy. Mr. and
Mrs. Merton were very much astonished at this, but they
forebore to enquire till the end of the service: then, as they were
going out of church together, Mr. Merton asked his son what
could be the reason of the general attention which he excited
at his entrance into church. Tommy had no time to answer,
for at that instant a very decent-looking woman ran up, and

threw herself at his feet, calling him her guardian-angel and preserver, and praying that Heaven would shower down upon his head all the blessings which he deserved. It was some time before Mr. and Mrs. Merton could understand the nature of this extraordinary scene; but when they at length understood the secret of their son's generosity, they seemed to be scarcely less affected than the woman herself; and shedding tears of transport and affection, they embraced their son, without attending to the crowd that surrounded them; but immediately recollecting themselves, they took their leave of the poor woman, and hurried to their coach with such sensations as it is more easy to conceive than to describe.

The summer had now completely passed away while Tommy was receiving these improvements at the house of Mr. Barlow. In the course of this time, both his body and mind had acquired additional vigour; for he was neither so fretful and humoursome, nor so easily affected by the vicissitudes of the season.

And now the winter had set in with unusual severity. The water was all frozen into a solid mass of ice; the earth was bare of food; and the little birds that used to hop about and chirp with gladness, seemed to lament in silence the inclemency of the weather. Tommy was one day surprised, when he entered his chamber, to find a very pretty little bird flying about it. He went down stairs and informed Mr. Barlow, who, after he had seen the bird, told him it was called a robin red-breast; and that it was naturally more tame and disposed to cultivate the society of men than any other species. But, at present, added he, the little fellow is in want of food, because the earth is too hard to furnish him any assistance, and hunger inspires him with this unusual boldness. "Why then," said Tommy, "sir, if you will give me leave, I will fetch a piece of bread and feed him." "Do so," answered Mr. Barlow, "but first set the window open, that he may see you do not intend to take him prisoner." Tommy accordingly opened his window, and, scattering a few crumbs of bread about the room, had the satisfaction of seeing his guest hop down and make a very hearty meal. He then flew out of the room and settled upon a neighbouring tree, singing all the time, as if to return thanks for the hospitality he had met with.

Tommy was greatly delighted with his new acquaintance, and from this time never failed to set his window open every morning, and scatter some crumbs about the room; which the bird perceiving hopped fearless in, and regaled himself under the protection of his benefactor. By degrees, the intimacy increased so much, that little Robin would alight on Tommy's shoulder, and whistle his notes in that situation, or eat out of his hand; all which gave Tommy so much satisfaction, that he would frequently call Mr. Barlow and Harry to be witness of his favourite's caresses; nor did he ever eat his own meals without reserving a part for his little friend.

It however happened that one day Tommy went up stairs after dinner, intending to feed his bird as usual; but as soon as he opened the door of his chamber, he discovered a sight that pierced him to the very heart. His little friend and innocent companion lay dead upon the floor and torn in pieces; and a large cat taking that opportunity to escape, soon directed his suspicions towards the murderer. Tommy instantly ran down with tears in his eyes, to relate the unfortunate death of his favourite to Mr. Barlow, and to demand vengeance against the wicked cat that had occasioned it. Mr. Barlow heard him with great compassion, but asked what punishment he wished to inflict upon the cat.

Tommy. Oh! sir, nothing can be too bad for that cruel animal. I would have her killed, as she killed the poor bird.

Mr. Barlow. But do you imagine that she did it out of any particular malice to your bird, or merely because she was hungry and accustomed to catch her prey in that manner?

Tommy considered some time, but at last he owned that he did not suspect the cat of having any particular spite against his bird, and therefore he supposed she had been impelled by hunger.

Mr. Barlow. Have you never observed that it was the

property of that species to prey upon mice and other little animals?

Tommy. Yes, sir, very often.

Mr. Barlow. And have you ever corrected her for so doing, or attempted to teach her other habits?

Tommy. I cannot say I have.—Indeed I have seen little Harry, when she had caught a mouse and was tormenting it, take it from her and give it liberty. But I have never meddled with her myself.

Mr. Barlow. Are you not then more to be blamed than the cat herself?—You have observed that it was common to the whole species to destroy mice and little birds, whenever they could surprise them, yet you have taken no pains to secure your favourite from the danger; on the contrary, by rendering him tame, and accustoming him to be fed, you have exposed him to a violent death which he would probably have avoided had he remained wild. Would it not then be just and more reasonable to endeavour to teach the cat that she must no longer prey upon little birds, than to put her to death for what you have never taught her was an offence?

Tommy. But is that possible?

Mr. Barlow. Very possible I should imagine. But we may at least try the experiment.

Tommy. But why should such a mischievous creature live at all?

Mr. Barlow. Because if you destroyed every creature that preys upon others, you would perhaps leave few alive.

Tommy. Surely, sir, the poor bird which that naughty cat has killed, was never guilty of such a cruelty?

Mr. Barlow. I will not answer for that. Let us observe what they live upon in the fields, we shall then be able to give a better account.

Mr. Barlow then went to the window, and desired Tommy to come to him and observe a robin which was then hopping upon the grass with something in its mouth, and asked him what he thought it was.

Tommy. I protest, sir, it is a large worm. And now he has swallowed it! I should never have thought that such a pretty bird could be so cruel.

Mr. Barlow. Do you imagine that the bird is conscious of all that is suffered by the insect?

Tommy. No, sir.

Mr. Barlow. In him then it is not the same cruelty which it would be in you, who are endowed with reason and reflection. Nature has given him a propensity for animal food, which he obeys in the same manner as the sheep and ox when they feed upon grass, or the ass when he browses upon the furze or thistles.

Tommy. Why then, perhaps, the cat did not know the cruelty she was guilty of in tearing that poor bird to pieces.

Mr. Barlow. No more than the bird we have just seen is conscious of his cruelty to the insect. The natural food of cats consists in rats, mice, birds, and such small animals as they can seize by violence, or catch by craft. It was impossible she should know the value you set upon your bird, and therefore she had no more intention of offending you, than had she caught a mouse.

Tommy. But if that is the case, should I have another tame bird, she will kill it as she has done this poor fellow.

Mr. Barlow. That, perhaps, may be prevented—I have heard people, that deal in birds, affirm, there is a way of preventing cats from meddling with them.

Tommy. Oh! dear sir! I should like to try it. Will you not show me how to prevent the cat from killing any more birds?

Mr. Barlow. Most willingly.—It is certainly better to correct the faults of an animal than to destroy it. Besides, I have a particular affection for this cat, because I found her when she was a kitten, and have bred her up so tame and gentle that she will follow me about like a dog. She comes every morning to my chamber door and mews till she is let in; and she sits upon the table at breakfast and dinner, as grave and polite as a visitor, without offering to touch the meat. Indeed, before she was guilty of this offence, I have often seen you stroke and caress her with great affection; and puss, who is by no means of an ungrateful temper, would always purr and arch her tail, as if she were sensible of your attention.

In a few days after this conversation, another robin suffering like the former, from the inclemency of the season, flew into the house and commenced acquaintance with Tommy. But he, who recollected the mournful fate of his former bird, would not encourage it to any familiarity, till he had claimed the promise of Mr. Barlow, in order to preserve it from danger. Mr. Barlow, therefore, enticed the new guest into a small wire cage, and as soon as he had entered it shut the door in order to prevent his escaping. He then took a small iron gridiron, such as is used to broil meat upon, and having almost heated it red-hot, placed it erect upon the ground, before the cage in which the bird was confined. He then contrived to entice the cat into the room, and observing that she fixed her eye upon the bird, which she destined to become her prey, he withdrew the two little boys in order to leave her unrestrained in her operations. They did not retire far, but observed her from the door fix her eyes upon the cage, and begin to approach it in silence, bending her body to the ground, and almost touching it as she crawled along. When she judged herself within a proper distance, she exerted all her agility in a violent spring, which would probably have been fatal to the bird, had not the gridiron placed before the cage received the impression of her attack. Nor was this disappointment the only punishment she was destined to undergo: the bars of the machine had been so thoroughly heated, that in rushing against them she felt herself burned in several parts of her body; and retired from the field of battle, mewing dreadfully and full of pain; and such was the impression which this adventure produced, that from this time, she was never known again to attempt to destroy birds.

The coldness of the weather still continuing, all the wild animals began to perceive the effects, and compelled by hunger, approached nearer to the habitations of man and the places they had been accustomed to avoid. A multitude of hares, the most timorous of all animals, were frequently seen scudding about the garden, in search of the scanty vegetables which the severity of the season had spared. In a short time, they had devoured all the green herbs which could be found, and hunger still oppressing them, they began to gnaw the very bark of the trees for food. One day, as Tommy was walking in the garden, he found that even the beloved tree which he had planted with his own hands, and from which he had promised himself so plentiful a produce of fruit, had not escaped the general depredation, but had been gnawed round at the root and killed. Tommy, who could ill brook disappointment, was so enraged to see his labours prove abortive, that he ran with tears in his eyes to Mr. Barlow, to demand vengeance against the devouring hares. "Indeed," said Mr. Barlow, "I am sorry for what they have done, but it is now too late to prevent it." "Yes," answered Tommy, "but you may have all those mischievous creatures shot, that they may do no farther damage." "A little while ago," replied Mr. Barlow, "you wanted to destroy the cat because she was cruel and preyed upon living animals, and now you would murder all the hares, merely because they are innocent, inoffensive animals, that subsist upon vegetables." Tommy looked a little foolish, but he said, that he did not want to hurt them for living upon vegetables, but for destroying his tree. "But," said Mr. Barlow, "how can you expect the animal to distinguish your trees from any other? You should therefore have fenced them round in such a manner as might have prevented the hares from reaching them. Besides, in such extreme distress as animals now suffer from the want of food, I think they may be forgiven if they trespass a little more than usual." Mr. Barlow then took Tommy by the hand, and led him into a field at some distance which belonged to him, and which was sown with turnips. Scarcely had they entered the field, before a flock of larks rose up in such innumerable quantities as almost darkened the air. "See," said Mr. Barlow, "these little fellows are trespassing upon my turnips in such numbers, that in a short time they will destroy every bit of green about the field; yet I would not hurt them upon any account. Look round the whole extent of the country, you will see nothing but a barren waste, which presents no food either to bird or beast. These little creatures therefore assemble in multitudes here, where they find a scanty subsistence, and though they do me some mischief they are welcome to what they can find. In the spring they will enliven our walks by their agreeable songs."

Tommy.   How dreary and uncomfortable is this season of winter! I wish it were always summer.

Mr. Barlow.   In some countries it is so: but there the inhabitants complain more of the intolerable heat than you do of the cold. They would with pleasure be relieved by the agreeable variety of cooler weather, when they are panting under the violence of a scorching sun.

Tommy.   Then I should like to live in a country that was never either disagreeably hot or cold.

Mr. Barlow.   Such a country is scarcely to be found; or if there is, it contains so small a portion of the earth, as to leave room for very few inhabitants.

Tommy.   Then I should think it would be so crowded that one could hardly stir; for everybody would naturally wish to live there.

Mr. Barlow.   There you are mistaken, for the inhabitants of the finest climates are often less attached to their country than those of the worst. Custom reconciles people to every kind of life, and makes them equally satisfied with the place in which they are born. There is a country called Lapland, which extends a great deal farther North than any part of England, which is covered with perpetual snows during all the year, yet the inhabitants would not exchange it for any other portion of the globe.

Tommy.   How do they live in so disagreeable a country?

Mr. Barlow.   If you ask Harry he will tell you. Being a farmer, it is his business to study the different methods by which men find subsistence in all the different parts of the earth.

Tommy.   I should like very much to hear, if Harry will be so good as to tell me.

Harry.   You must know then, Master Tommy, that in

the greatest part of this country which is called Lapland, the inhabitants neither sow nor reap; they are totally unacquainted with the use of corn, and know not how to make bread. They have no trees which bear fruit, scarcely any of the herbs which grow in our gardens in England, nor do they possess either sheep, goats, hogs, cows, or horses.

Tommy. That must be a disagreeable country indeed! What then have they to live upon?

Harry. They have a species of deer which is bigger than the largest stags which you may have seen in gentlemen's parks in England, and very strong. These animals are called rein-deer, and are of so gentle a nature that they are easily tamed and taught to live together in herds, and to obey their masters. In the short summer which they enjoy, the Laplanders lead them out to pasture in the valleys, where the grass grows very high and luxuriant. In the winter, when the ground is all covered over with snow, the deer have learned to scratch away the snow, and find a sort of moss which grows underneath it, and upon this they subsist. These creatures afford not only food, but raiment, and even houses to their masters. In the summer the Laplander milks his herds and lives upon the produce; sometimes he lays by the milk in wooden vessels to serve him for food in winter. This is soon frozen so hard, that when they would use it, they are obliged to cut it in pieces with an hatchet. Sometimes the winters are so severe that the poor deer can scarcely find even moss; and then the master is obliged to kill part of them and live upon the flesh. Of the skins he makes warm garments for himself and family, and strews them thick upon the ground to sleep upon.

Their houses are only poles stuck slanting into the ground, and almost joined at top, except a little hole which they leave to let out the smoke. These poles are either covered with the skins of animals, or coarse cloth, or sometimes with turf and the bark of trees. There is a little hole left in one side, through which the family creep into their tent, and they make a comfortable fire to warm them in the middle. People that are so easily contented, are totally ignorant of most of the things that are thought so necessary here. The

Laplanders have neither gold, nor silver, nor carpets, nor carve-work in their houses. Every man makes for himself all that the real wants of life require, and with his own hands performs everything which is necessary to be done. Their food consists either in frozen milk, or the flesh of the rein-deer, or that of the bear, which they frequently hunt and kill. Instead of bread, they strip off the bark of firs, which are almost the only trees which grow upon those dismal mountains, and boiling the inward and more tender skin, they eat it with their flesh. The greatest happiness of these poor people is to live free and unrestrained: therefore, they do not long remain fixed to any spot, but taking down their houses, they pack them up along with the little furniture they possess, and load them upon sledges to carry and set them up in some other place.

Tommy. Have you not said that they have neither horses nor oxen? Do they then draw these sledges themselves?

Harry. I thought I should surprise you, Master Tommy. The rein-deer which I have described are so tractable that they are harnessed like horses, and draw the sledges with their masters upon them near thirty miles a day. They set out with surprising swiftness, and run along the snow which is frozen so hard in winter that it supports them like a solid road. In this manner do the Laplanders perform their journeys, and change their places of abode as often as is agreeable. In the spring they lead their herds of deer to pasture upon the mountains; in the winter they come down into the plains, where they are better protected against the fury of the winds. For the whole country is waste and desolate, destitute of all the objects which you see here. There are no towns, nor villages; no fields inclosed or cultivated; no beaten roads; no inns for travellers to sleep at; no shops to purchase the necessaries or conveniences of life at; the face of the whole country is barren and dismal; wherever you turn your eyes, nothing is to be seen but lofty mountains white with snow and covered with ice and fogs. Scarcely any trees are to be seen except a few stunted fir and birch. These mountains afford a retreat to thousands of bears and wolves, which are continually pouring down and prowling about to prey upon the herds of deer: so that the Laplanders are continually obliged to fight them in their own defence. To do this, they fix large pieces of flat board about four or five feet long to the bottom of their feet; and thus secured they run along without sinking into the snow, so nimbly, that they can overtake the wild animals in the chase. The bear they kill with bows and arrows which they make themselves. Sometimes they find out the dens where they have laid themselves up in the winter, and then they attack them with spears, and generally overcome them. When a Laplander has killed a bear, he carries it home in triumph, boils the flesh in an iron pot, which is all the cooking they are acquainted with, and invites all his neighbors to the feast. This they account the greatest delicacy in the world, and particularly the fat, which they melt over the fire and drink; then, sitting round the flame, they entertain each other with stories of their own exploits in hunting or fishing, till the feast is over. Though they live so barbarous a life, they are a good-natured, sincere, and hospitable people. If a stranger comes among them, they lodge and entertain him in the best manner they are able, and generally refuse all payment for their services, unless it be a little bit of tobacco, which they are immoderately fond of smoking.

Tommy.   Poor people, how I pity them to live such an unhappy life! I should think the fatigues and hardships they undergo, must kill them in a very short space of time!

Mr. Barlow.   Have you then observed that those who eat and drink the most, and undergo the least fatigue, are the most free from diseases?

Tommy.   Not always; for I remember that there are two or three gentlemen that come to dine at my father's, who eat an amazing quantity of meat, besides drinking a great deal of wine; and these poor gentlemen have lost the use of almost all their limbs. Their legs are so swelled that they are almost as big as their bodies; their feet are so tender that they cannot set them to the ground, and their knees so stiff that they cannot bend them. When they arrive, they are obliged to be helped out of their coaches by two or three people, and they come hobbling in upon crutches. But I never heard them talk about anything but eating and drinking in my life.

Mr. Barlow. And did you ever observe that any of the poor had lost the use of their limbs by the same disease?

Tommy. I cannot say I have.

Mr. Barlow. Then perhaps the being confined to a scanty diet, to hardship, and to exercise, may not be so destructive as you imagine. This way of life is even much less so than the intemperance in which too many of the rich continually indulge themselves. I remember lately reading a story upon this subject, which if you please you shall hear. Mr. Barlow then read the following:

> *History of a surprising* CURE *of the* GOUT.
> [*This and other stories are omitted.*]

And now the time arrived, when Tommy was by appointment to go home and spend some time with his parents. Mr. Barlow had been long afraid of this visit, as he knew he would meet a great deal of company there, who would give him impressions of a very different nature from what he had with so much assiduity been labouring to excite. However, the visit was unavoidable, and Mr. Merton sent so pressing an invitation for Harry to accompany his friend, after having obtained the consent of his father, that Mr. Barlow, with much regret, took leave of both his pupils. Harry, from the experience he had formerly acquired of polite life, had no great inclination for the expedition; however, his temper was too easy and obliging to raise any objections, and the real affection he now entertained for Master Merton, rendered him less averse than he would otherwise have been.

When they arrived at Mr. Merton's, they were introduced into a crowded drawing-room, full of the most elegant company which that part of the country afforded; among whom were several young gentlemen and ladies of different ages, who had been purposely invited to spend their holidays with Master Merton. As soon as Master Merton entered, every tongue was let loose in his praise; he was grown, he was improved, he was such a charming boy; his eyes, his hair, his teeth, his every feature was the admiration of all the ladies. Thrice did he make the circle in order to receive the congratulations of the company and to be introduced to the young ladies. As to Harry, he had the good fortune to be taken notice of by nobody except Mr. Merton, who received him with great cordiality. A lady however, that sat by Mrs. Merton, asked her in a whisper, which was loud enough to be heard all over the room, whether that was the little plough-boy which she had heard Mr. Barlow was attempting to breed up like a gentleman. Mrs. Merton answered it was. "I protest," said the lady, "I should have thought so by his plebeian look and vulgar air. But I wonder, my dear madam, that you will suffer your son, that without flattery is one of the most accomplished children I ever saw in my life, with quite the air of fashion, to keep such company. Are you not afraid that Master Merton should insensibly contract bad habits and a groveling way of thinking? For my own part, as I think a good education is a thing of the utmost consequence in life, I have spared no pains to give my dear Matilda every possible advantage." "Indeed," replied Mrs. Merton, "one may see the excellence of her education in everything that Miss Matilda does. She plays most divinely upon the harpsichord, talks French even better than she does English, and draws in the style of a master. Indeed, I think that last figure of the naked gladiator the finest thing I ever saw in my life."

While this conversation was going on in one part of the room, a young lady observing that nobody seemed to take the least notice of Harry, advanced towards him with the greatest affability, and began to enter into conversation with him. This young lady's name was Simmons: her father and mother had been two of the most respectable people in the country, according to the old style of English gentry; but having died while she was young, the care of her had devolved upon an uncle, who was a man of sense and benevolence, but a very great humourist. This gentleman had such peculiar ideas of female character, that he waged war with most of the polite and modern accomplishments. As one of the first blessings of life, according to his notions, was health, he endeavoured to prevent that sickly delicacy, which is considered as so great an ornament in fashionable life, by a more robust and hardy education. His niece was accustomed from her earliest years to plunge into the cold bath at every season of the year, to rise by candlelight in winter, to ride a dozen miles upon a trotting horse, or to walk as many even with the hazard of being splashed or soiling her clothes.

By this mode of education Miss Sukey, for so she had the misfortune to be named, acquired an excellent character, accompanied however with some dispositions, which disqualified her almost as much as Harry, for fashionable life. She was acquainted with all the best authors in our own language, nor was she ignorant of those in French; although she could not speak a word of the language. Her uncle, who was a man of sense and knowledge, had besides instructed her in several parts of knowledge, which rarely fall to the lot of ladies; such as the established laws of nature and a small degree of geometry. She was, besides, brought up to every species of household employment, which is now exploded by ladies in every rank and station, as mean and vulgar; and taught to believe, that domestic economy is a point of the utmost consequence to every woman that intends to be a wife or mother. As to music, though Miss Simmons had a very agreeable voice, and could sing several simple songs in a very pleasing manner, she was entirely ignorant of it; her uncle used to say, that human life is not long enough, to throw away so much time upon the science of making a noise. Nor would he permit her to learn French, although he understood it himself; women, he thought, are not birds of passage, that are to be eternally changing their place of abode. "I have never seen any good," would he say, "from the importation of foreign manners; every virtue may be learned and practiced at home; and it is only because we do not choose to have either virtue or religion among us, that so many adventurers are yearly sent out to smuggle foreign graces. As to various languages, I do not see the necessity of them for a woman. My niece is to marry an Englishman, and to live in England. To what purpose then should I labour to take off the difficulty of conversing with foreigners, and to promote her intercourse with barbers, valets, dancing-masters, and adventurers of every description, that are continually doing us the honour to come amongst us? As to the French nation, I know and esteem it on many accounts; but I am very doubtful whether the English will ever gain much by adopting either their manners or their government; and when respectable foreigners choose to visit us, I see no reason why they should not take the trouble of learning the language of the country."

Such had been the education of Miss Simmons, who was the only one of all the genteel company at Mr. Merton's that thought Harry deserving the least attention. This young lady, who possessed an uncommon degree of natural benevolence of character, came up to him, and addressed him in such a manner as set him perfectly at his ease. Harry was destitute of the artificial graces of society; but he possessed that natural politeness and good-nature, without which all artificial graces are the most disgusting things in the world. Harry had an understanding naturally strong; and Mr. Barlow, while he had with the greatest care preserved him from all false impressions, had taken great pleasure in cultivating the faculties of his mind. Harry indeed never said any of those brilliant things which render a boy the darling of the ladies; he had not that vivacity, or rather impertinence, which frequently passes for wit with superficial people: but he paid the greatest attention to what was said to him, and made the most judicious observations upon subjects he understood. For this reason, Miss Simmons, although much older and more improved, received great satisfaction from conversing with him, and thought little Harry infinitely more agreeable and judicious than any of the smart young gentlemen she had hitherto seen at Mr. Merton's.

But now the company was summoned to the important business of dinner. Harry could not help sighing, when he reflected upon what he had to undergo; however, he determined to bear it with all imaginable fortitude for the sake of his friend Tommy. The dinner indeed was, if possible, more dreadful than anything he had before undergone; so many fine gentlemen and fine ladies; so many powdered servants to stand behind their chairs; such an apparatus of dishes that Harry had never tasted before, and that almost made him sick when he did taste; so many removes; such pomp and solemnity about what seemed the easiest thing in the world; that Harry could not help envying the condition of his father's labourers, who when they are hungry, can sit at their ease under an hedge, and make a dinner, without plates, table-cloths, or compliments. In the meantime his friend Tommy was received amid the circle of the ladies, and attended to as a prodigy of wit and ingenuity. Harry could not help being surprised at this; his affection for his friend was totally unmixed with the meanness of jealousy, and he received the sincerest pleasure from every improvement which Tommy had made; however, he had never discovered in him any of those surprising talents, and when he could catch anything that Tommy said, it appeared to him rather inferior to his usual method of conversation: however, as so many fine ladies were of a different opinion, he took it for granted that he must be mistaken. But if Harry's opinion of his friend's abilities was not much improved by this exhibition, it was not so with Tommy. The repeated assurances which he received that he was indeed a little prodigy, began to convince him that he really was so. When he considered the company he came from, he found that infinite injustice had been done to his merit; for at Mr. Barlow's he was frequently contradicted and obliged to give a reason for what he said; but here in order to be admired, he had nothing to do but talk; whether he had any meaning or not, his auditors always found either wit, or sense, or a most entertaining sprightliness in all he said.

Nor was Mrs. Merton herself deficient in bestowing marks of admiration upon her son. To see him before improve in health, in understanding, in virtue, had given her a pleasurable sensation, for she was by no means destitute of good dispositions; but to see him shine with such transcendent brightness, before such excellent judges and in so polite a company, inspired her with raptures she had never felt before. Indeed, in consequence of this success, the young gentleman's volubility improved so much, that before the dinner was over, he seemed disposed to engross the whole conversation to himself; and Mr. Merton, who did not quite relish the sallies of his son so much as his wife, was once or twice obliged to interpose and check him in his career. This Mrs. Merton thought very hard, and all the ladies, after they had retired into the drawing-room, agreed, that his father would certainly spoil his temper by such improper contradiction.

As to little Harry, he had not the good fortune to please the greater number of the ladies; they observed that he was awkward and ungenteel, and had an heavy clownish look; he was also silent and reserved, and had not said a single agreeable thing: if Mr. Barlow chose to keep a school for carters and threshers, nobody would hinder him; but it was not proper to introduce such vulgar people to the sons of persons of fashion. It was therefore agreed, that Mr. Barlow ought either to send little Harry home to his friends, or to be no more honoured with the company of Master Merton. Indeed, one of the ladies hinted that Mr. Barlow himself was but an odd kind of man, that never went to assemblies, and played upon no kind of instrument. "Why," answered Mrs. Merton, "to tell the truth, I was not over fond of the scheme: Mr. Barlow, to be sure, though a very good, is a very odd kind of man; however, as he is so disinterested, and would never receive the least present from us, I doubt whether we could with propriety insist upon his turning little Sandford out of the house." "If that is the case, madam," answered Mrs. Compton, for that was the name of the lady, "I think it would be infinitely better to remove Master Merton, and place him in some polite seminary; where he might acquire a knowledge of the world, and make genteel connections. This will be always the greatest advantage to a young gentleman, and will prove of the most essential service to him in life. For though a person has all the merit in the world, without such acquaintance it never will push him forward, or enable him to make a figure. This is the plan which I have always pursued with Augustus and Matilda; I think I may say, not entirely without success; for they have both the good fortune to have formed the most brilliant acquaintances. As to Augustus, he is so intimate with young Lord Squander,

who you know is possessed of the greatest parliamentary interest, that I think his fortune is as good as made."

Miss Simmons, who was present at this refined and wise
conversation, could not help looking with so much significance
at this mention of Lord Squander, that Mrs. Compton coloured
a little, and asked with some warmth, whether she knew anything of that young nobleman. "Why, madam," answered the
young lady, "what I know is very little; but if you desire me
to inform you, it is my duty to speak the truth." "Oh! to be
sure, miss," replied Mrs. Compton, a little angrily; "we all
know that your judgment and knowledge of the world are
superior to what anybody else can boast; and therefore, I shall
be infinitely obliged to you for any information you may be
pleased to give." "Indeed, madam," answered the young lady,
"I have very little of either to boast, nor am I personally acquainted with the nobleman you are talking of; but I have a
cousin, a very good boy, that is at the same public school with
his lordship, who has given me such a character of him as does
not much prepossess me in his favour."—"And what may this
wise cousin of yours, have said of his lordship?"—"Only,
madam, that he is one of the worst boys in the whole school.
That he has neither genius, nor application for anything that
becomes his rank and situation. That he has no taste for anything but gaming, horse-racing, and the most contemptible
amusements. That though his allowance is so large, he is eternally running in debt with everybody that will trust him; and
that he has broken his word so often that nobody has the least
confidence in what he says. Added to this, I have heard that
he is so haughty, tyrannical, and overbearing, that nobody can
long preserve his friendship, without the meanest flattery and
subservience to all his vicious inclinations. And to finish all,
that he is of so ungrateful a temper, that he was never known
to do an act of kindness to anyone, or to care about anything
but himself.—"

Here Miss Matilda could not help interposing with
warmth: she said, that his lordship had nothing in his character
or manners that did not perfectly become a nobleman of the
most elevated soul. Little, groveling minds, indeed, which are

always envious of their superiors, might give a disagreeable turn to the generous openness of this young nobleman's temper. That as to gaming and running in debt, they were so essential to a man of fashion, that nobody who was not born in the city, and oppressed by city prejudices, would think of making the least objection to them. She then made a panegyric upon his lordship's person, his elegant taste in dress, his new phaeton, his entertaining conversation, his extraordinary performance upon the violin, and concluded that, with such abilities and accomplishments, she did not doubt of one day seeing him at the head of the nation. Miss Simmons had no desire of pushing the conversation any farther, and the rest of the company coming in to tea, the disquisition about Lord Squander finished.

After tea, several of the young ladies were desired to amuse the company with music and singing: among the rest, Miss Simmons sang a little Scotch song, called Lochaber, in so artless, but sweet and pathetic a manner, that little Harry listened almost with tears in his eyes, though several of the other young ladies, by their significant looks and gestures, treated it with ineffable contempt. After this Miss Matilda, who was allowed to be a perfect mistress of music, played and sang several celebrated Italian airs. But as they were in a language totally unintelligible to him, Harry received very little pleasure, though all the rest of the company were in raptures. She then proceeded to play several pieces of music, which were allowed by all connoisseurs to require infinite skill to execute.

The audience seemed all delighted, and either felt or pretended to feel, inexpressible pleasure; even Tommy himself, though he did not know one note from another, had caught so much of the general enthusiasm, that he applauded as loud as the rest of the company: but Harry, whose temper was not quite so pliable, could not conceal the intolerable weariness that over-powered his senses during this long exhibition. He gaped, he yawned, he stretched, he even pinched himself, in order to keep his attention alive, but all in vain; the more Miss Matilda exercised her skill in playing pieces of the most difficult execution, the more did Harry's propensity to drowsiness increase. At length, the lateness of the hour, which much exceeded Harry's time of going to bed, conspiring with the opiate charms of music, he could resist no longer, but insensibly fell back upon his chair, fast asleep. This unfortunate accident was soon remarked by the rest of the company, and confirmed them very much in the opinion they had conceived of Harry's vulgarity; while he, in the meantime, enjoyed the most placid slumber, which was not dissipated till Miss Matilda had desisted from playing.

Thus was the first day passed at Mr. Merton's, very little to the satisfaction of Harry; the next, and the next after, was only a repetition of the same scene. The little gentry, whose tastes and manners were totally different from his, had now imbibed a perfect contempt for Harry, and it was with great difficulty that they would condescend to treat him even with common civility. In this laudable behaviour they were very much confirmed by Master Compton and Master Mash. Master Compton was reckoned a very genteel boy, though all his gentility consisted in a pair of buckles so big that they almost crippled him, in a slender, emaciated figure, and a look of consummate impudence. He had almost finished his education at a public school, where he had learned every vice and folly which is commonly taught at such places, without the least improvement either of his character or his understanding. Master Mash was the son of a neighbouring gentleman who had considerably impaired his fortune by an inordinate love of horse-racing. Having been from his infancy accustomed to no other conversation than about winning and losing money, he had acquired the idea that to bet successfully was the summit of all human ambition. He had been almost brought up in the stable, and therefore had imbibed the greatest interest about horses; not from any real affection for that noble animal, but merely because he considered them as engines for the winning of money. He too was now improving his talents by a public education, and longed impatiently for the time when he should be set free from all restraint, and allowed to display the superiority of his genius at Ascot and Newmarket.[4] These two young gentlemen had conceived the most violent dislike to Harry, and lost no occasion of saying or doing everything they had in their power to mortify him.

To Tommy they were in the contrary extreme, and omitted no opportunity of rendering themselves agreeable. Nor was it long before their forward, vivacious manners, accompanied with a knowledge of many of those gay scenes which acted forcibly upon Tommy's imagination, began to render their conversation highly agreeable. They talked to him about public diversions, about celebrated actresses, about parties of pleasure and parties of mischief. Tommy began to feel himself introduced to a new train of ideas and a wider range of conduct; he began to long for the time when he should share in the glories of robbing orchards, or insulting passengers, with impunity; but when he heard that little boys, scarcely bigger than himself, had often joined in the glorious prospect of forming open rebellions against their masters, or of disturbing a whole audience at a play-house, he panted for the time when he might have a chance of sharing in the fame of such achievements. By degrees he lost all regard for Mr. Barlow, and all affection for his friend Harry: at first, indeed, he was shocked at hearing Mr. Barlow mentioned with disrespect; but, becoming by degrees more callous to every good impression, he at last took infinite pleasure in seeing Master Mash, who, though destitute of either wit or genius, had a great taste for mimicry, take off the parson in the middle of his sermon. Harry perceived and lamented this change in the manners of his friend; he sometimes took the liberty of remonstrating with him upon the subject, but was only answered with a contemptuous sneer; and Master Mash, who happened once to be present, told him that he was a monstrous bore.

It happened that while Harry was at Mr. Merton's, there was a troop of strolling players at a neighbouring town. In order to divert the young gentry, Mr. Merton contrived that they should make a party to see a play. They went accordingly, and Harry with the rest. Tommy, who now no longer condescended to take any notice of his friend, was seated between his two inseparable companions. These young gentlemen first began to give specimens of their politeness by throwing nuts and orange peel upon the stage, and Tommy, who was resolved to profit by such excellent example, threw nuts and orange peel with infinite satisfaction. As soon as the curtain drew up, and the actors appeared, all the rest of the audience observed a decent silence; but Mash and Compton, who were now determined to prove the superiority of their manners, began to talk so loud, and make so much noise, that it was impossible for anyone near them to hear a word of the play. This also seemed amazingly fine to Tommy; and he too talked and laughed as loud as the rest. The subject of their conversation was the audience and the performers, neither of which these polite young gentlemen found bearable.

The company was chiefly composed of the tradesmen of the town, and the inhabitants of the neighbouring country: this was a sufficient reason for these refined young gentlemen to speak of them with the most insufferable contempt. Every circumstance of their dress and appearance was criticised with such a minuteness of attention, that Harry, who sat near, and very much against his inclinations was witness to all that passed, began to imagine that his companions, instead of being brought up like the sons of gentlemen, had only studied under barbers and tailors; such amazing knowledge did they display in the history of buckles, buttons, and dressing of hair. As to the poor performers, they found them totally undeserving mercy; they were so shocking awkward, so ill dressed, so low-lived, and such detestable creatures, that it was impossible to bear them with any patience. Master Mash, who prided himself upon being a young gentleman of great spirit, was of opinion that they should kick up a riot and demolish all the scenery. Tommy, indeed, did not very well understand what the expression meant, but he was so intimately persuaded of the merit and genius of his companions, that he agreed that it would be the properest thing in the world, and the proposal was accordingly made to the rest of the young gentlemen.

But Harry, who had been silent all the time, could not help remonstrating at what appeared to him the greatest cruelty and injustice. "These poor people," said he, "are doing all they can to entertain us; is it not very unkind to treat them in return with scorn and contempt? If they could act better, even as well as those fine people you talk of in London, would they not willingly do it; and therefore why should we be angry at them for what they cannot help? And as to cutting the scenes to pieces, or doing the house any damage, have we any more right to attempt it, than they would have to come into your father's dining-room and break the dishes to pieces, because they did not like the dinner?—While we are here let us behave with good manners; and if we do not like their acting, it is our own faults if ever we come to see them again." This method of reasoning was not much relished by those to whom it was addressed, and it is uncertain how far they might have proceeded, had not a decent, plain looking man, who had been long disturbed with the noise of these young gentry, at length taken the liberty of expostulating with them upon the subject. This freedom or impertinence, as it was termed by Master Mash, was answered by him with so much rudeness, that the man, who was a neighbouring farmer, was obliged to reply in an higher strain.

Thus did the altercation increase every minute, till Master Mash, who thought it an unpardonable affront that anyone in an inferior station should presume to think or feel for himself, so far lost all command of his temper as to call the man a blackguard, and strike him upon the face. But the farmer, who possessed great strength and equal resolution, very deliberately laid hold of the young gentleman who had offered him the insult, and without the smallest exertion, laid him sprawling upon the ground, at his full length under the benches, and setting his feet upon his body, told him that since he did not know how to sit quiet at a play, he would have the honour of teaching him to lie; and that if he offered to stir, he would trample him to pieces, a threat which was very evident he could find no difficulty in executing.

This unexpected incident struck an universal damp over the spirits of the little gentry; and even Master Mash himself so far forgot his dignity, as to supplicate in a very submissive manner for a release: in this he was joined by all his companions, and Harry among the rest. "Well," said the farmer, "I should never have thought that a parcel of young gentlemen, as you call yourselves, would come into public to behave with so much rudeness; I am sure, that there is ne'er a plough-boy at my house, but what would have shown more sense and manners: but since you are sorry for what has happened, I am very willing to make an end of the affair; more especially for the sake of this little master here, who has behaved with so much propriety, that I am sure he is a better gentleman than any of you, though he is not dressed so much like a monkey or a barber." With these words he suffered the crest-fallen Mash to rise, who crept from his place of confinement, with looks infinitely more expressive of mildness than he had brought with him: nor was the lesson lost upon the rest, for they behaved with the greatest decency during all the rest of the exhibition. However, Master Mash's courage began to rise as he went home, and found himself farther from his formidable farmer; for he assured his companions, that if it had not been so vulgar a fellow, he would certainly call him out and pistol him.

The next day at dinner, Mr. Merton, and the ladies who had not accompanied the young gentlemen to the play, nor had yet heard of the misfortune which had ensued, were very inquisitive about the preceding night's entertainment. The young people agreed that the performers were detestable, but that the play was a charming piece, full of wit and sentiment, and extremely improving: this play was called *The Marriage of Figaro,* and Master Compton had informed them, that it was amazingly admired by all the people of the fashion in London. But Mr. Merton, who had observed that Harry was totally silent, at length insisted upon knowing his opinion upon the subject. "Why, sir," answered Harry, "I am very little judge of these matters, for I never saw a play before in my life, and therefore I cannot tell whether it was acted well or ill; but as to the play itself, it seemed to me to be full of nothing but cheating and dissimulation, and the people that come in and out, do nothing but impose upon each other, and lie, and trick, and deceive. Were you or any gentleman to have such a parcel of servants, you would think them fit for nothing in the world; and therefore

I could not help wondering, while the play was acting, that people would throw away so much of their time upon sights that can do them no good; and send their children and their relations to learn fraud and insincerity." Mr. Merton smiled at the honest bluntness of Harry; but several of the ladies, who had just been expressing an extravagant admiration of this piece, seemed to be not a little mortified; however, as they could not contradict the charges which Harry had brought against it, they thought it more prudent to be silent.

In the evening, it was proposed that all the little gentry should divert themselves with cards; and they accordingly sat down to a game which is called Commerce. But Harry, who was totally ignorant of this accomplishment, desired to be excused; however, his friend Miss Simmons offered to teach him the game, which she assured him was so easy, that in three minutes he would be able to play as well as the rest. Harry, however, still continued to refuse, and at length confessed to Miss Simmons, that he had expended all his money the day before, and therefore was unable to furnish the stake which the rest deposited. "Don't let that disturb you," said she, "I will put down for you with a great deal of pleasure." "Madam," answered Harry, "I am very much obliged to you, I am sure; but Mr. Barlow has always forbidden me either to receive or borrow money of anybody, for fear in the one case I should become mercenary, or in the other, dishonest; and therefore, though there is nobody here, whom I esteem more than yourself, I am obliged to refuse your offer." "Well," replied Miss Simmons, "that need not disturb you, for you shall play upon my account; and that you may do without any violation of your principles."

Thus was Harry, though with some reluctance, induced to sit down to cards with the rest. The game, indeed, he found no difficulty in learning, but he could not help remarking with wonder, the extreme solicitude which appeared in the face of all the players at every change of fortune. Even the young ladies, all but Miss Simmons, seemed to be equally sensible of the passion of gaining money with the rest; and some of them behaved with a degree of asperity which quite astonished him.

After several changes of fortune, it happened that Miss Simmons and Harry were the only remaining players; all the rest,
by the laws of the game, had forfeited all pretensions to the
stake, the property of which was clearly vested in these two,
and one more deal was wanting to decide it. But Harry with
great politeness rose from the table, and told Miss Simmons,
that as he had only played upon her account, he was now no
longer wanted, and that the whole undoubtedly belonged to her.
Miss Simmons refused to take it, and when she found that
Harry was not to be induced to play any more, she at last
proposed to him to divide what was left. This also Harry declined, alleging that he had not the least title to any part. But
Miss Simmons, who began to be uneasy at the observation
which this extraordinary contest produced, told Harry that he
would very much oblige her by taking his share of the money,
and laying it out in any manner for her that he judged best.
"Upon this condition," answered Harry, "I will take it; and I
think I know a method of laying it out, which you will not
entirely disapprove."

The next day, as soon as breakfast was over, Harry disappeared; nor was he come back when the company were assembled at dinner. At length he came in, with a glow of health
and exercise upon his face, and that disorder of dress which is
produced by a long expedition. The young ladies eyed him
with great contempt, which seemed a little to disconcert him;
but Mr. Merton speaking to him with great good humour, and
making room for him to sit down, Harry soon recovered from
his confusion. In the evening, after a long conversation among
the young people about public diversions, and plays, and
dancers, and actors, they happened to mention the name of a
celebrated performer, who at this time engaged the whole
attention of the town. Master Compton, after expatiating with
great enthusiasm upon the subject, added that nothing was so
fashionable as to make great presents to this person, in order to
show the taste and elegance of the giver. He then proposed, that
as so many young gentlemen and ladies were here assembled,
they should set an example which would do them infinite
honour, and probably be followed throughout the kingdom, of

making a little collection among themselves to buy a piece of plate, or a gold snuff-box, or some other trifle, to be presented in their name. He added, that though he could ill spare the money, having just laid out six guineas upon a new pair of buckles, he would contribute a guinea to so excellent a purpose, and that Master Mash and Merton would do the same.

This proposal was universally approved of by all the company; and all, but Harry, promised to contribute in proportion to their finances. This Master Mash observing, said, "Well, farmer, and what will you subscribe?" Harry answered, that upon this occasion he must beg to be excused, for he had nothing to give. "Here is a pretty fellow!" answered Mash; "last night we saw him pouch thirty shillings of our money, which he cheated us out of at Commerce, and now the little stingy wretch will not contribute half a crown, where we are giving away whole guineas." Upon this, Miss Matilda said, in an ironical manner, that Master Harry had always an excellent reason to give for his conduct; and she did not doubt but he could prove to all their satisfaction, that it was more liberal to keep his money in his pocket than to give it away. Harry, who was a little nettled at these reflections, answered, that though he was not bound to give any reason, he thought he had a very good one to give; and that was, that he saw no generosity in thus bestowing money. "According to your own account," added he, "the person you have been talking of, gains more than fifty poor families have in the country to maintain themselves; and therefore, if I had any money to give away, I should certainly give it to those that want it most." With these words, Harry went out of the room, and the rest of the gentry, after abusing him very liberally, sat down to cards. But Miss Simmons, who imagined that there was more in Harry's conduct than he had explained, excused herself from cards, and took an opportunity of talking to him upon the subject. After speaking to him with great good-nature, she asked him, whether it might not have been better to have contributed something along with the rest, than to have offended them by so free an exposition of his sentiments; even though he did not entirely approve of the scheme.

"Indeed, madam," said Harry, "this is what I would gladly have done, but it was totally out of my power." "How can that be, Harry; did you not win the other night near thirty shillings?" "That, madam, all belonged to you; and I have already disposed of it in your name, in a manner that I hope you will not disapprove." "How is that!" answered the young lady with some surprise. "Madam," said Harry, "there was a young woman that lived with my father as a servant, and always behaved with the greatest honesty and carefulness. This young woman had an aged father and mother, who for a great while were able to maintain themselves by their own labour; but at last the poor old man became too weak to do a day's work, and his wife was afflicted with a disease they call the palsy. Now, when this good young woman saw that her parents were in such great distress, she left her place and went to live with them, on purpose to take care of them; and she works very hard, whenever she can get work, and fares very hard, in order to maintain her parents; and though we assist them all we can, I know that sometimes they can hardly get food and clothes. Therefore, madam, as you were so kind to say, that I should dispose of this money for you, I ran over this morning to these poor people, and gave them all the money in your name: and I hope you will not be displeased at the use I have put it to." "Indeed," answered the young lady, "I am much obliged to you for the good opinion you have of me; and the application of it does me a great deal of honour: I am only sorry, you did not give it in your own name." "That," replied Harry, "I had not any right to do; it would have been attributing to myself what did not belong to me, and equally inconsistent with truth and honesty."

In this manner did the time pass away at Mr. Merton's, while Harry received very little satisfaction from his visit, except in conversing with Miss Simmons. The affability and good sense of this young lady had entirely gained his confidence. While all the other young ladies were continually intent upon displaying their talents and importance, she alone was simple and unaffected. But what disgusted Harry more than ever was, that his refined companions seemed to consider themselves, an?

a few of their acquaintance, as the only beings of any consequence in the world. The most trifling inconvenience, the being
a little too hot, a little too cold, the walking a few hundred
yards, the waiting a few minutes for their dinner, the having a
trifling cold, or a little head-ache, were misfortunes so feelingly
lamented, that he would have imagined they were the most
tender of the human species, had he not observed that they
considered the sufferings of all below them with a profound
indifference. If the misfortunes of the poor were mentioned, he
heard of nothing but the insolence and ingratitude of that class
of people, which seemed to be a sufficient excuse for the want
of common humanity. Surely, said Harry to himself, there cannot be so much difference between one human being and
another; or if there is, I should think that part of them the most
valuable, which cultivates the ground and provides necessaries
for all the rest: not those, who understand nothing but dress,
walking with their toes out, staring modest people out of
countenance, and jabbering a few words of a foreign language.

But now the attention of all the younger part of the company was fixed upon making preparations for a ball; which
Mrs. Merton had determined to give in honour of Master
Tommy's return. The whole house was now full of milliners
mantua-makers, and dancing masters. All the young ladies were
employed in giving directions about their clothes, or in practicing the steps of different dances. Harry now, for the first time,
began to comprehend the infinite importance of dress. Even the
elderly ladies seemed to be as much interested about the affair
as their daughters; and instead of the lessons of conduct and
wisdom which he expected to hear, nothing seemed to employ
their attention a moment, but French trimmings, gauzes, and
Italian flowers. Miss Simmons alone appeared to consider the
approaching solemnity with perfect indifference. Harry had
never heard a single word drop from her that expressed either
interest or impatience; but he had for some days observed her
employed in her room, with more than common assiduity. At
length, upon the very day that was destined for this important
exhibition, she came to him with a benevolent smile, and spoke
to him thus: "I was so much pleased with the account you gave

me the other day, of that poor young woman's duty and affection towards her parents, that I have for some time employed
myself in preparing for them a little present, which I shall be
obliged to you, Master Harry, to convey to them. I have unfortunately never learned either to embroider or to paint artificial flowers; but my good uncle has taught me, that the best
employment I can make of my hands is to assist those that cannot assist themselves." Saying this, she put into his hands a
parcel that contained some linen and other necessaries for the
poor old people; and bade him tell them not to forget to call
upon her uncle, when she was returned home; as he was always
happy to assist the deserving and industrious poor. Harry received her present with gratitude, and almost with tears of joy;
and looking up in her face imagined that he saw the features of
one of those angels which he had read of in the scriptures: so
much does real, disinterested benevolence improve the expression of the human countenance.

But all the rest of the young gentry were employed in
cares of a very different nature, the dressing their hair and
adorning their persons. Tommy himself had now completely
resumed his natural character, and thrown aside all that he had
learned during his residence with Mr. Barlow. He had contracted an infinite fondness for all those scenes of dissipation
which his new friends daily described to him, and began to be
convinced that one of the most important things in life is a
fashionable dress. In this most rational sentiment he had been
confirmed by almost all the young ladies, with whom he had
conversed since his return home. The distinctions of character,
relative to virtue and understanding, which had been with so
much pains inculcated upon his mind, seemed here to be entirely unheeded. No one took the trouble of examining the real
principles or motives from which any human being acted; while
the most minute attention was continually given to what regarded merely the outside. He observed that the omission of
every duty towards our fellow-creatures, was not only excused,
but even to a certain degree admired, provided it was joined
with a certain fashionable appearance; while the most perfect
probity, or integrity, was mentioned with coldness or disgust,

and frequently with open ridicule, if unconnected with a brilliant appearance.

As to all the common virtues of life, such as industry, economy, a punctuality in discharging our obligations or keeping our words, these were qualities which were treated as fit for nothing but the vulgar. Mr. Barlow, he found, had been utterly mistaken in all the principles which he had ever inculcated. The human species, said Mr. Barlow, can only be supplied with food and necessaries, by a constant assiduity in cultivating the earth and providing for their mutual wants. It is by labour that everything is produced; without labour, these fertile fields which are now adorned with all the luxuriance of plenty, would be converted into barren heaths or impenetrable thickets; these meadows, the support of a thousand herds of cattle, be covered with stagnated waters, that would not only render them uninhabitable by beasts, but corrupt the air with pestilential vapours. Even these innumerable flocks of sheep, that feed along the hills, would disappear along with that cultivation, which can alone support them, and secure their existence. For this reason, would Mr. Barlow say, labour is the first and most indispensable duty of the human species, from which no one can have a right entirely to withdraw himself.

But, however true might be these principles, they were so totally inconsistent with the conduct and opinions of his new friends, that it was not possible for Tommy long to remember their force. He had been near a month with a few young gentlemen and ladies of his own rank, and, instead of their being brought up to produce anything useful, he found that the great object of all their knowledge and education was only to waste, to consume, to destroy, to dissipate what was produced by others. He even found that this inability to assist either themselves or others, seemed to be a merit upon which everyone valued himself extremely; so that an individual that could not exist without having two attendants to wait upon him, was superior to him that had only one; but was obliged in turn to yield to another that required four. And, indeed, this new system seemed much more easy than the old; for instead of giving himself any trouble about his manners or understanding, he might with safety indulge all his caprices; give way to all his passions; be humour-some, haughty, unjust, and selfish to the extreme; he might be ungrateful to his friends, disobedient to his parents, a glutton, an ignorant blockhead, in short everything which to plain sense appears most frivolous or contemptible, without incurring the least imputation, provided his hair hung fashionably about his ears, his buckles were sufficiently large, and his politeness unimpeached to the ladies.

Once indeed, Harry had thrown him into a disagreeable train of thinking, by asking him with great simplicity, what sort of a figure these young gentlemen would have made in the army of Leonidas, or these young ladies upon a desert island, where they would be obliged to shift for themselves. But Tommy had lately learned that nothing spoils the face more than intense reflection; and therefore as he could not easily resolve the question, he wisely determined to forget it.

And now the important evening approached; the largest room in the house was lighted up for the dancers, and all the little company assembled. Tommy was that day dressed in an unusual style of elegance; and had submitted without murmuring to be under the hands of an hair-dresser for two hours. But what gave him the greatest satisfaction of all, was an immense pair of new buckles, which Mrs. Merton had sent for on purpose to grace the person of her son. Several minuets were danced, to the great admiration of the company; and among the rest Tommy, who had been practicing ever since he had been at home, had the honour of exhibiting with Miss Matilda. He indeed began with a certain degree of diffidence, but was soon inspired with a proper degree of confidence by the applauses which resounded on every side. "What an elegant little creature!" cried one lady. "What a shape is there!" said a second. "I protest, he puts me in mind of Vestris[5] himself." "Indeed," said a third, "Mrs. Merton is a most happy mother to be possessed of such a son, who wants nothing but an introduction to the world, to be one of the most elegant creatures in England, and the most accomplished." As soon as Tommy had finished his dance, he led his partner to her seat, with a grace that surprised all the company anew; and then with the sweetest condescension imaginable, he went from one lady to another, to receive the praises which they liberally poured out; as if it was the greatest action in the world to draw one foot behind another and to walk on tiptoe. Harry, in the meantime, had shrouded himself in the most obscure part of the room, and was silently gazing upon the scene that passed. He knew that his company would give no pleasure among the elegant figures that engrossed the foremost seats, and felt not the least inclination for such an honour.

In this situation he was observed by Master Compton; who, at the same instant, formed a scheme of mortifying Miss Simmons, whom he did not like, and of exposing Harry to the general ridicule. He therefore proposed it to Mash, who had partly officiated as Master of the Ceremonies, who agreed to assist him, with all the readiness of officious malice. Master Mash, therefore, went up to Miss Simmons, and with all the solemnity of respect invited her out to dance: which she, although indifferent about the matter, accepted without hesitation. In the meantime, Master Compton went up to Harry with the same hypocritical civility, and in Miss Simmons' name invited him to dance a minuet. It was in vain that Harry assured him he knew nothing about the matter; his perfidious friend told him, that it was an indispensable duty for him to stand up; that Miss Simmons would never forgive him if he should refuse; that it would be sufficient if he could just describe the figure, without embarrassing himself about the steps. In the meantime, he pointed out Miss Simmons who was advancing towards the upper end of the room, and taking advantage of his confusion and embarrassment, led him forward and placed him by the young lady's side. Harry was not yet acquainted with the sublime science of imposing upon unwary simplicity, and therefore never doubted that the message had come from his friend; and as nothing could be more repugnant to his character than the want of compliance, he thought it necessary at least to go and expostulate with her upon the subject. This was his intention when he suffered himself to be led up the room; but his tormentors did not give him time, for they placed him by the side of the young lady, and instantly called to the music to begin. Miss Simmons, in her turn, was equally surprised at the partner that was provided for her; she had never imagined minuet dancing to be one of Harry's accomplishments; and therefore instantly suspected that it was a concerted scheme to mortify her.

However, in this she was determined they should be disappointed, as she was destitute of all pride and had the sincerest regard for Harry. As soon, therefore, as the music struck up, the young lady began her reverence; which Harry, who found he was now completely caught, and had no time for explanation, imitated as well as he was able, but in such a manner as set the whole room in a titter. Harry, however, arming himself with all the fortitude he possessed, performed his part as well as could be expected from a person that had never learned a single step of dancing. By keeping his eye fixed upon his partner, he made a shift at least to preserve something of the figure, although he was terribly deficient in the steps and graces of the dance. But his partner, who was scarcely less embarrassed than himself, and wished to shorten the exhibition, after crossing once, presented him with her hand. Harry had unfortunately not remarked the nature of this manœuvre with perfect accuracy; and therefore imagining that one hand was just as good as the other, he offered the young lady his left, instead of his right hand. At this incident, an universal peal of merriment, which they no longer laboured to conceal, burst from almost all the company; and Miss Simmons wishing at any rate to close the scene, presented her partner with both her hands, and abruptly finished the dance. The unfortunate couple then retreated to the lower end of the room, amid the jests and sneers of their companions, particularly Mash and Compton, who assumed unusual importance upon the credit of such a brilliant invention.

When they were seated, Miss Simmons could not help asking Harry, with some displeasure, why he had thus exposed himself and her, by attempting what he was totally ignorant of; and added, that though there was no disgrace in not being able to dance, it was very great folly to attempt it without having learned a single step. "Indeed, madam," answered Harry, "I never should have thought of trying to do what I knew I was totally ignorant of; but Master Compton came to me, and told me, that you particularly desired me to dance with you, and led me to the other end of the room; and I only came to speak to you and to inform you that I knew nothing about the matter, for fear you should think me uncivil; and then the music began to play and you to dance, so that I had no opportunity of speaking; and I thought it better to do the best I could, than to stand still, or leave you there." Miss Simmons instantly recovered her former good humour, and said, "Well, Harry, we are not the first, nor shall be the last by hundreds, that have made a ridiculous figure in a ball-room, without so good an excuse. But I am sorry to see so malicious a disposition in these young gentlemen, and that all their knowledge of polite life has not taught them a little better manners." "Why, madam," answered Harry, "since you are so good as to talk to me upon the subject, I must confess that I have been very much surprised at many things I have seen at Mr. Merton's. All these young gentlemen and ladies are continually talking about genteel life and manners, and yet they are frequently doing things which surprise me. Mr. Barlow has always told me that politeness consisted in a disposition to oblige everybody around us, and to say or do nothing which can give them disagreeable impressions. Yet I continually see these young gentlemen striving to do and say things, for no other reason than to give pain. For not to go any farther than the present instance, what motive can Master Compton and Mash have had, but to mortify you by giving you such a partner? You, madam, too, that are so kind and good to everybody, that I should think it impossible not to love you."

"Harry," answered the young lady, "what you say about politeness is perfectly just. I have heard my uncle and many sensible people say the same. But in order to acquire this species of it, both goodness of heart and a just way of thinking are required; and therefore many people content themselves with aping what they can pick up in the dress, or gestures, or cant expressions of the higher classes: just like the poor ass that dressed in the skin of a lion was taken for the lion himself, till his unfortunate braying exposed the cheat." "Pray, madam, what is that story?" said Harry. "It is a trifling one that I have read," answered Miss Simmons, "of somebody, that having procured a lion's skin, fastened it round the body of an ass, and then turned him loose to the great affright of the neighbourhood. Those who saw him first, imagined that a monstrous lion had invaded the country, and fled with precipitation. Even the very cattle caught the panic, and were scattered by hundreds over the plains. In the meantime, the victorious ass pranced and capered along the fields, and diverted himself with running after the fugitives. But, at length, in the gaiety of his heart, he broke out into such a discordant braying, as surprised those that were nearest, and expected to hear a very different noise from under the terrible skin. At length a resolute fellow ventured by degrees nearer to this object of their terror, and discovering the cheat that had been practiced upon them, divested the poor ass of all his borrowed spoils, and drove him away with his cudgel."

"This story," continued Miss Simmons, "is continually coming into my mind, when I see anybody imagine himself of great importance, because he has adopted some particular mode of dress, or the grimaces of those that call themselves fashionable people. Nor do I ever see Master Mash, or Compton, without thinking of the lion's skin, and expecting every moment to hear them bray." Harry laughed very heartily at this story; but now their attention was called towards the company, who had ranged themselves by pairs for country-dancing. Miss Simmons, who was very fond of this exercise, then asked Harry if he had never practiced any of these dances. Harry said it had happened to him three or four times at home, and that he believed he should not be puzzled about any of the figures. "Well then," said the young lady, "to show how little I regard their intended mortification, I will stand up, and you shall be my partner." So they rose, and placed themselves at the bottom of the whole company, according to the laws of dancing, which appoint that place for those who come last. And now the music began to strike up in a more joyous strain; the little dancers exerted themselves with all their activity, and the exercise diffused a glow of health and cheerfulness over the faces of the most pale and languid. Harry exerted himself here, with much better success than he had lately done in the minuet. He had great command over all his limbs, and was well versed in every play that gives address to the body; so that he found no difficulty in practicing all the varied figures of the dances; particularly with the assistance of Miss Simmons, who explained to him everything that appeared embarrassing.

But now, by the continuance of the dance, all who were at first at the upper end had descended to the bottom; where, by the laws of the diversion, they ought to have waited quietly, till their companions, becoming in their turn uppermost, had danced down to their former places. But, when Miss Simmons and Harry expected to have had their just share of the exercise, they found that almost all their companions had deserted them, and retired to their places. Harry could not help wondering at this behaviour; but Miss Simmons told him with a smile, that it was only of a piece with the rest; and that she had often remarked it at country assemblies, where all the gentry of a county were gathered together. "This is frequently the way," added she, "that those who think themselves superior to the rest of the world, choose to show their importance." "This is a very bad way, indeed," replied Harry: "people may choose whether they will dance or practice any particular diversion; but if they do, they ought to submit to the laws of it, without repining: and I have always observed among the little boys that I am acquainted with, that wherever this disposition prevails it is the greatest proof of a bad and contemptible temper."

"I am afraid," replied Miss Simmons, "that your observations will hold universally true; and that those who expect so much for themselves, without being willing to consider their fellow-creatures in turn, in whatever station they are found, are always the most mean, ignorant, and despicable of the species." "I remember," said Harry, "reading a story of a great man, called Sir Philip Sydney. This gentleman was reckoned not only the bravest, but the politest person in all England. It happened that he was sent over the sea to assist some of our allies against their enemies. After having distinguished himself in such a manner as gained him the love and esteem of all the army, this excellent man one day received a shot, which broke his thigh as he was bravely fighting at the head of his men. Sir Philip Sydney felt that he was mortally wounded, and was obliged to turn his horse's head and retire to his tent, in order to have his wound examined. By the time that he reached the tent, he not only felt great agonies from his wound, but the heat of the weather, and the fever which the pain produced, had excited an intolerable thirst; so that he prayed his attendants to fetch him a little water. With infinite difficulty some water was procured and brought to him; but, just as he was raising the cup to his lips, he chanced to see a poor English soldier, who had been mortally wounded in the same engagement, and lay upon the ground, faint and bleeding, and ready to expire. The poor man was suffering like his general, from the pain of a consuming thirst; and therefore, though respect prevented him from asking for any, he turned his dying eyes upon the water, with an eagerness which sufficiently explained his sufferings. Upon this, the excellent and noble gentleman took the cup, which he had not yet tasted, from his lips, and gave it to his attendants; ordering them to carry it to the wounded soldier, and only saying, 'This poor man wants it still more than I do.' "

"This story," added Harry, "was always a particular favourite with Mr. Barlow, and he has often pointed it out to me, as an example not only of the greatest virtue and humanity, but also of that elevated method of thinking which constitutes the true gentleman. For what is it, I have heard him say, that gives a superiority of manners, but the inclination to sacrifice our own pleasures and interests to the well-being of others? An ordinary person might have pitied the poor soldier, or even have assisted him, when he had first taken care of himself: but who, in such a dreadful extremity as the brave Sydney was reduced to, would be capable of even forgetting his own sufferings to relieve another, that had not acquired the generous habit of always slighting his own gratifications for the sake of his fellow-creatures?"

As Harry was conversing in this manner, the little company had left off dancing, and were refreshing themselves with a variety of cakes and agreeable liquors, which had been provided for the occasion. Tommy Merton and the other young gentlemen were now distinguishing themselves by their attendance upon the ladies, whom they were supplying with everything they chose to have; but no one thought it worth his while to wait upon Miss Simmons. When Harry observed this, he ran to the table, and upon a large waiter brought her cakes and lemonade, which he presented, if not with a better grace, with a sincerer desire to oblige than any of the rest. But, as he was stooping down to offer her the choice, Master Mash unluckily passed that way, and, elated by the success of his late piece of ill-nature, determined to attempt a second still more brutal than the first. For this reason, just as Miss Simmons was helping herself to some wine and water, Mash pretending to stumble, pushed Harry in such a manner, that the greater part of the contents of the glasses was discharged full into her bosom. The young lady coloured at the insult, and Harry, who instantly perceived that it had been done on purpose, being no longer able to contain his indignation, seized a glass that was only half emptied, and discharged the contents full into the face of the aggressor. Mash, who was a boy of violent passions, exasperated at this retaliation, which he so well deserved, instantly catched up a drinking glass and flung it full at the head of Harry. Happy was it for him, that it only grazed his head without taking the full effect. It however laid bare a considerable gash, and Harry was in an instant covered with his own blood. This sight only provoked him the more, and made him forget both the place and company where he was; so that flying upon Mash with all the fury of just revenge, a dreadful combat ensued, which put the whole room into a consternation.

But Mr. Merton soon appeared, and with some difficulty separated the enraged champions. He then enquired into the subject of the contest, which Master Mash endeavoured to explain away as an accident. But Harry persisted in his account with so much firmness, in which he was corroborated by the testimony of Miss Simmons, that Mr. Merton readily perceived the truth. Mash however apologized for himself in the best manner he was able, by saying, that he had only meant to play Master Harry an innocent trick, but that he had undesignedly injured Miss Simmons. Whatever Mr. Merton felt, he did not say a great deal; he, however, endeavoured to pacify the enraged combatants, and ordered assistance to Harry to bind up the wound, and clean him from the blood which had now disfigured him from head to foot.

Mrs. Merton in the meantime, who was sitting at the upper end of the room amidst the other ladies, had seen the fray, and been informed that it was owing to Harry's throwing a glass of lemonade in Master Mash's face. This gave Mrs. Compton an opportunity of indulging herself again in long invectives against Harry, his breeding, family, and manners. She never, she said, had liked the boy, and now he had justified all her forebodings upon the subject. Such a little vulgar wretch could never have been witness to anything but scenes of riot and ill-manners; and now he was brawling and fighting in a gentleman's house, just as he would do at one of the public houses to which he was used to go with his father. While she was in the midst of this eloquent harangue, Mr. Merton came up, and gave a more unprejudiced narrative of the affair; he acquitted Harry of all blame, and said, that it was impossible, even for the mildest temper in the world, to act otherwise upon such unmerited provocation. This account seemed wonderfully to turn the scale in Harry's favour; though Miss Simmons was no great favourite with the young ladies, yet the spirit and gallantry which he had discovered in her cause began to act very forcibly upon their minds. One of the young ladies observed, that if Master Harry was better dressed, he would certainly be a very pretty boy; another said, she had always thought that he had a look above his station; and a third remarked, that considering he had never learned to dance, he had by no means a vulgar look.

This untoward accident having thus been amicably settled, the diversions of the evening went forward. But Harry, who had now lost all taste for genteel company, took the first opportunity of retiring to bed; where he soon fell asleep, and forgot both the mortification and bruises he had received. In the meantime, the little company below found means to entertain themselves till past midnight, and then retired to their chambers.

The next morning they rose later than usual: and, as several of the young gentlemen who had been invited to the preceding evening's diversion, were not to return till after dinner, they agreed to take a walk into the country. Harry went with them as usual, though Master Mash by his misrepresentations had prejudiced Tommy and all the rest against him. But Harry, who was conscious of his own innocence, and began to feel the pride of injured friendship, disdained to give an explanation of his behavior; since his friend was not sufficiently interested about the matter to demand one. But while they were slowly walking along the common, they discovered at a distance a prodigious crowd of people, that were all moving forward in the same direction. This attracted the curiosity of the little troop; and upon enquiry they found there was going to be a bull-baiting. Instantly an eager desire seized upon all the little gentry to see the diversion. One obstacle alone presented itself, which was that their parents, and particularly Mrs. Merton, had made them promise that they would avoid every species of danger. This objection was however removed by Master Billy Lyddal, who observed that there could be no danger in the sight, as the bull was to be tied fast, and could therefore do them no harm. "Besides," added he smiling, "what occasion have they to know that we have been at all? I hope we are not such simpletons as to accuse ourselves, or such tell-tales as to inform against one another."

No! no! no! was the universal exclamation from all but Harry, who had remained profoundly silent upon the occasion. "Master Harry has not said a word," said one of the little folks, "sure he will not tell of us." "Indeed," said Harry, "I don't wish to tell of you; but if I am asked where we have been, how can I help telling?"—"What," answered Master Lyddal, "can't you say, that we have been walking along the road, or across the common, without mentioning anything farther?"—"No," said Harry, "that would not be speaking truth: besides, bull-baiting is a very cruel and dangerous diversion, and therefore none of us should go to see it; particularly Master Merton, whose mother loves him so much and is so careful about him."

This speech was not received with much approbation by those to whom it was addressed. "A pretty fellow," said one, "to give himself these airs and pretend to be wiser than every one else!—" "What," said Master Compton, "does this beggar's brat think he is to govern gentlemen's sons, because Master Merton is so good as to keep company with him?"—"If I were Master Merton," said a third, "I'd soon send the little impertinent jackanapes home to his own blackguard family."—And Master Mash, who was the biggest and strongest boy in the whole company, came up to Harry, and grinning in his face, said, "So all the return that you make to Master Merton for his goodness to you, is to be a spy and an informer, is it, you little dirty blackguard?"—Harry, who had long perceived and lamented the coolness of Master Merton towards him, was now much more grieved to see that his friend was not only silent, but seemed to take an ill-natured pleasure in these insults, than at the insults themselves which were offered to him. However, as soon as the crowd of tormentors which surrounded him, would give him leave to speak, he coolly answered, that he was as little of a spy and informer as any of them; and as to begging, he thanked God, he wanted as little of them, as they did of him: besides, added he, "were I even reduced so low as that, I should know better how to employ my time, than to ask charity of anyone here."

This sarcastic answer, and the reflections that were made upon it, had such an effect upon the too irritable temper of Master Merton, that in an instant forgetting his former obligations and affection to Harry, he strutted up to him, and clenching his fist, asked him, whether he meant to insult him? "Well done, Master Merton," echoed through the whole society; "thresh him heartily for his impudence." "No, Master Tommy," answered Harry, "it is you and your friends here that insult me." "What," answered Tommy, "arc you a person of such consequence, that you must not be spoken to? You are a prodigious fine gentleman indeed."—"I always thought you one, till now," answered Harry. "—How, you rascal," said Tommy, "do you say that I am not a gentleman?—Take that," and immediately struck Harry upon the face with his fist. His fortitude was not proof against this treatment; he turned his face away, and only said in a low tone of voice, "Master Tommy, Master Tommy, I never should have thought it possible you could have treated me in this unworthy manner": then covering his face with both his hands, he burst into an agony of crying.

But the little troop of gentlemen, who were vastly delighted with the mortification which Harry had received, and had formed a very indifferent opinion of his prowess, from the patience which he had hitherto exerted, began to gather round, and repeat their persecutions. Coward, and blackguard, and tell-tale, echoed in a chorus, through the circle; and some, more forward than the rest, seized hold of him by the hair, in order that he might hold up his head, and show his pretty face. But Harry, who now began to recollect himself, wiped his tears with his hand, and looking up, asked them with a firm tone of voice and a steady countenance, why they meddled with him; then swinging round, he disengaged himself at once, from all who had taken hold of him. The greatest part of the company gave back at this question, and seemed disposed to leave him unmolested; but Master Mash, who was the most quarrelsome and impertinent boy present, advanced, and looking at Harry with a contemptuous sneer, said, "This is the way we always treat such little blackguards as you; and if you have not had enough to satisfy you, we'll willingly give you some more." "As to all your nick-names and nonsense," answered Harry, "I don't think it worth my while to resent them; but though I have suffered Master Merton to strike me, there's not another in the company shall do it; or if he chooses to try, he shall soon find whether or not I am a coward."

Master Mash made no answer to this but by a slap of the face, which Harry returned by a punch of his fist, which had almost overset his antagonist, in spite of his superiority of size and strength. This unexpected check from a boy so much less than himself might probably have cooled the courage of Mash, had he not been ashamed of yielding to one whom he had treated with so much unmerited contempt. Summoning, therefore, all his resolution, he flew at Harry like a fury; and, as he had often been engaged in quarrels like this, he struck him with so much force, that with the first blow he aimed, he felled him to the ground. Harry, foiled in this manner but not dismayed, rose in an instant and attacked his adversary with redoubled vigour, at the very moment when he thought himself sure of the victory. A second time did Mash, after a short but severe contest, close with his undaunted enemy, and, by dint of superior strength, roughly hurl him to the ground. The little troop of spectators who had mistaken Harry's patient fortitude for cowardice, began now to entertain the sincerest respect for his courage, and gathered round the combatants in silence. A second time did Harry rise and attack his stronger adversary, with the cool intrepidity of a veteran combatant.

The battle now began to grow more dreadful and more violent. Mash had superior strength and dexterity, and greater habitude of fighting; his blows were aimed with equal skill and force; and each appeared sufficient to crush an enemy so much inferior in size, in strength, in years: but Harry possessed a body hardened to support pain and hardship; a greater degree of activity, a cool, unyielding courage, which nothing could disturb or daunt. Four times had he been now thrown down by the irresistible strength of his foe; four times had he risen stronger from his fall, covered with dirt and blood, and panting with fatigue, but still unconquered. At length from the duration of the combat and his own violent exertions, the strength of Mash began to fail: enraged and disappointed at the obstinate resistance he had met with, he began to lose all command of his temper and strike at random; his breath grew short, his efforts were more laborious, and his knees seemed scarcely able to sustain his weight. But actuated by rage and shame, he rushed with all his might upon Harry, as if determined to crush him with one last effort. Harry prudently stepped back, and contented himself with parrying the blows that were aimed at him; till seeing that his antagonist was almost exhausted by his own impetuosity, he darted at him with all his force, and, by one successful blow, levelled him with the ground.

An involuntary shout of triumph now burst from the little assembly of spectators; for such is the temper of human beings that they are more inclined to consider superiority of force than justice; and the very same boys who just before were loading Harry with taunts and outrages, were now ready to congratulate him upon his victory. He, however, when he found his antagonist no longer capable of resistance, kindly assisted him to rise, and told him he was very sorry for what had happened; but he, oppressed at once with the pain of his bruises and the disgrace of his defeat, observed an obstinate silence.

Just in this moment, their attention was engaged by a new and sudden spectacle. A bull of the largest size and greatest beauty was led across the plain, adorned with ribbons of various colours. The majestic animal suffered himself to be led along an unresisting prey, till he arrived at the spot which was destined for the theatre of his persecutions. Here he was fastened to an iron ring, which had been strongly let into the ground, and whose force they imagined would be sufficient to restrain him, even in the midst of his most violent exertions. An innumerable crowd of men, of women, of children, then surrounded the place, waiting with eager curiosity for the inhuman sport which they expected. The little party, which had accompanied Master Merton, were now no longer to be restrained; their friends, their parents, admonition, duty, promises, were all forgotten in an instant, and, solely intent upon gratifying their curiosity, they mingled with the surrounding multitude.

Harry, although reluctantly, followed them at a distance; neither the ill-usage he had received, nor the pain of his wounds, could make him unmindful of Master Merton, or careless of his safety. He knew too well the dreadful accidents which frequently attend these barbarous sports, to be able to quit his friend, till he had once more seen him in a place of safety. And now the noble animal, that was to be thus wantonly tormented, was fastened to the ring by a strongly-twisted cord; which, though it confined and cramped his exertions, did not entirely restrain them. Although possessed of almost irresistible strength, he seemed unwilling to exert it; and looked round upon the infinite multitude of his enemies with a gentleness that ought to have disarmed their animosity. Presently, a dog of the largest size and most ferocious courage was let loose; who, as soon as he beheld the bull, uttered a savage yell, and rushed upon him with all the rage of inveterate animosity. The bull suffered him to approach with the coolness of deliberate courage; but just as the dog was springing up to seize him, he rushed forward to meet his foe, and putting his head to the ground, canted him into the air several yards; and had not the spectators run and caught him upon their backs and hands, he would have been crushed to pieces in the fall. The same fate attended another, and another dog, which were let loose successively; the one was killed upon the spot, while the other, who had a leg broken in the fall, crawled howling and limping away. The bull, in the meanwhile, behaved with all the calmness and intrepidity of an experienced warrior; without violence, without passion, he waited every attack of his enemies, and then severely punished them for their rashness.

While this was transacting, to the diversion not only of the rude and illiterate populace, but to that of the little gentry with Master Merton, a poor half-naked black came up, and humbly implored their charity. He had served, he told them, on board an English vessel, and even showed them the scars of several wounds he had received; but now he was discharged, and without friends, without assistance, he could scarcely find food to support his wretched life, or clothes to cover him from the wintry wind. Some of the young gentry, who from a bad education had been little taught to feel or pity the distress of others, were base enough to attempt to jest upon his dusky colour and foreign accent; but Master Merton, who, though lately much corrupted and changed from what he had been with Mr. Barlow, preserved a great degree of generosity, put his hand into his pocket in order to relieve him, but unfortunately found nothing to give; the foolish profusion which he had lately learned from the young gentlemen at his father's house, had made him waste in cards, in play-things, in trifles, all his stock of money; and now he found himself unable to relieve that distress which he pitied. Thus repulsed on every side, and unassisted, the unfortunate black approached the place where Harry stood, holding out the tattered remains of his hat, and imploring charity. Harry had not much to give, but he took sixpence out of his pocket, which was all his riches, and gave it with the kindest look of compassion, saying, "Here, poor man, this is all I have; if I had more, it should be at your service." He had no time to add more, for at that instant, three fierce dogs rushed upon the bull at once, and by their joint attacks rendered him almost mad. The calm deliberate courage, which he had hitherto shown, was now changed into rage and desperation; he roared with pain and fury; flashes of fire seemed to come from his angry eyes, and his mouth was covered with foam and blood. He hurried round the stake with incessant toil and rage, first aiming at one, then at another, of the persecuting dogs, that harassed him on every side, growling and baying incessantly, and biting him in every part. At length, with a furious effort that he made, he trampled one of his foes beneath his feet, and gored a second to that degree, that his bowels came through the wound; and at the same moment, the cord which had hitherto confined him, snapped asunder, and let him loose upon the affrighted multitude.

It is impossible to conceive the terror and dismay which instantly seized the crowd of spectators. Those, who before had been hallooing with joy, and encouraging the fury of the dogs with shouts and acclamations, were now scattered over the plain, and fled from the fury of the animal, whom they had been so basely tormenting. The enraged bull, meanwhile, rushed like lightning over the plain, trampling some, goring others, and taking ample vengeance for the injuries he had received. Presently, he rushed, with headlong fury, towards the spot where Master Merton and his associates stood; all fled with wild affright, but with a speed that was not equal to that of the pursuer. Shrieks, and outcries, and lamentations were heard on every side; and those, who a few minutes before had despised the good advice of Harry, would now have given the world to be safe in the houses of their parents. Harry alone seemed to preserve his presence of mind; he neither cried out nor ran; but when the dreadful animal approached, leaped nimbly aside, and the bull passed on, without embarrassing himself about his escape.

Not so fortunate was Master Merton; he happened to be the last of the little troop of flyers, and full in the way which the bull had taken. And now his destruction appeared certain; for as he ran, whether through fear or the inequality of the ground, his foot slipped, and down he tumbled, in the very path of the enraged pursuing animal. All, who saw, imagined his fate inevitable; and it would certainly have proved so, had not Harry, with a courage and presence of mind above his years, suddenly seized a prong, which one of the fugitives had dropped, and at the very moment when the bull was stooping to gore his defenceless friend, advanced and wounded him in the flank. The bull, in an instant, turned short, and with re-doubled rage made at his new assailant; and it is probable that, notwithstanding his intrepidity, Harry would have paid the price of his assistance to his friend with his own life, had not an unexpected succour arrived. But, in that instant, the grateful black rushed on like lightning to assist him, and assailing the bull with a weighty stick which he held in his hand, compelled him to turn his rage upon a new object. The bull indeed attacked him with all the impetuosity of revenge, but the black jumped nimbly aside and eluded his fury. Not contented with this, he wheeled round his fierce antagonist, and seizing him by the tail, began to batter his sides with an unexpected storm of blows. In vain did the enraged animal bellow and writhe himself about in all the convulsions of madness; his intrepid foe, without ever quitting his hold, suffered himself to be dragged about the field, still continuing his discipline, till the creature was almost spent with the fatigue of his own violent agitations. And now some of the boldest of the spectators, taking courage, approached to his assistance, and throwing a well-twisted rope over his head, they at length, by the dint of superior numbers, completely mastered the furious animal, and bound him to a tree.

In the meanwhile, several of Mr. Merton's servants who

had been sent out after the young gentlemen, approached and took up their young master, who, though without a wound, was almost dead with fear and agitation. But Harry, after seeing that his friend was perfectly safe, and in the hands of his own family, invited the black to accompany him, and instead of returning to Mr. Merton's, took the way which led to his father's house.

While these scenes were passing, Mrs. Merton, though ignorant of the danger of her son, was not undisturbed at home. Some accounts had been brought of Harry's combat, which served to make her uneasy and to influence her still more against him. Mrs. Compton too and Miss Matilda, who had conceived a violent dislike to Harry, were busy to inflame her by their malicious representations. While she was in these dispositions Mr. Merton happened to enter, and was at once attacked by all the ladies upon the subject of this improper connection. He endeavoured, for a long time, to remove their prejudices by reason, but when he found that to be impossible, he contented himself with telling his wife, that a little time would perhaps decide which were the most proper companions for their son; and that till Harry had done something to render himself unworthy of their notice, he never could consent to the treating him with coldness or neglect.

At this moment a female servant burst into the room with all the wildness of affright, and cried out with a voice that was scarcely articulate, "Oh! madam, madam! such an accident— poor, dear Master Tommy . . . . ." "What of him, for God's sake?" cried out Mrs. Merton, with an impatience and concern that sufficiently marked her feelings. "Nay, madam," answered the servant, "he is not much hurt they say; but little Sandford has taken him to a bull-baiting, and the bull has gored him, and William and John are bringing him home in their arms." These words were scarcely delivered when Mrs. Merton uttered a violent shriek, and was instantly seized with an hysteric fit. While the ladies were all employed in assisting her and restoring her senses, Mr. Merton, who, though much alarmed, was more composed, walked precipitately out, to learn the truth of this imperfect narration. He had not proceeded far, before he met the crowd of children and servants, one of whom carried Tommy Merton in his arms. As soon as he was convinced that his son had received no other damage than a violent fright, he began to enquire into the circumstances of the affair, but before he had time to receive any information, Mrs. Merton, who had recovered from her fainting, came running wildly from the house. When she saw that her son was safe, she caught him in her arms, and began to utter all the incoherent expressions of a mother's fondness. It was with difficulty that her husband could prevail upon her to moderate her transports till they were within. Then she gave a loose to her feelings in all their violence; and, for a considerable time, was incapable of attending to anything but the joy of his miraculous preservation.

At length, however, she became more composed, and observing that all the company were present except Harry Sandford, she exclaimed with sudden indignation: "So, I see that little abominable wretch has not had the impudence to follow you in; and I almost wish that the bull had gored him as he deserved." "What little wretch, mamma," said Tommy, "do you mean?" "Whom can I mean," cried Mrs. Merton, "but that vile Harry Sandford, that your father is so fond of, and who had nearly cost you your life, by leading you into this danger?" "He! mamma," said Tommy, "he lead me into danger! He did all he could to persuade me not to go; and I was a very naughty boy indeed, not to take his advice." Mrs. Merton stood amazed at this information; for her prejudices had operated so powerfully upon her mind, that she had implicitly believed the guilt of Harry upon the imperfect evidence of the maid. "Who was it then," said Mr. Merton, "could be so imprudent?" "Indeed, papa," answered Tommy, "we were all to blame, all but Harry, who advised and begged us not to go, and particularly me, because he said it would give you so much uneasiness when you knew it, and that it was so dangerous a diversion."

Mrs. Merton looked confused at her mistake, but Mrs.

Compton observed that she supposed Harry was afraid of the danger, and therefore had wisely kept out of the way. "Oh! no, indeed, madam," answered one of the little boys; "Harry is no coward, though we thought him so at first, when he let Master Tommy strike him; but he fought Master Mash in the bravest manner I ever saw, and though Master Mash fought very well, yet Harry had the advantage; and I saw him follow us at a little distance, and keep his eye upon Master Merton all the time, till the bull broke loose; and then I was so frightened that I do not know what became of him." "So, this is the little boy," said Mr. Merton, "that you were for driving from the society of your children! But let us hear more of the story, for as yet I know neither the particulars of his danger nor his escape." Upon this, one of the servants, who from some little distance had seen the whole affair, was called in and examined. He gave them an exact account of all; of Tommy's misfortune; of Harry's bravery; of the unexpected succour of the poor black; and filled the whole room with admiration that such an action, so noble, so intrepid, so fortunate, should have been achieved by such a child.

Mrs. Merton was now silent with shame at reflecting upon her own unjust prejudices, and the ease with which she had become the enemy of a boy who had saved the life of her darling son; and who appeared as much superior in character to all the young gentlemen at her house, as they exceeded him in rank and fortune. The young ladies now forgot their former objections to his person and manners, and such is the effect of genuine virtue, all the company conspired to extol the conduct of Harry to the skies. But Mr. Merton, who had appeared more delighted than all the rest with the relation of Harry's intrepidity, now cast his eyes around the room, and seemed to be looking for his little friend. But when he could not find him, he said, with some concern, "Where can be our little deliverer? Sure he can have met with no accident that he has not returned with the rest!" "No," said one of the servants, "as to that, Harry Sandford is safe enough, for I saw him go towards his own home in company with the black." "Alas!" answered Mr. Merton, "surely he must have received some unworthy treatment that could make him thus abruptly desert us all. And now I recollect that I heard one of the young gentlemen mention a blow that Harry had received; surely, Tommy, you could not have been so basely ungrateful as to strike the best and noblest of your friends!"

Tommy, at this, hung down his head; his face was covered with a burning blush, and the tears began silently to trickle down his cheeks. Mrs. Merton remarked the anguish and confusion of her child, and, catching him in her arms, was going to clasp him to her bosom with the most endearing expression; but Mr. Merton, hastily interrupting her, said, "It is not now a time to give way to fondness for a child, that, I fear has acted the basest and vilest part that can disgrace an human being; and who, if what I suspect is true, can be only a dishonour to his parents." At this Tommy could no longer contain himself, but burst out into such a violent transport of crying, that Mrs. Merton, who seemed to feel the severity of Mr. Merton's conduct with still more poignancy than her son, caught her darling up in her arms, and carried him abruptly out of the room, accompanied by most of the ladies, who pitied Tommy's abasement, and agreed that there was no crime he could have been guilty of which was not amply atoned for by such a charming sensibility.

But Mr. Merton, who now felt all the painful interest of a tender father, and considered this as the critical moment which was to give his son the impression of worth or baseness for life, was determined to examine the affair to the utmost. He therefore took the first opportunity of drawing the little boy aside who had mentioned Master Merton's striking Harry, and questioned him upon the subject. But he, who had no particular interest in disguising the truth, related the circumstances nearly as they had happened; and, though he a little softened matters in Tommy's favour, yet, without intending it, he held up such a picture of his violence and injustice as wounded his father to the soul. While Mr. Merton was occupied by these uneasy feelings, he was agreeably surprised by a visit from Mr. Barlow, who came accidentally to see him, with a perfect ignorance of all the great events which had so recently happened. Mr. Merton received this worthy man with the sincerest cordiality; but there was such a gloom diffused over all his manners, that Mr. Barlow began to suspect that all was not right with Tommy, and therefore purposely enquired after him, to give his father an opportunity of speaking. This Mr. Merton did not fail to do; and taking Mr. Barlow affectionately by the hand, he said, "Oh! my dear sir, I begin to fear that all my hopes are at an end in that boy, and all your kind endeavours thrown away. He has just behaved in such a manner as shows him to be radically corrupted, and insensible of every principle but pride." He then related to Mr. Barlow every incident of Tommy's behaviour, making the severest reflections upon his insolence and ingratitude, and blaming his own supineness that had not earlier checked these boisterous passions, that now burst forth with such a degree of fury and threatened ruin to his hopes.

"Indeed," answered Mr. Barlow, "I am very sorry to hear this account of my little friend; yet, I do not see it quite in so serious a light as yourself: and, though I cannot deny the dangers that may arise from a character so susceptible of false impressions, and so violent at the same time, yet I do not think the corruption either so great, or so general, as you seem to suspect. Do we not see, even in the most trifling habits of body or speech, that a long continual attention is required, if we would wish to change them; and yet our perseverance is in the end generally successful? Why then should we imagine that those of the mind are less obstinate, or subject to different laws? Or, why should we rashly abandon ourselves to despair, from the first experiments that do not succeed according to our wishes?" "Indeed," answered Mr. Merton, "what you say is perfectly consistent with the general benevolence of your character, and most consolatory to the tenderness of a father. Yet, I know too well the general weakness of parents in respect to the faults of their children, not to be upon my guard against the delusions of my own mind. And when I consider the abrupt transition of my son into everything that is most inconsistent with goodness; how lightly, how instantaneously he seems to have forgotten everything he had learned with you, I cannot help forming the most painful and melancholy presages of the future."

"Alas, sir," answered Mr. Barlow, "what is the general malady of human nature but this very instability which now appears in your son? Do you imagine that half the vices of men arise from real depravity of heart? On the contrary, I am convinced that human nature is infinitely more weak than wicked; and that the greater part of all bad conduct springs rather from want of firmness than from any settled propensity to evil." "Indeed," replied Mr. Merton, "what you say is highly reasonable; nor did I ever expect that a boy so long indulged and spoiled should be exempt from failings. But what particularly hurts me is, to see him proceed to such disagreeable extremities without any adequate temptation; extremities that I fear imply a defect of goodness and generosity, virtues which I always thought he had possessed in a very great degree." "Neither," answered Mr. Barlow, "am I at all convinced that your son is deficient in either. But you are to consider the prevalence of example, and the circle to which you have lately introduced him. If it is so difficult even for persons of a more mature age and experience to resist the impressions of those with whom they constantly associate, how can you expect it from your son? To be armed against the prejudices of the world, and to distinguish real merit from the splendid vices which pass current in what is called society, is one of the most difficult of human sciences. Nor do I know a single character, however excellent, that would not candidly confess he has often made a wrong election, and paid that homage to a brilliant outside which is only due to real merit."

[A story is omitted here.]

This conversation being finished, Mr. Merton introduced Mr. Barlow to the company in the other room. Mrs. Merton, who now began to be a little staggered in some of the opinions she had been most fond of, received him with uncommon civility, and all the rest of the company treated him with the greatest respect. But Tommy, who had lately been the oracle and the admiration of all this brilliant circle, appeared to have lost all his vivacity. He indeed advanced to meet Mr. Barlow with a look of tenderness and gratitude, and made the most respectful answers to all his enquiries; but his eyes were involuntarily turned to the ground, and silent melancholy and dejection were visible in his face. Mr. Barlow remarked with the greatest pleasure these signs of humility and contrition, and pointed them out to Mr. Merton the first time he had an opportunity of speaking to him without being overheard; adding, that unless he was much deceived, Tommy would soon give ample proofs of the natural goodness of his character, and reconcile himself to all his friends. Mr. Merton heard this observation with the greatest pleasure, and now began to entertain some hopes of seeing it accomplished.

After the dinner was over, most of the young gentlemen went away to their respective homes. Tommy seemed to have lost much of the enthusiasm which he had lately felt for his polite and accomplished friends; he even appeared to feel a secret joy at their departure, and answered with a visible coldness all their professions of regard and repeated invitations. Even Mrs. Compton herself and Miss Matilda, who were also departing, found him as insensible as the rest; though they did not spare the most extravagant praises and the warmest professions of regard.

And now the ceremonies of taking leave being over, and most of the visitors departed, a sudden solitude seemed to have taken possession of the house which was lately the seat of noise, and bustle, and festivity. Mr. and Mrs. Merton and Mr. Barlow were left alone with Miss Simmons and Tommy, and one or two others of the smaller gentry who had not yet returned to their friends. As Mr. Barlow was not fond of cards, Mr. Merton proposed, after the tea-table was removed, that Miss Simmons, who was famous for reading well, should entertain the company with some little tale or history, adapted to the comprehension even of the youngest.

[*The story, and an account of Tommy's horsemanship, are omitted.*]

In the meantime, Tommy walked pensively along the common, reflecting upon the various accidents which had befallen him, and the repeated disappointments he had found in all his attempts to distinguish himself. While he was thus engaged, he overtook a poor and ragged figure, the singularity of whose appearance engaged his attention. It was a man of middle age, in a dress he had never seen before, with two poor children that seemed with difficulty to keep up with him, while he carried a third in his arms, whose pale, emaciated looks, sufficiently declared disease and pain. The man had upon his head a coarse blue bonnet instead of an hat; he was wrapped round by a tattered kind of garment, striped with various colours, and, at his side, hung down a long and formidable sword. Tommy surveyed him with such an earnest observation, that, at length, the man took notice of it, and, bowing to him with the greatest civility, ventured to ask him if he had met with any accident, that he appeared in a disorder which suited so little with his quality. Tommy was not a little pleased with the discernment of the man, that could distinguish his importance in spite of the dirtiness of his clothes and therefore mildly answered, "No, friend, there is not much the matter.—I have a little obstinate horse that ran away with me, and, after trying in vain to throw me down, he plunged into the middle of that great bog there, and so I jumped off for fear of being swallowed up, otherwise I should soon have made him submit; for I am used to such things, and don't mind them in the least." Here the child that the man was carrying began to cry bitterly, and the father endeavoured to pacify him, but in vain. "Poor thing," said Tommy, "he seems not to be well—I am heartily sorry for him!"—"Alas! master," answered the man, "he is not well, indeed; he has now a violent ague fit upon him, and I have not had a morsel of bread to give him, or any of the rest, since yesterday noon."

Tommy was naturally generous, and now his mind was unusually softened by the remembrance of his own recent distresses; he therefore pulled a shilling out of his pocket and gave it to the man, saying, "Here, my honest friend, here is something to buy your child some food, and I sincerely wish he may soon recover." "God bless your sweet face!" said the man; "you are the best friend I have seen this many a day; but for this kind assistance we might have all been lost." He then, with many bows and thanks, struck across the common into a different path; and Tommy went forward, feeling a greater pleasure at this little act of humanity than he had long been acquainted with among all the fine acquaintance he had lately contracted. But he had walked a very little way with these reflections, before he met with a new adventure; a flock of sheep was running with all the precipitation which fear could inspire from the pursuit of a large dog, and just as Tommy approached, the dog had overtaken a lamb, and seemed disposed to devour it. Tommy was naturally an enemy to all cruelty, and therefore running towards the dog, with more alacrity than prudence, he endeavoured to drive him from his prey. But the animal, who probably despised the diminutive size of his adversary, after growling a little while and showing his teeth, when he found that this was not sufficient to deter him from intermeddling, entirely quitted the sheep; and making a sudden spring, seized upon the skirt of Tommy's coat, which he shook with every expression of rage. Tommy behaved with more intrepidity than could have been expected, for he neither cried out nor attempted to run, but made his utmost efforts to disengage himself from his enemy. But as the contest was so unequal, it is probable he would have been severely bitten, had not the honest stranger, whom he had relieved, come running up to his assistance, and seeing the danger of his benefactor, laid the dog dead at his feet by a furious stroke of his broadsword.

Tommy, thus delivered from the impending danger, expressed his gratitude to the stranger in the most affectionate manner, and desired him to accompany him to his father's house; where he and his wearied children should receive whatever refreshment they wished. He then turned his eyes to the lamb, which had been the cause of the contest, and lay panting upon the ground, bleeding and wounded, but not to death, and remarked, with astonishment, upon his fleece, the well-known characters of H.S. accompanied with a cross! "As I live," said Tommy, "I believe this is the very lamb which Harry used to be so fond of, and which used sometimes to follow him to Mr. Barlow's. I am the luckiest fellow in the world to have come in time to deliver him; and now, perhaps, Harry may forgive me all the ill usage he has met with." Saying this, he took the lamb up, and kissed it with the greatest tenderness; nay, he would have even borne it home in his arms had it not been rather too heavy for his strength: but the honest stranger, with a grateful officiousness, offered his services, and prevailed on Tommy to let him carry it, while he delivered his child to the biggest of its brothers.

When Tommy was now arrived within a little distance of his home, he met his father and Mr. Barlow, who had left the house to enjoy the morning air before breakfast. They were surprised to see him in such an equipage; for the dirt, which had bespattered him from head to foot, began to dry in various places, and gave him the appearance of a farmer's clay-built wall in the act of hardening. But Tommy, without giving them time to make enquiries, ran affectionately up to Mr. Barlow, and taking him by the hand, said; "Oh, sir! here is the luckiest accident in the world—poor Harry Sandford's favourite lamb would have been killed by a great mischievous dog, if I had not happened to come by and save his life." "And who is this honest man," said Mr. Merton, "whom you have picked up upon the common? He seems to be in distress, and his famished children are scarcely able to drag themselves along." "Poor man," answered Tommy, "I am very much obliged to him; for, when I went to save Harry's lamb, the dog attacked me and would have hurt me very much, if he had not come to my assistance, and killed him with his great sword. So I have brought him with me that he might refresh himself with his poor children, one of which has a terrible ague. For I knew, papa, though I have not behaved well of late, you would not be against my doing an act of charity." "I am, on the contrary, very glad," said Mr. Merton, "to see you have so much gratitude in your temper. But what is the reason that I see you thus disfigured with dirt? Surely you must have been riding, and your horse have thrown you. And so it is, for here is William following with both the horses in a foam."

William at that moment appeared, and, trotting up to his master, began to make excuses for his own share in the business. "Indeed, sir," said he, "I did not think there was the least harm in going out with Master Tommy; and we were riding along as quietly as possible, and master was giving me a long account of the Arabs; who, he said, lived in the finest country in the world, which does not produce anything to eat, or drink, or wear; and yet they never want or come upon the parish; but ride the most mettled horses in the world, fit to start for any plate in England. And just as he was giving me this account, Punch took it into his head to run away, and while I was endeavouring to catch him, he jumped into a quagmire, and shot Master Tommy off in the middle of it." "No," said Tommy, "there you mistake; I believe I could manage a much more spirited horse than Punch; but I thought it prudent to throw myself off, for fear of his plunging deeper in the mire." "But how is this?" said Mr. Merton. "The pony used to be the quietest of horses; what can have given him this sudden impulse to run away? Sure, William, you were not so imprudent as to trust your master with spurs." "No, sir," answered William, "not I, and I can take my oath he had no spurs on when we set out." Mr. Merton was convinced there was some mystery in this transaction, and looking at his son to find it out, he, at length, discovered the ingenious contrivance of Tommy to supply the place of spurs, and could hardly preserve his gravity at the sight. He, however, mildly set before him his imprudence, which might have been attended with the most fatal consequences, the fracture of his limbs, or even the loss of his life, and desired him for the future to be more cautious. They then returned to the house, and Mr. Merton ordered the servants to supply his guests with plenty of the most nourishing food.

After breakfast, they sent for the unhappy stranger into the parlour, whose countenance now bespoke his satisfaction and gratitude; and Mr. Merton, who by his dress and accent discovered him to be an inhabitant of Scotland, desired to know by what accident he had thus wandered so far from home with these poor helpless children, and had been reduced to so much misery. "Alas! your honour," answered the man, "I should ill deserve the favours you have shown me, if I attempted to conceal anything from such worthy benefactors. My tale, however, is simple and uninteresting, and I fear there can be nothing in the story of my distress the least deserving of your attention." "Surely," said Mr. Merton, with the most benevolent courtesy, "there must be something in the distress of every honest man which ought to interest his fellow creatures: and if you will acquaint us with all the circumstances of your situation, it may perhaps be within our power, as it certainly is in our inclinations, to do you farther service. The man then bowed to the company with an air of dignity which surprised them all, and thus began:

—I was born in that part of our island which is called the North of Scotland. The country there, partly from the barrenness of the soil and the inclemency of the seasons, and partly from other causes which I will not now enumerate, is unfavourable to the existence of its inhabitants. More than half the year our mountains are covered with continual snows, which prohibit the use of agriculture, or blast the expectations of an harvest. Yet the race of men which inhabit these dreary wilds, are perhaps not more undeserving the smiles of fortune than many of their happier neighbours. Accustomed to a life of toil and hardship, their bodies are braced by the incessant difficulties they have to encounter, and their minds remain untainted by the example of their more luxurious neighbours. They are bred up from infancy with a deference and respect for their parents, and with a mutual spirit of endearment towards their equals, which I have not remarked in happier climates. These circumstances expand and elevate the mind, and attach the highlanders to their native mountains with a warmth of affection, which is scarcely known in the midst of polished cities and cultivated countries. Every man there is more or less acquainted with the history of his clan, and the martial exploits which they have performed. In the winter season we sit around the blazing light of our fires, and commemorate the glorious actions of our ancestors; the children catch the sound, and consider themselves as interested in supporting the honour of a nation, which is yet unsullied in the annals of the world, and resolve to transmit it equally pure to their posterity.

With these impressions, which were the earliest I can remember, you cannot wonder, gentlemen, that I should early imbibe a spirit of enterprise and a love of arms. My father was, indeed, poor, but he had been himself a soldier, and therefore did not so strenuously oppose my growing inclinations. He, indeed, set before me the little chance I should have of promotion, and the innumerable difficulties of my intended profession. But what were difficulties to a youth brought up to subsist upon an handful of oatmeal, to drink the waters of the stream, and to sleep, shrouded in my plaid, beneath the arch of an impending rock! I see, gentlemen, continued the highlander, that you appear surprised to hear a man, who has so little to recommend him, express himself in rather loftier language than you are accustomed to among your peasantry here. But you should remember that a certain degree of education is more general in Scotland than where you live; and that, wanting almost all the gifts of fortune, we cannot afford to suffer those of nature to remain uncultivated. When, therefore, my father saw that the determined bent of my temper was towards a military life, he thought it vain to oppose my inclinations. He even, perhaps, involuntarily cherished them, by explaining to me, during the long leisure of our dreary winter, some books which treated of military sciences and ancient history. From these I imbibed an early love of truth and honour, which I hope has not abandoned me since; and, by teaching me what brave and virtuous men have suffered in every age and country, they have, perhaps, prevented me from entirely sinking under my misfortunes.

One night in the autumn of the year, as we were seated round the embers of our fire, we heard a knocking at the door. My father rose, and a man of a majestic presence came in and requested permission to pass the night in our cottage. He told us he was an English officer who had long been stationed in the highlands; but now, upon the breaking out of war, he had been sent for in haste to London, whence he was to embark for America as soon as he could be joined by his regiment. "This," said he, "has been the reason of my travelling later than prudence permits in a mountainous country with which I am imperfectly acquainted. I have unfortunately lost my way, and, but for your kindness," added he, smiling, "I must here begin my campaign, and pass the night upon a bed of heath amid the mountains." My father rose and received the officer with all the courtesy he was able; for in Scotland every man thinks himself honoured by being permitted to exercise his hospitality; he told him his accommodations were mean and poor, but what he had was heartily at his service. He then sent me to look after his visitor's horse, and set before him some milk and oaten bread, which were all the dainties we possessed: our guest, however, seemed to feed upon it with an appetite as keen as if he had been educated in the highlands; and, what I could not help remarking with astonishment, although his air and manners proved that he could be no stranger to a more delicate way of living, not a single word fell from him that intimated he had ever been used to better fare.

During the evening he entertained us with various accounts of the dangers he had already escaped, and the service he had seen. He particularly described the manners of the savage tribes he was going to encounter in America, and the nature of their warfare. All this, accompanied with the tone and look of a man that was familiar with great events, and had borne a considerable share in all he related, so enflamed my military ardour, that I was no longer capable of repressing it. The stranger perceived it, and, looking at me with an air of tenderness and compassion, asked if that young man was intended for the service. My colour rose, and my heart immediately swelled at the question; the look and manner of our guest had strangely interested me in his favour, and the natural grace and simplicity with which he related his own exploits put me in mind of the great men of other times. Could I but march under the banners of such a leader, I thought nothing would be too arduous to be achieved. I saw a long perspective before me of combats, difficulties, and dangers; something, however, whispered to my mind that I should be successful in the end, and support the reputation of our name and clan.

Full of these ideas, I sprang forwards at the question, and told the officer that the darling passion of my life would be to bear arms under a chief like him; and that, if he would suffer me to enlist under his command, I should be ready to justify his kindness by patiently supporting every hardship, and facing every danger. "Young man," replied he, with a look of kind concern, "there is not an officer in the army that would not be proud of such a recruit; but I should ill repay the hospitality I have received from your parents, if I suffered you to be deceived in your opinion of the military profession." He then set before me, in the strongest language, all the hardships which would be my lot; the dangers of the field, the pestilence of camps, the slow consuming languor of hospitals, the insolence of command, the mortification of subordination, and the uncertainty that the exertions of even a long life would ever lead to the least promotion. "All this," replied I, trembling with fear that my father should take advantage of these too just representations to refuse his consent, "I knew before; but I feel an irresistible impulse within me which compels me to the field. The die is cast for life or death, and I will abide by the chance that now occurs. If you, sir, refuse me, I will however enlist with the first officer that will accept me; for I will no longer wear out life amid the solitude of these surrounding mountains, without even a chance of meriting applause or distinguishing my name."

The officer then desisted from his opposition, and, turning to my parents, asked them if it were with their consent that I was going to enlist. My mother burst into tears, and my sisters hung about me weeping; my father replied, with a deep sigh, "I have long experienced that it is vain to oppose the decrees of Providence. Could my persuasions have availed, he would have remained contented in these mountains; but that is now impossible, at least till he has purchased wisdom at the price of his blood. If, therefore, sir, you do not despise his youth and mien, take him with you, and let him have the advantage of your example. I have been a soldier myself, and I can assure you, with truth, that I have never seen an officer under whom I would more gladly march than yourself." Our guest made a polite reply to my father, and instantly agreed to receive me. He then pulled out a purse, and, offering it to my father, said, "the common price of a recruit is now five guineas, but, so well am I satisfied with the appearance of your son, and the confidence you repose in me, that I must insist upon your accepting what is contained in this purse; you will dispose of it as you please for your mutual advantage. Before I depart tomorrow, I will give such directions as may enable him to join the regiment, which is now preparing to march."

He then requested that he might retire to rest, and my father would have resigned the only bed he had in the house to his guest; but he absolutely refused, and said, "Would you shame me in the eyes of my new recruit? What is a soldier good for that cannot sleep without a bed? The time will soon arrive when I shall think a comfortable roof and a little straw, an enviable luxury." I, therefore, raised him as convenient a couch as I was able to make with heath and straw; and, wrapping himself up in his riding coat, he threw himself down upon it, and slept till morning. With the first dawn of day he rose and departed, having first given me the directions which were necessary to enable me to join the regiment: but, before he went, my father, who was equally charmed with his generosity and manners, pressed him to take back part of the money he had given us; this, however, he absolutely refused, and left us full of esteem and admiration.

I will not, gentlemen, repeat the affecting scene I had to undergo in taking leave of my family and friends. It pierced me to the very heart; and then, for the first time, I almost repented at being so near the accomplishment of my wishes. I was, however, engaged, and determined to fulfill my engagement; I, therefore, tore myself from my family, having, with difficulty, prevailed upon my father to accept of part of the money I had received for my enrolment. I will not trespass upon your time to describe the various emotions which I felt at the crowd of new sensations, which entered my mind along our march. I arrived without an accident at London, the splendid capital of this kingdom; but I could not there restrain my astonishment, to see an immense people talking of wounds, of death, of battles, sieges, and conquests, in the midst of feasts, and balls, and puppet-shows; and calmly devoting thousands of their fellow-creatures to perish by famine or the sword, while they considered the loss of a dinner, or the endurance of a shower, as an exertion too great for human fortitude.

I soon embarked, and arrived, without any other accident than an horrible sickness, at the place of our destination in America. Here I joined my gallant officer, Colonel Simmons, who had performed the voyage in another ship.—Miss Simmons, who was present at this narration, seemed to be much interested at this mention of her own name; she, however, did not express her feelings, and the stranger proceeded with his story.—This gentleman was, with justice, the most beloved, and the most deserving to be so, of any officer I have ever known. Inflexible in everything that concerned the honour of the service, he never pardoned wilful misbehaviour, because he knew that it was incompatible with military discipline; yet, when obliged to punish, he did it with such reluctance, that he seemed to suffer almost as much as the criminal. But, if his reason imposed this just and necessary severity, his heart had taught him another lesson in respect to the private distresses of his men. He visited them in their sicknesses, relieved their miseries, and was a niggard of nothing but human blood;— but I ought to correct myself in that expression, for he was rashly lavish of his own, and to that we owe his untimely loss.

I had not been long in America before the colonel, who was perfectly acquainted with the language and manners of the savage tribes that border upon the British colonies, was sent upon an embassy to one of their nations, for the purpose of soliciting their alliance with Britain. It may, perhaps, be not uninteresting to you, gentlemen, and to this my honourable little master, to hear some account of a people whose manners and customs are so much the reverse of what you see at home. As my worthy officer, therefore, contented with my assiduity and improvement in military knowledge, permitted me to have the honour of attending him, I will describe some of the most curious facts which I was witness to.

You have, doubtless, heard many accounts of the surprising increase of the English colonies in America; and, when we reflect that it is scarcely an hundred years since some of them were established, it must be confessed that they have made rapid improvements in clearing the ground of woods and bringing it to cultivation. Yet, much as they have already done, the country is yet an immense forest, except immediately upon the coasts. These forests extend on every side to a distance that no human sagacity or observation has been able to determine. They abound in every species of tree which you see in England, to which may be added a great variety more which are unknown with us. Under their shade is generally found a rich luxurious herbage, which serves for pasture to a thousand herds of animals. Here are seen elks, a kind of deer of the largest size, and buffaloes, a species of wild ox, by thousands, and even horses, which, having been originally brought over by the Spaniards, have escaped from their settlements and multiplied in the woods.

"Dear," said Tommy, "that must be a fine country, indeed, where horses run wild; why a man might have one for nothing." "And yet," said Mr. Merton, "it would be but of little use for a person to have a wild horse, who is not able to manage a tame one."

Tommy made no answer to his father, and the man proceeded:—But the greatest curiosity of all this country is, in my opinion, the various tribes or nations which inhabit it. Bred up from their infancy to a life of equal hardiness with the wild animals, they are almost as robust in their constitutions. These various tribes inhabit little villages which generally are seated upon the banks of rivers, and, though they cultivate small portions of land around their towns, they seek the greater part of their subsistence from the chase. In their persons they are rather tall and slender, but admirably well proportioned and active, and their colour is a pale red, exactly resembling copper. Thus accustomed to roam about the woods, and brave the inclemencies of the weather, as well as continually exposed to the attacks of their enemies, they acquire a degree of courage and fortitude which can scarcely be conceived. It is nothing to them to pass whole days without a morsel of food, to lie whole nights upon the bare damp ground, and to swim the widest rivers in the depth of winter. Money, indeed, and the greater part of what we call the conveniencies of life, they are unacquainted with; nor can they conceive that one man should serve another merely because he has a few pieces of shining metal; they imagine that the only just distinctions arise from superior courage and bodily perfections, and therefore these alone are able to engage their esteem. I shall never forget the contempt which one of their chiefs expressed at seeing an officer who was rather corpulent at the head of his men: "What fools," said he, "are these Europeans, to be commanded by a man who is so unwieldy that he can neither annoy his enemies nor defend his friends, and who is only fit to be a scullion!" When they are at peace, they exercise the virtue of hospitality to a degree that might shame more polished nations: if a stranger arrives at any of their towns, he enters into the first habitation he pleases, and is sure to be entertained with all that the family possesses. In this manner he might journey from one end of the continent to the other, and never fail a friendly reception.

But, if their manners are gentle in peace, they are more dreadful when provoked than all the wildest animals of the forest. Bred up from infancy to suffer no restraint, and to give an unbounded loose to all their passions, they know not what it is to forgive an injury. They love their tribe with a degree of affection that is totally unknown in every other country; for that they are ready to suffer every hardship and danger; wounds, and pain, and death, they despise, as often as the interest of their country is concerned; but the same attachment renders them implacable and unforgiving to all their enemies: in short, they seem to have all the virtues and the vices of the ancient Spartans.

[Some narrative is omitted.]

And now the company being separated, Tommy, who had listened with silent attention to the story of the highlander, took an opportunity of following Mr. Barlow, who was walking out; and when he perceived they were alone, he looked at him as if he had some weighty matter to disclose, but was unable to give it utterance. Mr. Barlow, therefore, turned towards him with the greatest kindness, and, taking him tenderly by the hand, enquired what he wished. "Indeed, sir," answered Tommy, almost crying, "I am scarcely able to tell you. But I have been a very bad and ungrateful boy, and I am afraid you no longer have the same affection for me."

Mr. Barlow. If you are sensible of your faults, my little friend, that is a very great step towards amending them. Let me therefore know what it is, the recollection of which distresses you so much, and if it is in my power to assist in making you easy, there is nothing, I am sure, which I shall be inclined to refuse you.

Tommy. Oh! sir, your speaking to me with so much goodness hurts me a great deal more than if you were to be very angry. For when people are angry and passionate, one does not so much mind what they say. But, when you speak with so much kindness it seems to pierce me to the very heart, because I know I have not deserved it.

Mr. Barlow. But if you are sensible of having committed any faults, you may resolve to behave so well for the future, that you may deserve everybody's friendship and esteem. Few people are so perfect as not to err sometimes; and if you are convinced of your errors, you will be more cautious how you give way to them a second time.

Tommy. Indeed, sir, I am very happy to hear you say so—I will then tell you everything which lies so heavy upon my mind. You must know then, sir, that, although I have lived so long with you, and, during all that time, you have taken so much pains to improve me in everything, and teach me to act well to everybody, I had no sooner quitted your sight, than I became, I think, a worse boy than ever I was before.

Mr. Barlow. But why do you judge so severely of yourself, as to think you were become worse than ever? Perhaps you have been a little thoughtless and giddy, and these are faults which I cannot with truth say you were ever free from.

Tommy. No, sir, what I have been guilty of is infinitely worse than ever. I have always been very giddy and very thoughtless; but I never imagined I could have been the most insolent and ungrateful boy in the world.

Mr. Barlow. You frighten me, my little friend.—Is it possible you can have committed actions that deserve so harsh a name?

Tommy. You shall judge yourself, sir; for now I have begun, I am determined to tell you all. You know, sir, that when I first came to you, I had an high opinion of myself for being born a gentleman, and a very great contempt for every body in an inferior station.

Mr. Barlow. I must confess you have always had some tendency to both those follies.

Tommy. Yes, sir; but you have so often laughed at me upon the subject, and shown me the folly of people's imagining themselves better than others, without any merit of their own, that I was grown a little wiser. Besides, I have so often observed that those I despised could do a variety of things which I was ignorant of, while those who are vain of being gentlemen can do nothing useful or ingenious, that I had begun to be ashamed of my folly. But since I came home, I kept company with a great many fine young gentlemen and ladies that thought themselves superior to all the rest of the world, and used to despise everyone else, and they have made me forget every thing I learned before.

Mr. Barlow. Perhaps then I was mistaken, when I taught you that the greatest merit any person could have, is to be good and useful; these fine young gentlemen and ladies may be wiser, and have given you better lessons. If that is the case, you will have great reason to rejoice that you have changed so much for the better.

Tommy. No, sir, no; I never thought them either good or wise; for they know nothing but how to dress their hair and buckle their shoes. But they persuaded me that it was necessary to be polite, and talked to me so often upon the subject, that I could not help believing them.

Mr. Barlow. I am very glad to hear that; it is necessary for everybody to be polite. They therefore, I suppose, instructed you to be more obliging and civil in your manners than ever you were before. Instead of doing you any hurt, this will be the greatest improvement you can receive.

Tommy.   No, sir, quite the contrary—Instead of teaching me to be civil and obliging, they have made me ruder and worse behaved than ever I was before.

Mr. Barlow.   If that is the case, I fear these fine young gentlemen and ladies undertook to teach you more than they understood themselves.

Tommy.   Indeed, sir, I am of the same opinion myself. But I did not think so then, and, therefore, I did whatever I observed them do, and talked in the same manner as I heard them talk. They used to be always laughing at Harry Sandford; and I grew so foolish that I did not choose to keep company with him any longer.

Mr. Barlow.   That was a pity, because I am convinced he really loves you. However, it is of no great consequence, for he has employment enough at home; and, however ingenious you may be, I do not think that he will learn how to manage his land, or raise food, from your conversation. It will, therefore, be better for him to converse with farmers, and leave you to the society of gentlemen. Indeed, this, I know, has always been his taste, and had not your father pressed him very much to accompany you home, he would have liked much better to avoid the visit. However, I will inform him that you have gained other friends, and advise him, for the future, to avoid your company.

Tommy.   Oh, sir! I did not think you could be so cruel. I love Harry Sandford better than any other boy in the world, and I shall never be happy till he forgives me all my bad behavior, and converses with me again as he used to do.

Mr. Barlow.   But then, perhaps, you may lose the acquaintance of all those polite young gentlemen and ladies.

Tommy.   I care very little about that, sir. But, I fear, I have behaved so ill, that he never will be able to forgive me and love me as he did formerly.

Tommy then went on, and repeated with great exactness the story of his insolence and ingratitude, which had so great an effect upon him, that he burst into tears and cried a considerable time. He then concluded with asking Mr. Barlow if he thought Harry would be ever able to forgive him.

Mr. Barlow.   I cannot conceal from you, my little friend, that you have acted very ill indeed in this affair. However, if you are really ashamed of all your past conduct, and determined to act better, I do not doubt that so generous and good-natured a boy as Harry is, will forgive you all.

Tommy.   O, sir, I should be the happiest creature in the world—Will you be so kind as to bring him here to-day, and you shall see how I will behave?

Mr. Barlow.   Softly, Tommy, softly. What is Harry to come here for? Have you not insulted and abused him, without reason; and, at last, proceeded so far as to strike him, only because he was giving you the best advice, and endeavouring to preserve you from danger? Can you imagine that any human being will come to you in return for such treatment? at least till you have convinced him that you are ashamed of your passion and injustice, and that he may expect better usage for the future.

Tommy.   What then must I do, sir?

Mr. Barlow.   If you want any future connection with Harry Sandford, it is your business to go to him and tell him so.

Tommy.   What, sir, go to a farmer's, to expose myself before all his family?

Mr. Barlow.   Just now you told me you were ready to do everything, and yet you cannot take the trouble of visiting your friend at his own house. You then imagine that a person does not expose himself by acting wrong, but by acknowledging and amending his faults!

Tommy.   But what would everybody say, if a young gentleman like me, was to go and beg pardon of a farmer's son?

Mr. Barlow.   They will probably say that you have more sense and gratitude than they expected. However, you are to act as you please; with the sentiments you still seem to entertain, Harry will certainly be a very unfit companion, and you will do much better to cultivate the new acquaintance you have made.

Mr. Barlow was then going away, but Tommy burst again into tears and begged him not to go; upon which Mr. Barlow said, "I do not want to leave you, Tommy, but our conversation is now at an end. You have asked my advice, which I have given you freely. I have told you how you ought to act, if you would preserve the esteem of any good or sensible friend, or prevail upon Harry to excuse your past behavior. But as you do not approve of what I suggested, you must follow your own opinions."

"Pray, sir, pray, sir," said Tommy sobbing, "do not go. I have used Harry Sandford in the most barbarous manner; my father is angry with me; and if you desert me, I shall have no friend left in the world."

Mr. Barlow.   That will be your own fault, and, therefore, you will not deserve to be pitied. Is it not in your own power to preserve all your friends, by an honest confession of your faults? Your father will be pleased, Harry Sandford will heartily forgive you, and I shall retain the same good opinion of your character which I have long had.

Tommy.   And is it really possible, sir, that you should have a good opinion of me, after all I have told you about myself?

Mr. Barlow.   I have always thought you a little vain and careless, I confess; but, at the same time, I imagined you had both good sense and generosity in your character; I depended upon the first to make you see your faults, and upon the second to correct them.

Tommy.   Dear sir, I am very much obliged to you: but you have always been extremely kind and friendly to me.

Mr. Barlow.   And, therefore, I told your father yesterday, who is very much hurt at your quarrel with Harry, that though a sudden passion might have transported you too far, yet, when you came to consider the matter coolly, you would perceive your faults and acknowledge them: were you not to behave in this manner, I owned I could say nothing in your favour. And I was very much confirmed in this opinion, when I saw the courage you exerted in the rescue of Harry's lamb, and the compassion you felt for the poor highlander. A boy, said I, who has so many excellent dispositions, can never persist in bad behaviour. He may do wrong by accident, but he will be ashamed of his errors, and endeavour to repair them by a frank and generous acknowledgment. This has always been the conduct of really great and elevated minds; while mean and groveling ones alone imagine that it is necessary to persist in faults they have once committed.

Tommy. Oh, sir!—I will go directly, and entreat Harry to forgive me; I am convinced that all you say is right.—But will you not go with me? Do, pray, sir, be so good.—

Mr. Barlow. Gently, gently, my good friend; you are always for doing everything in an instant. I am very glad you have taken a resolution which will do you so much credit, and give so much satisfaction to your own mind: but before you execute it, I think it will be necessary to speak to your father and mother upon the subject, and, in the meantime, I will go and pay a visit to farmer Sandford, and bring you an account of Harry.

Tommy. Do, sir, be so good; and tell Harry, if you please, that there is nothing I desire so much as to see him; and that nothing shall ever make me behave ill again. I have heard too, sir, that there was a poor black, that came begging to us, who saved Harry from the bull; if I could but find him out, I would be good to him as long as I live.

Mr. Barlow commended Tommy very much for dispositions so full of gratitude and goodness, and taking leave of him, went to communicate the conversation he had just had to Mr. Merton. That gentleman felt the sincerest pleasure at the account, and entreated Mr. Barlow to go directly to prepare Harry to receive his son. "That little boy," added he, "has the noblest mind that ever adorned an human being; nor shall I be ever happy till I see my son acknowledging all his faults, and entreating forgiveness: for, with the virtues that I have discovered in his soul, he appears to me a more eligible friend and companion than noblemen or princes."

Mr. Barlow, therefore, set out on foot, though Mr. Merton would have sent his carriage and servants to attend him, and soon arrived at Mr. Sandford's farm. It was a pleasant spot, situated upon the gentle declivity of an hill, at the foot of which winded along a swift and clear little stream. The house itself was small, but warm and convenient, furnished with the greatest simplicity, but managed with perfect neatness. As Mr. Barlow approached, he saw the owner himself guiding a plough through one of his own fields, and Harry, who had now resumed the farmer, directed the horses. But when he saw Mr. Barlow coming across the field, he stopped his team, and letting fall his whip, sprang forward to meet him with all the unaffected eagerness of joy. As soon as Harry had saluted Mr. Barlow, and enquired after his health, he asked him with the greatest kindness after Tommy; "for I fancy, sir," said he, "by the way which I see you come, you have been at Mr. Merton's house." "Indeed I have," replied Mr. Barlow, "but I am very sorry to find that Tommy and you are not upon as good terms as you formerly were."

Harry. Indeed, sir, I am very sorry for it myself. But I do not know that I have given Master Merton any reason to change his sentiments about me: and though I do not think he has treated me as well as he ought to do, I have the greatest desire to hear that he is well.

Mr. Barlow. That you might have known yourself, had you not left Mr. Merton's house so suddenly, without taking leave of anyone, even your friend Mr. Merton, who has always treated you with so much kindness.

Harry. Indeed, sir, I shall be very unhappy if you think I have done wrong; but be so good as to tell me how I could have acted otherwise. I am very sorry to appear to accuse Master Merton, neither do I bear any resentment against him for what he has done, but since you speak to me upon the subject, I shall be obliged to tell the truth.

Mr. Barlow. Well, Harry, let me hear it. You know I shall be the last person to condemn you if you do not deserve it.

Harry. I know your constant kindness to me, sir, and I always confide in it: however, I am not sensible now that I am in fault. You know, sir, that it was with great unwillingness I went to Mr. Merton's, for I thought there would be fine gentlemen and ladies there that would ridicule my dress and manners:

and though Master Merton has been always very friendly in his behaviour towards me, I could not help thinking that he might grow ashamed of my company at his own house.

Mr. Barlow. Do you wonder at that, Harry, considering the difference there is in your rank and fortune?

Harry. No, sir, I cannot say I do, for I generally observe that those who are rich will scarcely treat the poor with common civility. But, in this particular case, I did not see any reason for it. I never desired Master Merton to admit me to his company or invite me to his house, because I knew that I was born and bred in a very inferior station. You were so good as to take me to your house, and there I became acquainted with him; and if I was then much in his company, it was because he seemed to desire it himself, and I always endeavoured to treat him with the greatest respect.

Mr. Barlow. That, indeed, is true, Harry; in all your little plays and studies I have never observed anything but the greatest mildness and good-nature on your part.

Harry. I hope, sir, it has never been otherwise. But though I have the greatest affection for Master Merton, I never desire to go home with him. What sort of a figure could a poor boy like me make at a gentleman's table, among little masters and misses that powder their hair, and wear buckles as big as our horses carry upon their harness? If I attempted to speak, I was always laughed at, or if I did anything, I was sure to hear something about clowns and rustics! And yet, I think, though they were all gentlemen and ladies, you would not much have approved of their conversation, for it was about nothing but plays, and dress, and trifles of that nature. I never heard one of them mention a single word about saying their prayers, or being dutiful to their parents, or doing any good to the poor.

Mr. Barlow. Well, Harry, but if you did not like their conversation, you surely might have borne it with patience for a little while: and then, I heard something about your being quarrelsome.

Harry. Oh, sir, I hope not.—I was to be sure once a little passionate, but that I could not help, and I hope you will forgive me. There was a modest, sensible young lady, that was the only person who treated me with any kindness; and a bold, forward, ill-natured boy, affronted her in the grossest manner, only because she took notice of me. Could I help taking her part? Have you not told me too, sir, that every person, though he should avoid quarrels, has a right to defend himself when he is attacked?

Mr. Barlow. Well, Harry, I do not much blame you, from the circumstances I have heard of that affair: but why did you leave Mr. Merton's family so abruptly, without speaking to anybody, or thanking Mr. Merton himself for the civilities he had shown you? Was that right?

Harry. Oh, dear, sir, I have cried about it several times, for I think I must appear very rude and ungrateful to Mr. Merton. But as to Master Tommy, I did not leave him while I thought I could be of any use. He treated me, I must say, in a very unworthy manner; he joined with all the other fine little gentlemen in abusing me, only because I endeavoured to persuade them not to go to a bull-baiting; and then at last he struck me. I did not strike him again, because I loved him so much, in spite of all his unkindness; nor did I leave him till I saw he was quite safe in the hands of his own servants. And, then, how could I go back to his house, after what he had done to me? I did not choose to complain of him to Mr. Merton; and how could I behave to him as I had done before without being guilty of meanness and falsehood? And therefore I thought it better to go home, and desire you to speak to Mr. Merton, and entreat him to forgive my rudeness.

Mr. Barlow. Well, Harry, I can inform you that Mr. Merton is perfectly satisfied upon that account. But there is one circumstance you have not mentioned, my little friend, and that is your saving Tommy's life from the fury of the enraged bull.

Harry. As to that, sir, I hope I should have done the same for any human creature. But I believe that neither of us would have escaped, if it had not been for the poor courageous black, that came to our assistance.

Mr. Barlow. I see, Harry, that you are a boy of a noble and generous spirit, and I highly approve of everything you have done: but, are you determined to forsake Tommy Merton forever, because he has once behaved ill?

Harry.   I, sir! no, I am sure. But, though I am poor, I do not desire the acquaintance of anybody that despises me. Let him keep company with his gentlemen and ladies, I am satisfied with companions in my own station. But surely, sir, it is not I that forsake him, but he that has cast me off.

Mr. Barlow.   But if he is sorry for what he has done and only desires to acknowledge his faults, and obtain your pardon?

Harry.   Oh, dear, sir! I should forget everything in an instant. I knew Master Tommy was always a little passionate and headstrong; but he is at the same time generous and good-natured; nor would he, I am sure, have treated me so ill, if he had not been encouraged to it by the other young gentlemen.

Mr. Barlow.   Well, Harry, I believe your friend is thoroughly sensible of his faults, and that you will have little to fear for the future. He is impatient till he sees you and asks your forgiveness.

Harry.   Oh, sir, I should forgive him if he had beaten me an hundred times. But, though I cannot leave the horses now, if you will be so kind to wait a little, I dare say my father will let me go when he leaves off ploughing.

Mr. Barlow.   No, Harry, there is no occasion for that. Tommy has indeed used you ill, and ought to acknowledge it; otherwise he will not deserve to be trusted again. He will call upon you, and tell you all he feels upon the occasion. In the meantime, I was desired, both by him and Mr. Merton, to enquire after the poor negro that served you so materially and saved you from the bull.

Harry.   He is at our house, sir; for I invited him home with me; and, when my father heard how well he had behaved, he made him up a little bed over the stable, and gives him victuals every day; and the poor man seems very thankful and industrious, and says he would gladly do any kind of work to earn his subsistence.

Mr. Barlow then took his leave of Harry, and, after having spoken to his father, returned to Mr. Merton. During his absence, Mr. Simmons had arrived there to fetch away his niece: but, when he had heard the story of the highlander, he perfectly recollected his name and character, and was touched with the sincerest compassion for his sufferings. Upon conversing with the poor man, he found that he was extremely well acquainted with agriculture, as well as truly industrious, and therefore instantly proposed to settle him in a small farm of his own, which happened to be vacant. The poor man received this unexpected change in his fortune with tears of joy, and every mark of unaffected gratitude; and Mr. Merton, who never wanted generosity, insisted upon having a share in his establishment. He proposed to supply him with the necessary instruments of agriculture, and a couple of horses, to begin the culture of his land. Just in that moment, Mr. Barlow entered, and, when he had heard, with the sincerest pleasure, the improvement of his circumstances, begged permission to share in so benevolent an action. "I have an excellent milch cow," said he, "which I can very well spare, whose milk will speedily recruit the strength of these poor children; and I have half a dozen ewes and a ram, which I hope, under Mr. Campbell's management, will soon increase to a numerous flock." The poor highlander seemed almost frantic with such a profusion of unexpected blessings, and said, that he wished nothing more than to pass the remainder of his days in such a generous nation, and to be enabled to show at least the sentiments which such undeserved generosity had excited.

[A section is omitted.]

Tommy now entered the room, but with a remarkable change in his dress and manner. He had combed the powder out of his hair, and demolished the elegance of his curls: he had divested his dress of every appearance of finery, and even his massy and ponderous buckles, so long the delight of his heart, and the wonder of his female friends, were taken from his shoes, and replaced by a pair of the plainest form and appearance. In this habiliment he appeared so totally changed from what he was, that even his mother, who had lately become a little sparing of her observations, could not help exclaiming,

"What, in the name of wonder, has the boy been doing now! Why, Tommy, I protest you have made yourself a perfect fright, and you look more like a ploughboy than a young gentleman!"

"Mamma," answered Tommy gravely, "I am only now what I ought always to have been. Had I been contented with this dress before, I never should have imitated such a parcel of coxcombs as you have lately had at your house; nor pretended to admire Miss Matilda's music, which, I own, tired me as much as Harry, and had almost set me asleep; nor should I have exposed myself at the play and the ball; and, what is worst of all, I should have avoided all my shameful behaviour to Harry at the bull-baiting. But, from this time, I shall apply myself to the study of nothing but reason and philosophy; and therefore I have bid adieu to dress and finery forever."

It was with great difficulty that the gentlemen could refrain from laughing at Tommy's harangue, delivered with infinite seriousness and solemnity; they, however, concealed their emotions, and encouraged him to persevere in such a laudable resolution. But, as the night was now pretty far advanced, the whole family retired to bed.

The next morning, early, Tommy arose and dressed himself with his newly adopted simplicity; and, as soon as breakfast was over, entreated Mr. Barlow to accompany him to Harry Sandford's. But he did not forget to take with him the lamb, which he had caressed and fed with constant assiduity ever since he had so valiantly rescued him from his devouring enemy. As they approached the house, the first object which Tommy distinguished was his little friend at some distance, who was driving his father's sheep along the common. At this sight, his impetuosity could no longer be restrained, and, springing forward with all his speed, he arrived in an instant, panting, and out of breath, and incapable of speaking. Harry, who knew his friend, and plainly perceived the dispositions with which he approached, met him with open arms; so that the reconciliation was begun and completed in a moment; and Mr. Barlow, who now arrived with the lamb, had the pleasure of seeing his little pupils mutually giving and receiving every unaffected mark of the warmest affection.

"Harry," said Mr. Barlow, "I bring you a little friend, who is sincerely penitent for his offences, and comes to own the faults he has committed." "That I am, indeed," said Tommy, a little recovered and able to speak. "But I have behaved so ill, and have been such an ungrateful fellow, that I am afraid Harry will never be able to forgive me." "Indeed, indeed," said Harry, "there you do me the greatest injustice; for I have already forgotten everything but your former kindness and affection." "And I," answered Tommy, "will never forget how ill, how ungratefully I have used you, nor the goodness with which you now receive me." Tommy then recollected his lamb, and presented it to his friend; while Mr. Barlow told him the story of its rescue, and the heroism exerted in its defence. Harry seemed to receive equal pleasure from the restoration of his favourite, and the affection Tommy had shown in its preservation, and, taking him by the hand, he led him into a small but neat and convenient house, where he was most cordially welcomed by Harry's family.

In a corner of the chimney sat the honest black who had performed so signal a service at the bull-baiting. "Alas!" said Tommy, "there is another instance of my negligence and ingratitude. I now see that one fault brings on another without end." Then, advancing to the black, he took him kindly by the hand, and thanked him for the preservation of his life. "Little master," replied he, "you are extremely welcome to all I have done. I would at any time risk my own safety to preserve one of my fellow-creatures; and, if I have been of any use, I have been amply repaid by the kindness of this little boy, your friend, and all his worthy family." "That is not enough," said Tommy, "and you shall soon find what it is to oblige a person like. . . ." Here a stroke of presumption was just coming out of Tommy's mouth, but, recollecting himself, he added, "a person like my father." And now he addressed himself to Harry's mother, a venerable, decent woman, of a middle age, and his two sisters, plain, modest, healthy-looking girls, a little older than their

brother. All these he treated with so much cordiality and attention, that all the company were delighted with him; so easy is
it for those who possess rank and fortune to gain the good-will
of their fellow-creatures; and so inexcusable is that surly pride
which renders many of them deservedly odious.

When dinner was ready, he sat down with the rest, and as
it was the custom here for everybody to wait upon himself,
Tommy insisted upon their suffering him to conform to the
established method. The victuals were not indeed very delicate,
but the food was wholesome, clean, and served up hot to the
table; an advantage which is not always found in elegant apartments. Tommy ate with a considerable appetite, and seemed to
enjoy his new situation as much as if he had never experienced
any other. After the dinner was removed, he thought he might
with propriety gratify the curiosity he felt to converse with the
black upon fighting bulls, for nothing had more astonished him
than the account he had heard of his courage, and the ease
with which he had subdued so terrible an animal. "My friend,"
said he, "I suppose in your own country you have been very
much used to bull-baitings; otherwise you never would have
dared to encounter such a fierce creature; I must confess,
though I can tame most animals, I never was more frightened
in my life, than when I saw him break loose; and without your
assistance, I do not know what would have become of me."

"Master," replied the black, "it is not in my own country,
that I have learned to manage these animals. There, I have
been accustomed to several kinds of hunting much more
dangerous than this; and considering, how much you white
people despise us blacks, I own, I was very much surprised to
see so many hundreds of you running away from such an in-
significant enemy as a poor tame bull."

Tommy blushed a little at the remembrance of the prejudices he had formerly entertained, concerning blacks and his
own superiority; but not choosing now to enter upon the subject, he asked the man where then he had acquired so much
dexterity in taming them.

[*A portion is omitted.*]

Tommy expressed the greatest admiration at this recital; and now, as the evening began to advance, Mr. Barlow invited him to return. But Tommy, instead of complying, took him by the hand, thanked him for all his kindness and attention, but declared his resolution of staying some time with his friend Harry. "The more I consider my own behaviour," said he, "the more I feel myself ashamed of my folly and ingratitude. But you have taught me, my dear sir, that all I have in my power is to acknowledge them, which I most willingly do before all this good family, and entreat Harry to think that the impressions I now feel are such as I shall never forget." Harry embraced his friend, and assured him once more of his being perfectly reconciled; and all the family stood mute with admiration at the condescension of the young gentleman, who was not ashamed of acknowledging his faults even to his inferiors.

Mr. Barlow approved of Tommy's design, and took upon him to answer for the consent of Mr. Merton to his staying some time with Harry; then, taking his leave of all the company, he departed.

But Tommy began now to enter upon a course of life which was very little consistent with his former habits. He supped with great cheerfulness, and even found himself happy with the rustic fare which was set before him, accompanied as it was with unaffected civility and an hearty welcome. He went to bed early and slept very sound all night; however, when Harry came to call him the next morning at five, as he had made him promise to do, he found a considerable difficulty in rousing himself at the summons. Conscious pride, however, and the newly-acquired dignity of his character, supported him; he recollected that he should disgrace himself in the eyes of his father, of Mr. Barlow, and of all the family with which he now was, if he appeared incapable of acting up to his own declarations: he therefore made a noble effort, leaped out of bed, dressed himself, and followed Harry. Not contented with this, he accompanied him in all his rustic employments, and, as no kind of country exercise was entirely new to him since his residence with Mr. Barlow, he acquitted himself with a degree of dexterity which gained him new commendations.

Thus did he pass the first day of his visit, with some little difficulty indeed, but without deviating from his resolution. The second, he found his change of life infinitely more tolerable; and, in a very little space of time, he was almost reconciled to his new situation. The additional exercise he used improved his health and strength, and added so considerably to his appetite, that he began to think the table of farmer Sandford exceeded all he had ever tried before.

By thus practicing the common useful occupations of life, he began to feel a more tender interest in the common concerns of his fellow-creatures. He now found, from his own experience, that Mr. Barlow had not deceived him in the various representations he had made of the utility of the lower classes, and consequently of the humanity which is due to them when they discharge their duty. Nor did that gentleman abandon his little friend in this important trial. He visited him frequently, pointed out everything that was curious or interesting about the farm, and encouraged him to persevere by his praises.

"You are now," said Mr. Barlow, one day, "beginning to practice those virtues which have rendered the great men of other times so justly famous. It is not by sloth, nor finery, nor the mean indulgence of our appetites, that greatness of character, or even reputation, is to be acquired. He that would excel others in virtue or knowledge, must first excel them in temperance and application. You cannot imagine that men fit to command an army, or to give laws to a state, were ever formed by an idle and effeminate education. When the Roman people, oppressed by their enemies, were looking out for a leader able to defend them, and change the fortune of the war, where did they seek for this extraordinary man? It was neither at banquets, nor in splendid palaces, nor amid the gay, the elegant, or the dissipated; they turned their steps towards a poor and solitary cottage, such as the meanest of your late companions would consider with contempt; there they found Cincinnatus, whose virtues and abilities were allowed to excel all the rest of his citizens, turning up the soil with a pair of oxen, and holding the plough himself. This great man had been inured to arms and the management of public affairs, even from his infancy; he had repeatedly led the Roman legions to victory; yet in the hour of peace, or when his country did not require his services, he deemed no employment more honourable than to labour for his own subsistence.

"What would all your late friends have said, to see the greatest men in England, and the bravest officers of the army, crowding round the house of one of those obscure farmers you have been accustomed to despise, and entreating him, in the most respectful language, to leave his fields, and accept of the highest dignity in the government or army? Yet this was actually the state of things at Rome, and it was characters like these, with all the train of severe and rugged virtues, that elevated that people above all the other nations of the world.— And tell me, my little friend, since chance, not merit, too frequently allots the situation in which men are to act, had you rather, in an high station, appear to all mankind unworthy of the advantages you enjoy, or, in a low one, seem equal to the most exalted employments by your virtues and abilities?"

Such were the conversations which Mr. Barlow frequently held with Tommy, and which never failed to inspire him with new resolution to persevere. Nor could he help being frequently affected by the comparison of Harry's behaviour with his own. No cloud seemed ever to shade the features of his friend, or alter the uniform sweetness of his temper. Even the repeated provocations he had received were either totally obliterated, or had made no disagreeable impressions. After discharging the necessary duties of the day, he gave up the rest of his time to the amusement of Tommy, with so much zeal and affection, that he could not avoid loving him a thousand times better than before.

During the evening he frequently conversed with the honest negro concerning the most remarkable circumstances of the country where he was born. One night that he seemed peculiarly inquisitive, the black gave him the following account of himself.

"I was born," said he, "in the neighbourhood of the river Gambia in Africa. In this country people are astonished at my colour, and start at the sight of a black man, as if he did not belong to their species: but there, everybody resembles me, and when the first white men landed upon our coast, we were as much surprised with their appearances as you can be with ours. In some parts of the world I have seen men of a yellow hue, in others of a copper colour, and all have the foolish vanity to despise their fellow creatures as infinitely inferior to themselves. There indeed they entertain these conceits from ignorance; but in this country, where the natives pretend to superior reason, I have often wondered they could be influenced by such a prejudice. Is a black horse thought to be inferior to a white one, in speed, or strength, or courage? Is a white cow thought to give more milk, or a white dog to have an acuter scent in pursuing the game? On the contrary, I have generally found, in almost every country, that a pale colour in animals is considered as a mark of weakness and inferiority. Why then should a certain race of men imagine themselves superior to the rest, for the very circumstance they despise in other animals?

"But in the country where I was born, it is not only man that differs from what we see here, but every other circumstance. Here, for a considerable part of the year, you are chilled by frosts and snows, and scarcely behold the presence of the sun during that gloomy season that is called the winter. With us the sun is always present, pouring out light and heat, and scorching us with his fiercest beams. In my country we know no difference in the length of nights and days: all are of equal length throughout the year, and present not that continual variety which you see here. We have neither ice, nor frost, nor snow; the trees never lose their leaves, and we have fruits in every season of the year. During several months, indeed, we are scorched by unremitting heats, which parch the ground, dry up the rivers, and afflict both men and animals with intolerable thirst. In that season, you may behold lions, tigers, elephants, and a variety of other ferocious animals, driven from their dark abodes in the midst of impenetrable forests, down to the lower grounds and the sides of rivers. Every night we hear their savage yells, their cries of rage, and think ourselves scarcely safe in our cottages. In this country you have reduced all other animals to subjection, and have nothing to fear except from each other. You even shelter your-selves from the injuries of the weather in mansions that seem calculated to last forever, in impenetrable houses of brick or stone, that would have scarcely anything to fear from the whole animal creation; but, with us, a few reeds twisted together, and perhaps daubed over with slime or mud, compose the whole of our dwellings. Yet there the innocent negro would sleep as happy and contented as you do in your palaces, provided you did not drag him by fraud and violence away, and force him to endure all the excesses of your cruelty.

"It was in one of these cottages that I first remember any-thing of myself. A few stakes set in the ground, and inter-woven with dry reeds, covered at top with the spreading leaves of the palm, composed our dwelling. Our furniture consisted of three or four earthen pipkins, in which our food was dressed; a few mats woven with a silky kind of grass to serve as beds; the instruments with which my mother turned the ground, and the javelin, arrows, and lines, which my father used in fishing or the chase. In this country, and many others where I have been, I observe that nobody thinks himself happy till he has got together a thousand things which he does not want, and can never use; you live in houses so big, that they are fit to contain an army; you cover yourselves with superfluous clothes that restrain all the motions of your bodies: when you want to eat, you must have meat enough served up to nourish a whole village; yet I have seen poor famished wretches starving at your gate, while the master had before him at least an hundred times as much as he could consume. We negroes, whom you treat as savages, have different manners and different opinions. The first thing that I can remember of myself was the running naked about such a cottage as I have described, with four of my little brothers and sisters. I have observed your children here with astonishment: as soon as they are born, it seems to be the business of all about them, to render them weak, help-less, and unable to use any of their limbs. The little negro, on the contrary, is scarcely born before he learns to crawl about upon the ground. Unrestrained by bandages or ligatures, he comes as soon and as easily to the perfect use of all his organs as any of the beasts which surround him. Before your children here are taught to venture themselves upon their feet, he has the perfect use of his, and can follow his mother in her daily labours.

"This I remember was my own case. Sometimes I used to go with my mother to the field, where all the women of the village were assembled to plant rice for their subsistence. The joyful songs which they used to sing, amid their toils, delighted my infant ear; and, when their daily task was done, they danced together under the shade of spreading palms. In this manner did they raise the simple food, which was sufficient for themselves and their children; yams, a root resembling your potato, Indian corn, and, above all, rice; to this were added the fruits which nature spontaneously produced in our woods, and the produce of the chase and fishing. Yet with this we are as much contented as you are with all your splendid tables, and enjoy a greater share of health and strength. As soon as the fiery heat of the sun declined, you might behold the master of every cottage reposing before his own door, and feasting upon his mess of roots or fruits, with all his family around. If a traveller or stranger happened to come from a distant country, he was welcome to enter into every house and share the provisions of the family. No door was barred against his entrance, no surly servant insulted him for his poverty; he entered wherever he pleased, sat himself down with the family, and then pursued his journey, or reposed himself in quiet till the next morning. In each of our towns there is generally a large building, where the elder part of the society are accustomed to meet in the shade of the evening, and converse upon a variety of subjects; the young and vigorous divert themselves with dances and other pastimes, and the children of different ages amuse themselves with a thousand sports and gambols adapted to their age: some aim their little arrows at marks, or dart their light and blunted javelins at each other, to form themselves for the exercises of war and the chase; others wrestle naked upon the sand, or run in sportive races, with a degree of activity which I have never seen among the Europeans, who pretend to be our masters.

"I have described to you the building of our houses;

simple as they are, they answer every purpose of human life, and every man is his own architect. An hundred or two of these edifices compose our towns, which are generally surrounded by lofty hedges of thorns to secure us from the midnight attacks of wild beasts, with only a single entrance, which is carefully closed at night."

"You talk," said Tommy, "of wild beasts; pray have you many of them in your country?" "Yes," said the black, "master, we have them of many sorts, equally dreadful and ferocious. First, we have the lion, which I dare say you have heard of, and perhaps seen. He is bigger than the largest mastiff, and infinitely stronger and more fierce; his paws alone are such, that with a single blow, he is able to knock down a man, and almost every other animal; but these paws are armed with claws so sharp and dreadful, that nothing can resist their violence. When he roars, every beast of the forest betakes himself to flight, and even the boldest hunter can scarcely hear it without dismay. Sometimes, the most valiant of our youth assemble in bands, arm themselves with arrows and javelins, and go to the chase of these destructive animals. When they have found his retreat, they generally make a circle round, uttering shouts and cries, and clashing their arms, to rouse him to resistance. The lion, meanwhile, looks round upon his assailants with indifference or contempt; neither their number, nor their horrid shouts, nor the glitter of their radiant arms, can daunt him for an instant. At length he begins to lash his sides with his long and nervous tail, a certain sign of rising rage, his eyes sparkle with destructive fires, and, if the number of the hunters is very great, he perhaps moves slowly on. But this he is not permitted to do; a javelin, thrown at him from behind, wounds him in the flank, and compels him to turn. Then you behold him roused to fury and desperation; neither wounds, nor streaming blood, nor a triple row of barbed spears, can prevent him from springing upon the daring black who has wounded him. Should he reach him, in the attack, it is certain death; but generally the hunter, who is at once contending for glory and his own life, and is inured to danger, avoids him by a nimble leap, and all his companions hasten to his assistance.

Thus is the lion pressed and wounded on every side, his rage is ineffectual, and only exhausts his strength the faster; an hundred wounds are pouring out his blood at once, and at length he bites the ground in the agonies of death, and yields the victory though unconquered.

"When he is dead, he is carried back in triumph by the hunters, as a trophy of their courage. All the village rushes out at once; the young, the old, women and children, uttering joyful shouts, and praising the valour of their champions. The elders admire his prodigious size, his mighty limbs, his dreadful fangs, and perhaps repeat tales of their own exploits; the women seem to tremble at their fierce enemy even in his death; while the men compel their children to approach the monster, and tinge their little weapons in his blood. All utter joyful exclamations, and feasts are made in every house, to which the victors are invited as the principal guests. These are intended at once to reward those who have performed so gallant an achievement, and to encourage a spirit of enterprise in the rest of the nation."

[A crocodile hunt is omitted.]

Such was the account which the negro gave to Tommy, in different conversations, of his birth and education. His curiosity was gratified with the recital, and his heart expanded in the same proportion that his knowledge improved. He reflected, with shame and contempt, upon the ridiculous prejudices he had once entertained; he learned to consider all men as his brethren and equals; and the foolish distinctions which pride had formerly suggested were gradually obliterated from his mind. Such a change in his sentiments rendered him more mild, more obliging, more engaging than ever; he became the delight of all the family; and Harry, although he had always loved him, now knew no limits to his affection.

One day he was surprised by an unexpected visit from his father, who met him with open arms, and told him, that he was now come to take him back to his own house. "I have heard," said he, "such an account of your present behaviour, that the past is entirely forgotten, and I begin to glory in owning you for a son." He then embraced him with the transports of an affectionate father who indulges the strongest sentiments of his heart, but sentiments he had long been forced to restrain. Tommy returned his caresses with genuine warmth, but with a degree of respect and humility he had once been little accustomed to use. "I will accompany you home, sir," said he, "with the greatest readiness; for I wish to see my mother, and hope to give her some satisfaction of my future behaviour. You have both had too much to complain of in the past; and I am unworthy of such affectionate parents." He then turned his face aside, and shed a tear of real virtue and gratitude, which he instantly wiped away as unworthy of the composure and fortitude of his new character.

"But, sir," added he, "I hope you will not object to my detaining you a little longer, while I return my acknowledgements to all the family, and take my leave of Harry." "Surely," said Mr. Merton, "you can entertain no doubt upon that subject: and, to give you every opportunity of discharging all your duties to a family, to which you owe so much, I intend to take a dinner with Mr. Sandford, whom I now see coming home, and then returning with you in the evening."

At this instant farmer Sandford approached, and very respectfully saluting Mr. Merton, invited him to walk in. But Mr. Merton, after returning his civility, drew him aside as if he had some private business to communicate. When they were alone, he made him every acknowledgement that gratitude could suggest; "but words," added Mr. Merton, "are very insufficient to return the favours I have received; for it is to your excellent family, together with the virtuous Mr. Barlow, that I owe the preservation of my son. Let me, therefore, entreat you to accept of what this pocket-book contains, as a slight proof of my sentiments, and lay it out in whatever manner you please, for the advantage of your family."

Mr. Sandford, who was a man both of sense and humour, took the book, and, examining the inside, found that it contained bank-notes to the amount of some hundred pounds. He then carefully shut it up again, and, returning it to Mr. Merton, told him that he was infinitely obliged to him for the generosity which prompted him to such a princely act; but, as to the present itself, he must not be offended if he declined it. Mr. Merton, still more astonished at such disinterestedness, pressed him with every argument he could think of; he desired him to consider the state of his family; his daughters unprovided for; his son himself, with dispositions that might adorn a throne, brought up to labour; and his own advancing age, which demanded ease and respite, and an increase of the conveniencies of life.

"And what," replied the honest farmer, "is it, but these conveniencies of life, that are the ruin of all the nation? When I was a young man, Master Merton, and that is near forty years ago, people in my condition thought of nothing but doing their duty to God and man, and labouring hard: this brought down a blessing upon their heads, and made them thrive in all their worldly concerns. When I was a boy, farmers did not lie droning in bed as they do now till six or seven; my father, I believe, was as good a judge of business as any in the neighbourhood, and turned as straight a furrow as any ploughman in the county of Devon; that silver cup, which I intend to have the honour of drinking your health out of to-day at dinner, that very cup was won by him at the great ploughing-match near Axminster—Well, my father used to say, that a farmer was not worth a farthing that was not in the field by four; and my poor dear mother too, the best-tempered woman in the world, she always began milking exactly at five; and if a single soul was to be found in bed after four in summer, you might have heard her from one end of the farm to the other.—I would not disparage anybody, or anything, my good sir; but those were times indeed; the women, then, knew something about the management of an house: it really was quite a pleasure to hear my poor mother lecture the servants; and the men were men, indeed; pray, did you ever hear the story of my father's being at Truro, and throwing the famous Cornish wrestler, squinting Dick the miner?"

Mr. Merton began to be convinced, that, whatever other qualities good Mr. Sandford might have, he did not excel in brevity; and therefore endeavoured in still stronger terms to overcome the delicacy of the farmer, and prevail upon him to accept his present.

But the good farmer pursued his point thus; "Thank you, thank you, my dear sir, a thousand times, for your good will; but, as to the money, I must beg your pardon if I persist in refusing it. Formerly, sir, as I was saying, we were all happy and healthy, and our affairs prospered, because we never thought about the conveniencies of life: now, I hear of nothing else. One neighbour, for I will not mention names, brings his son up to go a shooting with gentlemen; another sends his to market upon a blood horse, with a plated bridle; and then the girls, the girls!—There is fine work, indeed; they must have their hats and feathers, and riding-habits; their heads as big as bushels, and even their hind-quarters stuck out with cork or pasteboard; but scarcely one of them can milk a cow, or churn, or bake, or do any one thing that is necessary in a family; so that unless the government will send them all to this new settlement, which I have heard so much of, and bring us a cargo of plain, honest housewives, who have never been at boarding-schools, I cannot conceive how we farmers are to get wives."

Mr. Merton laughed very heartily at this sally, and told him, that he would venture to assert it was not so at his house. —"Not quite so bad, indeed," said the farmer; "my wife was bred up under a notable mother, and, though she must have her tea every afternoon, is, in the main, a very good sort of woman. She has brought her daughters up a little better than usual; but I can assure you she and I have had many a good argument upon the subject. Not but she approves their milking, spinning, and making themselves useful; but she would fain have them genteel, Master Merton: all women now are mad after gentility; and, when once gentility begins, there is an end of industry. Now, were they to hear of such a sum as you have generously offered, there would be no peace in the house. My wenches, instead of Deb and Kate, would be Miss Deborah and Miss Catharine; in a little time, they must be sent to boarding-school, to learn French and music, and wriggling about the room. And, when they come back, who must boil the pot, or make the pudding, or sweep the house, or serve the pigs?—Did you ever hear of Miss Juliana, or Miss Harriet or Miss Carolina, doing such vulgar things?"

Mr. Merton was very much struck with the honest farmer's method of expressing himself, and could not help internally allowing the truth of his representations; yet he still pressed him to accept his present, and reminded him of the improvement of his farm.

"Thank you again, and again," replied the farmer; "but the whole generation of the Sandfords have been brought up to labour with their own hands for these hundred years; and, during all that time, there has not been a dishonest person, a gentleman, or a madman amongst us. And shall I be the first to break the customs of the family, and perhaps bring down a curse on all our heads?—What could I have more, if I were a lord, or a macaroni,[6] as I think you call them?—I have plenty of victuals and work, good firing, clothes, a warm house, a little for the poor, and, between you and I, something, perhaps, in a corner to set my children off with, if they behave well.—Ah! neighbour, neighbour, if you did but know the pleasure of holding plough after a good team of horses, and then going tired to bed, perhaps you'd wish to have been brought up a farmer too.—But in one word, as well as a thousand, I shall never forget the extraordinary kindness of your offer; but, if you would not ruin a whole family of innocent people that love you, ev'n consent to leave us as we are."

Mr. Merton then seeing the fixed determination of the farmer, and feeling the justice of his coarse but strong morality, was obliged, however reluctantly, to desist; and Mrs. Sandford coming to invite them to dinner, he entered the house, and paid his respects to the family.

After the cloth was removed, and Mr. Sandford had twice or thrice replenished his silver mug, the only piece of finery in his house, little Harry came running in, with so much alacrity and heedlessness, that he tore Miss Deborah's best apron, and had nearly precipitated Miss Catharine's new cap into the fire, for which the young ladies and his mother rebuked him with some acrimony. But Harry, after begging pardon with his usual good humour, cried, "Father, father, here is the prettiest team of horses, all matched, and of a colour, with new harness, the most complete I ever saw in my life; and they have stopped at our back-door, and the man says they are brought for you." Farmer Sandford was just then in the middle of his history of the ploughing-match at Axminster; but the relation of his son had such an involuntary effect upon him, that he started up, overset the liquor and the table, and, making an hasty apology to Mr. Merton, ran out to see these wonderful horses.

Presently he returned, in equal admiration with his son. "Master Merton," said he, "I did not think you had been so good a judge of an horse. I suppose they are a new purchase, which you want to have my opinion upon; and, I can assure you, they are the true Suffolk sorrels, the first breed of working horses in the kingdom; and these are some of the best of their kind." "Such as they are," answered Mr. Merton, "they are yours; and I cannot think, after the obligations I am under to your family, that you will do me so great a displeasure as to refuse." Mr. Sandford stood for some time in mute astonishment; but, at length, he was beginning the civilest speech he could think of to refuse so great a present, when Tommy coming up, took him by the hand, and begged him not to deny to his father and himself the first favour they had ever asked. "Besides," said he, "this present is less to yourself than to little Harry; and, surely, after having lived so long in your family, you will not turn me out with disgrace, as if I had misbehaved." —Here Harry himself interposed, and, considering less the value of the present than the feelings and intentions of the giver, he took his father by the hand, and besought him to oblige Master Merton and his father. "Were it anyone else, I would not say a word," added he; "but I know the generosity of Mr. Merton, and the goodness of Master Tommy so well, that they will receive more pleasure from giving, than you from taking the horses. Though, I must confess, they are such as would do credit to anybody; and they beat farmer Knowles's all to nothing, which have long been reckoned the best team in all the country."

This last reflection, joined with all that had preceded, overcame the delicacy of Mr. Sandford; and he at length consented to order the horses to be led into his stables. And now Mr. Merton, having made the most affectionate acknowledgements to all this worthy and happy family, among whom he did not forget the honest black, whom he promised to provide for, summoned his son to accompany him home. Tommy arose, and, with the sincerest gratitude, bade adieu to Harry and all the rest. "I shall not be long without you," said he to Harry; "to your example I owe most of the little good that I can boast; you have taught me how much better it is to be useful than rich or fine; how much more amiable to be good than to be great.—Should I be ever tempted to relapse, even for an instant, into any of my former habits, I will return hither for instruction; and I hope you will again receive me." Saying this, he shook his friend Harry affectionately by the hand, and, with watery eyes, accompanied his father home.

NOTES

A Sentimental Journey through France and Italy

1. Mrs. Elizabeth Draper, whom Sterne had recently met and to whom he wrote a number of sentimental letters, which were collected together and called the *Journal to Eliza.*
2. Guido Reni, seventeenth-century Italian painter.
3. Tartuffe, a religious hypocrite in a comedy by Molière.
4. Tobias Smollet, whose *Travels Through France And Italy* appeared in 1766. Mundungus is Sterne's reference to *Letters From Italy* by Samuel Sharp, also published in 1766.
5. John Home, Scottish dramatic poet, and David Hume, philosopher and historian, whose surnames were pronounced alike.
6. *spatter* plus *dash,* that is, leggings.
7. In dice, throwing a pair. The metaphor is continued in "my *cast,*" that is, "chance from the fall of dice."
8. The wife or daughter of a tradesman.
9. John Hall-Stevenson, Sterne's Yorkshire friend who appears in *Tristram Shandy.*
10. Uncle Toby of *Tristram Shandy.*
11. Or cicisbeo, "The name formerly given in Italy to the recognized gallant or *cavalier servente* of a married woman," *OED.*
12. Comfort; with a pun on "house or seat of ease," relieving the bowels.
13. "(Among women) to ease oneself in open air," E. Partridge, *Dictionary of Slang.*
14. Soldier's ornamental outfitting.
15. Stocking: "The original word seems to be *stock,* whence *stocks,* a prison for the legs," Johnson's *Dictionary.* Hussive or hussy is a "kind of book, used by women for holding thread . . . sometimes called a *huswife.*"

16. A stone believed by alchemists to be able to turn base metals into gold.

17. A "bag" is an ornament tied to men's wigs; "solitaire" is a neck ornament.

18. Jan Gruter (d. 1627), a Dutch classicist; Jacob Spon (d. 1686), a French antiquarian.

19. A fine hat made of beaver fur.

20. Sterne is capitalizing on a famous sentimental scene in *Tristram Shandy*.

21. Don Quixote.

22. Wooden shoes.

23. Driver of a carriage.

The Man of Feeling

1. A small four-sided disc with letters on each side, which was twirled like a top; the letter that lay uppermost when it fell decided the player's fortune.

2. In later editions Mackenzie explained the reference to the political debating society, The Robinhood, held in a house in Butcher Row.

3. Richard Bentley (1662–1742), the famous classical scholar, who was satirized as a pedant by Pope and Swift.

4. One of the most popular mid-eighteenth-century coffee houses.

5. "A man deceived or imposed upon; as by sharpers or a strumpet," Johnson's *Dictionary*.

6. Salvator Rosa, seventeenth-century Italian painter whose landscapes were prized for their romantic quality.

7. "Certain observable years are supposed to be attended with some considerable change in the body; as the seventh year; the twenty-first, made up of three times seven; the forty-ninth, made up of seven times seven; the sixty-third, being nine times seven; and the eighty-first, which is nine times nine: which two last are called the *grand climatericks*." Johnson's *Dictionary*.

The History of Sandford and Merton

1. Or Maybug; a large, whirring beetle.
2. *Letters Written by the Earl of Chesterfield to His Son* (1774).
3. Day's optimistic theory about animals unfortunately led to his own death. He was thrown by a half-broken colt and died almost immediately from a concussion.
4. Famous eighteenth-century race courses.
5. Gaétan Balthazar Vestris (d. 1808), a famous French dancer, sometimes called "the god of dance."
6. Stylish; a fop or dandy who affected continental manners: compare "stuck a feather in his hat, And called it macaroni."

Rinehart Editions